D0802816

THE BLADE OF THE FLAME

BY ACCLAIMED AUTHOR
TIM WAGGONER

Thieves of Blood

Forge of the Mindslayers

Sea of Death
(February 2008)

EBERRON

TIM WAGGONER

FORGE
OF THE
MINDSLAYERS

BLADE OF THE FLAME

BOOK
2

Wizards
OF THE COAST

FORGE OF THE MINDSLAYERS
The Blade of the Flame · Book 2

©2007 Wizards of the Coast, Inc.

Cover art by Raymond Swanland
Map by Robert Lazzaretti
First Printing: March 2007

9 8 7 6 5 4 3 2 1

ISBN: 978-0-7869-4313-5
620-95971740-001-EN

U.S., CANADA,
ASIA, PACIFIC, & LATIN AMERICA
Wizards of the Coast, Inc.
P.O. Box 707
Renton, WA 98057-0707
+1-800-324-6496

EUROPEAN HEADQUARTERS
Hasbro UK Ltd
Caswell Way
Newport, Gwent NP9 0YH
GREAT BRITAIN
Save this address for your records.

Visit our web site at www.wizards.com

ACKNOWLEDGEMENTS

Once again, I'd like to thank Mark Sehestedt for editorial guidance par excellence. Having an editor as good as you, Mark, means never having to write STET.

DEDICATION

For Robert L. Snead, Im Specialist U.S. Army infantry. Here's something else for you to read, Rob!

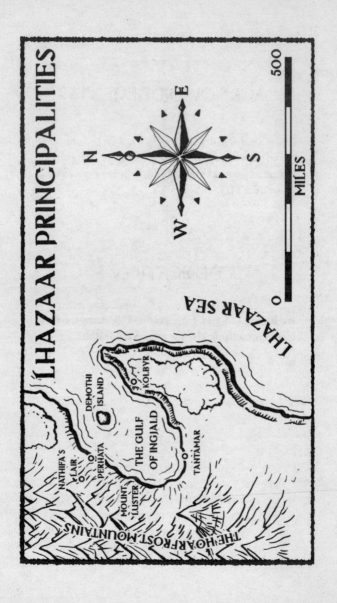

CHAPTER

ONE

Chagai crouched behind a rocky outcropping near the summit of a small mountain, a perfect vantage point to observe the party of four men traveling by foot through the canyon below. Two were human—one in the prime of his life, dressed all in black, with long ebon hair, while the other was a white-beard, thin of frame, and from the way he lagged behind his companions, not very strong. A halfling and a half-orc accompanied the humans. Chagai's upper lip curled in disgust. Even from this height he could smell the half-blood's stink, and without his realizing it, a growl rumbled deep in his chest.

The half-blood paused and cocked his head. He gazed up at the mountain—directly where Chagai hid—eyes furrowed, nostrils flaring as he read the scents on the wind. Chagai stopped breathing and held himself as motionless as the rocks around him. The orc wore a mottled gray cloak over his chain-mail armor, and he had the hood up. The cloak's color blended with the mountain's surface, and Chagai was confident that the

1

half-blood wouldn't be able to detect him. Still, even a half-orc possessed senses far stronger than those of a human, and Chagai knew better than to underestimate him, especially *this* half-orc—for Chagai recognized the other's scent, recognized the way he moved, even the way he breathed. The half-breed's name was Ghaji, and years ago he had come close to slaying Chagai. *Very* close.

Too bad for Ghaji that he'd failed.

"Something wrong, my friend?"

Ghaji didn't take his gaze from the mountainside as he answered. "I'm not sure. For a moment, I thought I saw something up there, but now . . ."

Diran Bastiaan came over and stood next to the half-orc. The black-garbed priest looked toward the spot on the mountain where Ghaji was staring, shielding his eyes with one hand to block out the rays of the setting sun. Dusk was rapidly approaching, and while the valley in which they stood was already draped in shadow, orange-red sunlight shone from behind the mountain, making it difficult to see.

"It's nothing," Ghaji decided at last. "A trick of the light, nothing more."

Though they were but in the foothills of the Hoarfrost Mountains, the canyon terrain was rocky and barren, save for a scattering of scraggly trees and tufts of coarse scrub grass that had pushed their way up through the stony ground. It was late autumn, and in the Lhazaar Principalities that meant the air already held more than a hint of winter's bite. The four companions were garbed in heavy clothes, fur cloaks, and thick, sturdy boots. Even so, Ghaji—the only one of the quartet not born in the Principalities—still shivered with every blast of wind, the cold air cutting through him like one of Diran's daggers. Chalk up one more disadvantage to his half-blood status.

The other two members of their party joined them. Though they'd been trekking through the foothills for the better part of a day, the halfling appeared as fresh as when they'd started out. The older human, however, looked as if he were about ready to drop from exhaustion.

"Maybe it's an animal of some kind," Hinto said. The halfling sounded excited, as if he might race up the hillside any moment to go check.

The human, whose name was Tresslar, spoke in a breathless, raspy voice. "The only animals we've encountered today are hares, foxes, and mountain goats." He paused to catch his breath. "And we've seen precious few of those."

Ghaji turned away from the mountain to look at Tresslar. The artificer was in his late sixties, and while he was in generally good health, the day's journey through the mountains had taken its toll on him. Though they'd rested regularly and drank often from their waterskins, Tresslar's face was gaunt and pale. His legs trembled, and Ghaji feared the man might collapse any moment.

Ghaji turned toward Diran, hoping to communicate to his friend that Tresslar was in dire need of his assistance, but Diran was already ahead of him. The priest carried a bow and quiver of arrows, and he now slipped them off his shoulder and placed them on the ground. Ordinarily, divesting one's self of weapons while being stalked by a hidden opponent wasn't the wisest of moves. Though Diran carried a bow and practiced with it, he did so only because it was the signature weapon of his order. In truth, he was only middling skilled at its use. While this fact vexed him, Diran wasn't foolish or stubborn enough to rely on his unremarkable archery skills in a dangerous situation—not that he needed to, for he possessed other weapons with which he was far more proficient.

Diran stepped to Tresslar's side and laid a hand on the artificer's shoulder.

"I know what you intend to do," Tresslar protested, "but I am hardly in need of healing." The artificer reached up to push Diran's hand away, but Diran caught his wrist with his free hand and gently but firmly kept him from doing so.

"There is no shame in admitting one's needs," Diran said. "Besides, when we locate what we've come here for, we'll need to be at our full fighting strength."

As a youth, Tresslar had sailed with the legendary explorer Erdis Cai, and though that had been many decades ago, the artificer sometimes pushed himself as if he thought only a handful of years had passed. Still, while Tresslar was a proud man, he was also a practical one, and he sighed and nodded his acceptance of Diran's words. The priest smiled, released his grip on Tresslar's wrist, and closed his eyes.

Ghaji had seen Diran perform healings many times, and he'd been the beneficiary of the priest's otherworldly powers on more than one occasion himself, but no matter how often he'd seen Diran at work, he was always impressed by the profound simplicity of the act. Diran never made a great show of healing. He didn't speak prayers, didn't wave his hands about in the air, didn't loudly beseech the holy Silver Flame to work its wonders through him. All he did was touch the person he wished to heal, close his eyes, and then several moments later, it was done.

It was at moments like those when Ghaji was struck afresh by the dichotomy his friend represented. During the Last War, Diran had served as a mercenary assassin—a damn fine one—and there was still much of the killer's mien to him. His long black hair framed a face that was lean and wolfish, with eyes that were dark, cold, and calculating. He always wore black, and he moved with the precision and grace of someone whose body was the most important weapon he owned. But after the War, Diran abandoned the life of a killer-for-hire and became a priest of the Silver Flame, an order dedicated to purging evil from the world. It was this power Diran channeled when he healed others. At those times his touch was gentle, his voice warm and soothing, his expression one of beatific contentment. It was almost enough to make a hard-headed skeptic like Ghaji take up the worship of the Silver Flame himself. Almost.

Diran opened his eyes and removed his hand from Tresslar's shoulder. "Better?"

Tresslar's face no longer looked so drawn, his color had returned to normal, and his legs were once more sure and steady. "Yes, thank you." Despite his earlier protestation, the artificer sounded relieved.

Diran smiled, nodded, then returned to Ghaji's side.

"Well, if it isn't an animal," Hinto said, "then maybe it's the thing we've come hunting for. The lyke, lihk, however you pronounce it."

"Lich," Diran said, "and I seriously doubt it. According to the stories we heard back in Perhata, this particular lich rarely strays from its lair."

"If you can trust a bunch of tall tales told by drunken sailors," Tresslar muttered.

They'd first heard tell of the lich in a seedy tavern in the sea-side city of Perhata. It was an all-too-familiar story: an undead creature had holed up in cave somewhere in the mountains outside the city, where it used its hoard of fabulous wealth to lure greedy treasure-seekers to their unspeakably horrible dooms. If Ghaji had a copper crown for every time they'd heard a similar story . . .

Of course, now that he thought of it, most of the time the stories had turned out to be true.

"Are you *sure* it's not a lich, Diran?"

There was a small tremor to Hinto's voice, and Ghaji gazed down with concern at the halfling pirate's brown, sun-weathered face. Ever since his time shipwrecked in the Mire—where Hinto had watched his crewmates captured and devoured one by one—the halfling had been prone to sudden attacks of paralyzing panic. Over the last several months, Diran had been working with Hinto, teaching him meditation techniques that the Purified used to center and calm themselves. Diran's tutelage had helped somewhat, but Hinto still suffered bouts of panic from time to time.

"Positive," the priest said. "As Ghaji said, what he saw was likely nothing more than a trick of light and shadow, caused by—"

Diran's words were cut off by the sound of a shrill scream, but the cry came from behind them, not from the mysterious figure on the mountainside.

Ghaji whirled about, drawing his axe as he turned. With a thought, he activated the mystic weapon and flames wreathed the axe-head. Diran also spun around, a pair of silver daggers in his hands, the blades pulled from two of the many sheaths sewn into the priest's clothing. Tresslar yanked a two-foot iron rod from beneath his belt and pointed the end—which terminated in a golden dragon's head—toward the direction of the scream. Ghaji glanced at Hinto and was gratified to see that the halfling had drawn the long knife he used as a sword. Hinto trembled like a leaf caught in a windstorm, but he stood his ground, determined not to let his fear get the best of him.

Before them the canyon wall rose at a sloping angle, the gray stone painted black by the shadow of the mountain opposite. A dozen feet above the ground was a cleft in the rock, and hanging half out of the narrow opening was a small humanoid figure with orange-tinted skin, a flat face, broad nose, pointed ears, and tiny fangs protruding from its lower jaw. The creature's face was distorted by pain and terror, and it reached out toward them with long simian-like arms.

"Help me, please! She's going to kill me!" Its voice was a shrill whine, the words spoken with an odd accent that Ghaji couldn't place.

"It's a goblin," Hinto said. The halfling started forward, obviously intending to go to the creature's aid, but Diran put a hand on the little pirate's shoulder to stop him.

"Perhaps," Diran said. "Perhaps not." The priest gazed intently at the distressed goblin, an appraising look in his eyes.

"What's wrong?" Tresslar asked.

"It could be a trap," Ghaji said.

Tears streamed down the goblin's face. "Please! I can pay you! There's treasure in here, tons of it! I'll share it with you! You can have it all, just don't let her—" With a sudden motion the goblin disappeared into the cleft, as if something inside had violently yanked him backward. Another shriek echoed through the canyon, this one short-lived, and then there was only silence.

Ghaji and Diran looked at each other, smiled, and spoke at the same time.

"Definitely a trap," they said.

❋ ❋ ❋ ❋ ❋ ❋ ❋

The sloping surface of the canyon wall provided enough hand and footholds that the four companions were able to climb up to the opening without any trouble. Even Tresslar had no difficulty, thanks to the fresh infusion of strength granted to him by Diran's healing touch. Ghaji went first, elemental axe deactivated and tucked once more beneath his belt. Diran came second, daggers temporarily returned to their sheaths, then came Tresslar and Hinto.

They didn't attempt to enter right away. Diran and Ghaji remained to the right of the cleft, while Tresslar and Hinto stayed on the other side. Ghaji then eased toward the opening and activated his elemental axe. Flames flared to life, and he held the burning axe toward the cleft. The light chased away the shadows huddling around the entrance, and Ghaji could see that the opening was wider than it had first appeared from the canyon floor. They wouldn't have any trouble getting inside, but then the intention had never been to keep them out.

"How do you know it's a trap?" Tresslar asked as they clung to the rocky surface.

"It's quite simple," Diran answered. "A lone goblin could never have escaped from a lich to call out for help. He would've been too paralyzed by fear in her presence to speak, let alone move."

"Doesn't it strike you as awfully convenient that the goblin just happened to get free while we were in the vicinity?" Ghaji added. "Not to mention all that talk about treasure. He's just a lure, maybe even an illusion conjured by the lich."

Ghaji extended his axe into the opening and saw that beyond the cleft was a passageway large enough for two men to walk side by side, if only just. Of the goblin—or anything else for that matter—he saw no sign. He examined the floor of the passageway beyond the entrance and saw no scratch marks in the rock. A goblin fighting for his life would've scuffed the floor somehow, perhaps even torn his claws and left behind spots of blood, but the half-orc saw nothing.

"Looks clear," Ghaji said. "I'm going in."

"Be careful," Diran warned, "and don't go too far inside. Wait for the rest of us to join you."

Ghaji turned to his friend and gave the priest a withering look. "I'm not stupid, Diran. I'm not about to go dashing off into a monster's lair on my own."

"That's what you said last month," Diran pointed out, "when we dealt with that nest of ghouls in the sewers of Skairn."

Ghaji scowled. "That was different. I—"

Diran continued. "What about the time we went after the pack of yeth hounds that was attacking ships off the coast?"

"All right, I'll admit to that one, but I'd gotten our plan confused—"

"And then there was that wraith on the isle of—"

"Very well!" Ghaji snapped. "I'll wait!"

Hinto snickered, but the halfling instantly shut up when Ghaji glared at him. Muttering to himself, Ghaji climbed through the cleft and into the passageway beyond. It was a bit of a squeeze for the half-orc, but once he was inside, the tunnel opened up sufficiently to allow him to stand without slouching. The light cast by his fire-axe revealed the gray stone of the passage to be rough and uneven, but the tunnel's shape was uniform enough for Ghaji to guess it wasn't a natural formation. This passageway had been carved into the hillside, but who had done it—and how long ago—Ghaji couldn't say. He took a breath and regretted it as the stench of ancient rot and decay assailed his nostrils. Ghaji had fought evil alongside Diran long enough to recognize the stink of undeath when he smelled it. If this wasn't a lich's lair, it was surely home to some creature equally as foul.

The axe-flame illuminated the passageway for a good dozen feet. Beyond that, the tunnel veered to the left, cutting off Ghaji's view. Anything might be around that bend—and probably was.

He turned to speak over his shoulder, keeping one eye fixed on the passageway before him. "The entrance is clear," he told his companions then stepped forward to make room for them in the tunnel.

Diran entered first, followed by Tresslar and then Hinto. There wasn't enough room in the passage for the four of them to walk shoulder to shoulder, so Ghaji and Diran went first, with Tresslar and Hinto coming after. They moved into the tunnel slowly, all of them armed, senses alert for the slightest sign of danger.

As they neared the bend in the tunnel, Ghaji glanced back at Hinto to see how the little pirate was doing. He was trembling, and his lips moved soundlessly as he mouthed one of the calming meditative prayers Diran had taught him. Not for the first time, Ghaji questioned the wisdom of allowing the halfling to join them on this hunt, but Hinto had insisted, and Diran had finally agreed, saying the journey might help the halfing further progress in mastering his fear. Ghaji's own fear was that Hinto might get one or more of them killed should he suffer a bout of panic while they were within the lich's lair. Ghaji trusted Diran with his life, but in this case he hoped the priest knew what he was doing.

As they rounded the bend, a low moan drifted from somewhere ahead of them, and Ghaji recognized the sound of the goblin's voice. The cry was soft and weak, as if the goblin was near death.

Diran started forward, but before the priest could take more than a single step, Ghaji reached out with his free hand and grabbed hold of his friend's elbow.

"It's probably a trap, remember?" the half-orc said.

"I know, but if there's even a chance that it isn't, I must go to the goblin's aid."

Diran's face was mask of grim determination, and Ghaji knew there would be no arguing with him. "Very well then. Let's go."

Diran took off down the passageway at a run, Ghaji at his side, Hinto and Tresslar following close behind.

The tunnel curved twice more—right then left—before opening up into a crudely hewn stone chamber a dozen feet high and a hundred feet across. Hanging from the ceiling was a colony of sleeping bats, each one the size of a small rat-hound. Though it was not yet dark outside, already the bats were stirring, shifting their bodies, stretching out wings, yawning mouths wide to expose sharp fangs. The chamber floor was covered with the creatures' droppings, along with parts of dismembered skeletons, dozens of them—skulls, rib cages, spines, arms, legs, pelvises—most human, some not. The bones protruded from the thick layer of muck created by the bat-droppings. The stench was unbearable, and Ghaji was glad that all they'd had to eat this day was trail rations, for if his stomach had been any fuller, he'd have been forced to empty it now. He wished his elemental axe produced mundane fire instead of magic. If so, the flame might've produced enough smoke to leaven the stink—but then, it might have also ignited some of the gases protruding from the muck.

Rising above the horrid muck in the middle of the chamber sat a large rock about three feet high. The goblin crouched on top, obviously unharmed. He fixed them with a baleful amber-eyed gaze and grinned maliciously.

"Stupid, stupid, stupid, but then I suppose I shouldn't complain, should I? For if it wasn't for idiots like you, my mistress and I wouldn't have any fun."

Diran gave no sign that he was upset at having fallen for the goblin's ruse. "I give you fair warning, goblin. I've come to slay the lich that inhabits this lair. If you get in my way, I'll kill you, too." Diran's tone was matter-of-fact, as if he were discussing something of no more import than the weather, and was all the more chilling for it.

The goblin let out a snuffling laugh. "You could try." His form blurred, and orange skin and mismatched scraps of leather armor shifted, melded, and reformed until the creature that crouched atop the rock was no longer a goblin but instead a lupine beast with blue-tinged fur, humanoid hands, and a goblinish face.

"He's a werewolf!" Hinto cried out.

"No," Diran said. "The priests of my order hunted Khorvaire's lycanthropes to extinction many years ago. That creature is a barghest—though it's just as deadly as any lycanthrope and in some ways more so."

The barghest inclined its head as if acknowledging a compliment. "I can't tell you how happy I am that there are four of you." The barghest's voice had become a rumbling growl. "That means my mistress might give me one of you when she's done. It's been so long since I've had a juicy soul to feed upon. So very long." The barghest licked its muzzle with a long black tongue that appeared more serpentine than wolf-like.

"You keep speaking of this mistress of yours," Diran said, "yet aside from your leather-winged friends hanging from the ceiling, you appear to be alone. Only moments ago you attempted to deceive us by pretending to be in danger. Perhaps the lich and her treasure are also part of your deception, nothing more than stories designed to lure prey to you."

The barghest laughed, the sound emerging from its lupine throat as a snuffling whine. "You aren't that fortunate, I'm afraid."

As if in response to some unseen signal, the entire colony of bats released its grip on the ceiling and took flight. The ebon creatures swirled around the chamber, black wings beating wildly as they darted through the fetid air. The four companions held their weapons at the ready, but none of the creatures made a move to attack them. As the bats continued to fly, they began to lose definition, their features becoming smooth and indistinct, their color darkening even further until they were nothing more than patches of deep shadow whipping about the chamber. Then the shadow-fragments came together and coalesced into a single dark form that hovered in the air next to the still-laughing barghest.

Burning orbs of crimson light blazed at them from within hollow eye sockets, and desiccated bone-white lips stretched into a hideous parody of a smile.

"I am Nathifa, and you are trespassing in my home." The lich's voice was cold and whisper-soft, a winter wind blowing across a barren field filled with unmarked graves. "Now your lives belong to me."

Ghaji knew what was coming next, but even so, the knowledge didn't insulate the half-orc from the terror that crashed into him like a frigid wave. Paralyzing fear engulfed him, threatening to force him to his knees and reduce him to a trembling, mewling child, but Ghaji had faced fear more times than he could count—both on the battlefield and off—and if it wasn't exactly an old friend, he knew it well enough not to let it get the better of him. This terror, though, wasn't natural; it was created by the lich's dark magic. The undead fiend was burrowing into their minds, attempting to drive them mad with fear and render them helpless so that she might dispose of them at her leisure, a spider spinning a web of terror to ensnare four hapless flies. Still, he gritted his teeth and fought back the fear with all his strength.

Ghaji heard Hinto cry out as he fell, caught in the grip of the lich's presence. Tresslar held his mystic rod before him, a thin sheen of blue light glimmering around the dragonhead. The artificer's eyes were squeezed shut, his brow furrowed, and sweat beaded on his forehead as he used the magic stored within the dragonwand to attempt to ward off the lich's magic. From the look of it, Tresslar was only having partial success.

Ghaji concentrated on drawing back his fire-axe and hurling it toward the lich. He knew his weapon wouldn't kill the fiend, but a blow from the flaming axe might distract her long enough to allow the four of them to break free of her fear casting. The half-orc's body refused to obey him. Even using the full force of his will, it was all he could do to pull the axe back a couple inches. The lich's power was simply too strong.

Ghaji managed to turn his head just far enough to see Diran drop the dagger he held in his right hand and slowly reach into one of his tunic pockets. The priest's face was contorted with the strain of resisting the lich's fear-spell as his fingers groped for the object within the pocket. His hand closed around the object, and then, as if touching it granted Diran the strength to further resist the lich's power, he pulled it out swiftly and held it out toward the lich. The object was a metallic arrowhead, the symbol of the Order of the Silver Flame.

The lich's crimson-fire eyes narrowed to tiny pinpoints as she looked upon the holy object, and the tatters of black shadow that cloaked her body stirred restlessly as if a sudden wind passed through the chamber.

"Is that the best you can do, priest?" she said, her voice dripping with contempt.

"Not . . . at . . . all . . ." Diran gritted the words through clenched teeth and then closed his eyes. Bright silver light burst forth from the arrowhead and washed over the lich in a brilliant spray of blue-white illumination.

The undead fiend shrieked as the power of the Silver Flame struck her. She spun away from the light, raising an arm of her shadow-cloak to shield herself from its holy power.

"Skarm!" she cried out. "Attack!"

Ghaji felt the lich's fear-spell begin to dissipate just as the barghest leaped off the rock to do its mistress's bidding. Eyes glowing orange in excitement, the lupine creature bounded across the chamber floor toward them, splashing through horrid muck and scattering skeletal fragments as it came. Ghaji knew the barghest would attack Diran first, for if the creature could knock the metallic arrowhead from the priest's grip—or better yet slay him—then the silver light would be extinguished, and the lich would be free to kill the rest of them.

Diran still held a dagger in his left hand. Ordinarily he'd be able to defend himself with it, but the lich's fear-spell, while weakening, still affected them. Channeling the power of the Silver Flame through the arrowhead, there was no way he'd also be able to fight off the remnants of the fear-spell fast enough to employ his dagger. However, Ghaji wasn't as preoccupied as his friend.

As the barghest leaped for Diran's throat, Ghaji broke free of the lich's power and swung his flaming axe at the lupine creature. The blade struck the barghest in the neck and sank into its flesh. Black blood burst from the wound, and the barghest's blue-tinged fur caught fire. The creature howled with pain as the momentum of Ghaji's strike sent it slamming to the floor. The mystic flames spread rapidly across the surface of the barghest's body, and the creature rolled about in the muck that covered the chamber floor in an attempt to extinguish the fire and save itself. The elemental flames, however, were stronger than ordinary fire, and the barghest was only partially successful in putting them out. Its agonized howls rose an octave as it rolled to its feet and rushed past the four companions into the passageway, trailing flames behind it as it fled.

Ghaji looked to Diran, and the priest gave the half-orc a grateful nod before turning his attention back to the lich. The light pouring forth from the silver arrowhead doubled its intensity, and the lich screamed, the sound so loud and high-pitched that it felt as if red-hot spikes had been shoved into Ghaji's ears. Just as Ghaji thought he might go deaf from the noise, the lich burst apart into shadow-fragments that resolved into dozens of small black mice that scurried toward the chamber walls and swiftly squeezed into thin cracks in the stone and disappeared.

The light blazing from the arrowhead winked out, and Diran lowered a hand that trembled from the effort he'd expended. The four companions then stood in silence, waiting to see if the lich was truly gone. After several moments passed without hint of another attack, Diran tucked the holy symbol into his tunic pocket and turned to Ghaji.

"It's over."

The half-orc warrior looked down at Hinto. Though the danger had passed, the halfling remained curled into a ball on the chamber floor, pale and shivering.

Not for all of us, Ghaji thought.

CHAPTER

TWO

The lich was only banished, not destroyed. To finish the job, they had to find her phylactery, Diran said.

"Her what?' Hinto was still pale, but at least he was able to move and speak once more, though his eyes kept darting about, as if he were expecting the shadows to come to life any second and try to slay him. Ghaji had deactivated his fire-axe after the lich fled, and now Hinto held an everbright lantern to illuminate the chamber for them. The soft green glow made the chamber seem even more eerie than it had when they'd first entered—a detail, Ghaji was certain, that wasn't lost on the halfling.

"Phylactery." Diran was slowly walking around the chamber, slogging through the muck that covered the floor as he ran his hands over the walls. "Part of the process of transforming oneself into a lich requires that one's life force be preserved in a mystic container of some sort. That container is called a phylactery."

Ghaji stepped through the foul-smelling ooze to the nearest wall and joined Diran in examining the stone surface.

"The only way to completely destroy a lich is to destroy its phylactery," said Diran, "but liches don't keep their phylacteries in plain sight—though they do keep them nearby. She must have a hidden chamber behind these walls or perhaps beneath the floor."

Hinto looked down at the layer of muck. "You mean we're going to have to search under *that?*"

"If we must," Diran said. "We cannot allow the lich to continue preying on travelers."

The halfling grimaced. "I don't suppose any of you thought to bring a shovel?"

"No," Tresslar said, "but I do have this." He held up his dragonwand. "And I believe I have a spell or two that might suit our needs."

Tresslar had been traveling with them for several months now, but even after all that time, Ghaji still didn't understand how the artificer's magic device worked. He knew that Tresslar was able to absorb magical energy and store it inside the rod for later use, but how Tresslar released that power—or by what method he was able to choose which specific spell came forth—the half-orc had no idea.

Tresslar held the rod out at arm's length, closed his eyes, and concentrated. At first nothing happened, but then wisps of smoke curled out of the golden dragonhead's nostrils. The tendrils of smoke lengthened and extended from the dragonhead and began undulating through the air like serpents, going first this way then that, searching, searching . . .

Finally the smokewisps stopped at a section of wall that neither Diran nor Ghaji had examined yet. The ends of the tendrils brushed against the stone, seeming almost to caress it before finally dissipating in the air.

Tresslar lowered the dragonwand. "Search there."

Diran and Ghaji made their way to the section of wall that the smoke-wisps had indicated, and before long they found a section of stone the size of a man's palm that gave slightly when pushed. Ghaji pressed hard on the spot, and the wall swung slowly inward with a sound of grinding stone. They'd found the lich's hidden chamber.

Diran turned to Tresslar. "Well done. Can you use another such spell to locate the phylactery?"

"I could, but I'd rather we search by more mundane means first. I'd hate to waste a spell."

Ghaji shook his head. "You have to be the stingiest artificer I've ever meant. Most of them are only too happy to show off what their toys can do."

Tresslar snorted. "Such artificers are idiots. Magic is a tool that should be employed wisely and sparingly."

"I'm only too happy to look in there," Hinto said, eyeing the open doorway suspiciously. "As long as the floor isn't covered with bat droppings."

"Shall we find out?" Diran asked.

Hinto nodded and slogged through the muck, holding his breath the entire way. When he reached the doorway, he held the lantern forth and shone its greenish light into the chamber beyond. Hinto's hand trembled, causing the light to waver, but the halfling held his ground and did his job.

Ghaji and Diran had no problem looking over Hinto to peer into the hidden chamber. The room was smaller than the outer chamber—about half the size, Ghaji guessed—though the ceiling was just as high. No bats or other creatures were hanging from the ceiling, but that didn't mean other dangers weren't waiting for them.

Ghaji turned to Diran, and the priest shook his head. "I sense no evil within."

Ghaji knew his friend spoke of supernatural evil, not mundane, but he saw no reason to mention this with Hinto close by.

"I'll go first," said Ghaji.

The half-orc gripped his elemental axe as he stepped through the doorway and into the hidden chamber. The floor was blessedly free of muck, save what Ghaji tracked in on his boots, so if he had to fight, at least he'd have decent footing. Not that he'd have a lot of room to maneuver, for the chamber was filled with clothing, armor, and weapons, all cast about the room in haphazard piles—the possessions the lich had taken from her victims. The barghest had spoken of treasure, though from what Ghaji could see there was little of value in the piles.

Even so, that didn't stop Hinto from rushing into the chamber before Ghaji could tell his companions that it was safe to enter.

"Look at all this!" Hinto raised the everbright lantern higher to better illuminate the room's contents. The halfling's eyes gleamed in the greenish lantern light as he gazed upon the items. Before becoming trapped in the Mire, Hinto had been a sailor. Life was harsh in the northern waters of the Principalities, and those who plied the Lhazaar Sea did what was necessary to survive. No sailor—even one as prone to panic as Hinto—would be foolish enough to pass up an opportunity for salvage.

The halfling started toward a pile of clothes, but before he could reach it, Diran took hold of his arm and stopped him.

"Be careful," the priest said. "Just because these items once belonged to mortal men doesn't make them safe. If this chamber is where the lich keeps her phylactery, then it's likely that she's set traps to protect it. We must proceed with caution."

Hinto nodded, a chastened look on his face.

"What precisely should we look for?" Tresslar asked. "I assume the lich wasn't considerate enough to label her phylactery for us."

"Heh. No. You're right about that. Often an object that was important to a lich in life serves as the phylactery, but it could be anything," Diran said. "Something as simple as a locked chest or as ornate as a piece of sculpture. We won't know for certain until we find it, but whatever object is used, it is always cold to the touch."

"Then let's get to it," Ghaji said, nose wrinkling as he caught a whiff of the muck clinging to his boots. "I want to destroy the phylactery and get out of here before my sense of smell is completely gone."

With that, the four companions began carefully searching through the collection of items in the lich's hidden chamber. There was no treasure, though they did find purses containing various types and amounts of currency.

"I think we should take some of this money, Diran," Hinto said. "We're always short on funds since you refuse to charge for your services."

"Sorry, my friend," the priest said. "While I appreciate your Lhazaarite frugality, the money is tainted by the lich's evil, thus we must leave it."

With a regretful sigh, Hinto nodded.

While they looked for the phylactery, Tresslar also kept an eye out for magic items whose power he could absorb with his dragonwand, but the artificer found none. Either the lich's victims hadn't possessed such items or she'd done something else with them besides storing them here.

It was Ghaji who finally found the phylactery. The only armor he wore was a battered breastplate that he'd had since his days as a soldier. Despite Diran's warning to Hinto about the items in the chamber being tainted, when he came across a cuirass that looked to be his size—one that was better-made than his breastplate and relatively unscathed—he couldn't help picking it up to admire it. That's when he noticed three things: the front and back plates of the cuirass had been welded together, the openings for the wearer's head, arms, and trunk had been sealed with plugs of wax, and most telling of all, the metal was cold to the touch.

Ghaji carried the cuirass to Diran, and when the priest saw it, he couldn't help smiling.

"It seems our lich has a sense of humor. She stored her life force—her heart and soul—inside a human torso, albeit a metal one. Would you do the honors, Ghaji?"

The half-orc put the cuirass on the floor, placing it on its side so one of the welded seams was on top. Then he raised his axe and with a single blow split the front and back plates apart. Wisps of what looked like ebon smoke curled forth from inside the cuirass, filling the chamber with a foul smell like rotten eggs before finally dissipating

Diran said, "The lich is no more. Let us depart this place, seal the outer entrance, and . . ." He glanced down at his muck-covered boots.

"And find something to wipe this off," Ghaji finished for him.

Diran grinned. "Indeed."

⊛ ⊛ ⊛ ⊛ ⊛ ⊛ ⊛

Chagai watched as Ghaji and his three companions exited the cleft in the hillside. They'd been gone for some time, and the orc mercenary had been starting to wonder if they were ever going to return. From what he'd overheard before they'd gone in, a lich laired within the hillside. He didn't know if it was true. He rarely came to this part of the foothills, for the hunting was poor here. But after seeing the goblin appear from the cleft then be pulled back inside—not to mention witnessing the fiery exit of some wolf-like creature that dashed away trailing flame behind it—Chagai had no trouble believing the hillside was home to a lich. He did, however, have a great deal of trouble understanding why anyone, even a half-blood like Ghaji, would willingly enter a lich's lair. He puzzled over the idea while he waited to see if the four would exit alive.

Though it was now full night, Chagai still crouched behind the outcropping. The moons shone bright this evening, and while he doubted the humans would spot him even if he stood up and waved his arms about, he knew Ghaji and the halfling both had better night-vision. Thus, Chagai kept still and watched as Ghaji and his companions moved well away from the cleft. The older human pointed a weapon of some sort at the opening in the hillside, and a bolt of lightning surged forth to strike the cleft. The air filled with the sizzle of released power and the stink of scorched rock, and the opening exploded in a shower of rock shards and dust. When the air cleared, Chagai could see that the cleft had been sealed. Whatever lay inside the hillside—lich or something else—it seemed Ghaji and his friends wanted it to remain there.

After that, the four began heading off in the direction they'd originally come from. Chagai guessed that they were bound for Perhata, if only because there was nowhere else for them to go. Chagai was torn about what he should do next. He knew what he *wanted* to do: follow Ghaji and the others into Perhata and wait for the right opportunity for him to become reacquainted with his old friend. He had been out hunting earlier that afternoon when Ghaji and the others had come near a place where Chagai often caught mountain goats. They hadn't detected him. He was a full-blooded orc warrior, after all, and he was only seen when he wished to be. Still, they'd been close enough for him to catch and recognize Ghaji's scent, and he had abandoned one hunt for another, careful to remain hidden as he followed their trail.

He hadn't been out hunting goats for himself . . . at least, not only for himself. His employer had sent him out to bring back dinner, and while he was confident that Cathmore would understand why he'd allowed himself to become distracted, the man's patience only extended so far. If Chagai followed Ghaji and his friends back to Perhata, it would be a day or more before he returned to Mount Luster, and Cathmore wouldn't tolerate that long a delay.

"Go back to the city, Ghaji," whispered Chagai, "and celebrate your victory with your friends. You and I will meet again soon enough."

Chagai moved away from his hiding place and began heading in the direction of Mount Luster, hoping he'd come across a goat or two along the way.

❋ ❋ ❋ ❋ ❋ ❋ ❋

Much later that night, Skarm padded back to the entrance to his mistress's lair. His lupine body had healed much since the half-orc had set him afire, but he was still covered with suppurating blisters, and his fur—what there was of it—was scorched and blackened. The pain was excruciating, and the barghest whined softly with every step he took.

He wasn't surprised to discover that the hillside entrance had been destroyed, nor was he dismayed. His mistress had long ago prepared for such an eventuality. Skarm climbed up the hillside, picking his way through the rubble that covered the main entrance, moving past it, going higher and higher until he was close to the summit. The ground sloped more sharply here, and it took an effort for Skarm to maintain his footing, injured as he was. He reached a rocky ledge and climbed onto it, then stretched out a clawed hand and pressed the blistered palm against a section of stone in front of him that was slightly darker than what surrounded it. The dark spot subsided with an audible click, and a small doorway opened inward, just large enough for a lupine creature—or perhaps a small goblin—to squeeze through. Skarm wriggled through the entrance, hissing in pain as his injured sides scraped stone, massive blisters popping, clear serum trickling down his burnt skin. Once he was all the way inside, the door closed behind him.

Skarm padded along the narrow, cramped passageway as it spiraled downward. He came to another opening no wider than the first, and he was forced to squeeze through again, gritting wolfish teeth against the pain. The serum from his running blisters helped him slide through the opening, but it still hurt like blazes.

He stood inside a chamber lit by the flickering blue light of mystic gems set into the smooth stone walls at regular intervals. The light was dim, but it was enough for the barghest to see by, and surely it was more than enough for his mistress, whom he suspected had no need for illumination to see in darkness. This chamber was smaller than either of the other two, but then those were just for show. This was where Nathifa actually lived—if such a word could be applied to a lich. There were plush chairs upholstered with fine silk, a highly polished cherry wood table, several mahogany bookcases filled with leather-bound volumes, and a large canopy bed stuffed with soft down and covered in satin sheets. Skarm wondered why she had the latter, for as far as he knew, his mistress had no need of rest. There were other ornate and elegant objects displayed in Nathifa's living chamber—masterful paintings and tapestries, detailed sculptures, and trunks filled with gold and jewels, but all of this finery, beautiful as it was, displayed the taint of age and rot. The leather covering Nathifa's books was cracked, the pages yellowed at the edges. The colors of the paintings had grown dull, and the sculptures had lost definition. The cherry wood table was warped, as was the bookcase, and the upholstery of the chairs and the sheets on the bed showed signs of fraying. One object alone seemed to have escaped the corruption that affected all the rest. Sitting atop the table, mounted on an obsidian pedestal so it would be at eye level, was Nathifa's most prized possession: an obsidian skull.

The lich sat at the table now, elbows on the wood, chin resting on fists, as she stared into the smooth hollow sockets of the skull. The intertwining strands of shadow that served as her robe undulated like black kelp stirred by the motion of a slow current. Skarm knew they did this whenever his mistress was lost in thought.

Skarm forsook his natural form and assumed his goblin aspect. While he could also become a true wolf when he wished, the goblin was his favorite persona. Not only could he more effectively communicate while wearing this body, it was also much easier to stir up mischief. Though it had been his barghest form that had been burned, his goblin body was marked by the same injuries. Because it was physically weaker than either of his others forms, Skarm now experienced the pain of his burns far more intensely. He took in a hissing breath; he might have screamed but he didn't wish to disturb Nathifa. He stood there for a moment, gritting his teeth as he struggled to adjust to the pain. Only when he thought he had it under some measure of control did he allow himself to speak.

"I am glad to see that you are unharmed, my mistress."

Nathifa didn't take her gaze from the ebon skull as she answered. "It's not for lack of trying on that priest's part, I assure you. He's stronger than I would have given him credit for. Stronger, perhaps, than even he knows . . ."

Her voice trailed off, her manner dreamy and distracted. If he didn't keep her talking, she might well drift away into her own thoughts, not emerging for hours, perhaps even days, for she was undead and did not experience time the same way mortals did.

"Did they find the false phylactery?" the barghest asked.

"Hmmm? Oh, yes, they did."

Nathifa often said the skull, which she called Espial, spoke to her. Skarm had never heard the obsidian sculpture do so clearly, but he believed it, for sometimes he thought he detected a faint whispering coming from the thing, a sibilant voice muttering darkly in a language he didn't recognize. Like now.

"Did it take them long to find it?" Skarm asked, a hint of eagerness in his voice.

Nathifa finally turned away from the ebon skull to fix Skarm with an irritated glance. "I didn't remain behind to observe them as they searched. Suffice it to say that your deception fulfilled its purpose."

Skarm smiled but then grimaced as his burnt lips cracked and began bleeding. "I thought the cuirass was a nice touch. I hope they weren't too rough with it. We can make use of it again after we . . . I mean I repair the main entrance."

"There is no need. Our false lair has done its work." Nathifa turned away from Skarm to look once more into Espial's empty sockets. At least they were empty to Skarm. Who knew what Nathifa saw in their black depths?

"But that would make you vulnerable, my mistress!" the barghest objected. "A false phylactery is the perfect way to ensure that your true phylactery is safe!"

What Skarm didn't add was that if they didn't repair the main entrance, they wouldn't have any more visitors, and if they didn't have any visitors, he would be deprived of sustenance. Barghests survived by devouring both the flesh and souls of the living. No entrance, no foolish treasure-seekers. No treasure-seekers, no food for Skarm.

"Your concern for me is touching," the lich said, her voice dripping sarcasm, "though I wager your true concern is your perpetually empty belly. You forget the reason I built the false chambers in the first place."

"Of course I haven't. You built them—" *Though I did most of the work,* Skarm added mentally—"in order to draw adventurers to you because the skull told you to do so."

Nathifa reached out and gently stroked the smooth surface of Espial's skull with dead-white fingers. "Do you remember why Espial so advised?"

Skarm could feel the chamber growing colder: a sure sign that Nathifa was beginning to become irritated with him. "Because one day a certain man would come, a man bearing a golden dragon's head." Skarm's eyes widened in realization. "The old man! He carried such an object!"

Nathifa continued stroking Espial's gleaming black surface. "Indeed."

Skarm frowned and winced as the blisters on his brow burst. He wiped away the serum that threatened to drip into his eyes. "But if the man was here and he had the dragonhead, why didn't you take it from him?"

The temperature took a sudden sharp drop, and Skarm could see his breath mist in the air.

"The old man had companions. I . . . wished to take their measure before I acted."

Skarm understood. Nathifa hadn't expected one of those companions to be a priest and such a powerful one at that. She hadn't taken the dragonhead because she couldn't. It seemed that Espial didn't know—or at least didn't tell Nathifa— everything. Skarm would've smiled if he hadn't feared it would anger Nathifa further.

"What do we do now?" he asked.

"*We* don't do anything. Espial says the old man and his friends are bound for Perhata. You will go there and keep watch on them for me, learn what you can about them, and if the opportunity presents itself for you to take the Amahau—the dragonhead—do it and bring it directly to me."

Skarm didn't relish the prospect of trekking to Perhata—especially in his current condition. "I would be most happy to do as you bid, Mistress, but the old man and the others have already seen me. I fear they will recognize me if I attempt to spy on them."

"They saw you because they were distracted by the orc watching from the western mountainside. I sent you out to lure them in before they could head off to investigate who was tracking them." She glanced at the barghest. "And might I add that your performance was clumsy at best."

Skarm bristled. "But you must admit it was sufficient to draw them in."

Nathifa waved Skarm's words away. "Yes, yes." She sighed, the sound like winter wind whistling through hollow bone. "It's not like the orc to venture this close to our domain. Our neighbors on Mount Luster must be up to something. The question is, will it interfere with my plans?"

Skarm smiled, revealing teeth larger and sharper than a goblin should possess. "If it does, I am certain you will make them regret it, my mistress."

Nathifa placed her hands on either side of the ebon skull before her, cradling Espial's face in her hands as if it belonged to a loved one, and her dry dead lips slowly stretched into a bloodless smile.

CHAPTER

THREE

The four companions—their boots now relatively clean—sat around a small fire, huddled in their heavy cloaks against the cold night air. They ate a supper of tasteless trail rations while they debated whether to make camp for the evening or continue on to Perhata. Since they were no longer searching through the foothills, they could head directly to the city and reach it in a few hours' time. The moons were bright, and though the area was draped in shadows cast by the hills and small mountains all around them, both Ghaji and Hinto would be able to guide the other two with little trouble. Fatigue wasn't an issue, either, for since Diran had dispelled Tresslar's weariness, the older man was fresh and full of energy. Hinto didn't care one way or another, but the way the halfling kept gazing nervously into the darkness, as if he expected some terrible monster to come roaring out of the night, told a different story.

"I'm inclined to make camp," Diran said, "if for no other reason than that we haven't located the body of the barghest that Ghaji set aflame. It's possible the foul creature survived, and if so, it would need to feed right away in order to begin healing its injuries. If we remain here in the foothills, there's a good chance the barghest might attack our camp during the night, giving us an opportunity to finish it off."

Diran waited for the others to react, but no one said anything right away. Hinto kept his gaze cast downward as he nibbled without enthusiasm on a biscuit. Tresslar stared into the fire, his lips pressed together tight as if he were fighting to hold back words. Only Ghaji looked directly at him, and the half-orc was scowling. Of course, a scowl was Ghaji's most common facial expression, but even for him, this was an especially angry one.

Ghaji rose to his feet. "Before we decide one way or the other, we should check the area to make certain it's a suitable campsite, and by *we*, I mean you and I, Diran."

Without waiting for Diran to respond, Ghaji turned and walked away from the fire.

Diran waited a moment before standing. He looked at Tresslar and Hinto and said, "We'll be back soon."

Neither of them responded, and they still pointedly avoided meeting the priest's gaze. Something was obviously wrong, but Diran had no idea what it might be. He followed after Ghaji, who by now was only a silhouette in the darkness. Diran caught up with his friend, but Ghaji continued apace, saying nothing. He just kept walking. Diran fell into step beside the half-orc, knowing that his friend would speak when he was ready and not before.

When they had walked far enough that the campfire seemed but a candle flame on the horizon, Ghaji stopped and turned to Diran.

"You're driving them too hard, Diran. Tresslar and Hinto . . . especially Hinto."

Diran frowned. "What do you mean? We took periodic rest breaks throughout the day, and when Tresslar grew too weary, I restored his strength."

"I'm not talking about today, at least, not just about it. You've always been dedicated to combating evil, but ever since Grimwall, you've become almost obsessed with it. In these last few months, I think we've slain more undead creatures and fought more than in all the time I traveled with you before we battled Erdis Cai. I'm not complaining, mind you. Who likes a good fight more than me? But the constant traveling and ceaseless slaying have taken a toll on Tresslar and Hinto. It's affected the halfling even more than the artificer. At least Tresslar was an adventurer in his youth, but as you've pointed out to me on more than one occasion, Hinto was mentally scarred by his time shipwrecked in the Mire, and he's traveled with us ever since. He's had no time to rest and recover from his ordeal—how can he when we're always racing to kill one monster after another?"

Diran felt anger rising within him, and he struggled to keep an even tone as he replied. "Neither Tresslar nor Hinto has been forced to accompany us. They've done so of their own free will."

"They've done so because they believe in you, Diran . . . in what you do. Hinto most of all." Ghaji's voice softened. "He practically worships you. He'd follow you anywhere, do whatever you ask of him, regardless of the price to his mind and soul."

Diran thought about the way the halfling had fallen to the floor in the lich's chamber, how he'd lain there shivering, unable to fight, unable even to defend himself. If Diran and the others hadn't been able to draw the attention of both the barghest and the lich, Hinto would've been easy pickings for either of the foul creatures. This hadn't been the first time that Hinto's fear had gotten the better of him at a dangerous moment. Far from it.

Diran's anger faded to be replaced by guilt. As if sensing his friend's change of emotion, Ghaji put a hand on Diran's shoulder.

"You're not to blame for what happened to Makala," the half-orc said. "You did everything you could to save her."

"My *everything* wasn't enough, was it?" Diran said. He wanted to pull away from Ghaji and stalk off into the night. But instead he took a deep breath, centered himself, and let the air out slowly. When he spoke again, his voice was calm and more than a touch weary. "Are you suggesting I'm driving us all so hard because I'm trying to make up for failing her?"

Ghaji smiled. "I'm just a dumb half-orc, remember?"

Diran laughed. "Very well. We shall leave it up to Tresslar and Hinto. If they want to stay the night, we shall. If not, we'll start back for Perhata. Agreed?"

"Agreed." Ghaji's smile fell away then. "At the risk of straining our friendship even further, I think you should consider having a talk with Hinto. If he continues to accompany us on our 'hunts,' he's going to get hurt, perhaps even killed." The half-orc paused before adding, "Or worse."

Diran didn't have to ask his friend what he meant by *or worse.* He meant something like what had happened to Makala. Diran remembered the last time he'd seen her face—skin pale, canine teeth elongated, eyes blazing with hunger . . .

He'd already failed one of his companions. He wasn't going to fail another.

"I'll talk to him the next chance I get," Diran said.

Ghaji nodded and the two companions started back toward the campfire, walking together, but each alone with his own thoughts.

❂ ❂ ❂ ❂ ❂ ❂ ❂

Hinto and Tresslar opted to remain camped for the night and get an early start come dawn. They spread out their bedrolls around the fire and decided in what order they'd stand watch. As a priest, Diran could erect certain wards about their camp— some mystical, some physical—but these would only fend off undead or infernal creatures. More mundane threats would have to be detected by eyes and ears and met with cold steel. Diran selected the first watch, Ghaji the second, Tresslar the third, and Hinto the last. As the others settled into their bedrolls and drifted off to sleep, Diran sat cross-legged on the ground and concentrated on entering a meditative trance that would allow him to remain in a state of semi-wakefulness, senses alert, mind vigilant, for the entire night. Letting his friends have their sleep might not make up for the way he'd been driving them the last few months, but it would be a start. On the morrow, Ghaji would likely accuse Diran of taking the entire night's watch as a way to punish himself, and the half-orc would be right, but then, Diran thought with a smile, a little self-flagellation was good for the soul. He closed his eyes halfway, slowed his breathing, and settled in to keep watch over his friends.

And so the night passed.

⬤ ⬤ ⬤ ◉ ⬤ ⬤ ⬤

The four companions reached the outskirts of Perhata by noon. Their journey back had been uneventful, and if it hadn't been for the cold winds blowing down from the north, it might have been almost pleasant.

Though the citizens of Perhata referred to their home as a "city," in truth it was more like a ramshackle village. The docks were old and badly in need of repair or complete replacement. The outer buildings were unpainted shacks, their wood worn and weathered, the structures so rickety they looked as if a strong rainfall might batter them to the ground. The buildings in the center of Perhata were somewhat sturdier, though hardly more attractive: square gray-stone buildings of one or two stories. Even the baron's "palace" was of similarly plain construction, though it stood three stories high and was surrounded by a stone wall topped with rusty iron spikes to discourage unwanted visitors. The streets of central Perhata were paved, though their brick surface was often cracked and warped. The streets in the rest of the city were nothing but dirt and mud—given the city's proximity to the sea, more of the latter than the former. A cold breeze wafted in off the Lhazaar, filling the air with the salty tang of seawater. From any point in the city one could hear the cries of gulls, the shouts of sailors, and the lap of waves breaking against the pier.

The companions had a pair of rooms at a dockside inn called the King Prawn. The establishment's grandiose name belied the rather modest accommodations it offered, but it was the best they could afford, which meant they probably wouldn't contract a fatal disease by staying there. As they walked down the street toward the inn, they passed men and women of various races—humans, half-elves, and gnomes being the most common. Most were dressed warmly and huddled within cloaks of thick cloth or fur with the hoods up. With everyone garbed thus, it appeared the street was filled with shady characters of dubious intent which, given Perhata's reputation as a place where any type of business could be conducted without questions asked, seemed only appropriate.

Diran and the others entered the King Prawn and stepped into the common room. Sailors, traders, and low-level merchants sat drinking and playing games of chance, speaking to one another in low tones so no one else might overhear the plans they made. Cast-off bones and dropped bits of food covered the bare earth floor, all marinating in a stew of spilled ale and other less savory liquids. Despite the chill outside, the logs in the fireplace remained unlit, and the cold air smelled of sweat, desperation, and dark intent.

The four companions made their way through the crowd as they headed for the stairs, intending to go up to their rooms and divest themselves of their packs before coming back down to eat. But just as they were about to mount the stairs, someone in the crowd called out, "Hey, half-orc!"

Ghaji sighed. Normally he enjoyed dealing with the idiots who taunted him about his half-blood status, but he was tired and hungry and didn't have the patience for it right now.

He turned around. "Yes?"

A gnome stood up on his chair. He was smaller than Hinto, which made him short even for one of his people. He wore brown boots, brown pants, a white shirt, and a black leather vest. His bald head was adorned with an octopus tattoo, the tentacles reaching down across both of cheeks. From the way he wobbled unsteadily on his chair, it was clear the man was drunk.

"I got a question for you!"

Everyone in the common room grew silent as they waited to see what the gnome was going to say. Ghaji figured that more than a few of them were hoping to see the little man torn apart by an enraged half-breed beast-man.

"Since you're a *half*-orc, are your manly bits *half*-sized?"

Delighted with his display of wit, the inebriated gnome barked out a laugh and looked around the room to see what reaction his joke had gotten. A few of the men and women in the room laughed along with the little man, but most kept their gazes fixed on Ghaji, anticipating his violent reaction.

Ghaji turned to Diran. "What is it with gnomes and size jokes?"

"A racial inferiority complex would be my guess," the priest said.

"You're probably right." Ghaji considered drawing his axe and setting it aflame to scare the gnome, but he decided against it. It wouldn't be the wisest move to advertise he possessed such a rare weapon, especially not in a place like this. Since "borrowing" the axe from a guard on the prison island of Dreadhold several months ago, Ghaji had been forced more than once to prevent someone from trying to "borrow" it from him.

Instead, he reached down, undid his belt buckle, and allowed his pants to drop around his ankles. The crowd let out gasps of surprise and more than a few murmurs of appreciation. The gnome's eyes goggled as he took in Ghaji's "manly bits."

"As you can see," Ghaji said, "I received the best of both worlds."

A moment passed, and then the patrons in the common room broke into applause—and no one applauded louder than the gnome with the octopus tattoo.

● ● ● ◉ ● ● ●

Diran and Ghaji reached their room first, and Tresslar and Hinto continued down the hall to theirs. As Ghaji opened the door to the room, Diran said, "If I were you, I'd prepare myself to be visited by any number of ladies tonight . . . and perhaps even a few gentlemen."

Ghaji was about to tell Diran that he wasn't any funnier than the gnome, but before he could do so, a feminine voice came from within the room.

"He's already got a visitor, though I'm not sure too many people would call me a lady."

Ghaji and Diran stepped into the room and saw a slender elf-woman sitting atop one of their straw-filled sleeping pallets. Her chestnut-colored hair was braided in colorful beaded strands, as was the custom in the Principalities. She wore a white shirt with long billowy sleeves, tight black pants, knee-high black boots, and a wide black belt with an iron buckle. Hanging from the belt was a leather pouch that Ghaji knew was filled with any number of surprises.

"Yvka!" Ghaji broke into a broad grin upon seeing the elf-woman. The sight of an orc—even a half-orc—baring his teeth normally would've sent a shiver of fear through even the most seasoned of warriors, but Yvka returned the grin, hopped lightly to her feet, and ran over to embrace Ghaji. Despite the elf-woman's thin frame, she nearly knocked Ghaji off his feet as she threw herself into his arms. They kissed, and when they were done, they kissed again.

Diran cleared his throat. "I'll just go on down and have something to eat while you two finish saying hello."

● ● ● ◉ ● ● ●

Diran, Tresslar, and Hinto sat at a table in the common room, their meal long finished. They were drinking ale and talking when Ghaji and Yvka at last came downstairs. There was a scattering of laughter and raised mugs from the other patrons when they saw Ghaji, and the half-orc waved good-naturedly as he led Yvka over to his friends' table.

"What was that all about?" the elf-woman asked as they sat.

"There was this drunken gnome," Hinto began, but Ghaji shot him a dark look and the halfling mumbled, "Never mind" and turned his attention back to his ale.

"It's good to see you again, my dear," Tresslar said. "It's been far too long."

Ykva smiled. "I'm afraid the life of an entertainer is an uncertain one. It seems I'm always moving from one town to another in search of my next job."

Hinto put down his mug and wiped a smear of foam off his upper lip. "What are you talking about? I thought you worked for—"

The halfling cried out in pain as Ghaji's boot connected solidly with his shin.

"Hinto, while I may, upon occasion, perform certain tasks not related to entertaining, I'd appreciate it if you could avoid speaking of them aloud."

"Our friend is a juggler and acrobat," Diran said. "Remember? And one who possesses more than a touch of wanderlust, I might add."

Understanding shown on Hinto's face at last, and he gave the elf-woman a wink. "No problem. I'll be as quiet as a Tantamar brothel after an outbreak of fire-fungus."

"Thank you." Yvka smiled at the halfling sailor.

She seemed amused by Hinto, but Ghaji didn't think the situation was funny. Though she'd never come out and said so to any of them—not even him— she was an operative who worked for the Shadow Network, an organization of mercenaries, spies, and assassins that didn't officially exist. The most valuable weapon an operative possessed was secrecy, and if Yvka's true profession became known, she could be placed in grave danger. While the elf-woman could handle herself well in just about any situation, given how Ghaji felt about her, he couldn't help feeling at least a little protective.

Ghaji decided to change the subject. "So what were you three talking about before we got here?"

"We were taking bets on how long it would be before you came down from the room," Hinto said. "Tresslar won."

Ghaji scowled as Hinto and Diran tossed coins over to Tresslar, but Yvka just laughed.

"That means the next round of drinks is on me." The artificer raised his hand to catch a serving woman's attention.

"Before that, we were talking about yesterday's expedition," Diran said. "I assume you didn't get the opportunity to tell Yvka about it?"

Ghaji shook his head and Diran gave the elf-woman a quick run-down of their battle with the lich in her mountain lair.

During the telling, Tresslar ordered more ales, and the serving woman went off to fetch them. Diran was finished with the story by the time their drinks arrived.

Yvka lifted her clay mug and sniffed the contents with suspicion. "Is the ale any good in this place?"

Tresslar took a sip of his and grimaced. "If by *good* you mean *awful,* then yes."

Yvka considered tasting her ale, but then put the mug back down on the table. It seemed even an operative of the infamous Shadow Network was only so brave. "It sounds as if you four had quite an adventure yesterday. Sorry I missed it."

Ghaji listened as Diran filled in Yvka about their hunt for the lich, and from the tone of his voice, Ghaji guessed something was bothering his friend. "It's not like you to sit with a mug of ale in your hand and relive old glories, Diran. There had to be some other reason why you were discussing the lich."

"There was. Did you notice anything strange about her lair?"

"You're joking, right? It was a lich's home—the whole *place* was strange."

Diran smiled. "I meant anything unusual for a lich."

Ghaji thought for a moment. "Now that you mention it, her lair seemed overdone, almost as if it were something out of a child's tale."

Diran nodded. "It takes a strong will and a great amount of mystic knowledge for someone to transform herself into a lich. In life, such individuals are usually devoted to the acquisition of power in all its forms: political and economic, as well as magical. After they enter a state of undeath, they are loath to give up the riches they stockpiled in life. They surround themselves with finery . . . ornate clothes, luxurious furnishings, rare and beautiful artifacts of all sorts, though it's only a short time before the lich's corruption begins to taint those possessions with rot and decay."

"There was plenty of rot and decay in the lich's lair," Ghaji said, "but not so much in the way of finery. Even the objects in the chamber that held her phylactery seemed more like a collection of odds and ends taken from her victims over the years than a hoard of prized possessions."

"Precisely my thinking," Diran said. "It was almost as if she purposely constructed her chambers to resemble a fiend's lair, like a set built for a play."

"I acknowledge that hunting and dispatching the undead is your area of expertise," Tresslar said, "but during my time with Erdis Cai, we ran into more than a few such fiends ourselves. While they often do conform to certain patterns of behavior—much like animals follow their instinctive nature—they once were human, and some remnant of that remains buried inside them. Because of this, the undead sometimes defy expectations, and you find a ghoul that resists its craving for human flesh, a zombie that refuses to obey its creator's orders, a vampire . . ." Tresslar broke off, suddenly uncomfortable.

Ghaji glanced at Diran to see if Tresslar's words had disturbed him, but the priest's expression was unreadable.

Tresslar cleared his throat and hurried on. "My point is that this particular lich, for whatever reasons, chose to create a lair that was different from what most liches would have. Perhaps she built her chambers according to her own expectations of what a fiend's lair should look like."

Diran seemed to consider the artificer's point for several moments before slowly nodding. "Perhaps so." He said no more on the matter, and an awkward silence descended over the table.

It was Yvka who finally broke the quiet. "I wish I could say that I have come here solely to see the four of you again"—she flashed Ghaji a smile—"but I cannot. Instead I've come on business. Certain friends of mine have come into possession of knowledge that I think will be of interest to all of you, but most especially to Diran."

The priest, who'd been lost in thought, looked up in surprise. "Indeed?"

Yvka nodded. "Tell me, is the name Aldarik Cathmore familiar to you?"

Diran didn't answer, but his shocked expression spoke for him. Ghaji was about to ask his friend what was wrong, when the door to the common room burst open and a group of men and woman entered, bringing a chill breeze with them. There were six of them—four male, two female. Garbed in thick red waterproof cloaks, they carried long-swords belted around their waists, though Ghaji doubted the swords were the sole extent of their weapons. As the six red-cloaks came inside, they pulled back their hoods to reveal they all bore the same tattoo on their forehead: a stylized blue skull.

One of the newcomers, a broad-shouldered man with a blond beard, appeared to be the leader. He looked around the room, taking the measure of its patrons, and then said, "I bring you greetings from your neighbors across the Gulf of Ingjald! The Coldhearts have just made port and we have a ravenous thirst for some fine ale, but since the best drink can only be found in the taverns of Kolbyr, I suppose we'll have to make do with the piss-water you people serve!"

Blond-Beard's companions laughed as if their leader had just made the funniest jest in the history of the Principalities. But none of the King Prawn's customers came even close to smiling.

Diran looked at Ghaji. "How long do you think it'll be before a fight breaks out?"

"Less than a minute. Better get ready." Ghaji drew his axe, though he didn't activate its flames. Diran's hands disappeared beneath the tabletop and remained there, out of sight. Ghaji knew the priest had drawn a pair of daggers and was ready to use them should the need arise.

Tresslar sighed. "I'll say one thing. My life hasn't been dull since I joined up with you two." The artificer left his dragon-wand tucked beneath his belt—for the moment, at least. Tresslar wasn't one to expend magic unless it was absolutely necessary.

Ghaji glanced at Hinto, but the halfling showed no signs of panic. He was a sailor, and to him this was just another tavern fight in the offing. Nothing out of the ordinary and thus nothing to fear.

Yvka leaned close and whispered in Ghaji's ear. "First a thoroughly invigorating greeting, and now a swordfight in a seedy tavern. You sure know how to show a woman a good time."

"What can I say? Only the best for my girl."

That's when the first drunken fool leaped up from his table, drew his sword, and ran at the leader of the Coldhearts, bellowing a battle-cry.

"Let's go," Diran said.

As Ghaji and the priest jumped to their feet, the half-orc was glad to see that his friend smile grimly. Whoever Aldarik Cathmore was, they could worry about him later. Right now they had work to do—the kind they did best.

Weapons in hand, the two companions rushed forward, side by side.

CHAPTER

FOUR

It's cold."

"Nonsense. This chamber is directly above a thermal vent. If anything, it's sweltering in here."

Cathmore drew his bearskin cloak tighter around his cadaverously thin frame. He didn't reply to Galharath because he knew the kalashtar was right. Though he couldn't feel the heat himself, he could see the sweat running down the other man's slightly angular face. Cathmore was envious. It had been a long time since he'd felt warm, and he almost couldn't remember what it was like.

Galharath possessed the physical traits common to kalashtar men—tall, slim, clean-shaven, and handsome. He wore his long brown hair in a braid with crystal shards of various colors woven in. Open-fingered leather gloves covered each hand, with eight more crystals affixed to the knuckles. Yet another crystal—this one large and emerald green—was embedded in the center of the black leather vest worn over his gray tunic. Cathmore didn't fully understand the nature of the crystals or how they aided Galharath in his work, but then he knew little of magic and even less of the psionic artificer's craft—and he didn't care to learn. All that mattered to him were results.

The two men stood surrounded by the darkness of a vast mountain cavern, awash in an island of pale green light cast by a series of everbright light-poles bolted to the stone floor. The light-poles surrounded and illuminated a large spherical structure twenty feet high and ten feet wide. The object was fashioned from thousands of hair-thin crystalline strands woven together to form a solid, gleaming surface. Four large crystal struts extended from the top of the sphere and stretched up into the darkness where they were embedded in the ceiling's rough stone. A dozen smaller struts protruded from the sphere's base, curved downward, and penetrated the cavern floor. Though Cathmore had never asked, he assumed these smaller struts connected the sphere to the thermal vent that was making his kalashtar associate sweat so. In the middle of the sphere was an eight-foot by four-foot opening, and visible within—for the sphere was hollow—lay a crystal table with a series of indecipherable runes carved into its sides.

Galharath stood before the sphere's entrance, eyes closed, hands held out before him, his thin, graceful fingers moving through the air as if he were a musician delicately plucking the strings of an invisible, silent instrument.

Cathmore disliked being near Galharath when the kalashtar was working, which was why he stood a dozen feet away from the artificer at the edge of the pool of light. The atmosphere always felt charged like after a violent thunderstorm, and there was an irritating insect-like drone in the air that Cathmore sometimes thought seemed to issue from inside his own mind. These visits often left him with a headache, but Cathmore had made an investment of both time and resources in this project—a great deal of each, as a matter of fact—and he was determined to oversee its progress.

"So? Have you managed to repair it?"

Galharath didn't open his eyes as he replied. "I've fixed the outer shell, but that's the easy part. There's also a lattice of psionic energies that must be perfectly aligned in order for the forge to function. Adjusting this lattice is painstakingly delicate work, requiring as much instinct as skill, and despite what you might think, that process isn't sped up by you constantly looking over my shoulder as I work."

Cathmore clenched his jaw in anger. There had been a time when someone who spoke to him like that would've been well advised to hire himself a food taster, but though the kalashtar was technically employed by Cathmore, the psionic artificer viewed himself as an equal partner in this endeavor, and since Cathmore had need of the man's undeniable expertise, he chose not to make an issue of Galharath's impertinence. This time.

Forget the fool, you don't need him. You don't need anyone or anything . . . except me.

The voice that whispered in Cathmore's mind was a familiar one, and he knew it as well as he did his own, in many ways better.

It would be so simple. All you'd have to do is remove the vial of yellow death-spores from your doublet pocket, pry out the cork, and release a few into the air. You took the antidote years ago and are immune, but Galharath isn't. All the kalashtar's psionic abilities couldn't prevent the spores from seeking him out, finding their way into his lungs, and swiftly beginning to reproduce. In only a few moments, Galharath would die gasping for air, his throat and lungs filled with newly born spores.

Without even realizing he was doing so, Cathmore's hand reached toward the pocket of his brown doublet.

Galharath's hand motions stopped. He opened his eyes and turned to face Cathmore. "Don't do it, old man. I'm well aware of the dark voice that speaks to you and what it urges you to do. It would only take me an instant's thought to reduce your brain to steaming jelly."

At first Cathmore had no idea what the artificer was talking about, but then he realized his fingers had slid inside his pocket. It took an effort of will, but he withdrew them and allowed his hand to drop to his side. Though Cathmore's hands weren't visible beneath his bearskin cloak, Galharath nevertheless relaxed.

"You're bluffing," Cathmore said. "You don't possess that kind of power."

The kalashtar gave him a thin smile.

They locked gazes for several moments, but it was Cathmore who looked away first. "I . . . apologize, Galharath. It was a momentary lapse of control on my part. It won't happen again."

The kalashtar's smile took on a mocking edge. "It *will* happen again, and more frequently. Hosting an entity such as the one that dwells within you comes with a price. Just look at you. How old are you? Sixty? Seventy? You look closer to a hundred, and not a very healthy hundred at that."

Cathmore was fifty-nine, but he knew Galharath wasn't overstating the case. He was a skeleton of a man, little more than parchment-thin skin stretched tight over brittle bone. He had only wisps of white hair clinging to his bald pate, and a patchy white beard that refused to grow any fuller. Most telling of all were his eyes. They were a sour yellow-green, like pus-filled wounds ready to burst at any moment. Cathmore was struck anew by the irony that he, a master of poisons, had been infected with a toxin. That this toxin wasn't derived from a chemical but was instead of a spiritual nature didn't matter. In the end, poison was poison: the only question was how long it took to kill, and the dark spirit that shared Cathmore's body hadn't killed him yet.

"How much longer do you think you can go on, Cathmore?" Galharath asked.

Cathmore's reply was as cold as steel. "As long as I must." He continued in a softer tone, surprising himself by how weary he sounded. "I'll leave you to your work. Keep me informed of your progress."

Without waiting for the kalashtar's reaction, Cathmore turned and walked away from the crystalline sphere, his footsteps echoing in the cavern air. The mountain cave was huge, and as far as Cathmore could tell, completely natural. The ceiling was so high and the walls so far apart that the everbright light-poles stationed around the sphere couldn't illuminate the entire place. Galharath had told him that the cavern needed to be this large, that its shape and size—not to mention the mineral deposits within its stone—made it perfect for channeling and focusing psionic energy. That might be, Cathmore thought, but it still seemed like a waste of space to him.

He was halfway to the stairs that led to the facility's upper levels when he saw the dim form of Chagai coming toward him out of the cavern gloom. Cathmore's mouth wrinkled in distaste. While the orc made an effective servant, his attitude left a great deal to be desired. Cathmore wasn't particularly fond of the creatures. Oh, they could fight well enough and they were cunning, he'd give them that, but they possessed precious little stealth and even less self-control. Worse, they stank like a wet hound that had rolled back and forth over a dead animal carcass several dozen times.

Chagai stopped when he reached Cathmore and nodded once. It was as close as the orc mercenary would get to a sign of respect. "I've laid in supplies for the next several days. Salted meat, fresh water. I've also checked all the levels and made certain they're secure. I'm going into Perhata for some other things. Fruits and vegetables, maybe some fish, and we're running low on wine. I'll bring back a few bottles."

Cathmore didn't trust the orc to tell the difference between a fine wine and basilisk urine. "There's no need to go into the city. We're getting by well enough on what you provide, Chagai, and the less any of us are seen outside Mount Luster, the better—at least until we get this facility operational."

The orc scowled, but he didn't bare his teeth, so Cathmore knew that he wasn't angry, merely thinking. "I'll be cautious. Perhata is a rough town where people know better than to ask too many questions. No one will pay any attention to a lone orc buying a few supplies."

"Your . . . *people* aren't that common in the Principalities. You might draw more attention than you think. I prefer that you remain in the facility."

Chagai's scowl deepened, and this time he bared his teeth. "And I prefer to go."

Cold anger gripped Cathmore. There had been a time when he wouldn't have had to associate with such a creature, let alone put up with one defying him.

You still have that vial of death-spores, reminded the dark spirit that shared his soul.

Cathmore struggled to control his anger, always a difficult task when the dark spirit goaded him. He thought of the facility, of the riches it would bring him once it was up and running again, but most of all, he thought of the revenge that would be his after he'd become the Lord of Mount Luster. He imagined the look on his dear half-brother's face when one of Cathmore's creations stalked into his bedchamber one night—after having penetrated the supposedly impregnable security of his manor home—just before the creature stopped his heart with but a single thought.

It was an image that Cathmore hoped to make reality sooner rather than later. It was a gentler death than Emon deserved, Cathmore supposed, but he preferred his kills to be clean and tidy. Poisons were so much more subtle and elegant than the garish brutality of the blade.

"I'm going now."

Cathmore was startled out of his thoughts by Chagai's declaration. Without another word, the orc turned and began walking toward the stairs. The fury that Cathmore had worked to suppress flared bright and strong then, and he reached out and grabbed hold of Chagai's shoulder. He hadn't the strength to stop the orc, let alone turn him around, but the mere act of laying his hand upon Chagai's person was enough to make him halt.

The orc didn't turn to face Cathmore, but the emaciated old man could feel Chagai tremble with rage beneath his touch.

"I may work for you, but that does not give you the right to insult me," the orc growled. "Remove your hand or I will tear your arm from its socket."

The death-spores . . . urged the dark spirit.

With his free hand, Cathmore reached into his doublet pocket and closed his skeletal fingers around the vial within, but before he could remove the spores, Galharath was suddenly standing next to them. Cathmore hadn't seen or heard the artificer cross the cavern to reach them, and he wondered if that was because he had been too caught up in his anger to notice, or because the kalashtar had used his psionic abilities to mask his approach.

"I'm tempted to let you two kill each other," Galharath said, "but then I wouldn't get paid. Take your hand away from the orc's shoulder, Cathmore . . . and Chagai, don't use the opportunity to spin around and attack."

Cathmore took a deep breath, released it, then did as the kalashtar asked.

The orc turned slowly to face Galharath. "I don't like having my mind read, artificer."

The kalashtar laughed. "I didn't need to pry into your thoughts to divine your intent. You *are* an orc, after all."

Chagai's upper lip curled in irritation, but he didn't dispute Galharath's statement.

Cathmore decided to start over. "I understand that you wish to go to Perhata, Chagai."

"I *am* going," the orc corrected.

Cathmore ignored the comment and continued. "I doubt simply buying a few supplies could inspire such . . . determination on your part. Why not tell us the true reason for your trip?"

Chagai glanced back and forth between Cathmore and Galharath, and then let out a disgusted snort.

"When I was out hunting yesterday, I caught a familiar scent."

The orc spoke for a while, and when he was finished, it was Galharath's turn to be angry.

"You spotted strangers snooping around the foothills, and you didn't bother to tell us?" The crystals affixed to the kalashtar's gloves began to pulse with smoldering light, as if responding to the strength of their wearer's emotion.

"Peace, Galharath," Cathmore said, barely able to contain a sense of mounting excitement. "I understand something about wishing to settle old grudges, and to that point, it would appear that our orc associate and I have something in common. Based on his description of the four men who entered the lich's lair, I believe that I also know one of them, though he was but a child when last I saw him. Still, I've made it my business to keep informed of his activities over the years, and I know that of late he's been traveling with a half-orc. I wonder if it truly is him . . ."

Cathmore trailed off in thought. As much as he wished to have revenge on Emon Gorsedd, he also had a score to settle with this man in black who traveled with a half-orc warrior.

"Who is this man?" Galharath asked.

"Diran Bastiaan," Cathmore said. "One of the finest assassins I helped train"—he paused—"and the only one who ever killed me."

* * * ◉ * * *

Enshrouded within the cavern's darkness, a large figure stood watching the three talk. He tried to understand their words, but it was so difficult for him to concentrate with the voices swirling around in his head like a multitude of leaves tossed about in a windstorm. The voices were always with him, shouting, whispering, screaming, but never silent. Never.

He wasn't concerned that the strangers would detect him, not even the kalashtar. The three had come to the Mount Luster weeks ago, and he'd been observing them ever since, and not once in all that time had any of them noticed him. Their eyes saw him, of course, the kalashtar's included, but their minds refused to acknowledge his presence—precisely as Solus wished it. He understood that they intended to repair the forge and activate it once more, but he was unclear on their reasons for doing so. Didn't they understand the dangers involved? Didn't they know what had happened the last time?

Solus knew. He was the only one left alive who did. And the voices, of course. They knew, and they never let him forget it, not for a single second.

He watched as the strangers finished their conversation and headed for the stairs. Then, after a moment's hesitation, he followed, his iron footsteps loud on the stone floor, yet still unheard.

CHAPTER

FIVE

The man attacking the leader of the Coldhearts was a short, portly sailor with an unkempt black beard and one milky-white eye. He brandished a long knife whose dull blade looked to be in dire need of sharpening. Even if the weapon had been well cared for, it wouldn't be a match for the Coldheart's sword. The blond-bearded warrior watched in amusement as the sailor came barreling toward him, gut bobbling seismically with every step he took. The warrior deliberately waited to draw his sword to show his contempt for his fat opponent.

Diran knew that while the fat man might be able to give a good enough account of himself in a normal tavern brawl, he'd prove no challenge to the blond-bearded warrior. Diran also knew that no matter how fast he and Ghaji moved, they couldn't reach the two in time to keep the fat man from getting spitted on Blond-Beard's sword. Diran held a pair of daggers in his hands, and as he ran toward the two men, Ghaji at his side, the priest hurled one of his blades at the fat man. The gleaming dagger streaked through the air and struck the fat man's long knife with a loud clang of metal. The impact knocked the weapon out of the man's hand and both blades tumbled to the filthy dirt floor.

The sailor stopped and stared mystified at his empty hand, as if he'd just witnessed his long knife disappear into thin air and couldn't believe it. The man was still trying to puzzle out what had happened when Diran and Ghaji finally reached him.

Diran put a hand on the fat man's shoulder. "Collect your weapon and go."

The sailor looked at Diran, his one good eye struggling to focus on the priest's face. The man was obviously drunk, which hardly came as a surprise. A sober man would've thought twice about trying to attack a half dozen well-armed warriors by himself.

"Yeah . . . sure . . ." the sailor mumbled.

He bent down to retrieve his long knife, tucked it into his belt sheath, and then without another look at Diran or the blond-bearded warrior, he staggered to the common room's door, opened it to a cold blast of wind, and stepped out into the street, drunk but still alive.

"You spoiled my fun, friend."

Diran turned to the blond-bearded warrior. The man was glaring at him, and while he hadn't yet drawn his sword, his hand lay on the pommel.

"Are you upset that I stopped you from killing that man, or because I ruined your entrance?" Diran asked.

"Both would be my guess," Ghaji said.

Diran knew his friend was right. Everyone in the common room was staring at the scene unfolding in their midst, and more than a few patrons were smirking at the Coldhearts where before they'd been either intimidated or angered.

The blond-bearded warrior leaned toward them, though he didn't actually take a step in their direction. "Do you know who I am?" he asked in a low, threatening voice.

"A loudmouth who's starting to annoy me," Ghaji growled.

The man's face turned crimson. "I am Haaken Sprull, leader of the Coldhearts." He nodded toward his five companions. "We are the warrior fleet of Baroness Calida, ruler of Kolbyr."

Diran understood now why the men and women in the common room had reacted so negatively to the Coldhearts' entrance. The barons of Perhata and Kolbyr had been vying for control of the Gulf of Ingjald for decades, and there was little love lost between the peoples of the two cities.

"Now tell me who you are," Haaken demanded. "Whenever possible, I like to learn the names of the men I'm going to kill." Haaken glanced at Ghaji. "Well, one man and one halfbreed, in this case."

The other Coldhearts laughed at their leader's dazzling display of wit.

Ghaji sighed. "Do you have any idea how many variations on that joke I've heard over the years? Bad enough that you're stupid, but do you have to be unoriginal too?"

Haaken clenched his teeth. "Listen, you filthy—"

Diran's hand blurred and Haaken found a daggerpoint dimpling the flesh just above his throat apple.

"I am Diran Bastiaan, and my companion's name is Ghaji. Now that the introductions are over, please continue with what you were about to say to my friend."

A hiss of steel filled the air as the other Coldhearts drew their weapons.

"You saw Diran disarm that drunk," Ghaji said. "Do you really think any of you are fast enough to stop him from giving your commander a second smile? Not to mention that you'd have to get through me first."

One of the Coldhearts—a woman with a patch over her left eye—sneered. "You're not so tough, halfbreed."

Ghaji's axe erupted in flames.

The Coldheart didn't say anything, but her sneer fell away, and her remaining eye widened in surprise.

Diran took the opportunity to glance over at their table. Tresslar, Hinto, and Yvka were still sitting and watching, but they all had weapons in hand now. Tresslar held his dragonwand, Hinto gripped the long knife he used in place of a sword, and Yvka held three playing cards—all the triad of shards. Diran knew they were no ordinary cards but rather mystical weapons of some sort designed by Shadow Network artificers. Precisely what the cards would do, Diran had no idea, but whatever it was, he knew from experience that it was bound to be deadly. He also knew his companions were merely waiting for a signal from him or Ghaji to come to their aid, but Diran hoped to resolve this conflict without bloodshed, so he gave the others a quick shake of his head. They nodded to acknowledge his signal and remained seated, but they didn't put away their weapons.

Diran returned his attention to Haaken Sprull. "Now are you going to finish insulting my friend, or are you and your subordinates going to leave peacefully?"

"I'll give you a hint," Ghaji said. "Pick the right one and you get to live a little longer."

Haaken's eyes darted back and forth between Diran and those Coldhearts that were in range of his vision. Diran could see the man weighing his options. Haaken wanted to live, but he also didn't want to lose face in front of the men and women he commanded. Unfortunately, given the increasing desperation in his gaze, the Coldheart leader was beginning to realize that those two goals were mutually exclusive.

Before Haaken could reach a decision, the door to the common room burst open and a woman with close-cropped strawberry-blond hair entered, followed by a half dozen others. Including the strawberry-blonde, there were three women and four men in the group, all of them armed with long swords and wearing red cloaks and black tabards over mail armor. Each bore the tattoo of a scorpion on the back of the right hand.

The newcomers quickly surrounded the Coldhearts—as well as Diran and Ghaji—and drew their swords. The patrons in the common room grew deathly silent, and more than a few of those sitting at tables closest to the red-cloaked warriors stood and began backing away with slow, precise steps.

"Greetings, Haaken," the strawberry-blonde said. "I see you and your crew have finally realized what a rancid tide pool Kolbyr is and have come to settle here in Perhata."

The woman's tone was flippant, but her gaze was cold and steady, just like the sword held in her relaxed grip. Diran marked her at once as a professional warrior who was all business: the opposite of an arrogant blowhard like Haaken. Diran also noted, almost without realizing it consciously, that the woman was quite attractive.

Haaken responded to her without taking his gaze off Diran, careful to remain still so he wouldn't cut himself on the priest's knife point. "Hello, Asenka. Wish I could say it's good to see your Sea Scorpions again, but then it never is. My crew and I happened to be in the vicinity of Perhata's waters when we realized we were out of wine. We decided to make berth at that collection of rotting driftwood you call a dock, and visit one of the oversized latrines you call taverns." He gave her a mocking smile. "All in the interests of furthering good relations between our two cities, of course."

Asenka seemed unfazed by Haaken's taunts. She looked at Diran next. "And you are . . . ?"

"Diran Bastiaan."

"And the reason you have a dagger pressed to Haaken's throat is . . . ?"

Ghaji answered for Diran. "Because he's the southbound end of a northbound jackass." The half-orc paused. "Haaken, I mean. Not Diran."

Asenka looked at Ghaji for a moment as if trying to decide whether he was feeble-minded or not. Finally, she said, "I can't argue with that." She turned to Diran once more. "As much as I would like to see Haaken's blood soaking into the floor, I'm afraid I'm going to have to ask you to remove your dagger from his throat."

Diran did as she asked, returning the blade to its hidden pocket within his cloak with an unnecessary flourish. Ghaji raised a curious eyebrow, but Diran, embarrassed at having been caught showing off, ignored him.

Asenka nodded to Ghaji, or more accurately, to his axe. "And if you wouldn't mind dousing your weapon before you set the whole place aflame?"

Ghaji nodded and with a thought extinguished the elemental axe's fire.

Asenka turned her attention back to Haaken. "I suggest that you and your people forget about procuring wine, head back to the dock, get in your sorry excuse for a ship, and leave as swiftly as wind and tide can take you."

Haaken, emboldened once more now that he no longer had a dagger-point touching his throat, asked, "And if we don't?"

"My people and I will leave and let these two"—she nodded to Diran and Ghaji—"do whatever it was they were going to do before we interrupted them."

Haaken glared at Asenka, then at Diran and Ghaji. "Sheathe your swords, Coldhearts," he said, eyes blazing with fury, jaw muscles tight. "Time to set sail."

His people did as they were told—though not without casting a few glares of their own at those who had insulted their commander—and then Haaken turned and walked out the door into the bitterly cold air, his men and women following behind. The last Coldheart to leave slammed the door so hard it tore halfway off its hinges.

Asenka addressed her people. "Why don't you go along to make sure they reach the docks without any more trouble? I'll stay here. I have a few more questions to ask these two."

The six warriors under her command sheathed their weapons and, without saying a word, left the inn to carry out their orders. Asenka then turned to Diran and Ghaji. "I assume you two have a table?"

❁ ❁ ❁ ❁ ❁ ❁ ❁

Skarm sat alone, huddled within a thick cloak. Though his burns had mostly healed by now, as a precaution he wore the cloak's hood up to conceal his features. Even if the priest and his companions marked him as a goblin, he thought it unlikely that they'd recognize him for who and what he truly was. While goblins weren't common in the Principalities, they were hardly unknown. There were two other goblins in the room right this very moment. Of course, those were true goblins and not barghests in disguise.

His table was only two away from where the priest and his friends sat—close enough for him to overhear what they talked about, but not so close that they'd notice him . . . he hoped.

Following the priest and his companions back to Perhata without being seen hadn't been difficult for a creature of his abilities, especially since they had chosen to spend the night in the foothills. Skarm had been grateful for a chance to rest, for it had given him time to heal the worst of his burns, but now that he was here, with the dragon-headed wand so close, he wasn't certain how to go about getting his hands on it. He'd been too weak to make a try for it last night, but he'd since fed on a pair of unfortunate drunkards who'd had the misfortune to pass out in an alley not far from here, and their flesh, blood, and most importantly, their life energy, had restored his strength.

Still, now that he was back to his full power, he couldn't come up with a suitable plan for snatching the wand, at least not one more sophisticated than grab-it-and-run-fast. That was the problem with being a shapeshifter. Not only did he change outwardly, but his mental and emotional state transformed to suit his new shape. As a wolf, he was a cunning hunter primarily interested in running free through the wild and filling his belly. As a goblin, he was crafty but cautious to the point of timidity. As a barghest, he was a ravenous killer that devoured its prey body and soul.

Skarm wore the shape of a goblin now, which meant that caution was his byword. It would do him—or his mistress—no good if he attempted to snatch the dragonwand only to be caught before he could make off with it. Better to sit, listen to the priest and the others talk, and hope that he learned something that would be of use to him in obtaining his goal.

So he sat and listened.

* * * ◉ * * *

"You're a *priest?*" Asenka said, then laughed at herself. "My apologies. I didn't mean for it to come out like that."

Diran smiled. "I'm used to that reaction."

"It's just that when you see a man holding a dagger against another's throat, 'priest' isn't the first profession that you associate him with." Asenka looked at Ghaji. "Let me guess: you're a bishop."

Yvka snorted, and Ghaji frowned at the elf-woman in irritation. He then replied to Asenka. "Diran's the only one of us who's taken vows, holy or otherwise."

The commander of the Sea Scorpions smiled with amusement. "Just asking. So the five of you were sitting here, talking and minding your own business, when Haaken and his crew came in and started to stir up trouble, and when trouble began, you"—she nodded to Diran—"decided to intervene."

"I'm a priest of the Silver Flame, one of the Purified. It's my job to combat evil wherever I find it."

Asenka looked at him for a long moment, and Diran wondered if he'd said something wrong.

"If anyone else told me that, I'd say they were full of bilge water, but you sound so . . . *sincere*." She stressed this last word as if it were foreign to her.

"Is that so hard to believe?" Diran asked.

"In Perhata, yes," Asenka answered. "In this town, people would slit their own mother's throats to make a few extra coppers. That is, if dear old Mommy didn't cut theirs first. Qualities like honesty and sincerity are in short supply around here."

"I don't know about that," Diran said. "You're being both right now, aren't you?"

"I suppose," Asenka admitted, "but it comes with the territory. I'm commander of the baron's fleet, and Mahir doesn't take kindly to his servants lying to him."

"You strike me as someone who does what she believes is best, regardless of what anyone else thinks. Barons included."

Asenka smiled then and gazed into his eyes. Diran returned both her gaze and her smile, and they sat like that for several moments until Diran became aware that they were being stared at. He broke eye contact with Asenka and turned to see that his companions were looking at him and smiling pleased, knowing, almost smirking smiles. Diran scowled, but his friends only smiled wider.

Irritated, though unsure exactly why, he returned his attention to Asenka. "I take it that it's not uncommon for you to have trouble with the Coldhearts."

"Every few months they sail into Perhata, stroll into the city, and make some noise, but they usually depart before causing any serious damage. They do it just to prove they can—and to annoy us, of course. As soon as they make port, the dockmaster sends a runner to inform me, then I bring some of my people around to tell Haaken to weigh anchor, and that's the end of it. Out on the open water, it's a different story. The Coldhearts periodically stage raids on our fishing and cargo ships, and they harass merchant vessels in an attempt to deter them from coming here to trade."

"Do you harass back?" Ghaji asked.

Asenka shook her head. "Mahir's father believed in striking back, a raid for a raid, a life for a life, but Mahir has more restraint. When he became baron, he decreed that we were only to strike back at the Coldhearts themselves, and that Kolbyr's fishing and trading vessels were to be left in peace."

"He sounds like a reasonable man," Tresslar said. "For a baron, that is."

"It must be frustrating for you and the Sea Scorpions," Diran said to Asenka, "unable to fight back as completely as you might wish."

"I'll admit it's not much fun at times," she said, "but I can see the wisdom in Mahir's thinking. We've been at undeclared war with Kolbyr for close to a century now, and while both cities still survive, neither has been able to thrive the way others in the Principalities have. Mahir isn't foolish enough to believe that we'll become friends with Kolbyr anytime soon, but he hopes to eventually establish a truce, one that will allow both cities to conduct their business without interference—at least from each other."

"I would think that progress toward such a truce would be difficult at best," Yvka said, "given how strong the enmity between your two cities is, and how long it's lasted."

Hinto nodded. "Every salt on the Lhazaar knows that the Gulf of Ingjald is rough sailing—and not because of the waters."

Asenka sighed. "Progress has been minimal, to say the least. I'm afraid that while Mahir has good intentions, a truce simply isn't possible until something can be done about the curse."

"Curse?" Diran asked.

"A hundred years or more ago, a trio of sea raiders sailed into the gulf. There were only a few fishing villages here at the time, and the three newcomers—impressed with the quality of fishing in the gulf—decided this would be an excellent location to settle and begin building their own empire. The three were family, two brothers and a sister, and their surname was Ingjald. As you might guess, they named the gulf after themselves. They selected a suitable village, one that wasn't too small but which also wasn't large enough to put up much resistance. They took over the village and renamed it after the oldest brother: Perhata. Perhata grew swiftly under the guiding hands of its new rulers, and the people, who had been unhappy at first to have their village usurped by the three raiders, became content."

"The younger brother, Kolbyr, had never really gotten along with Perhata, and he wanted a city of his own, so after convincing his sister to join him, he sailed across the gulf with her. They found a village to conquer and set up their own domain. The newly named city of Kolbyr also grew swiftly, and its people also eventually accepted their new rulers. The two cities competed for control of the gulf, but their forces were equally matched, so a balance of power was struck, and aside from the occasional raid by one side or the other, things were peaceful enough for the next several decades.

"As Kolbyr grew older it became clear that, despite a succession of wives, he was unable to produce an heir. His sister, however, had married and had a son, and she tried to convince Kolbyr to make him the next baron, for the boy was, after all, of his bloodline. Kolbyr had accumulated a great deal of power over the years, and he was determined not to share it with anyone other than his true heir. To make certain his sister's offspring could never succeed him, he had her son killed, as well as her husband. He tried to have her killed as well, but she managed to escape and fled to Perhata where she sought refuge from her other brother. Perhata was a more forgiving man than Kolbyr, and he gladly took his sister in.

"The deaths of her husband and son had driven the sister mad with desire for revenge. She began studying dark magic and eventually sought the help of infernal powers to gain her vengeance. Those powers listened. Kolbyr became fertile, and his latest wife had a child, but the child was born a misbegotten monstrosity, one that could not be slain by any known means, whether mundane or mystical. Kolbyr commanded that the creature be imprisoned, locked away to never more see the light of the sun. His wife became pregnant with another child, and though they feared the worst, this baby was born normal, as were her others. Only the firstborn was cursed. Though nothing could kill the creature, it eventually died of old age, and everyone thought that was the end of the curse, until Kolbyr's heir took over as the new baron of the city and had a child.

"For the last century, the firstborn child of each one of Kolbyr's descendents who've ascended to the barony has been born just like the first: a horrible, indestructible monster. Because the sister was living in Perhata as she learned the dark arts—and because she made no secret of who had laid the curse on her brother's house and why—the barons of Kolbyr knew exactly who was to blame for their misfortune. Over the years, the citizens of Kolbyr came to transfer the blame for the curse from the sister to the barons of Perhata, until now the cities simply hate each other on general principles. The curse of Kolbyr continues to this day, and the current baroness will not even consider peace as long as her firstborn remains a monster." Asenka smiled sadly. "So you see why peace is just a dream in the Gulf of Ingjald."

Diran considered the tale that Asenka had told him. After a time, he asked, "What became of the sister?"

Asenka shrugged. "No one knows for certain. The legend is that she just disappeared one night from her quarters in the baron's palace, never to return."

"What was the sister's name?" Hinto asked.

Asenka frowned. "Didn't I tell you? It's Nathifa."

A burst of laughter broke into their conversation. The companions turned their heads, curious who made the sound, but everyone around them was busy talking or drinking and seemed to be paying them no attention whatsoever. The only even remotely suspicious person they saw was a small cloaked figure sitting at a table alone, nursing a mug of ale, and he appeared lost in his own thoughts, though it was difficult to tell since his features were obscured by his hood.

* * * * * * *

Asenka bid them farewell soon after that, urging them to stay out of trouble during the remainder of their stay in Perhata—an admonition which elicited a snort of laughter from Ghaji. Asenka gave Diran a last lingering look, said, "See you around, Priest," and then left the inn.

Diran watched her go, then turned to see his friends grinning at him. He scowled. "Whatever you're thinking, I wish you all would stop."

"We're not thinking anything," Ghaji said, "are we?"

Yvka and Hinto shook their heads in mock innocence, still grinning. Tresslar, however, said, "Well, I'm thinking that it's getting near the dinner hour and that we should eat soon."

Diran, glad for the opportunity to change the subject, said, "I agree." He raised his hand and motioned to attract the attention of one of the inn's servers. A young man came over to take their orders, which, considering that all the inn had to offer this night was fish stew and hard-crust bread, didn't take long. As the server headed away from their table, Diran turned to Ykva.

"You were saying something before the Coldhearts barged in." He leaned forward, eyes narrowing. "Something about Aldarik Cathmore."

CHAPTER

SIX

Diran stood shivering on the raised wooden platform. He was dressed only in his breechcloth, and though the dank air raised goosebumps on his bare skin, it wasn't the cold that made him shiver. It was fear.

Standing next to him was a brown-haired man who also wore nothing but a breechcloth. Unlike Diran, the man's wrists and ankles weren't bound together by leather thongs.

"Take a good look at him, folks!" the man said. "He may be young, but he comes to us from the Lhazaar Principalities. Life's rough up there, so you know he comes from hardy stock!"

"He's too skinny!" someone shouted from the crowd.

Diran tried to see who it was, but while the platform he stood on had light-stones embedded along the edges, their radiance was somehow directed inward, illuminating only the platform itself. The area beyond was shrouded in shadow, and though Diran could tell that the chamber was crowded with people, they were only silhouettes in the darkness to him. He could hear some of them whispering to one another, and he could smell the tang of human sweat and nonhuman musk.

"True, but then he's only a child." The man turned to face the crowd and chuckled. "Which, of course, is why you've all come here tonight."

There was a scattering of dark laughter throughout the crowd. Before being brought here, Diran had spent several days in another chamber, bound in darkness within a large cage. He hadn't been alone. Inside the cage with him had been a number of boys and girls, some older than him, many younger, all similarly bound, all wearing only undergarments. They sat and talked in the darkness, with no food or water, and they saw no sign of their captors until tonight when an everbright lantern lit the chamber, carried by a grim-faced half-elf. He unlocked the cage door, entered, chose a child seemingly at random, and carried her off through a tunnel entrance, taking the light with him. The half-elf returned three more times, taking a different child every time. The fourth time he'd picked up Diran and carried him out of the cage, through the tunnel, and into this chamber where he was placed on this wooden platform next to the brown-haired man.

While Diran didn't know exactly where he was, he understood what was happening. This was a slave auction, and he was the one currently up for bid.

"I have no doubt he'll grow up to be a strong one," the slave-trader said, "assuming you're looking for a worker, that is." More laughter from the crowd. "But you don't have to take my word for it. See for yourselves."

The man's facial features began to blur, shift, and reform. His brown hair became thick and black, and he grew taller, his lean arms and legs taking on muscle. His chest became broader, his abdominal muscles more defined. When he was finished, he looked like a human male in his mid-twenties, with shoulder-length black hair, and a lean, almost wolfish face, with a penetrating intelligence in his gaze.

Diran couldn't believe it; the slave-trader wasn't human at all but rather a changeling!

Women in the crowd—and some of the men—let out appreciative whistles.

"Spare us the parlor tricks, Rawiri!" a voice called out. "Do you really expect us to believe you know what the boy will grow up to look like?"

The changeling turned to face the challenger. "You must be a first-timer—and a latecomer to boot." Though Rawiri appeared different—*Am I really going to look like that someday?* Diran thought—his voice remained unchanged. "This is the fourth time tonight that I've done this. I could defend my methods, but there are many buyers present this evening who have been valued customers of mine for years. They can speak to the accuracy of my predictions as well as I, if not better."

People spoke up from within the darkness that hid them from Diran's view.

"It's true!"

"The changeling has a gift for it!"

"I've been buying from him for the last twenty years, and he's never wrong!"

Rawiri bowed in appreciation of his audience's support. He straightened and said, "If you have no further objections, I will continue."

The challenger, whether convinced or merely silenced by the crowd's support of Rawiri, said nothing.

"Very good. Now, who wants to start the bidding at one hundred gold?"

People in the crowd began to call out offers. The changeling remained in Diran's form—or rather, his extrapolation of Diran's adult form—during the bidding, perhaps as a reminder to the audience of what they were buying. In the cage, Diran had heard some of the older children talk about what uses they might be put to after they were sold. Physical labor was the least of it. They might be put to work in brothels or used as pleasure-toys by their new owners. They might be sold to wizards for experimentation or to dark priests for sacrifice. There was even talk that they might be sold as food for those with very particular tastes. Whichever one of these awful fates might be his, Diran was determined to avoid it.

He'd done more during his time imprisoned with the other children besides listen to their dire predictions for the future. He'd worked slowly and methodically on loosening the leather thongs that bound his wrists and ankles, stretching, twisting, pulling, all the while feeling the leather chafe his skin raw. When the pain became too much to bear, he switched to gnawing on the thongs binding his wrists. When the pain become tolerable again, he returned to stretching and pulling. His plan was simple: when an opportunity came along, he'd break free of the weakened thongs around his wrists, then use his hands to pull off the loosened restraints around his ankles. After that, he'd run as fast and far as he could.

He'd been lucky so far. Neither the half-elf nor the changeling had noticed what he'd done, but Diran knew his luck wasn't going to hold out for much longer. If he was going to escape, he'd have to do it now, before he was bought and his new owner decided to inspect his purchase.

Diran rolled his eyes upward and allowed his body to go limp, not a difficult accomplishment given that he'd had nothing to eat or drink for several days. As he fell toward the platform's surface, he pulled his wrists away from each other, and the leather thongs tore like wet vellum. He hit the platform, reached down to his ankles, and yanked the loosened thongs over his bare feet. The leather straps were still tight enough to take skin with them as they came off, but Diran didn't care, didn't even feel it. All that mattered was he'd made his opportunity, and he knew he had only seconds to take advantage of it.

He jumped to his feet and scanned the darkness beyond the platform, hoping to detect some indication of a doorway or opening through which the crowd had entered the auction chamber. He saw no sign of a door in the chamber's gloom, though, and decided he had no choice but to rush into the crowd, shove his way through as best he could, and hope that he stumbled across a way out of this nightmarish place. Before he could take a step toward freedom, he felt a strong hand clamp down on his shoulder.

"Not so fast, my spirited young—" Rawiri was interrupted by Diran ramming the heel of his hand into the changeling's throat. The slave-trader's voice cut off with a wet glurk, and he staggered back, releasing his hold on Diran.

Diran didn't hesitate. He ran to the edge of the platform and leaped . . . right into the waiting arms of the half-elf. The changeling's partner enfolded Diran in a crushing bear-hug, pinning his arms to his sides so that he was unable to strike the slaver. Diran tried kicking, thrashing, biting, but the half-elf had seen what the boy had done to his partner and was careful to avoid Diran's attacks. Diran was considering trying to tear out the half-elf's jugular, but the man—as if reading Diran's mind or perhaps simply divining his intent from his gaze—pulled back his head and slammed his forehead into Diran's. Bright light flashed behind the boy's eyes and a roaring noise not unlike churning ocean waves sounded in his ears. Diran fell limp in the half-elf's arms, and the man carried him back to the platform and tossed him onto it none too gently. Diran hit the wood with a dull thump and lay there, struggling to hold onto consciousness, fighting to roll over onto his hands and knees so that he might make another grab for freedom, futile as it might be.

"How much for the boy?"

A man stepped out of the gloom and up to the edge of the platform. Diran looked at him, but his vision was blurry and all he could make out were the man's eyes: cold, sharp, gaze penetrating. They were predator's eyes, wolf's eyes.

Rawiri had reassumed the shape of a brown-haired human male once more, but when he answered, his voice was a raspy whisper. "This brat's not for sale." The changeling bared teeth that would've been at home in the mouth of a shark. "I intend to keep this one for myself."

From the tight fury in the slaver's voice, Diran didn't think the changeling planned to keep him as a servant.

Through eyes still blurry, Diran saw a flash of motion and heard a muffled clank-clink as an object landed on the platform only a few inches from where he lay. Coins, Diran realized, in a leather purse.

"If that's not enough to make you change your mind, I have more," said the man standing at the edge of the platform. His words were neutral enough, but his tone said that the amount had damned well better be sufficient.

Rawiri knelt to pick up the purse. He looked inside and grinned.

"That will do fine, Master Cathmore. Quite fine, indeed." The slave-trader tossed the purse to his half-elf partner, and the man snatched it out of the air as if he feared it might vanish if he didn't get a firm grip on it fast enough. "Mark my words: that boy is going to be nothing but trouble."

Diran's vision had cleared to the point where he could make out the feral smile of his new owner.

"I'm counting on it."

". . . hear me, Diran?"

"Hmm?" The priest looked at Yvka as if just realizing she was present. "Sorry. I was just thinking about the first time I met Cathmore. My parents were fishers, and one day out on the Lhazaar, we were attacked by raiders. They killed my mother and father, but they let me live, not because they couldn't bring themselves to slay a child, but because they could make a profit on me. They sold me to a slaver who specialized in procuring children, and I ended up for sale in a secret slave market in Karr-nath. It was Cathmore who bought me."

"What did Cathmore want with you?" Tresslar asked.

"Aldarik Cathmore is an assassin. He's also Emon Gorsedd's half-brother. They were partners—or at least, they were back then. Cathmore's job was to find new students for Emon's academy in Atur. Quite often these students were purchased from slavers, but sometimes they were simply abducted or in rare cases adopted after one of Emon's operatives killed the rest of their family. Cathmore did more than just find students for Emon, though. He also taught the new recruits, introducing them to life in the Brotherhood of the Blade."

"Then what's he doing in the Principalities?" Ghaji asked.

For that was the news that Yvka had come to deliver: the Shadow Network had learned that a man called Aldarik Cathmore had passed through Perhata several weeks ago, accompanied by an orc and a kalashtar. They'd purchased numerous supplies in Perhata, and the orc still made an occasional supply run, but as for Cathmore, no one—not a single operative in the entire Network—had any inkling of why the man was in the area or what he was doing.

"I can help a bit with the why," Diran said. "Cathmore and Emon had a falling out when I was still a child. Neither of them agreed on the best way to run the academy. Emon believed in keeping his organization small, lean, and mobile, while Cathmore wanted to expand the Brotherhood. Business was good during the final years of the Last War, and Cathmore hoped to establish his own academy elsewhere in Khorvaire. When Emon refused to support him financially, Cathmore tried to have him killed. After he failed, Emon gave his half-brother a choice: leave or die. Cathmore left." Diran paused, remembering. Then he pushed the memories aside and turned to Yvka. "What I don't understand is how you knew of my connection to Cathmore."

Yvka smiled. "I make it my business to know. I probably know things about you that you don't know yourself."

"Do you think Cathmore's running an assassins' academy here in Perhata?" Ghaji asked.

'It's possible. He's had twenty years to set himself up in business, and since Emon operates out of Karrnath, perhaps Cathmore decided to carve out his own territory here in the Principalities." Diran smiled grimly. "I wouldn't be surprised if he did so as a way of getting back at me, at least in part. He knew I hailed from here. Perhaps he even had hopes of luring me back."

"Why would he want to do that?" Hinto asked.

"Because I'm the one who stopped him from killing Emon Gorsedd."

❋ ❋ ❋ ❋ ❋ ❋ ❋

Eneas staggered down the street, but he had no trouble remaining on his feet. Like most Lhazaarites, he'd spent his lifetime on the deck of one sailing vessel or another, and he actually felt more at home on dry land when he was drunk. The way the world spun around him and the ground dipped and rolled beneath his feet felt not only natural but comforting, and Eneas could use some comfort right now. Not because of his run-in with the thrice-damned Coldhearts or the man in black with the steel-gray eyes—Eneas wasn't one to back down from a fight—especially when he'd swallowed a bit too much ale. Even so, though the man in black had interfered and sent him on his way, Eneas wasn't so drunk that he didn't realize the man had done him a favor. What bothered Eneas right now was what waited for him at the docks. That was the real reason he'd been drinking so heavily throughout the day.

The sun had already dipped below the Hoarfrost Mountains to the west, and night was settling over Perhata. Shadows lengthened, thickened, and deepened, like chill dark waters slowly seeping through the streets. The wind blowing in off the Gulf of Ingjald cut into Eneas's skin like tiny slivers of ice, and though he was a Lhazaarite born and bred, and cold normally didn't bother him overmuch, he shivered. He was a free-hire merchant, which meant that he'd haul any cargo for the right price and no questions asked. He owned a small sailing craft called the *Boundless*, and his boat—and the freedom she represented—meant more to him than anything in this life. Even so, he considered turning around, walking away from the docks, heading inland, and never returning to the sea or his beloved boat.

The shadows were omnipresent now, and though purple tinged the sky, it was beginning to edge toward black. Eneas used to love the night, used to love being out on the Lhazaar, sail billowing in the wind as he charted his course by gazing up at the canopy of stars above, but he didn't like the night anymore. He doubted he ever would again.

He reached the main docks of Perhata. There were private docks elsewhere, of course, but these were the ones where most residents and visitors moored their craft. This was also where the fishmarkets were located, as well as taverns so seedy they made the common room of the King Prawn look like the most elegant Sharn teahouse. Normally Eneas patronized these taverns—the ale was lousy, but there was always a rowdy good time to be had, along with an invigorating fight or two. Today, however, he hadn't been able to stand the thought of remaining close to the docks, so he'd been forced to go further into the city in search of refreshment. He wouldn't be returning now if he hadn't needed to. No, been *compelled* to.

He reached up, pulled down the collar of his tunic, and scratched at a pair of small bite marks positioned along the thick blood vessel between shoulder and neck. The marks itched and throbbed, but no amount of scratching provided relief. Eneas wondered if he'd ever know relief again.

By the time he'd walked down the dock to the slip where he'd moored the *Boundless*, full night had descended. At least he wouldn't keep his passenger waiting. Perhaps she'd release him out of appreciation for his promptness. Unfortunately, he feared she had other plans for him.

Fog was rolling in off the Lhazaar, and though everbright lanterns stationed at periodic intervals lit the dock, their softly glowing light did little to penetrate the mist. If anything, they only made visibility worse by coloring the fog an eerie, sour green, but Eneas didn't need to see to find his boat. He could feel it, or rather he felt *her*, calling to him, impatient for his return. He reached the slip where his vessel was moored. The *Boundless* wasn't anything special: one mast, small hold, even smaller cabin. The boat had a few minor touches added by a shipwright who was also an artificer, but nothing extraordinary—spells to make the mast stronger, the hull barnacle-resistant, the sail less prone to tears, that sort of thing. The *Boundless* was hardly an elemental galleon or a shard-racer, Eneas knew, but he loved the old boat as fiercely as he'd ever loved anything in his life. All he wanted now was to get rid of the creature that lay within her hold and have the *Boundless* all to himself again.

Eneas jumped onto the deck with a surprising grace that belied both his heavy frame and drunken state. The fog was moving in so fast now that he could barely see more than a foot in front of his face as he moved toward the hull, but he was on the *Boundless* and could find his way around her with both eyes put out if he had to. The fog seemed to cling unnaturally to his body, forming a slimy cold film on his flesh that set him to shivering. He opened the hatch and still trembling—though perhaps not entirely from the fog's chill now—he climbed down the short ladder into the hold.

Once inside, he reached into his tunic pocket and brought out a small light gem. He waved his hand over it, and the gem began to give off a flickering orange light not unlike that produced by a candle, though there was no heat. The hold was empty, save for a large obsidian object that resembled a coffin, only with rounded edges. Strange runes were carved around the sides of the sarcophagus, and if Eneas looked at them too long, his head would start to hurt.

He told himself that he didn't have to do it. Without him to unlock the sarcophagus and deactivate the enchantment suffusing the obsidian stone, she couldn't get out. She would be trapped forever, and he would be safe. He could haul the coffin out by a winch and dump it in the sea. If worse came to worst and he couldn't offload his strange cargo, he could scuttle the whole damned ship and let her go down to the bottom, taking the obsidian box and its inhabitant along as she descended into the cold, dark depths of the Lhazaar. He didn't have to obey—he didn't!

Nevertheless, he stepped forward, took hold of the lid's edge and raised it up an inch.

Eneas stepped back quickly as pale white fingers—feminine fingers—emerged. They curled around the edge of the lid and lifted it the rest of the way off the sarcophagus. The lid wasn't attached, and the heavy stone cover fell off to the side, striking the floor of the wooden hull with a loud thump that made Eneas wince. Then *she* sat up and stared straight ahead, motionless, unblinking, as if she wasn't aware of his presence. Then slowly she turned to look at Eneas, her head pivoting on her neck with unnaturally smooth precision, as if she weren't a being of flesh and blood but rather some sort of mechanical construct in human form. She blinked once, twice, and then awareness returned to her gaze. She recognized him, and she smiled, displaying long, white incisors.

Then, moving with the speed and grace of a jungle cat, she leaped out of the coffin and rushed at Eneas. He dropped the light gem, and as physical contact with the mystical object was broken, its illumination winked out. Eneas felt the woman's small hands take hold of him in grips of iron, felt her teeth sink into the soft flesh of his neck, and then a darkness far worse than the absence of light came for him and he felt nothing more.

❀ ❀ ❀ ❀ ❀ ❀ ❀

Makala raised her head and with the back of a hand wiped a smear of blood from her mouth. She looked down at the fat man lying on the floor of the hold next to her, his skin pale, breathing shallow, blood oozing from the twin puncture marks on his throat. Without realizing it, she leaned forward, intending to lick the wounds clean, but she stopped herself. She might not be human anymore, but that didn't make her an animal.

She stood and took three steps back from Eneas, lest she be tempted to feed on him further. What she'd already taken from the man would have to suffice; if she drank anymore, there was a good chance he would die. There was a time when that wouldn't have made a difference to her, a time when she would've taken his life as casually as she might snap her fingers and for lesser reason than ensuring her own survival. Regardless of what she'd become, she was no longer a killer, at least, not a mindless one.

If she was going to kill, then she would do so when and where she chose and for justifiable reasons—not simply because she was hungry.

She felt Eneas's blood suffusing her body, lessening but not alleviating the pervasive chill in her undead flesh. In many ways, that was the worst part about being a vampire. No matter the temperature, no matter how much she fed, she was always cold. She felt the boat rock beneath her feet as a wave rolled in to shore, and sudden nausea twisted her gut, threatening to make her vomit the blood she'd taken from Eneas. She clamped her mouth shut tight, and though she no longer had any reason to breathe, she took slow, even breaths until the boat stopped rocking and her nausea subsided.

For all their strengths, vampires had a surprising number of weaknesses, as Makala had found out over the last several months. One of those was an aversion to crossing running water. Why that should be, she didn't know, but she'd experienced the discomfort too often to dismiss it as merely her imagination. She'd been lucky, though. She'd discovered the obsidian sarcophagus on one of the elemental galleons that Diran and the others had left behind when they'd departed Grimwall after defeating Erdis Cai. Once a vampire lay inside and the sigil of Vol affixed to the lid was activated, he or she could cross running water without the least discomfort. She believed that the vampire sailor Onkar—once Edris Cai's first mate and the one who'd changed her—had employed the sarcophagus in order to continue plying the waters of the Lhazaar Sea. Unfortunately, the sarcophagus had one serious drawback: once the lid was sealed and the enchantment activated, it could not be opened from within. Whoever rested inside the sarcophagus was dependent on someone outside to release her, hence her need for Eneas. Not only did he transport her across water, he also released her when they arrived at their destination.

The attack of nausea had taken the edge off her hunger, so she felt safe in approaching Eneas and kneeling next to him once more.

"You've done well," she said in a soft, almost dreamy voice. "Now I want you to remain on the ship until I return. You will then seal me into the sarcophagus before dawn and release me once again the following sunset. Do you understand?"

Eneas's eyes fluttered open. They were wide and staring, but he nodded once.

"Very good. Rest now—you've earned it."

Eneas's eyes closed and a moment later he began snoring.

Makala stood and regarded her—for lack of a better word—servant. Then she turned toward the open hatch above her, crouched, and with an effortless grace leaped onto the deck. She silently disembarked the *Boundless* and walked down the dock to shore, her footsteps making no sound on the weathered wooden planks.

CHAPTER

SEVEN

"What are we going to do?"
Ghaji asked.

He and Diran stood in the street outside the King Prawn.
The others were still inside, watching as Yvka performed a
juggling act for the inn's patrons. While the elf-woman was
an operative of the Shadow Network—which officially didn't
exist—she posed as a wandering player. It might be a disguise, but she was nevertheless a damn fine entertainer, and
Ghaji wished he was inside watching her along with everyone
else. Diran had asked him to step outside for a breath of fresh
air, and since fresh air was difficult to come by in this part of
Perhata, Ghaji had known his friend really wanted to talk to
him alone, so here Ghaji was, standing next to Diran, his back
against the stone wall of the inn, trying to ignore the sounds
of laughter and applause drifting from the common room as
Yvka performed.

Full night had fallen and a clammy fog was rolling in off
the Gulf of Ingjald, turning the world into an indistinct ghostly

image of itself. The fog muffled sound and defied even Ghaji's orcish night vision. He had the sensation that he and Diran were the only two living people left in Perhata, and though he knew it was only his imagination, the feeling was an eerie one and not easily dismissed.

"About what?" Diran said.

"Cathmore. Where do we start looking for him?"

Diran gazed into the fog, and Ghaji wondered what his friend saw in its roiling gray murk. "I'm not sure we should—at least not right away."

"I'm surprised. I thought you'd be ready to set out on the hunt right away."

Diran turned and smiled. "You've come to know me too well, Ghaji. You're right; ordinarily I would want to begin searching for Cathmore immediately, but I've been thinking about Asenka." He gave Ghaji a sideways look, then hurried to add, "I mean, ah, about what she told us regarding the origins of the enmity between Perhata and Kolbyr. Remember?"

"Sure, I remember. I especially remember the way the two of you looked at one another."

Diran scowled. "I have no idea what you're talking about."

Ghaji grinned. "Of course you don't."

In truth, he was pleased that Diran seemed attracted to the commander of the Sea Scorpions and she to him. The priest hadn't shown any interest in women at all since the night Makala had died and been reborn as a vampire. While Ghaji regretted what had happened to Makala, he knew it wasn't healthy for his friend to mourn her loss forever. Perhaps Diran was finally showing signs of putting his grief behind him and getting on with his life. Ghaji could only hope so.

"What about the conflict between the cities?" Ghaji asked.

Diran looked relieved that Ghaji had abandoned his teasing. "Asenka said it stems from a curse—a curse that has been carried down to this day. If the curse could somehow be removed . . ."

"The conflict might end," Ghaji finished.

Diran nodded. "Or at least peace negotiations might become possible. It seems to me that we would do more immediate good by investigating this curse than by haring off after Aldarik Cathmore."

Ghaji considered this. "Perhaps, but the curse has lasted for almost two centuries. What would a few more days or even weeks matter?"

Diran smiled gently. "Don't you think two centuries is more than long enough for the people of two cities to be at war?"

Ghaji and Diran had both seen their share of conflict during the War—the half-orc as a mercenary soldier, the priest as a hired assassin—and both of them had participated in far too much mindless slaughter.

"Yes, I do." Ghaji sighed. "Very well, now that Yvka's here, perhaps she'll ferry us over to Kolbyr on the *Zephyr*. Once there . . ."

His voice trailed off as a familiar scent came to his nose: thick, musky, and earthy. He hadn't smelled this scent for close to twenty years, but he remembered it just the same. Orcs— even half-orcs—never forget a smell.

"Something wrong?" Diran asked.

"I'm . . . not sure. There's something I need to check out, Diran. Alone, if you don't mind."

The priest frowned, but he said, "Of course, but if you should need me . . ."

Ghaji nodded. "I'll let you know." He turned away from his friend and moved off into the fog, following the scent of a ghost from the past.

● ● ● ◉ ● ● ●

Diran watched his friend disappear into the gray murk, torn as to what he should do. It wasn't like Ghaji to run off on a whim, so something was up, and that something might well prove dangerous. Whether Ghaji wanted to admit it or not, there was a good chance he'd need Diran's help. But Ghaji had asked to go alone, and Diran had acquiesced. To follow Ghaji now would be to break a trust between them, and Diran didn't wish to do that if he could avoid it.

As he stood outside the King Prawn trying to make up his mind, he heard footsteps approaching. At first, he thought Ghaji had returned, but the sound of the boots scuffing against dirt sounded wrong—lighter, the stride measured and patient. Diran had no idea whether whoever it was approaching was friend or foe, but at the Perhata Docks, one encountered more criminals than anywhere else in the Principalities. He drew a dagger from his belt sheath and palmed it, just in case.

The footsteps continued coming closer until the vague outline of a human body could be seen. A woman.

Diran's heart seized in his chest, and he whispered, "Makala?"

"Is that a dagger in your hand, or are you just glad to see me?"

The woman took a few more steps toward him, and Diran could make out enough of her features to recognize the commander of the Sea Scorpions. With a fluid motion, Diran returned the dagger to its sheath. If Asenka had heard him call her by a different name, she made no remark on it.

"Good evening, Asenka. Don't tell me you've returned because you can't get enough of the King Prawn's delicious ale."

Her laugh was warm and cheerful, and the sound helped diminish the fog's chill. "Hardly. Today wasn't the first time I have run off Haaken and his crew. In the past, they've been known to sneak back and cause further trouble. I've been keeping on eye on the King Prawn, figuring that if they did come back, they'd come for you and your friend."

Diran felt a sudden pang of worry. Could Ghaji have detected the Coldhearts lurking about? His half-orc senses were sharper than Diran's human ones, so it was quite possible, but why would Ghaji have gone off on his own to investigate? The man could be impulsive at times, but he wasn't foolish.

"Any sign of the Coldhearts?" Diran asked, trying not to let the worry he felt for his friend creep into his voice.

Asenka shook her head. "Aside from the usual drunken scuffles between sailors, it's been quiet tonight. It looks like Haaken may have actually gotten the message this time."

Diran was relieved to hear that. Hopefully, whatever had lured Ghaji away was something the half-orc warrior could deal with on his own.

A silence settled between them then, more companionable than awkward, despite the fact that this was only their second meeting. After a bit, Asenka said, "I have a confession to make."

"Oh? It's a good thing I'm a priest then."

She smiled, but she didn't laugh this time. "Earlier, I acted as if I didn't know you, but I did. I've heard of you and your friend. The two of you have been in the Principalities only a short time, but you're already gaining quite a reputation in certain circles."

"What circles would these be?" Diran kept his tone light, but he was on guard.

Since coming to the Principalities, he and Ghaji had done what they could to battle evil, but neither of them was overly concerned about whose toes they had to step on—or on occasion, cut off—in order to get the job done. That meant that they'd managed to make more than a few enemies among the Lhazaarites, and it was possible that Asenka was one of them.

"Let's just say that word has spread among the barons to keep a sharp eye out for a dagger-wielding priest and a half-orc who carries an elemental axe. It's said that whenever they sail into port, trouble comes blowing in after them."

It was Diran's turn to smile. "I wouldn't dispute that, though I'd argue any trouble is present long before we arrive."

Asenka narrowed her eyes and regarded Diran. "Are you saying there's trouble in Perhata?"

Diran thought about what Yvka had told him regarding Aldarik Cathmore. "I'm not sure yet."

"Promise me something: when you *are* sure, you'll let me know before you start hurling daggers about and turning the citizens of Perhata into pin cushions."

"Why? So you can run Ghaji and me out of town, like you did the Coldhearts?"

"No, silly." She stepped forward until only a few inches of foggy air separated their bodies. "So I can help you." Then she pressed her lips against his and kissed him. Diran was surprised, but not as surprised as when he found himself returning her kiss.

Asenka pulled away, gave him a last smile, then turned and walked away until she was swallowed by the fog. Diran stood staring into the gray nothingness where she had vanished, glad that Ghaji hadn't been present. If he had been, the half-orc never would have stopped teasing him.

* * * * * * *

Makala crouched on the roof of the King Prawn, fingernails sharp as claws digging into the thatch. Though she was unaware of it, her mouth was open and her fangs bared. Thick as it was, the fog was no impediment to her inhuman senses, and she'd been able to see, hear, and smell everything that had occurred between Diran and that . . . that *woman*. Cold fury gripped her, so strong that it was all she could do to keep from launching herself into the air and following after Asenka. She'd already fed tonight thanks to Eneas, but her belly was far from full, and she still hungered, and who better to slake her thirst than that over-eager tramp? The woman's words to Diran echoed in Makala's mind like a mocking whisper.

No, silly. So I can help you.

Makala's muscles tensed, and she was about to fling herself from the roof, but she stopped herself. She hadn't seen Diran since that night in Grimwall when she'd become a vampire, and it had been years before that since they'd been lovers. Though she still loved Diran Bastiaan, she had no claim on him—*could* have none as long as he was human and a priest of the Silver Flame, dedicated to eradicating evil in all its myriad forms. As a vampire, she definitely qualified as one of those forms, though she had done her best these last several months to keep the evil inherent in her nature from controlling her, so while the predator in her might like nothing better than to tear out Asenka's throat and guzzle her hot, sweet blood, she would restrain herself.

But that didn't mean she couldn't have a little fun.

She concentrated and her body became insubstantial as mist. She merged with the fog and drifted on the breeze, following Asenka.

Ghaji moved through the fog-enshrouded street silent as a shadow. He gripped his elemental axe in his right hand, but he hadn't activated it yet. The flames would cut through the fog like a beacon, alerting the one he hunted to the half-orc's presence, and if Ghaji was right about the identity of the man he tracked, then he would need every advantage he could get.

He sensed more than heard movement from his left, and he spun away as a broadsword blade hissed through the air. The steel struck the stone wall of the building where Ghaji had been standing, hitting with a ringing clang and setting off sparks.

Ghaji didn't wait for his attacker to recover his balance. With a thought he activated his axe and stepped forward, flames erupting along the blade and haft of his weapon, though his hand felt no heat. He swung the axe in a sweeping sideways arc designed to connect with his attacker's sword arm. A trail of fire followed the axe-blade, burning away the fog and illuminating the face of Ghaji's would-be assassin.

He was an orc—tall, broad-shouldered, well-muscled, an intimidating specimen even for one of his kind. His fur was thick and blackish gray, the skin underneath green. His beard was woven into a trio of braids, and a golden hoop earring dangled from his left earlobe. His lower incisors were massive, jutting up from his jaw and curving upward almost all the way to his small, hate-filled eyes. He wore a mail-shirt, black leather pants, and black boots, but his arms were bare to allow him freedom of movement in battle.

There were more strands of gray in the orc's fur than the last time Ghaji had seen Chagai of Striking Viper Clan, but otherwise he remained unchanged, which was too bad—Ghaji had hoped the son of a bitch would be dead by now.

Chagai didn't have time to bring his sword up to deflect Ghaji's strike, so he turned and took the impact on his chest. Fire flared bright as the flaming axe blade slammed into the mail shirt, driving Chagai back into the stone wall. The orc grunted as he collided with the wall, but he didn't cry out. There was no gushing blood, and worse yet, his mail-shirt didn't show the slightest sign of damage.

"Wearing enchanted armor these days, Chagai?" Ghaji said. "What would your clan say?" For an orc to use magical protection of any kind was considered a sign of weakness, an admission that one's own strength and battle skill weren't enough to defeat an opponent.

Chagai grinned. "I had to find something to replace the breastplate you stole from me."

Chagai swept his sword upward and knocked Ghaji's axe away from his chest. There was so much strength behind the blow that Ghaji had to move with the momentum lest he risk losing hold of his weapon. He took three steps to the side, giving Chagai the chance to move away from the wall and gain room to maneuver.

"You're a fine one to talk about my armor, half-blood," Chagai snarled. "You wield an elemental weapon!"

Ghaji turned to face Chagai and fell into a battle stance. "As you so often reminded me when we fought together, I'm only half-orc. I need every advantage I can get." He smiled grimly at his opponent. "So to what do I owe the displeasure of smelling your tick-ridden carcass again after all these years?"

"Unfinished business," Chagai growled.

He ran forward, broadsword raised, releasing the high-pitched cry known as the orc death scream. The sound was designed to terrify opponents so they died in fear. To an orc warrior, dying in a state of fright meant ultimate dishonor, denying one entrance to the afterlife. One's spirit would wander the world aimlessly for all eternity unseen, intangible, unable to interact with the physical world in any way. For an orc, there could be no worse fate.

Chagai, hardened warrior though he was, had always relied too much on his considerable strength and speed and not enough on skill, and the intervening years since they'd fought hadn't changed this. Ghaji sidestepped Chagai's attack easily, and the orc's broadsword whistled through empty air. Ghaji swung his axe, hoping to hit Chagai in the armpit where his armor didn't cover, but Chagai allowed the momentum of his failed strike to bring him around so that Ghaji's weapon struck his right shoulder. Again, the enchanted chain-mail protected the orc from the worst of the blow, but the impact sent him stumbling off balance. He let go of his sword and fell forward onto the earthen street.

Ghaji knew better than to give Chagai a chance to recover. He moved in for the kill.

Chagai rolled as he hit, came up on his feet, spun around, and flung his hand outward. Ghaji saw a shower of dirt coming toward his face and realized that Chagai had grabbed a handful of earth as he'd pretended to fall—a dirty trick by any standard, but an unforgivable breech of honor to an orc warrior. Ghaji tried to close his eyes and avert his face, but he was too slow. Bits of dirt and mud struck him and got in his eyes. He swung his axe in a sideways figure eight in front of him to keep Chagai away as he blinked furiously, trying to clear his vision. Tears filled his eyes, washing away the worst of the dirt, and when his vision was finally clear again, Ghaji saw that Chagai was gone. Ghaji stopped swinging his axe, though he did not douse its flame. It seemed Chagai had chosen to abandon the fight rather than slay Ghaji while he was temporarily blinded. Well, well, well. It seemed that Chagai had some small speck of honor left after all.

Then again, maybe Chagai doesn't want you to be an easy kill, Ghaji thought. Maybe he wants to make you suffer before you die.

Ghaji sighed. That sounded more like the Chagai he remembered.

With a thought, he extinguished the axe's flames and tucked the weapon handle-first into his belt. Chagai wouldn't make another try for him. Not tonight. Tonight had simply been Chagai's way of renewing their acquaintance and putting Ghaji on notice that he was being hunted. The *real* attack would come later, and Ghaji was almost looking forward to it. For the two of them indeed had unfinished business, and it was long past time that their account was settled.

● ● ● ◉ ● ● ●

Asenka wondered if Diran had bought her story. She was commander of the Sea Scorpions, not the city watch, and while it was within the scope of her duties to keep an eye out for Haaken and his crew in case they decided to cause more trouble tonight, walking a foot patrol of Perhata's dockside—and alone yet—wasn't exactly standard procedure. She'd returned to the vicinity of the King Prawn for one simple reason: she'd hoped to encounter Diran Bastiaan once more. Still, in order to complete the illusion that she was doing her job, she headed for the docks to check if the Coldhearts had made port once more. Assuming they hadn't, she would then head to the Scorpions' dockside quarters, open a bottle of wine, and think about why she'd done what she'd done this night.

It wasn't like her to show such obvious interest in a man, let alone do so while pretending she was acting in her official capacity. If Baron Mahir found out, he'd strip her of her command and assign her to scraping barnacles off fishing boats for the rest of her life. But Diran wasn't just any man, was he? Haaken and his crew might have been loudmouths, but they were as tough as they came. Diran and Ghaji had stood toe to toe with them without blinking . . . *and* made the Coldhearts back down. While Asenka had been impressed with Diran's courage, that alone hadn't stirred her interest in the priest. While speaking with him and his friends after the Coldhearts left the King Prawn, she'd sensed a sadness in the man, along with a gentleness that seemed at odds with his grim demeanor. It was a combination she found fascinating and, if she were to be honest with herself, irresistible.

She laughed as she neared the entrance to the docks. Look at me: Asenka, hard-bitten leader of the Sea Scorpions, acting like a love-sick child! And I've only just met the man!

Even so, she hoped Diran would remain in Perhata for a time. She'd like to see him again, though it would take some thought for her to come up with another excuse to visit the King Prawn. Maybe she could—

"I was watching you, Asenka."

The voice—a woman's—was soft, little more than a whisper, and it seemed to come from all around her. Asenka's long sword hissed as she drew it from its scabbard, and she held the weapon in front of her as she slowly turned in a circle, ready to meet an attack no matter from what direction it might come.

"Who are you?" Asenka demanded. She couldn't see anyone, but then the fog was so thick, an army could be surrounding her and she'd never know it.

The voice was louder now, more substantial somehow, though Asenka still couldn't see its owner. "Makala."

Asenka remembered that name: Diran had spoken it as she'd approached him back at the King Prawn. Foolish as it was, she'd experienced a tiny pang of jealousy that Diran's first thought as she came toward him was of another woman.

"What do you want?"

"A closer look at you. I don't blame you for showing interest in Diran. He's a fascinating man."

Makala's voice no longer seemed to be coming from all around her, but Asenka couldn't pinpoint the precise direction it *did* come from. One instant it seemed to be in front of her, the next behind her, off to her right then on her left. It was as if the woman were circling her, but moving so swiftly and silently that Asenka couldn't get a fix on her position. She had the eerie sensation that Makala was some sort of phantom, an ethereal presence without physical shape, but then a dark silhouette coalesced out of the fog in front of her, and Asenka could make out the woman's form.

Being able to see Makala—or at least her dim outline—allowed Asenka's boldness to return. "And you've come to tell me that he's yours, is that it?"

"He was. Once."

Asenka was surprised by the depth of sorrow in the woman's voice. Despite the situation, she found herself feeling sorry for Makala, though she wasn't quite sure why. Still, she wasn't about to relax her guard around the woman.

"And now?"

Makala didn't answer right away. "I don't know what we are to each other now, or if we can ever be anything to each other again. All I know is that I care for Diran and do not wish to see him hurt. If anyone does hurt him—for any reason—that person will have to answer to me."

Makala spoke these words calmly, but that made them all the more chilling, and Asenka had to suppress a shudder. "Brave talk from a woman hiding in the fog. Why don't you step closer so I can get a good look at you? Or are you afraid of stepping into range of my sword?"

"I'm afraid of very little anymore." Makala didn't approach, but twin pinpoints of crimson light flared within the fog, and Asenka knew she was looking at the woman's eyes. "I do not want to harm you, but remember what I said. I'll do anything to protect Diran." Her crimson eyes flashed like twin flares. *"Anything."*

Then, as if the woman simply melted into the fog, she was gone.

Asenka stood there for several long moments, gripping her sword in a trembling hand as she struggled to understand what she had just seen. Makala wasn't human, that was certain. She was some manner of fiend, and though she professed to care for Diran, she might in truth be a threat to him.

Asenka—her hand no longer shaking—sheathed her sword in a smooth, practiced motion.

"Seems to me that you're right," she said softly. "Diran *does* need protecting, but not from me."

The fog remained silent, and Asenka continued on her way to the Sea Scorpions' barracks. She was no longer contemplating having a bottle of wine, though. She intended to round up a squad of her people and keep watch on the King Prawn tonight. Just in case.

CHAPTER

EIGHT

Diran was already seated at their table when Ghaji returned to the common room of the King Prawn. Tresslar and Hinto sat with him, watching Yvka perform a juggling routine for the crowd. The half-orc warrior was still brooding over his less-than-tender reunion with Chagai, but the sight of the elf-woman tossing small wooden balls through the air with almost preternatural grace caused him to smile. It had been far too long since he had seen her perform, and he was glad that he hadn't missed it. He moved through the crowd, took the empty seat next to Diran, and waved for a mug of ale. While he waited for his drink to arrive, he concentrated on Yvka.

She was performing a routine that he'd seen before but which he still found fascinating. She appeared to be juggling—he did a quick count—fourteen balls, but as she threw them, they began to disappear one by one, until only two remained. Then the reverse happened: balls began to reappear one by one until once again all fourteen were circling through the air. On more than one occasion, Ghaji had asked her how she did it, but

Ykva would only grin and say, "Magic." Ghaji supposed that was always a possibility, but he had the feeling she was teasing him. He watched her closely now, determined to figure out how she performed the illusion through concentrated observation. Of course, the fact that she was incredibly beautiful might have had more than a little to do with his intense scrutiny as well.

A serving girl brought his ale, he took a deep draught, then he fixed his attention on one specific ball. If he could just keep his gaze on that one and follow it the entire time, he might able to finally figure this trick out.

Despite his best efforts, and without his even realizing it was happening, his thoughts began to drift back across the years, to a small farm in the Eldeen Reaches . . .

◎ ◎ ◎ ◉ ◎ ◎ ◎

Four orcs crouched in the grass at the edge of the valley. Well, three orcs and one half-orc. The orcs kept their distance from their half-brother whenever possible, keeping a minimum of two feet from him at all times, as if they believed he were tainted and unclean and his foulness might contaminate them if they got too close. Ghaji acted as if their aversion to his physical proximity didn't bother him, as if he accepted it as only right and proper, but inside he hated it—hated it like poison.

The moons were out tonight and the sky was nearly cloudless. To orc eyes that meant the valley was lit almost as bright as if it were a sunny day. Nestled within the small valley was a humble cottage of stone, wood, and thatch. The cottage was dark, save for the warm glow of lamplight filtering through the shutters of a single window. The land around the cottage had been cleared, and a well-worn trail wound from the cottage's front door, up and out of the valley. The trail was on the opposite side of the valley from where the orcs crouched. They were proud warriors and strong, but they weren't foolish enough to remain in plain sight while they were hunting. There was no trail here, but there were plenty of trees—oak and elm, mostly—and more than enough brush to provide cover. Despite the lateness of the hour, birds sang, and Ghaji found their mindless joy distracting and irritating. He chuffed air through his lips to frighten the foolish creatures into silence, but as soon as the sound came out of his mouth, he saw a blur of motion out of the corner of his eye and fiery pain erupted on the side of his head.

He turned to see Chagai glaring at him, teeth bared in fury. Ghaji's face stung from where Chagai's claws had raked the flesh, and he could feel blood trickling from the wounds. Though the scratches were deep and hurt like blazes, Ghaji was determined not to display any signs of discomfort. A *real* orc would scarcely feel the pain, let alone react to it.

The other two orcs—a female named Eggera and a male named Murtt, the latter of whom Ghaji had known since childhood—snuffled silent laughter. Ghaji was an adult by orc standards, if only barely, and he knew better than to make noise during a hunt. He really did, but he had allowed his excitement to get the better of him, and he'd forgotten himself. No doubt the others were thinking that the stupid half-blood had fouled up again, and were once more questioning why they allowed him to hunt with them—Chagai especially. While the four of them were currently in the employ of the bandit lord Medard the Strong, Chagai was the leader of their group, and Ghaji was permitted to fight with them only as long as Chagai allowed it. If he made too many mistakes Chagai would banish him without a second thought, and while Ghaji could always find work fighting alongside human mercenaries, he'd worked long and hard to get the chance to serve with full-blooded orcs. He was determined to stay with them no matter what it took, until they finally accepted him as one of their own.

Ghaji remembered something Chagai had said on another occasion when he'd made a mistake.

Too bad your father didn't have the good sense not to rape an orc—or at least know enough to use a charm to keep from getting the stupid sow pregnant!

Ghaji was grateful that all Chagai had done was strike him this time. Orc claws hurt far less than orc words.

Ghaji cast his gaze to the ground and nodded to Chagai in apology and obeisance. He kept his gaze lowered and waited to see if Chagai were going to hit him again, for the orc commander was well within his rights to do so, but Chagai let out a snort that was scarcely quieter than Ghaji's earlier chuff and then turned away. The message was clear: Ghaji wasn't worth dirtying Chagai's claws any further. Ghaji waited a few moments more, just to be sure, before raising his head.

The orcs were waiting for the lamplight in the cottage to be extinguished and the occupants to settle in for the night. Such stealth wasn't strictly necessary, of course. There were four of them, after all, and the man they had come to kill was only a simple wood-wright and not a warrior. Still, he was a shifter, and orcs respected the strength his kind were capable of summoning when need be, so they would try to gain every advantage they could before approaching the cottage. The wood-wright and his family would eventually go to sleep, then the orcs could take them by surprise. It wouldn't be as much fun—or gain them as much honor—as a direct assault, but then Medard was paying them for results, not for them to increase their honor.

The lamplight went out.

They waited an hour longer, telling time by the movements of the stars and moons, and then Chagai signaled for them to stand and follow him. Together, the three orcs and one half-blood drew their weapons and silently loped down into the valley toward the wood-wright's cottage. Ghaji wore a simple leather armor vest for protection and carried a hand axe, both of which he'd retrieved from the first soldier he'd ever killed, back before joining Chagai's group. Murtt and Eggera wore mail armor and helmets and carried broadswords which, with their strength, they could wield one-handed. Ghaji was stronger than a human, but not strong enough to wield a broadsword one-handed for very long. Chagai, as their leader, possessed the best equipment. His broadsword was of higher quality than the others, forged of finer steel and made with more skilled craftsmanship. His polished helm was adorned with two metal horns that jutted forward and which the orc commander could use as stabbing weapons if he wished. Best of all was the new breastplate he wore. Its shiny surface was smooth and unscratched, and Medard had given it to Chagai as a bonus for the numerous raids they'd conducted on supply caravans last month. Ghaji thought the breastplate looked magnificent, and he wondered what it would feel like to wear such a fine thing.

As they ran across the grass-covered ground, muscles moving in fluid harmony and hearts pounding in excitement, Ghaji felt as if he inhabited a timeless moment of perfection. The cool night air rushing past him, the moons and stars above, fellow orcs running by his side . . . well, running several steps ahead of him, as was only proper, but still, running *together*, at least . . . he didn't think anything could be better. If he were to die this night, he would die happy.

The odds of any of them dying tonight seemed slim indeed, though. Ruelo was a wood-wright, one known, among other things, for his ability to mystically craft arrows whose shafts were nigh unbreakable, and which flew faster and farther than ordinary arrows could. Medard had once purchased vast quantities of arrows from Ruelo, but the wood-wright claimed to have grown sick of the seemingly endless War, sick of using his skills to create instruments of death, and had sworn to never make another weapon of any sort ever again. Medard, however, believed that Ruelo was simply making an excuse, that the shifter had gotten a better deal with another of the bandit lords that harried the Eldeen Reaches. As far as Medard was concerned, if he couldn't have Ruelo's arrows, then no one could.

As the orcs drew near the cottage, Chagai motioned to Murtt and Eggera to head around the back. They veered away. When Ghaji had been younger, he would've thought it a mark of honor that their leader wished him to remain by his side. Now he knew it was because Chagai felt Ghaji needed watching. When they reached the cottage, Chagai—barely slowing—slammed his shoulder into the door, causing it to burst open in a shower of splintered wood. Chagai rushed inside and Ghaji followed, the thunder of his pulse sounding a bloodsong in his ears. The hunt was finished, and it was time for the killing to begin.

The one-room cottage was empty, save for simple wooden furniture—dining table and chairs, a long bench and several stools arranged in front of a cold hearth. A wooden ladder led to a sleeping loft just below the thatched ceiling. Atop the dining table was an everbright lantern that only a short time ago had been warming the cottage with its glow, along with a scattering of materials used in the wood-wright's art: narrow wooden shafts, feathers for fletching, metal arrowheads. Ghaji grinned. It appeared that Medard's suspicions about the shifter were correct after all.

Chagai rushed toward the ladder, and Ghaji followed, eager to wet his axe-blade in shifter blood, but before they could take more than a few steps, a male shifter wearing only a breech cloth stood up behind the loft's wooden railing. The shifter's fur was tinged with gray, but his muscles were still lean and strong. His full bestial aspect was upon him—face hirsute, features animalistic, fangs bared. The shifter held a bow with an arrow nocked, and his eyes blazed with fury as he lifted the weapon and aimed the shaft at Chagai's heart.

Ghaji didn't think. He hurled his axe at the shifter. The weapon flew upward, tumbling end over end, and the blade buried itself with a hollow thunk in the man's forehead. The shifter's eyes widened in surprise and he released his grip on the arrow. The shaft, regardless of any mystical properties it might have possessed, flew wild, missing Chagai entirely. Blood poured down the shifter's face, spattered onto his chest, but the wood-wright remained standing long enough to fix Ghaji with an accusing stare before the man's gaze dimmed and he pitched forward over the railing to fall with a dull thud on the dirt floor below.

Ghaji turned to Chagai, hoping to hear appreciation for the well-thrown strike that might very well have saved the orc leader's life, but a crash came from the roof of the cottage then, immediately followed by screams of terror. Ghaji knew what had happened: Murtt and Eggera had climbed onto the roof, torn through the thatch, and forced their way into the loft. Now they had begun their slaughter of the wood-wright's family.

Chagai leaped over the wood-wright's body, and rushed to the ladder, eager to join in the killing above. Ghaji hesitated only a second before following after Chagai. The walls of the loft were drenched with blood, as were Eggera and Murtt. They were practically covered from head to toe, as if they'd been bathing in gore. Chagai stood over the body of a female shifter lying on the loft's floor, her body nearly cut in two by his broadsword. Chagai's chest heaved with excitement, and his eyes were wild, those of a predator intoxicated by the thrill of bringing down its prey. There were four pallets in the loft, two of them small. Murtt and Eggera each stood over one of the small pallets, their swords slick with blood. Lying below them on the crimson-soaked bedding were the hacked-up remains of what had once been two shifter children, their bodies so mutilated that Ghaji couldn't even begin to guess their gender.

The female shifter—the children's mother, Ghaji supposed—lifted a trembling hand in the direction of her children, as if she still hoped to do something, anything to save them, or perhaps simply wanted to offer one last bit of motherly comfort to their departing souls. Chagai noted the movement and with a swift motion thrust his sword blade into the back of the woman's head. She shuddered once and then fell still.

Chagai then turned to Ghaji and gave him a wide grin. "Good sport tonight, eh?"

Ghaji knew the camaraderie in the orc leader's tone was meant as both a compliment and a thank-you for his slaying of the wood-wright. Chagai was, for the very first time, treating Ghaji as if he were an equal. It was what Ghaji had wanted so long and worked so hard for, so why didn't it mean anything to him now?

He stared at the red wet chunks of meat that only a short time ago had been a pair of children sleeping peacefully in their beds. Then he forced himself to return Chagai's grin, though he feared it came out more like a grimace.

"Good sport."

* * * ● * * *

Ghaji felt a small elbow jab him in the ribs, and he looked down to see Hinto frowning at him.

"Unless you want your lady love to think you're losing interest in her, you'd best pay more attention, Greenie," the halfling whispered.

Ghaji hated it when Hinto called him that, but he was so grateful to be pulled out of the memory of that awful night at the wood-wright's cottage that he nodded, took another sip of his bilge-water ale, and refocused his attention on Yvka. No matter how hard he tried, he couldn't completely chase away the image of the mother's trembling hand, reaching out to her children one last time before she died.

Skarm thanked whatever dark powers watched over barghests that the elf-woman had gotten up from her table, taken up a position in a corner of the common room, and started juggling. Her companions—including the elderly artificer—were watching her with rapt attention, providing him with a perfect distraction. He'd been observing the elf-woman's act along with the rest of the audience, and he noted that her tricks had become increasingly more complex, and she performed them with increasing speed. He sensed that she was building toward the climax of her act, and once she reached it . . .

The elf-woman was currently juggling a quintet of spheres that appeared to be formed of solid light. She hurled all five toward the ceiling of the common room, and they merged together, forming a large light sculpture of a dragon in flight. The drake's eyes blazed and a glittering stream of what seemed to be diamonds poured forth from its open mouth. There were awed murmurs of appreciated from the audience as the diamonds swirled through the air, circling the room above the people's heads, the illusion so realistic that more than a few men and women reached up to try to snag a diamond for themselves. The light dragon then began to glow bright as a summer sun, and all in attendance were utterly transfixed by the sight, breathless with anticipation of what would happen next . . .

Now! Skarm thought, and made his move.

Hinto knew that Yvka was performing a trick, that the dragon wasn't real and couldn't hurt him, but that knowledge did nothing to prevent the feeling of panic that coiled tight within his belly and which threatened to spring free any instant. As the light dragon glowed more intensely, he averted his gaze and stared down at the surface of the table, gripping its wooden edge tight. He told himself to hold on, to ride the panic out. He'd spent his lifetime on the sea, and he'd learned how to weather storms before he could walk. And not just any storms—those on the Lhazaar were rougher and deadlier than anywhere else in all the vast oceans of Eberron. If he could survive the Lhazaar's fury, he should be able to withstand something as simple as his own fear.

Since his time shipwrecked in the Mire, fear was no longer so simple for Hinto. Intense, overwhelming, paralyzing . . . it grabbed hold of him with ice-cold hands and crushed him in its grip, reducing him to a quivering mass of terror. He knew his friends understood—even Ghaji, who pretended to be gruff and unfriendly much of the time—and while Hinto appreciated their understanding, he didn't want them to pity him, and he didn't want his fear-attacks to cause him to let them down when they needed him, like yesterday in the lich's lair, the latest in a string of similar incidences over the last several months. So far, his panic and resultant inability to act hadn't caused injury or death to any of his friends, but Hinto feared that it was only a matter of time before it did. He had to get control of himself, had to learn to master his fear—not just for himself but for his friends.

Hinto was not looking at Yvka's light dragon when a cloaked and hooded goblin crept up next to Tresslar and snatched the artificer's dragonwand from under his belt. As soon as the goblin had the wand in hand, he dashed for the door.

Hinto cried out, "Tresslar, your wand!" and leaped out of his seat in pursuit of the thief. A lifetime at sea had kept Hinto strong and lean. He weaved between tables and chairs—sometimes ducking under tabletops if necessary—and caught hold of the goblin's cloak before the thief could reach the door.

Hinto spun the goblin around and took hold of his shoulders with a firm grip to make sure he didn't try to run again. "Here, now, what do you think—"

Hinto broke off as he saw the goblin's scarred visage, the eyes that blazed with orange fire, the mouthful of teeth far sharper than any ordinary goblin's should be. The halfling felt a sudden cold fluttering in his stomach and in his mind he saw tentacles rising out of the sea, swaying slowly in the darkness as they cast about in search of prey. The tentacles ended in tiny mouths that opened and closed hungrily . . .

Hinto let out a soft cry and released his hold on the goblin. He staggered back, his entire body shaking, his knees gone weak as water. His head swam, the world titled, and he collapsed to the earthen floor and shook like a leaf caught in a gale-force wind. He struggled to regain control of his body, but it was no good. His fear held him completely in thrall, and all he could do was watch in despair and shame as the goblin—or whatever it was—made for the door.

He's going to get away with Tresslar's wand, and it's all my fault!

Just as the goblin's hand—a hand that was now clawed and covered with gray fur—reached for the door handle, a small sphere came arcing from the far side of the common room. Yvka had hurled one of her juggling balls at the creature. The goblin looked up in time to see the smooth wooden sphere coming at him, and in reflex he lifted his free hand and caught the ball before it could strike him.

The goblin sneered. "Is that the best you can—"

Crackling tendrils of blue-white energy erupted from the ball, ran up his arm and covered his entire body. There was an acrid smell of burning fur, and the goblin let out an animalistic howl of pain. He dropped the dragonwand, but though he tried to let go of the lightning-ball, it seemed affixed to his hand, and no matter how hard he tried, he could not shake it loose.

Diran and Ghaji were up and moving toward the wounded goblin, weapons drawn and ready. Hinto tried once more to rise to his feet so he could help his friends, but his body still refused to obey him and all he could do was continue to lie trembling on the floor and observe.

Diran and Ghaji reached the goblin, and the creature slammed his wrist into the wall. There was a sickening sound of bones snapping, but the impact was sufficient to break the lightning-ball's hold, and the sphere tumbled from the goblin's hand. As soon as the ball was no longer in contact with the goblin's flesh, the lightning cocoon that surrounded him winked out, and he was free. He bent down to snatch up the dragonwand once more, but Diran hurled a dagger. The blade thunked into the ground next to the wand, sinking into the earth up the hilt, the cross-piece pinning the mystical object to the floor. The goblin looked up at Diran and snarled, and the orange light in his eyes seemed to blaze outward as if it were tongues of angry flame. The goblin's form blurred and shifted, and when it came into focus once more, the goblin had become a humanoid wolf-creature that Hinto recognized as a barghest—*the* barghest, he realized, the one they'd encountered yesterday in the lich's lair.

Ghaji stepped forward to attack the beast, his elemental axe bursting into flame, but the barghest, whose body still bore burnt patches from the wounds he'd suffered during their last battle, howled in frustration and threw itself back against the door. Already shaky from the appearance of the Coldhearts earlier, the door gave way easily beneath the barghest's weight, and the creature tumbled out into the street. Ghaji ran outside after it, Diran following close behind.

Tresslar ran past Hinto and crouched down next to his wand. He pried Diran's dagger free, then reclaimed his most prized mystical object, gripping it tight as if he feared someone else might attempt to steal it. Yvka came over and knelt down next to Hinto. The elf-woman slowly stroked his sweaty hair with one hand, while she gently took hold of his with the other.

"It's all right, Hinto. The creature didn't get Tresslar's wand, and Diran and Ghaji will take care of him."

Hinto gritted his teeth as a fresh wave of tremors wracked his body. It wasn't all right, and he didn't know if it was ever going to be again.

● ● ● ◉ ● ● ●

The fog still blanketed Perhata's dockside, and if it hadn't been for the light given off by Ghaji's blazing axe, Diran wouldn't have been able to see anything. As it was, he could see very little, and he certainly didn't see any sign of the barghest.

"I can't get his scent," Ghaji said. "Too many other smells here—the ocean, dead fish, and other odors I'd rather not discuss, so either you call upon the Silver Flame for guidance, or we pick a direction and start searching."

Diran considered. Barghests were infernal creatures, and while they were hardly all-powerful, they were swift—especially in full wolf form. The odds that he and Ghaji would be able to track a wolf, and an intelligent one at that, on a fog-shrouded night such as this were hardly favorable.

"We stopped it from taking Tresslar's dragonwand and drove it off," Diran said. "That's enough for one night, don't you think?"

Ghaji doused the flames of his axe, and the darkness closed in around them. "It galls me to let the creature go, especially since this is our second encounter with him. You think he followed us into town just to get hold of Tresslar's wand?"

"Perhaps. The barghest might wish to take revenge on the ones who destroyed his mistress and wounded him."

"Why try to steal the wand? That doesn't seem like much of a revenge to me."

"Barghests are magical creatures, and it's not unreasonable to think this one might have some mystical knowledge of his own. Perhaps he intended to use the dragonwand as a weapon against us." Even as he said it, Diran didn't think much of his theory. He sensed there was something more to the barghest's attempted theft of Tresslar's wand, but he couldn't say what. "Whatever the case, I think that we should make tracking down and slaying this barghest our next order of business."

Ghaji grinned and tightened his grip on his axe. "Where do we start?"

"I think you may have to put your plans on hold for a time—say, forever."

Diran still had hold of one of the daggers he'd drawn when Hinto had alerted them to the barghest's presence. Now he didn't hesitate; he threw the dagger in the direction the voice—Haaken's voice—came from, but before Diran could tell whether his blade had found its target, a large shape came at them out of the darkness, and he felt the heavy mesh of a fishing net descend upon them. The net was heavy enough on its own, but it was weighted down with lead balls at the edges to help it sink into the sea more effectively. It forced Diran and Ghaji to their knees. Ghaji's axe flared bright, and Diran knew his friend intended to burn their way free of the net. Not one to wait on someone else to save him, Diran pulled a dagger from one of the hidden sheathes sewn into the inner lining of his cloak and began sawing away at the net's mesh. They only needed a few seconds, and then they would—

Haaken stepped forward until Diran could make out the dim outline of his form. "You don't really think we'd give you a chance to escape, do you?"

His hand shot forth, and he released a fine amber powder into the air. The powder diffused into a small yellow cloud that surrounded Diran and Ghaji, and though the two companions knew enough to hold their breath, Haaken and another of the Coldhearts stepped forward—they had scraps of cloth tied over their noses and mouths, Diran saw—and kicked them in the ribs. Breath exploded from their lungs, and then in reflex, they breathed in. Whatever the drug was, it was powerful, and it took effect immediately. Diran saw Ghaji's axe-flame extinguish as the half-orc lost consciousness.

Diran felt his own body begin to go numb, and as darkness rushed in to take him, he heard Haaken say, "Well, that was easier than I thought it would be."

* * * * * * *

Asenka was on the way back to the King Prawn with a detachment of three Sea Scorpions when they nearly collided with Haaken and his people in the fog. The Coldhearts were carrying something wrapped in a fishing net—something that looked suspiciously like two bodies, and she had a damn good idea who those bodies belonged to.

Asenka drew her sword, and her people did the same. "If you want to leave Perhata alive, Haaken, you'll put them down now."

Haaken grinned. "We outnumber you two to one, Asenka." Only four of Haaken's people carried the net-wrapped bodies. The other four, Haaken included, had their swords in hand, and they now touched the points of their blades to their captives. "Unless you want us to gut these two here and now, I suggest you make way and allow us safe passage."

Asenka thought swiftly. If she let the Coldhearts go, they'd simply kill Diran and Ghaji later, but if she attempted to stop them here, Diran and Ghaji would be skewered, and she doubted she'd be able to get them to a healer before they perished. As much as it galled her, she didn't see how she had any choice.

"Very well, Haaken. You have safe passage." She stepped aside and motioned for her people to do the same. She lowered her sword, though she didn't sheathe it. She wasn't stupid enough to give Haaken the opportunity to kill her in the bargain.

"A wise decision, Asenka," the Coldheart leader said. "I always thought there was a reasonable person underneath that cold bitch exterior." He laughed, and his people joined in. "One more thing: I was thinking of just slicing your friends' throats and dumping them over the side for the sharks, but I've decided these two deserve something a bit more special, so we're going to drop them off on Demothi Island."

Asenka felt a cold stab of fear pierce her gut. "You can't be serious!"

Haaken laughed even harder. He motioned for his people to move out, and the Coldhearts continued on toward the docks, bearing their captives off to their horrible fate.

Demothi Island . . .

Asenka wondered if it wouldn't have been kinder to let Haaken kill Diran and Ghaji outright. She turned to her people. "Head for the barracks and alert the others that the Coldhearts are making for the dock. Stop them if you can. I'm going to the King Prawn to alert Diran's companions."

From what she'd learned about his friends during her conversation with Diran, she thought they might have just as good a chance of saving Diran and Ghaji as the Sea Scorpions would—maybe better.

As the rest of the detachment ran off to carry out their commander's order, Asenka ran in the direction of the King Prawn. She only hoped that she'd get there before Haaken and his people could make sail.

● ● ● ◉ ● ● ●

Makala soared above the buildings of dockside in bat form, wheeling and darting above the fog layer, exulting in the beauty of moon and starlight and the delicious freedom of not being shackled to the ground. She'd considered attempting to speak with Diran tonight, but it had been months since he'd allowed her to choose death at his hands or life as a vampire, and though she'd kept watch over him ever since, she hadn't so much as allowed him to see her, let alone speak to him. She thought perhaps he was aware of her presence from time to time, but if so, he'd never sought her out. Perhaps he didn't want to see her again. Perhaps he regretted his decision to let her live. He was a priest of the Silver Flame, one of the Purified, dedicated to destroying evil in all its myriad manifestations. Perhaps Diran had been avoiding her because he knew that if they encountered one another again, he'd be forced to destroy her.

Maybe she was simply afraid of witnessing the revulsion in his eyes once he saw how much she had become a creature of the night since they'd parted. Every night she awoke she felt there was less of the woman Makala left in her and more of the dark thing she was becoming. It had taken Erdis Cai the better part of four decades to lose the last shreds of his humanity. Makala, perhaps because of the dark spirit she'd once played host to, seemed to be changing far more swiftly. She wondered how much longer it would be before the woman she had been truly died at last, and she became a monster in both body and soul. Look at what she'd done—or almost done—to Asenka tonight. Simply because she'd been jealous, she'd threatened the woman, been tempted to feed on her, even though she'd fed on Eneas earlier.

No, she couldn't see Diran again, not in person. She would just have to content herself with acting as his unseen guardian, watching over him and helping him secretly whenever she could.

Though it was not yet midnight, Makala was weary—in spirit if not in body—and she decided to fly back to the dock and return to the *Boundless* and her obsidian sarcophagus. Perhaps if she were lucky, she'd fall into the torpor that vampires experienced instead of sleep before the dawn. If not . . . well, at least she'd be locked away where she could do no further harm this night.

As Makala drew near the docks, she felt the pull of the ocean. It tugged at her, as if exerting some form of magnetic force, urging her to come closer so that it could reach out with liquid hands and pull her down into its cold dark depths. It was as if all water—so vital to life—despised the undead and wanted nothing more than to destroy them. Though minor bodies of water such as streams and small rivers exerted the same pull, they were mere annoyances to vampires. Resisting the power of a sea took a great deal of strength. The sooner Makala was back aboard the *Boundless* and safe within her black coffin, the better.

She swooped down to the vessel, navigating by a complex interplay of bat senses, human intuition, and vampiric psychic abilities, but just as she reached the *Boundless* and was about to land upon the deck, she heard voices.

"Into the hold with those two, but go easy! I want the priest and his half-orc servant in the peak of health when we reach Demothi Island."

Makala didn't question how Diran and Ghaji had come to be captured. In life she had been more of a doer than a thinker, and death hadn't changed that quality in her. She banked upward, beating her wings as she flew toward the sound of wicked laughter. The ship was berthed at the furthermost end of the dock, and as Makala approached, she heard brisk movement—boots shuffling on deck, ropes being untied and cast off—and she knew that the vessel's occupants were preparing to get underway. Though she was only a few dozen yards closer to the open sea than where the *Boundless* was berthed, the mystic pull of the water was far stronger here, and as she angled down to the deck, she had to concentrate to resist the water's tug. It was as if the sea were interfering with her senses in an attempt to cause her to miss the ship and splash into the water, but she managed to make her descent—albeit an uncertain, wobbly one—and just as her tiny bat feet were about to come in contact with the wood, her form became living shadow that stretched and reformed itself into her natural shape.

It was part of a vampire's powers that personal items such as clothing and weaponry disappeared when one assumed an alternate shape and reappeared when one resumed human form. Makala had no idea where these objects went during her transformations, and she really didn't care. She was simply glad that the process worked the way it did. She drew her sword and cast about the deck, searching for the man who'd ordered Diran and Ghaji to be stowed in the hold. The fog was thinner at this end of the dock, and Makala, with her vampiric night-vision, had no trouble making out the forms of the ship's crew. They, however, being mere humans, could not see her. Makala decided to rectify that.

She willed the smoldering crimson flame that dwelt within her eyes to blaze and was rewarded with a shout of, "By the Host, what's *that?*"

It wasn't the captain's voice, so she assumed it was one of his underlings that spoke. No matter. She was certain the captain would hear her words.

"You've abducted two friends of mine." Makala spoke in a hollow-toned voice that seemed to issue forth from everywhere and nowhere all at once. She hoped the kidnappers would find the effect suitably chilling. "Release them and I'll allow you to depart in peace. Refuse, and I shall kill every one of you and then free them myself."

One of the crewmembers took several strides toward her, drawing his sword as he came. "Who might you be, missy? And more to the point, what makes you think you can scare us with your strangely spoken words and street-magician's light show?"

Makala smiled, revealing her fangs, though she doubted anyone could see them in the fog. "If you want to find out, just keep walking toward me."

The man hesitated. He was close enough now that Makala could make out his features despite the fog, and she saw he was tall, muscular, and blond-bearded. He carried a long-sword with the natural ease of someone who'd had so much practice wielding it over the years that the weapon had become virtually an extension of his own body. Not that it would do him any good.

She sniffed the air and smelled the blood coursing through the man's body. He was strong, in the prime of his life, and his blood smelled to her like the finest of wines. Makala's hunger welled within her, powerful and insistent, and for an instant she forgot about Diran and Ghaji. She pictured herself leaping upon the man and burying her fangs in the sweet-salty flesh of his neck, drinking deeply and letting the warm wet fluid that was life itself gush down her throat. She went so far as to take a step toward him, but she restrained herself. She wasn't an animal, and her friends—*Diran*—needed her.

"I have little patience," Makala said. "I'll say it one more time: release my friends or—"

She didn't get the chance to finish her ultimatum. A pair of sailors, both men and both as large and muscular as their captain—rushed at her from both sides and grabbed hold of her arms.

Blond-Beard grinned. "Looks like we have three passengers to ferry to Demothi Island now."

Unlike Diran, Makala hadn't been raised in the Principalities, and she'd never heard of Demothi Island. Whatever it was,

Blond-Beard acted as if going there was some sort of terrible fate. Not that it mattered, for Makala had no intention of letting Blond-Beard and his crew set sail.

Makala flexed her arms and slammed the two sailors that had hold of her into each other. Their skulls collided with a sickening hollow sound, and the men slumped motionless to the deck.

"Cast off!" Blond-Beard bellowed to his crew. "Cast off *now!*"

Makala didn't know whether Blond-Beard realized she was a vampire and understood she'd be weakened by being out on the open water or whether the man was simply acting on instinct. Either way, she couldn't afford to let this vessel get underway.

She stepped forward, intending to strike at Blond-Beard with her sword, but before she could attack, the man reached beneath his tunic collar and withdrew a small metal object that dangled from a chain. He held the object out toward her, and intense pain flared through Makala's entire body, as if her veins had suddenly become filled with molten fire. The pendant's shape—an iron spiral with a small indigo gem at the center—was unfamiliar to her.

She dropped her sword and raised her arms to block the spiral from her sight. That lessened the pain, but only a little. Hissing like an angry cat, she backed away from Blond-Beard, but he followed her, advancing slowly step by step, making sure not to get too close but still keeping up the pressure on her, not allowing her to find escape or respite from the pain that was burning her up from the inside out. She continued retreating until her lower back bumped into the ship's port railing. Without thinking, driven solely by the all-encompassing need to get away from the spiral, she turned, hopped up onto the railing with inhuman grace, and then leaped out into space. She intended to transform into a bat and fly away from the ship and the agonizing metal spiral as fast as she could, but she was too wracked with pain to manage the change, and she plunged into the sea.

Frigid water enveloped her, and she felt herself sinking. No, not sinking—being *drawn* downward, as if unseen tendrils had encircled her body and were dragging her deeper and deeper. The sea, the cradle from which some said all life had been born, was pulling her, a creature of death, down to where she could harm no one ever again. She struggled, thrashing her arms and legs, attempting to swim back to the surface, but it was so hard . . . her limbs felt like heavy lead weights, and she felt a weariness coming over her, not unlike the daylight torpor in which she slept. It would be so easy to give up, to surrender, let the Lhazaar take her and be done with it.

Then she remembered: Diran needed her help.

She renewed her efforts, swimming with all of her strength, and slowly, inch by inch, she felt herself rising back toward the surface. It felt as if she struggled against the sea's pull for hours, but finally her head broke the surface and, though she no longer had any need for air, she drew in a gasping breath. She swam to the edge of the dock, reached up, gripped its wooden edge, and hauled herself out of the water. She lay on the dock, wet, cold, and shivering, but still alive—or at least not dead. The fog had thinned out even further during her struggle to escape the Lhazaar's embrace, and she could clearly see a ship drawing away from the dock.

Makala rose unsteadily to her feet, turned back toward shore, and began staggering down the dock. Each step was an effort, but she couldn't afford to take time to rest. She had to reach the *Boundless* and rouse Eneas before the other vessel could get too far out to sea. She had enough faith in the old sailor's skills to believe he'd be able to track the ship if they could set sail soon enough, though what the two of them might be able to do on their own against Diran and Ghaji's captors—especially with her weakened as she would be by being out on the water—she didn't know, but she had to try.

She reached the *Boundless* and climbed aboard, nearly collapsing in the process. She managed to stay on her feet and made her way down into the hull where she'd left Eneas slumbering. She was relieved to find the old sailor still there, snoring away as if he didn't have a care in the world. All she had to do was wake him and then they could get underway. She crouched down and put her hand on his shoulder, intending to give him a shake . . .

And then she caught the scent of his blood.

She'd been greatly weakened by her plunge into the sea, and she desperately needed to rebuild her strength. She tried to resist the urge, but she was too weak to do so.

Just a little, she told herself. Enough to help me function, and no more.

She bent down over Eneas's neck, bit into his flesh, and began to feed. Blood poured into her, trickling through her body, filling her with warmth and life. She was unaware of time as she fed, but when she felt strong once more, she drew away from Eneas and wiped her mouth with the back of her hand. Then, without thinking, she licked the smear of blood from her hand.

She then took hold of Eneas's shoulder and gave him a shake.

"Wake up, Eneas! I need your help!"

But the old sailor did not wake. Makala shook him harder, and his head slumped forward and lolled back and forth. That's when Makala realized she could no longer smell his living blood, couldn't feel his pulse through her fingertips on his shoulder. She had taken too much.

Guilt and sorrow filled her unbeating heart, followed immediately by anger. How could she have been so foolish? Without Eneas, there was no way that she could go after Diran and Ghaji. Even if she knew how to sail, as a vampire she couldn't operate the *Boundless* on open water. She needed help, but first, she had a duty to attend to.

"I'm sorry, Eneas. You were a good servant, and you deserved better than this."

Makala took firm hold of the sailor's head and with a single swift violent motion broke his neck. She then picked up his lifeless body, threw it over her shoulder, and climbed up onto the deck of his ship . . . *her* ship now, she supposed. Though what she would be able to do with it on her own, she had no idea. Once on the deck, she lay his body down and removed a dagger from a sheath on her belt. The blade was sharp, and with her strength it took her little time to sever Eneas's head from his body. There was no blood, for there was none remaining in the corpse.

Though the blade wasn't stained, Makala wiped the dagger off on Eneas's clothes before returning it to its sheath. Now that Eneas had been beheaded, there was no chance that he would return to life as a vampire. Still, she wanted to make sure. First she threw his head out to sea as far as she could, and then she tossed his body after it. Instead of floating, Eneas's remains hit the water and sank like stones as the sea claimed them.

Makala gazed at the rippling water for a moment longer before casting aside her human form and rising into the air on leather wings, bound for the King Prawn.

CHAPTER

NINE

Cathmore stood at the open window, hands gripping the stone sill as he gazed westward. Galharath didn't have to read the old man's mind to know what he was searching for.

"You're wasting your time. You won't see Chagai approach in the dark."

Cathmore didn't turn away from the window. "It's my time to waste, isn't it?"

The two men stood in one of the highest chambers within Mount Luster: a stone room constructed near the pinnacle of the mountain, with a window that faced westward. There were three other chambers just like it, each with a window facing another point on the compass. These were watch chambers, with shutters painted on the outside to resemble the mountain's rocky surface. The shutters were open, and the late autumn wind blew cold and harsh. Cathmore, wrapped in his thick bearskin cloak, still shivered continuously, though he displayed no other sign of discomfort and made no complaint about the wind. So fierce was the old man's will and so intense his concentration that Galharath thought Cathmore capable of ignoring the temperature until he froze to death. As a kalashtar, Galharath could appreciate such disciplined focus, even when it was less than practical.

"Do you really believe that the half-orc Chagai recognized is in fact the partner of your former student?"

"I don't believe—I *know*." The old man glanced over his shoulder at Galharath. "Tell me, do your people believe in Fate?"

"Not by that name. *Fate* is far too simplistic a concept, but we recognize the existence of probability matrices that intersect with an individual's unique potential."

Cathmore scowled. "Forgive me for being so *simplistic*, but I have no idea what you just said. I believe that Fate is real and that it sweeps all of us along like the current of a vast river, and while we—the fish caught within its power—have some choice over how we swim, ultimately we are at the mercy of the river's force."

Galharath nodded his understanding. The metaphor was similar to something a kalashtar child might postulate but not altogether inaccurate. He was impressed anew by the keen intellect the old man possessed—for a human.

"I believe the river of Fate has swept both me and Diran to this point, and that soon we will be brought together to finish what we started so many years ago."

Galharath thought Cathmore had an exaggerated sense of his own importance in the complex and ever-shifting tapestry of events that made up what limited minds like his termed reality, but he could see no gain in bringing this point up, so he didn't. Galharath and Cathmore were not friends, and they weren't partners. Not really. They were two individuals currently working together for mutual advantage. Cathmore wished to repair and activate the psi-forge in order to create an army of unstoppable assassins—a goal Galharath found small-minded and ridiculous. Galharath was simply using the old man and his orc servant to provide him with supplies and protection while he studied the construction of the psi-forge. Galharath, like many kalashtar, was far more concerned with the advancement of his mind and the strengthening of his psionic abilities than he was in worldly achievements. The knowledge he would gain—had already gained—from helping Cathmore would prove invaluable in and of itself, but Galharath also had a practical application of his knowledge in mind.

Galharath's race, the kalashtar, had been born from a union of humans and quori, renegade spirits from Dal Quor, the Region of Dreams. The influence of the original quori spirits affected their descendants, so that while newborn kalashtar were distinct individuals, they possessed some of their ancestors' character traits and even fragmentary memories. They also possessed vast reserves of mental resources upon which they could draw, making them a race of powerful psionics, but the evil spirits that still remained in Dal Quor despised the kalashtar and sought their extermination. To further this aim, they possessed the bodies of physical beings on Eberron in order to operate on this dimensional plane, becoming a separate race of psionic beings known as the Inspired.

Galharath—or, as he thought of himself, Gal of the lineage of Harath, his original quori ancestor—had fought against the Inspired all his life. He had become a psionic artificer to discover and develop new weapons that might be used in his people's struggle for survival. When Cathmore approached him with an offer—working at a "site of singular interest to one of your kind," as the old man had put it—Galharath accepted without hesitation, especially since he'd been able to read the particulars of Cathmore's offer in his thoughts. Cathmore might have no greater vision for the psi-forge than producing mindslayers, but Galharath hoped to learn enough about the device in order to recreate it——or something very much like it——to construct beings that would fight the Inspired alongside the kalashtar.

"Do you think the stories are true?" Galharath asked. "Has Diran Bastiaan forsaken the ways of the Brotherhood of the Blade for priesthood within the Silver Flame? Or is it merely a ruse and he has come to Perhata to track you down and slay you once and for all?"

"Why do you bother asking questions when you already know the answers?" Cathmore said. "I hired you for your psionic abilities, and I have no illusion that you refrain from employing them on me. You'd be a fool not to."

Galharath's estimation of Cathmore went up a notch. "Then permit me to say this: I am well aware that yours is not the only spirit that inhabits your body. That much, at least, we have in common, but whereas my spirit is inextricably bound to that of my ancestor's, yours exists alongside a darker spirit that you allowed to be implanted within your body. Two spirits, connected but at the same time separate."

"So?"

"So your darker half knows that it has nearly used up your body and is hoping to find a replacement."

Cathmore turned away from the window again, but this time a darkness lurked in his eyes, and his smile was cold and feral. When he spoke, it sounded as if he did so in two distinct voices. "Of course. Why do you think we're so interested in being reunited with Diran——young, strong, healthy Diran—— once more?"

Cathmore laughed, the sound dry and brittle as ancient bone, before returning his attention to the darkness that lay beyond the window, a darkness, Galharath thought, that was bright as the sun compared to what dwelled inside the old man.

"I have something to tell you." Cathmore's voice had returned to normal, though it was no less chilling for that. "The spirit within me is sensitive to the unseen world. It's one of the reasons that the Brotherhood of the Blade uses them, and mine is whispering to me that we are not alone in this room."

Galharath frowned, his psionic senses sweeping through the chamber, and while he was normally acutely aware of his surroundings, this time he paid far closer attention to its minute details. At first, he detected nothing out the ordinary, and he began to wonder if perhaps Cathmore's dark spirit hadn't corrupted his mind to the point where the old man was starting to take leave of his senses, but then he found it: the merest flicker of a mental presence, so infinitesimal that even the most skilled psionicist would have been hard-pressed to notice it without conducting a careful search. The physical nexus for the presence lay in the far corner of the observation chamber. Galharath got a firm mental fix on the presence to make certain that it couldn't conceal itself from him once more, and then turned in its direction.

"We know you're there, and there's no way that you will be able to hide from me again. Show yourself."

At first nothing happened, and Galharath was contemplating a psionic strike against the presence when the air in the corner rippled, and a hulking stone and wood being with numerous multicolored crystals affixed to its body appeared. Galharath instantly recognized what he was looking at, though he wasn't sure he believed it. This was an artificial being produced by the crystalline forge that lay at the heart of Mount Luster. This was a psi-forged.

"How interesting," Cathmore said. If the master assassin was surprised by the sudden appearance of the psi-forged, Galharath couldn't tell it from the calm tone of his voice. "I wasn't aware that the forge was ever operational."

Galharath was intrigued, for there was so much they could learn about the forge and its processes from this being that had been born within its mystic fires, but he was also cautious. It was clear that the psi-forged was powerful, or else it wouldn't have been able to cloak itself from Galharath's perception for so long, and if Cathmore's dark spirit hadn't detected it, allowing Galharath to search for the creature, there was a good chance he might never have discovered it. That meant the psi-forged was extremely strong—and therefore extremely dangerous.

Galharath felt an itching sensation, as if hundreds of ants had somehow found their way into his skull and were crawling over the surface of his brain. The psi-forged was attempting to probe his mind. The technique was clumsy at best, but there was no denying the power behind the probe. The creature had been able to penetrate Galharath's standard defenses as easily as his physical body could pass through air. Already the itching sensation was beginning to hurt as the psi-forged intensified its probe. It now felt as if the ants were sinking their mandibles into the tender, moist flesh of his brain and tearing away chunks to devour. At this rate, if Galharath allowed the creature to persist in its attempt to explore his mind, there was a chance he would suffer significant brain damage.

Galharath concentrated on strengthening his psionic defenses, visualizing his head surrounded by an impenetrable globe of blazing light. He drew additional power from the psi-crystals he wore on his gloves and chest, as well as those shards woven into his hair. He used this power to increase the globe's density, adding layer upon layer to it, each layer vibrating at a different frequency, exponentially strengthening the whole. Galharath felt the pain of the psi-forged's mental probe begin to subside, and then it was gone. Before the psi-forged could renew its efforts to penetrate Galharath's defenses, the kalashtar went on the attack, both in an attempt to distract the creature as well as to conduct a probe of his own. His vision shifted, and he now saw the psi-forged not as a physical creature of darkwood, silver, obsidian, and stone but rather as a luminous being composed entirely of various hues of light.

And what light! Galharath's psychic vision was dazzled by the array of colors that comprised the creature's astral form: fiery reds, pulsating blues, glowing oranges, warm yellows, cool greens, and so many, many more—colors that Galharath had never seen, colors which he wasn't sure even had names . . . All were interwoven in a complex pattern that formed the true core of the psi-forged's self, what—for a lack of better term—could be called the creature's soul.

Galharath pictured tendrils of energy emerging from the globe surrounding his head like pseudopods. The tendrils lengthened and extended toward the multicolored patchwork of energy that was the psi-forged. The ends of the tendrils waved in the air around the creature's astral form, tentatively probing its outer defenses, searching for a weak point that might allow entry. No matter where the tendrils looked, they could find no weaknesses in the psi-forged's defenses, but Galharath did sense something odd about this creature . . .

He recoiled as images, thoughts, emotions, and sensations assaulted his mind. He tried to shut them out, to deny them entrance, but they crashed through the protective globe of mental energy protecting his brain as if it were the most fragile of glass. Galharath clasped his head in his hands and screamed.

● ● ● ◉ ● ● ●

The pieces had been crafted and assembled into a rough approximation of a humanoid shape. Now all that remained was to infuse the creature with the spark of life. The construct lay motionless atop a crystalline table in the middle of the spherical structure that was the psi-forge's main chamber. The crystal struts that connected the sphere to the cavern's ceiling and floor pulsated with soft illumination as they drew upon the vast thermal energies contained beneath the mountain, and the runes carved into the sides of the table glowed with eerie eldritch light. The atmosphere of the cavern was charged with the sensation of building power to the point where the air crackled with barely restrained energy.

Four people wearing protective crystal-lens goggles watched closely as the forge continued siphoning the mountain's power into itself. Three of them stood close to the forge's main chamber so that they might more closely observe the device's first test—and intervene in the unlikely event that anything went wrong. The fourth stood much farther back, almost with his back against the cavern's far wall. In addition to his goggles, this cautious individual wore a heavy cloak imbued with nearly a dozen different enchantments designed to safeguard the wearer from all harm, whether physical or mystical. This was Karnil of House Cannith, high-ranking member of the Fabricators Guild and overseer of this installation. He was a short man, though he thought himself of medium height. Ever since childhood he had endured jokes from people inquiring if he had any halfling blood in his ancestry, which was perhaps why his face seemed to be set in a permanent scowl. House Cannith carried the Mark of Making, and during its long and illustrious history, the House was responsible for some of Khorvaire's greatest achievements, including the towers of Sharn, the lightning rail, and the warforged.

It had been Karnil's task to shepherd this project from its inception to this moment, when the psi-forge was ready to become fully operational. It had taken a great deal of time to get to this point, and Karnil felt both pride and trepidation. If the psi-forge worked properly, House Cannith would be able to produce warriors the like of which Khorvaire had never seen, and his status within the House would rise immeasurably, but if the forge failed . . . Karnil thrust the thought away, lest he somehow jinx today's test by allowing his doubts to fully form in his mind. He rubbed the dragonmark on the back of his hand for luck, an unconscious habit he'd had most of his life. The forge would work because it *had* to work, he told himself. Simple as that.

The trio standing close to the forge were just as responsible for the device's creation as Karnil, but where he had served in primarily an administrative capacity, these three—kalashtar all—were the ones who'd done the actual design and construction. In their minds, that made the psi-forge *theirs*, but they wisely kept this feeling to themselves.

The first kalashtar's name was Banain, a telekineticist who specialized in animation psionics. He wore a silken robe of fiery red that rippled as if stirred by a gentle breeze, though the cavern air was still. This wasn't the first creation forge he had helped build, but it was certainly the most complex and challenging. If it worked, it would be the crowning achievement in a long, and if he did say so himself, distinguished career. His face betrayed none of the excitement that he felt, but his eyes gleamed with anticipation.

Next to Banain stood Evalina, a psionic artificer. She wore only a sleeveless black tunic and sandals, but her flesh was so covered with tattoos and piercings that it appeared she was clad in a multicolored body stocking from head to toe. She specialized in the miniaturization of psionic objects, and the myriad metal rings, studs, and pins embedded in her flesh were all devices of her own creation, each allowing her to perform psionic feats of various kinds. She had also developed a process—known only to herself—of mixing tiny shards of psionic crystals with ink, and the tattoos that adorned her skin were also powerful psionic devices in their own right. Evalina had a single driving purpose in her life: to do that which others thought impossible. Though this wasn't the first psi-forge ever built in the history of Khorvaire, all of the others had been failures and quite disastrous ones at that, but *she* had helped create this forge, therefore she knew it would work. In Evalina's mind, the only true impossibility in existence was that she could ever fail at something she attempted, so she waited for the psi-forge's successful activation, which in her mind was a certainty, a smug smile on her lips.

Turi was the last kalashtar's name, and he was a highly skilled and most powerful psionicist. He possessed no hair anywhere on his body, which was cadaverously thin. His only article of clothing was a white breech cloth, and it was all he ever wore, regardless of the climate. Turi sought to transcend his physical form and become a being of pure thought, and to this end he traveled the length and breadth of Khorvaire learning everything he could about the nature and practice of psionics. He had helped to create House Cannith's psi-forge not because he cared about the House's fortunes, and not because he cared who won the long war that had ravaged Khorvaire. He had done it for the knowledge he'd gained throughout the process, and because he saw the constructs the forge would produce as being a major step toward true psionic transcendence. If psi-forged could be born, perhaps he, Turi, could at last discover a way to achieve the apotheosis he so desired.

Banain, Evalina, and Turi monitored the complex interplay of energies—both mystical and psionic, visible and invisible—that coruscated across the psi-forge's surface. A few more seconds, and the forge would be up to full power, and then . . .

A burst of brilliant white light poured forth from the forge's main chamber, so intense that even though they wore protective goggles, the four in attendance were forced to avert their faces lest they risk blindness. They could feel the vast energies released by the forge as it worked to imbue the construct with life. Of the four, only Karnil knew that the true process by which life was granted to constructs remained a mystery. Oh, the Fabricators Guild pretended it understood, that House Cannith were the masters of the creation forges, but in reality the ultimate nature of how an inanimate being made of stone, metal, and wood became a living, sentient being was as much a mystery to them as to anyone else. Thus Karnil watched through eyes squeezed almost shut as the blazing light of life itself poured into the cavern, his heart filled with both awe and terror at the fearsome energies unleashed.

Then like a storm whose peak fury had passed, the light began to dim. A few moments more, and it had diminished to the point where the four could once more look upon the psi-forge. The crystalline structure continued to pulse with soft light, and the air was filled with the acrid smell of released energy, like after a lightning strike. More, each of the observers experienced a nauseating sensation of vertigo, though only Turi wasn't bothered by it. The dizziness was a result of energies that had rippled through the localized psi-scape as the forge discharged its power, affecting the mental equilibrium of the observers in the process. Turi was unconcerned; he knew the effect would soon pass.

The four waited, their gazes locked on the construct lying motionless upon the crystalline table inside the forge's main chamber. Several moments passed, during which the forge ceased to glow, and the vertiginous sensation in the observers subsided, but still the construct did not move. Karnil ground his teeth together in frustration. After all this time—all the careful preparation, all the exacting work—they couldn't have failed! He started forward, intending to enter the chamber and check on the construct himself, when the creature's left hand twitched.

Karnil froze, a hesitant smile on his lips. Had he imagined it or—There! The hand moved again!

Slowly, awkwardly, the construct sat up. It looked at the four observers, tiny pinpoints of light, of *life*, flickering deep within its eyes.

"We've done it!" Banain shouted. "It's alive!"

But before the others could echo the telekineticist's feeling of triumph, the crystals embedded in the psi-forged's body began to glow with multicolored light. The four observers screamed in a single voice, shrieking at the top of their lungs. Even after their bodies collapsed lifeless to the cavern floor, their minds continued screaming, only now the sound emerged from the throat of the newborn creature that stumbled forth from the crystalline forge.

● ● ● ◉ ● ● ●

Though it took every ounce of will and every iota of knowledge he possessed, Galharath managed to separate his awareness from the psi-forged's mind. Before the creature could pull him in again, he reached up to one of his braids and removed a small green crystal. He flicked it at the psi-forged, and as the shard flew, Galharath took hold of it in a telekinetic grip and drove it straight into the psi-forged's forehead. The creature's anguished bellow came out of its mouth in a blend of five different voices, then the crystals affixed to its body stopped glowing and the psi-forged froze, motionless as a statue. The shard that Galharath had struck the creature with, however, continued to glow a soft but steady green.

A wave of weakness washed over the kalashtar, and he collapsed to his knees, lungs heaving, heart pounding, body slick with sweat. He'd survived but it had been a near thing . . . too near.

"Have you neutralized it?" Cathmore's tone was casual, as if he were asking Galharath what time it was.

The master assassin didn't offer to help Galharath up, and the psionic artificer struggled to his feet on his own.

"For now. The shard I used enabled me to redirect the creature's higher brain functions inward." He wiped sweat from his forehead with a trembling hand. "Eventually he'll be able to free himself. How long it'll take, I can't say. Not long. He's extremely powerful."

Cathmore stepped up to the motionless psi-forged, displaying no fear of the creature whatsoever, but then Galharath knew the man didn't experience fear, thanks to the dark spirit that shared his body. "I assume this construct was produced by the psi-forge."

Galharath nodded. "The first and only one. The facility's original builders succeeded in creating a psi-forged, but they failed to take one thing into account: an organic psionicist is born as an infant, with parents to shepherd its mental development. They place psychic safeguards and blocks within the infant's mind to help protect the child—and those around it—as it grows and learns to master its abilities. The psi-forged was born fully developed in terms of power, but it was as an infant in terms of control. Its psychic abilities manifested wildly in the first few moments of its life, slaying its makers, or rather, their bodies. Their minds, their souls, if you will, were absorbed by the creature and still dwell within it to this day." Galharath stared at the motionless psi-forged. "What you see before you is five separate beings trapped within a single form."

It would have been six if Galharath hadn't managed to resist the psi-forged's power. As it was, the creature had nearly claimed his mind as well.

Cathmore looked into the psi-forged's eyes. The sockets were dark now and would remain so until Galharath freed the construct from the psychic trap that ensnared it.

"Fascinating," the old man said in a voice barely above a whisper. "In a sense, this is a child, isn't it?" He smiled. "How appropriate. I've always been good with the young ones." He turned to Galharath. "Did you learn anything else about our new friend?"

"A few things. He calls himself Solus. When representatives of House Cannith came to investigate why they'd ceased to receive communications from this facility, Solus hid, cloaking himself from their perceptions, just as he did with us. They found the bodies of the others, decided the project was a failure, and closed down the facility. They departed, unaware of Solus's existence. Solus has remained within Mount Luster ever since, rarely venturing outside. I'm not certain, but I got the sense that he's been trying to learn how to control his abilities so that he won't endanger anyone else. He has obtained a modicum of mastery over the years, but he still has quite a way to go."

Cathmore reached out and placed an arthritic claw on Galharath's shoulder. The assassin's touch was cold as ice. "Excellent, Galharath. Well done." The old man turned to regard Solus once more. "Remember what I told you about Fate? It appears that Fate has granted us an opportunity to learn more about psiforged before we begin producing our own. There is much we can learn from our new friend. Much indeed."

If he doesn't destroy us first, Galharath thought.

CHAPTER

TEN

Rocking, swaying ... wood creaking, wind howling, cold seeping into his bones, slowly turning them to ice. A ship—they were on a ship.

Diran struggled to open his eyes, but whatever drug the Coldhearts had used upon him and Ghaji was strong, and its hold was not easily broken. He fought to escape the black numbness that held him in its grip, but like a drowning man on the verge of going down for the third and final time, he was too weak. Despite his efforts he felt himself sink back down into nothingness.

❧ ❧ ❧ ❧ ❧ ❧

"Do you know why I summoned you here?" Cathmore asked.

Diran shook his head. He hadn't been in his new home long, but he'd already learned through painful experience that if he didn't know the right answer to a question, it was better not to say anything at all. He felt an urge to reach up and touch the bruised and swollen flesh of his face, but he resisted, not wishing to risk adding another injury by displaying weakness before Cathmore.

The two of them—man and boy—stood within a large room located on one of the lower levels of Emon Gorsedd's manor home. Diran had never been here before, but he'd heard of this place from the other students. It was called the Proving Room, though why it was named so, or what took place inside, no one would say. The ceiling was high, the walls and floor wooden and bereft of decoration of any sort. They weren't even painted. The only features in the room save for the cold fire globes hovering near the ceiling were a door on the far wall opposite from the one through which Diran had entered and a wide mahogany chest with double doors set against one wall.

Diran was a fisherman's son, and before coming here, he'd never seen anything as fine as the highly polished wood the chest was made from, but Emon Gorsedd was a man with, as he put it, "refined" tastes. Diran had quickly learned that *refined* really meant *expensive*. Diran wished Emon was here now. The man was warmer than Cathmore, and while Diran didn't exactly trust Emon, he wasn't terrified of him, not like he was of Cathmore. The man's eyes were cold and lifeless, like those of a dead fish, and his voice was flat and emotionless. Cathmore didn't seem altogether human to Diran, and he found it hard to believe that the man was Emon's half-brother. The two didn't seem to have anything in common at all.

Cathmore's eyes narrowed as he regarded Diran more closely, and Diran fought to suppress a shiver. "None of the other students told you what was going to happen to you in this room? Not even so much as a hint?"

Diran shook his head again. He'd been at the manse for two weeks, and during that time the other students, almost all of them older than Diran, had barely looked at him, let alone spoken to him. One girl around his own age had smiled at him a few times, though. He thought he'd heard another student call her Makala, but he wasn't sure that he'd heard right.

Cathmore's lips stretched into a thin lizard-like smile. "Good. That's as it should be."

Diran was startled by Cathmore's response, and for the first time since his arrival he wondered if the real reason none of the other students spoke to him wasn't because they were unfriendly but rather because they were afraid.

Diran wore a simple gray tunic and sandals; the outfit seemed to be the unofficial uniform of Emon Gorsedd's students. Cathmore, however, wore a light brown long-sleeved shirt, tan pants, and boots. Diran had noticed that Cathmore tended to dress in colors similar to his surroundings, and today his clothing matched well with the wood that this chamber had been made from. During his years on the Lhazaar fishing with his mother and father, Diran had witnessed how the octopus could blend into its surroundings by altering the color and even the texture of its skin. He wondered if Cathmore made his wardrobe choices for the same reason: protective coloration.

"What are you thinking right now?" Cathmore asked.

Diran didn't think it a good idea to share his observations about Cathmore's manner of dress, but he knew he couldn't remain silent any longer, not now that he'd been asked a direct question.

"I'm thinking about my parents." Saying the words turned the lie into reality, and he was filled with a sudden mixture of sorrow and anger.

"Do you miss them?"

Diran thought this an odd question. Was Cathmore simply asking as some sort of test? He sounded sincere, almost as if he didn't quite comprehend how one human being could mourn the loss of another.

Diran decided to put up a brave front. "I was raised in the Principalities. My parents taught me that life was harsh and death is only ever a heartbeat away."

Cathmore nodded slowly, as if considering Diran's reply. "Wise words, but I don't imagine such knowledge makes you miss your parents any less."

Diran didn't think Cathmore meant that as a question, but he responded anyway. "That's true."

"I doubt they're any more effective in quelling the anger surging within you . . . anger toward the raiders that killed your parents."

Diran gritted his teeth and balled his hands into fists. "Also true."

"There is one thing that will help, though, one thing that will give you the peace that you seek." Cathmore stepped toward Diran and when next he spoke, his voice was almost a purr. "Would you like to know what it is?"

Diran sensed that Cathmore had some sort of trick planned, but he knew he had no choice but to go along. Moreover, part of him—a cold dark part that had been born the day his parents died and their bodies left for the sharks—wanted to know.

"Yes," he said, his voice barely above a whisper.

Cathmore smiled, displaying his teeth, and Diran thought that not all sharks lived in water. Cathmore clapped his hands loudly and the door on the far side of the chamber opened. A pair of men garbed entirely in black entered carrying between them a naked man whose wrists and ankles were bound by leather thongs. The man was gagged, and though he struggled to break free from his captors, the men in black were too strong. The prisoner was bald, his bare scalp covered with a concentric tattoo, and he had a drooping black mustache. He was broad-shouldered and well-muscled, his skin bronzed and leathery from decades of living and working outside. His flesh was marked with criss-crossing scars which spoke of a life lived in conflict. The men in black dragged the prisoner to Cathmore then unceremoniously dumped him onto the floor. They then looked to Cathmore as if awaiting further instructions.

"That will be all."

The two men bowed then returned the way they'd come, closing the door behind them. The man got to his knees and glared at Cathmore, who paid him no attention. He stared at Diran with a penetrating gaze, as if he were trying to see inside Diran's mind.

"Do you recognize this man?" Cathmore asked.

Diran had trouble hearing Cathmore over the pounding of his pulse in his ears. His vision went gray around the edges, almost as if everything else had ceased to exist, save for the naked man bound before him. "He's the captain of the raiders who killed my parents."

"Yes, he is."

"How . . . why . . . ?" Diran was barely aware of speaking, but Cathmore answered, stepping closer to Diran and leaning down next to his ear, as if he understood that Diran might have difficulty hearing him.

"How scarcely matters, but I assure you, it wasn't difficult to locate him."

Diran stared into the raider captain's eyes. The man glared back at him with impotent fury but also, Diran thought, with growing fear. "What about his crew?"

"They're dead, as I ordered."

Diran looked at Cathmore, not comprehending what the man said.

"Think of it as a welcoming gift, but this one—his name is Bruk, by the way—I saved for you."

Diran frowned. "I-I don't . . ."

"Remember what I told you? That there was one thing that could make the pain and anger of losing your parents go away? It's called revenge."

Cathmore turned and walked to the mahogany chest. He flung the doors open and Diran saw that the chest was filled with all manner of weapons mounted inside: swords, maces, spears, hammers, axes, garroting wire, flails, whips, throwing stars . . . and daggers. So many daggers. Daggers with long blades, short blades, curved blades, straight . . . Daggers with golden pommels inlaid with jewels, and daggers with simple handles wrapped in leather, but no matter their differences in design and decoration, every one was sharp and deadly.

They were beautiful.

"Come here, boy," Cathmore said. "Take a closer look."

Diran hesitated, but he couldn't help himself. He joined Cathmore at the open chest.

"In your short time here, you've learned that we call ourselves the Brotherhood of the Blade," Cathmore said, "and you know what we do."

Though this was phrased as a statement, Diran understood that a response was required of him. "Yes. You kill people for money."

Cathmore looked at Diran for a moment without expression, and Diran feared that he was to be punished for his response, but then Cathmore's mouth stretched into a cold, mirthless smile. "I'll say one thing for you boy, you're direct. I like that. Allow me to be equally direct in turn. We are a brotherhood of assassins, and these—" Cathmore gestured at the chest's contents—"are the tools of our trade. You may choose any one of these weapons and slay Bruk. You may do the deed swiftly or take as much time as you wish. Whatever you prefer."

Cathmore reached into the bottom of the chest with both hands and brought forth a black laquer box. He cradled the box with one arm while he opened the lid with his free hand. Inside, resting on a bed of crimson velvet, were a dozen unmarked glass vials, each containing a different color of liquid: cerulean, amber, mauve, aquamarine and more.

"There are many approaches to the dark art of assassination. Some prefer to deal death with steel, while others—such as myself—prefer the refined subtlety to be found in the use of poisons." Cathmore gazed down upon the vials he displayed to Diran, his eyes gleaming with barely restrained excitement. It took an obvious effort for the master assassin to look up from his beloved poisons and meet Diran's gaze once more. "Still, as I said, it is your choice."

Diran pretended to consider his options for several moments, and then he stepped past Cathmore and his vials and reached into the chest. Almost of their own volition, his fingers stroked the cool, sleek metal of a dagger. Gently, almost reverently, he removed the blade from its niche on the inside of the chest door and gripped its handle tight. He expected the dagger's hilt to warm within his hand, but it remained cool, not cold, but soothing, almost as if it were trying to tell him that everything was going to be all right. Diran gazed down upon the blade, drinking in the way light played across the polished surface of the metal.

Then he lifted his head and turned to look at Bruk.

The sea raider remained on his knees, but he no longer glared at Diran. His eyes were now filled with fear and he was trembling. Diran recalled Bruk's face as he rammed his swordpoint into his father's chest, once more heard the cry of agony as blood bubbled past his father's lips . . . saw the light dim in his father's eyes as death came to claim him. Then Diran remembered what the raiders had done to his mother. Bruk had been the first to use her, but he had been far from the last.

Diran stepped toward Bruk, pulse pounding in his ears, dagger gripped tight in a palm slick with sweat. He stopped before the sea raider and looked deeply into the man's eyes. What he searched for, he didn't know. Some sign of remorse or regret, perhaps. An acknowledgement that here, at the end of his life, Bruk realized the grief he had caused so many and was sorry, but all Diran saw in the man's gaze was raw, naked fear.

He relaxed his grip and the dagger thunked to the wooden floor. He turned to Cathmore. "I know what this man did . . . I saw it, but I cannot kill him. To do so would make me no better than him."

Cathmore's face betrayed no hint of emotion as the master assassin regarded Diran for a long moment. Finally, he nodded and walked over to where Diran stood. Cathmore bent down and picked up the dagger that Diran had dropped. Diran feared that he had failed the assassin's test, and now Cathmore was going to kill him, but Diran didn't turn away, didn't avert his gaze from Cathmore. If the man intended to slay him, then so be it. Death would be preferable to a life as an acolyte in the Brotherhood of the Blade.

Cathmore turned and knelt next to Bruk, and with two swift, efficient strokes of the dagger, severed the bonds around the sea raider's wrists and ankles. Cathmore removed the man's gag, then stood and tossed the dagger onto the floor next to Bruk.

"Kill the boy and you can go free."

Diran stared at Cathmore in shock. Bruk looked confused for a moment, then he grinned and reached for the dagger.

❖ ❖ ❖ ◉ ❖ ❖ ❖

Ghaji lay next to Diran in the darkness of the ship's hold. His half-orc physiology was doing its best to fight off the effects of the drug the Coldhearts had used on him and Diran, but it was strong stuff, and he had no more success than his friend did, and like his friend, Ghaji found his semiconscious mind drifting on the tides of memory . . .

● ● ● ◉ ● ● ●

Ghaji walked into the clearing, his stride purposeful, head held high. Inwardly, he was afraid, but he knew that if he were to have any chance of surviving the next several moments, he couldn't afford to show it.

It was midmorning after the bloody raid on the wood-wright's cottage. The day was shaping up to be a pleasant one—sunny and mild, with a gentle breeze blowing. The trees were full and lush, their green leaves whispering in the wind. Birds sat on their branches, singing a counterpoint to the trees' whispering, their musical voices light and cheerful. After what the orcs had done last night, Ghaji found the beauty of the day revolting. It should be raining, the air cold, the sky overcast and gloomy. It was as if the world had taken no notice of the deaths of the wood-wright and his family . . . or worse, as if the world were actually celebrating their murders.

Eggera and Murtt reclined against the thick trunk of an old oak tree, eyes closed, chests rising and falling slowly as if they were napping. Ghaji knew better, though. The two orcs might appear to be resting, but Ghaji had fought alongside them for too many months not to know better. Both were surely aware of his approach and ready to leap up in an instant and fight if need be. Neither had bathed since last night's grisly work, and their clothes and armor were covered with dried blood, their fur matted with it. Flies buzzed around the pair, drawn by the rank stench of old blood, but if the insects bothered the orcs, they did nothing about the pests.

Chagai sat cross-legged in the middle of the clearing, hands on his knees, eyes closed, broadsword unsheathed on the ground at his side. He appeared to be meditating, and while the practice wasn't uncommon among certain orcs, Ghaji had never seen Chagai do it before. He guessed the mercenary leader was simply waiting . . . for him.

Ghaji crossed the clearing and walked up to Chagai, though he was careful to stop four feet from the orc. Coming any closer would be considered a challenge. Before Ghaji could say anything, Chagai spoke, though he did not open his eyes.

"Where have you been? We'd begun to think that you'd deserted us."

After the raid on the wood-wright's house, Ghaji hadn't been able to bring himself to spend the night with the other orcs, so he'd gone off on his own. He'd spent the time wandering mostly, though he finally did climb up into the branches of an elm tree a few hours before dawn and catch some fitful, restless sleep.

"Sneaking off in the night would not be honorable."

In truth Ghaji had contemplated doing that very thing, but while it might have been the wiser course, he hadn't been able to do it. He knew that Chagai and the others would have blamed what they saw as his betrayal on his half-blood nature. Plus, he knew that they would never allow him to break away from the company like that. They'd hunt him down, no matter where in Khorvaire he went and no matter how long it took. So both pride and pragmatism prompted Ghaji to return to speak with Chagai one last time.

"So you've come to tell me you're leaving."

Chagai still didn't open his eyes, but seeing the orc's muscles begin to tense up, Ghaji knew he had to be on his guard. Ghaji glanced over at Eggera and Murtt. They remained reclining against the oak tree, but both were now watching Ghaji with amused interest and, he thought, the beginnings of bloodlust.

"Yes."

Chagai at last opened his eyes. He looked up at Ghaji, his gaze unreadable. "I suppose this has something to do with last night's raid."

"It does."

Chagai unfolded his legs and rose to his feet. Though the mercenary captain left his broadsword lying on the ground, Ghaji still took a step backward, cursing himself for displaying such weakness.

Chagai's eyes narrowed and his lips curled back to display his teeth. "What's wrong? Spilling a little blood last night make you queasy?"

Eggera and Murtt barked out harsh laughter, but Ghaji didn't turn to look at them. He knew that taking his attention off Chagai even for a second could well prove to be a fatal mistake. "You have seen me in battle many times. Have I ever given you cause to doubt my courage?"

"Before last night? No." Chagai took a step toward Ghaji, a definite challenge. "But then perhaps you managed to keep your human half in check up to this point."

Ghaji gritted his teeth, but he refused to allow Chagai to bait him into attacking. "Orc, human, or in-between, it makes no difference. There was no honor in what we did last night. It was not a battle nor a hunt. It was slaughter, pure and simple."

Chagai shrugged. "That's what we were paid to do." He gave Ghaji a sharp-toothed grin.

"Strength without honor is meaningless. Killing without conscience or need is murder. I can no longer serve with you, Chagai. I'm leaving."

Ghaji had done what honor demanded and spoken directly to his commander before leaving. Now all that remained was to see if he could get out of here alive. He turned his back on Chagai and began walking toward the edge of the clearing, trying to hurry without looking like he was hurrying.

He heard a soft rustle of grass and knew that Chagai was coming for him. He feinted right then dodged left just as Chagai's broadsword whisked through the air where his neck had been an instant before. Ghaji hit the ground, rolled, and drew his axe as he came up onto his feet. He raised his weapon just in time to block Chagai's second swing. Chagai was a full orc and stronger than Ghaji, and the impact nearly caused Ghaji to lose his grip on his weapon. The broadsword was forged of superior steel and it cut a notch in Ghaji's axe-blade.

Chagai stepped back. "You're a disgrace, Ghaji. You never should have been born in the first place. The only way to redeem yourself is to surrender and allow me to end your misbegotten life."

Ghaji tightened his grip on his axe handle. "Maybe I shouldn't have been given life, but I was, and I'll be damned if I'll let the likes of you take it from me." He lifted his axe, bellowed a war-cry, and charged.

CHAPTER

ELEVEN

Yvka, Tresslar, and Hinto had run out of small talk and were getting tired of drinking the King Prawn's lousy ale. The broken door of the common room slammed inward.

As Asenka dashed in and ran over to their table, the three companions rose to their feet.

"Where are they?" Yvka demanded.

Asenka frowned in confusion. "Who?" she said between gasps for breath.

"Diran and Ghaji," Tresslar said. "We haven't seen them for a while, and from the way you burst in, it's obvious they're in trouble."

"She can tell us on the way!" Hinto said as he started for the door. "Come on!"

Yvka and Tresslar followed after the halfling, running past Asenka and leaving the woman standing alone at their abandoned table. She shrugged, turned, took a deep breath, and ran after them.

● ● ● ◉ ● ● ●

They were halfway to the dock by the time Asenka told the others what had happened to Diran and Ghaji. From what she'd heard of the priest and his half-orc friend, they weren't unfamiliar with trouble, and the speed at which their companions had reacted to Asenka's appearance told the Sea Scorpion commander just *how* familiar with trouble they truly were.

Yvka stopped and motioned for the others to do the same. The elfwoman swiveled her head slowly as she scanned their surroundings. Asenka knew that elves' vision was far keener than humans', especially in the dark, but she nevertheless wondered if Yvka could actually see anything. Though the fog had dissipated somewhat, the night was still murky, so that even elf eyes might have difficulty penetrating the mist roiling through Perhata's streets. Still, Asenka hadn't survived in the Sea Scorpions as long as she had by ignoring potential danger.

"What's wrong?" she asked as she drew her sword.

"I'm . . . not sure," Yvka admitted. "There's something . . ."

A figure stepped out of the fog then, seeming to coalesce out of the mist as if born of it. The figure came closer, and Asenka recognized the woman—if such a creature could be called a woman—who had confronted her before.

Yvka reached into the pouch hanging from her belt and withdrew a wooden juggling ball. Asenka noticed that the elfwoman's hand trembled. Tresslar stared open-mouthed at the blonde woman, his expression one of absolute shock. The old artificer recovered quickly and from his belt drew a wand that terminated in a golden dragonhead.

Asenka expected the halfling to react the same way as his two friends, but he didn't reach for a weapon, didn't gaze upon the blonde woman with fear. Instead, his mouth stretched into a wide grin.

"You're Makala, right? Will Diran ever be surprised to see you! I never got a chance to meet you, at least not formally." He stepped and held out his hand. "But I looked in on you a couple times while Diran tried to . . . tried to . . ." His hand began to shake then, and the tremors quickly spread to the rest of his body until the halfling was trembling so hard Asenka feared his small heart might burst.

The woman smiled sadly at Hinto. "While Diran tried to prevent my becoming a vampire."

Hinto nodded, but he didn't lower his trembling hand.

"There is no need to fear me," Makala said. "I know what's happened to Diran and Ghaji, and I wish to help."

"How can we trust you?" Yvka said. Her voice was firm, but there was a trace of fear in her eyes. "You're not human anymore."

For an instant, Makala's eyes flashed crimson, but then they returned to normal. "You're not human either, but I don't hold that against you."

"Elves may not be human," Tresslar said, "but they aren't blood-drinking monsters."

The vampire turned to the artificer. "If I wished to harm any of you, I could've done so long before now. All that need concern you—" she glanced at Asenka—"*all* of you, is that I wish to use my abilities to help rescue our friends. If you can't accept what I've become, perhaps you can at least accept that."

The tension in the air was far thicker than any sea fog could ever be. Yvka, Tresslar, and Hinto exchanged glances, and Asenka could guess what they were thinking: if it came down to it, could they stand against Makala without Diran and Ghaji's aid?

"We're wasting time," Asenka said. "While we stand here talking, the Coldhearts are sailing farther out to sea. We can worry later about whether or not we can trust one another."

The elfwoman, the halfling, and the artificer exchanged glances once more then nodded in silent agreement.

Makala smiled grimly. "Good. I'll meet you at the *Zephyr*. I have something I need to put aboard first if I'm to sail with you." The woman made no outward display of power, but her form grew hazy and indistinct, and then her body separated into shreds of mist that curled away and vanished into the night.

"What's the *Zephyr*?" Asenka asked, but the other three were already running again, and she hurried to keep up with them.

CHAPTER

TWELVE

Diran watched as Bruk picked up the dagger and rose to his feet. The boy raised his hands and took a step backward.

"But I spared your life!"

"You're a fool," the sea raider said as he slowly advanced. "You should've slit my throat from ear to ear and laughed as my life's blood splashed onto the floor." He smiled. "That's what I would've done."

Bruk lunged at Diran with the dagger, but the man's balance was off, making Diran wonder just how long the Brotherhood of the Blade had held him captive and how often he'd been fed during that time. Bruk listed to the left, and his legs wobbled as if they were having a hard time supporting his weight. Diran lashed out with a foot and kicked Bruk's left leg out from under him, causing the sea raider to fall to the floor. Bruk hadn't completely forgotten his fighting skills, though, and managed to keep hold of the dagger and avoid skewering himself with it as he hit.

Bruk glared at Diran, baring his teeth as if he were a wild animal. Appropriate, Diran thought, considering what the bastard had done to his parents.

"Just for that, I'll take my time gutting you, boy." Bruk began to pull himself up on his feet.

Diran remembered something his father had told him—

Sometimes when you're out on the water, everything will seem calm one moment, and then a storm will blow up out of nowhere. It's times like those when you most need to keep your wits about you. Giving in to fear is the fastest way to find yourself at the bottom of the Lhazaar.

Diran forced himself to remain calm and consider his options, such as they were. He knew there was no point trying to reach either door. Even if they were unlocked, which he very much doubted, surely some of the older acolytes—such as the ones who'd brought Bruk in—were waiting on the other side to prevent him from escaping. He also knew that there was no point in trying to appeal to Cathmore's sympathies, for the elder assassin had none. The only resources available to him were what lay inside the weapons chest . . . and in the box Cathmore held in his hands.

Diran ran toward Cathmore just as Bruk got to his feet and slashed out with the dagger. Diran heard the hiss of the blade parting air behind him and felt the breeze of its passage on the back of his neck. Bruk had missed, but not by much. As Diran approached Cathmore, the assassin stood motionless, though his gaze was riveted on Diran, almost as if he were studying the boy and assessing his actions.

Diran reached into the box and grabbed several vials at random. He turned to see Bruk charging, eyes blazing with anger, dagger raised for a killing strike.

Diran hurled the vials at Bruk's face.

Without thinking, Bruk lashed out with the dagger to protect himself, and the blade struck several of the vials. Glass shattered, liquid splattered—some of it onto Bruk's face and into his eyes. The other vials either missed him or bounced off his chest to burst apart harmlessly against the floor, but the poison that Bruk's blow had released was more than sufficient.

The sea raider screamed, dropped the dagger, and clapped his hands to his face. The skin around his eyes, nose, and mouth turned greenish-black and began to swell. He collapsed onto his side, his body spasming wildly, as if the muscles were tearing free from his skeleton. Then Bruk made a strangled gurling noise deep in his throat, stiffened once, and went limp. The poison had finished doing its work.

Diran looked at the corpse of the man who was responsible for the deaths of his parents, and though he was shamed by it, he felt a deep sense of satisfaction mingled with relief.

I hope you can rest easier now, Mother and Father.

"Well done, lad."

Diran turned to Cathmore and was surprised to see the assassin grinning.

"You didn't have the training to fight Bruk hand to hand, so you used the only weapon that would even the odds between you." Cathmore's grin took on a hard edge. "That's another reason I favor poison: it doesn't matter how powerful or skilled its victims are. All must bow before its power."

Diran didn't respond. Instead he walked over to Bruk and knelt at the sea raider's side. He retrieved the dagger Bruk had dropped and rubbed its blade in a puddle of poison created when one of the vials that the sea raider had missed had fallen to the floor, then he spun, rising to his feet as he did so, and hurled the dagger at Cathmore. The blade flew straight and true and embedded itself in the poison-master's left shoulder. Cathmore's eyes widened in surprise and he dropped the box holding the remaining poisons. It crashed onto the floor, spilling the rest of its contents in a mess of broken glass and foul-smelling liquid.

Blood welled forth from the wound and Cathmore reached up with a trembling hand, as if he intended to grasp the hilt and pull the blade free. Then he drew in a shuddering breath, his eyes rolled white, and he fell to the floor and lay still.

Diran stepped over to Cathmore's body and looked down upon it, a grim smile spreading across his face. "I might not have the skill to fight someone like Bruk, but my father taught me how to use a knife. He said it was a good weapon for a fisherman to have. It was small enough to wield in tight quarters and you could always use it to gut fish if necessary."

Cathmore's eyes moved to focus on Diran. "Your father was a wise man."

Diran took several frightened steps backward as Cathmore sat up.

"I applaud your ingenuity and your ruthlessness," the master assassin said, "but did you truly think that I wouldn't have long ago made myself immune to my own poisons? Even if your dagger strike itself had killed me, Emon would've simply paid to have me resurrected, though my dear half-brother would undoubtedly insist I pay him back. Still, Diran Bastiaan, I am impressed. You alone of all the children I have taught have managed to come this close to killing me." He chuckled, then drew in a hiss of air. "It hurts like blazes, though." He held out his right hand. "Help me up and we'll see about getting me to a healer, eh?"

Diran looked at Cathmore's hand for a moment before finally taking it and steadying the man as he rose to his feet.

❀ ❀ ❀ ❀ ❀ ❀ ❀

Ghaji swung his axe at Chagai's unprotected neck. Orc necks were thick, their heads set close to their broad shoulders, so it wasn't the easiest target to hit. That didn't matter since Ghaji didn't expect his strike to connect.

Sure enough, Chagai pulled away and brought his broadsword up to defect Ghaji's blow, but at the last instant, Ghaji turned his axe downward, angled his shoulder toward Chagai, and slammed into the orc leader. Pain exploded through Ghaji's right shoulder all the way down his arm as he hit Chagai's breastplate, but the maneuver had the intended effect of throwing Chagai off balance. With his left hand Ghaji grabbed Chagai's sword arm by the wrist and twisted as hard as he could. The sound of snapping bone cut through the air, followed instantly by Chagai's agonized cry. His hand went limp and the broadsword slipped from his useless fingers.

A broken wrist wasn't enough to stop an orc warrior, though. Chagai bared his teeth and lunged, sinking them into Ghaji's right shoulder—the one already bruised and battered from his collision with Chagai's breastplate. Ghaji's hide was tougher than a human's but not as tough as a full orc's, and Chagai's teeth sliced into Ghaji's flesh as easily as a white-hot knife through butter. Now it was Ghaji's turn to bellow in pain.

He felt hot blood gush from his wound and splatter onto his chest. The agony was so intense that he thought for a moment that he might lose consciousness. Though he might be only half-orc, he was all warrior, so he fought to ignore the pain. He tossed his axe from his right hand to his left, then swung the butt-end of the weapon upward and smashed the handle into Chagai's right temple. The blow jarred Chagai's head, causing the teeth embedded into Ghaji's shoulder to jerk violently and send a fresh wave of agony surging though the half-orc's arm. He let out another bellow of pain, but he refused to yield. He hit Chagai in the head once, twice, three times more.

Chagai's eyes went wide, and Ghaji felt a soft chuff of air escape the orc's mouth and waft across his shoulder wound. Then Chagai collapsed, and since his teeth were still stuck in Ghaji's shoulder, the half-orc was pulled down with his foe. As they hit,

Chagai's teeth tore free from Ghaji, causing pain so intense that Ghaji blacked out.

When he came to, he was lying on his back looking up at a blue, cloud-dotted sky. He turned his head, though it hurt like blazes to do so, and saw that Chagai lay next to him. The orc's eyes were closed, and Ghaji couldn't tell if he were alive or dead, not that he much cared at this point; he was just glad Chagai wasn't trying to kill him. He pressed two fingers against the side of Chagai's neck and felt his pulse. It was weak but steady. It appeared the mercenary commander would live. Too bad.

Slowly, painfully, Ghaji rose to his feet. He'd dropped his axe when Chagai's dead weight had pulled him down, but he didn't bother to retrieve the weapon. Chagai was no longer a threat, at least for now. Besides, Ghaji was too weary from the battle and too weak from blood loss to wield the weapon. He pressed a hand to his shoulder wound to staunch the bleeding, then turned to see where Eggera and Murtt were. The two orcs remained by the oak tree, but now they were standing, swords in hand.

Ghaji sighed. "If you plan to kill me, get on with it. I'm too tired to stop you."

Eggera and Murtt glanced at each other, then shrugged and returned their swords to their scabbards.

"It was a fair fight," Eggera said.

"Chagai got what he deserved," Murtt said with a derisive snort. "He should never have attacked you . . . especially from behind. There was no honor in it."

Ghaji wanted to say that there was no honor in slaughtering a cottage full of innocents, but he didn't see much point in bringing that up right then.

"What will you do now, Ghaji?" Eggera asked.

The question was innocent enough, but there was something in the female orc's tone that added an extra layer of meaning to her words. Battle-prowess was a prime requisite for orcs when searching for a lover. It seemed even a half-orc could make himself attractive to the opposite sex if he bested a superior opponent. Ghaji didn't know whether to be pleased by this development or angered that it had taken his almost getting killed to get Eggera to notice him. In the end, he decided to ignore the matter entirely.

"There's a war on. I'm sure I'll find work elsewhere." *Once I heal,* he added. "What of you two? Will you still follow Chagai?"

Murtt's disdainful grimace was sufficient answer. Still, he said, "Chagai has been defeated and by a half-blood, no less. He is no longer worthy of leading us." He turned to Eggera. "Let's go."

Eggera looked at Ghaji once more, a question in her eyes. Ghaji responded by looking away. A moment later he heard the sound of the two orcs walking away. He didn't turn around again for several moments, lest he give Eggera the wrong impression, then he spent some time cleaning and bandaging his wound. When he was finished, he returned to Chagai's side. The orc was beginning to stir, though he had a way to go to reach full consciousness. Ghaji picked up his axe with his left hand and stared down at his former commander. There was no honor in slaying a defenseless foe, but then Chagai hadn't worried about that last night at the wood-wright's cottage, had he? Ghaji wasn't skilled with using his left hand to fight, but he thought he could wield his axe well enough to do what had to be done.

He pressed the edge of his axe blade to Chagai's throat, and in his mind he once more heard the screams of the wood-wright and his family as they died. Slaying Chagai would be justice, but slaying Chagai while he was helpless would make Ghaji just like him.

Ghaji hesitated. Finally, he pulled the axe away from Chagai's throat and tucked it beneath his belt. Let Chagai live with the knowledge that he'd been beaten by a half-blood. That would be far worse for him than death.

Ghaji turned to go, then he stopped. He turned back around and looked at Chagai's breastplate. There was a small dent from where Ghaji had slammed into the metal, but otherwise it was still good as new—if you didn't count the blood splashed on it from Ghaji's shoulder wound.

If I'm going to strike out on my own, I could use some armor, he thought.

He knelt down and began undoing the breastplate's leather straps.

● ● ● ◉ ● ● ●

Ghaji opened his eyes to darkness. His head throbbed and his throat felt as if he'd been gargling with the stomach acid of a purple worm. He tried to move and when he couldn't, he realized that his hands and feet were bound.

If I had a copper piece for every time I've been taken prisoner . . .

The last Ghaji remembered was being attacked by Haaken and the Coldhearts. If he had to bet where he was, he'd guess the hold of the Coldhearts' ship. Was Diran here as well? He opened his mouth to whisper his friend's name, but when Ghaji tried to speak, he started coughing, and it took several moments for him to regain control of himself.

"Don't worry. It's a side-effect of the drug the Coldhearts used." Diran's voice was soft and scratchy but audible. "It's called the amber sleep, and it's made from the leaves of a plant that grows in the jungles of Xen'drik. It's rare and quite expensive. I wonder how Haaken got hold of it."

"How do you know? Oh, right. Former assassin." Ghaji struggled to break free of his bonds, but they held tight. He gave up and turned toward Diran's direction. "Do you still have any of your daggers?"

"Unfortunately not. Haaken and his people not only removed the daggers I carried on my person, they also took my cloak."

Ghaji was disappointed but not surprised. After all, his axe had been taken as well. Still, they weren't completely without weapons. "If you're not already lying down, Diran, do so."

Ghaji heard rustling nearby. "Done," Diran said.

Ghaji sighed. He really didn't want to do this, but he could think of no other way that they could get free. He wriggled over to Diran, lay down on his side, and shifted position until his head was next to Diran's wrists. Then Ghaji opened his mouth, and using his sharp teeth, he began to carefully gnaw upon the rope binding his friend's arms behind his back. It only took a few moments for Ghaji to free Diran's hands, and after he shifted position once more, his feet.

Ghaji spat several times. "I hate the taste of rope."

"I appreciate your sacrifice, my friend. Allow me to return the favor."

"Nothing personal, Diran, but you don't have the teeth for it."

Diran chuckled. "Perhaps not, but allow me to see what I can find that might serve the same purpose."

Ghaji listened as Diran searched the hold. He heard boxes being moved, lids being opened, contents shifted about as Diran felt around for something that would cut Ghaji's bonds. The half-orc's night vision adjusted to the hold's darkness, and he was able to make out Diran's form as the priest moved silently among the cargo, searching. After some time had passed without Diran having any success, Ghaji began to think that maybe things would go faster if his friend did employ his blunt human teeth to gnaw through the rope binding his wrists and ankles, but finally Diran said, "Ah, here we are!"

"What did you find?"

Diran returned to Ghaji's side. The half-orc could see that his friend held some sort of object in his right hand, but Ghaji couldn't quite make out what it was.

"A broken sword. Someone must've left it down here in hopes of either repairing it or selling to a smith as scrap. The edge is somewhat dull, but it should serve."

Diran knelt down next to Ghaji and began sawing at his bonds with the broken sword. Diran only needed to cut partway through the rope, just enough to weaken it so Ghaji could break free, and within moments, Ghaji was standing next to Diran and rubbing his wrists.

"What now?" Ghaji asked. "Do we storm the deck without weapons and take on Haaken and his crew with our bare hands?"

"As emotionally satisfying as that might be, it hardly seems practical, does it?" Diran replied.

"So we wait down here for Haaken to come get us and try to take him by surprise? That doesn't seem like much of a plan, either."

"True," Diran admitted. "I found a crate of oil. I suppose we could use it to start a fire."

"And do what? Die of smoke inhalation? What if we survive the fire but the ship goes down? As cold as the Lhazaar is, we'd die."

Diran didn't disagree with him. "If Haaken simply wanted to kill us, he could have done so easily while we were unconscious. He's obviously got something else in mind for us, and I wouldn't be surprised if whatever it is lies at the end of our journey. Perhaps an opportunity for escape shall present itself once we arrive at our destination."

"What do we do in the meantime?" Ghaji asked. "Just sit here in the hold and twiddle our thumbs?"

"Well, I also found a crate of wine . . ."

Ghaji thought for a moment then shrugged. "Sounds like a plan."

❧ ❧ ❧ ❧ ❧ ❧ ❧

Skarm stood at the end of the dock in goblin form, watching as the elemental sloop sped silently out to sea. The barghest possessed many strengths, but flying wasn't among them, and while he could swim quite fast in his natural form, there was no way he could ever hope to catch up to a vessel as swift as that one. The dragonwand had eluded him again.

In frustration, he gnashed teeth that looked more lupine than goblin. He'd followed the priest's companions as they made their way to the dock and had observed their meeting with the female vampire—from a safe distance, of course. Skarm had considered making an attempt to snatch the dragonwand then, while everyone was preoccupied, but in the end he'd decided against it. If the vampire was another of the priest's allies—though Skarm didn't see how such a thing was possible—then she might well try to stop him. Barghests were strong enough to hold their own against a vampire if need be, but the outcome of such a battle would be in doubt. In the end, Skarm had decided against taking such a risk and had continued to observe and trail behind the others as they continued on to the dock, boarded the elemental sloop, and set sail, leaving Skarm behind.

The barghest was beginning to worry. Nathifa was extremely patient as only the undead could be. After all, she'd been scheming to get her hands on the dragonwand—or rather, the dragonhead affixed to it—for decades, but now that she was so close to achieving her goal, she wouldn't tolerate many more delays. If he didn't get his hands on the dragonhead soon, it would go badly for him.

From what Skarm had overheard while following the priest's friends, it sounded as if they intended to return to Perhata after rescuing the priest and his half-orc servant. Provided they weren't all killed in the attempt, of course. If so, then he would have another opportunity to take the dragonhead when they once more made port. All he had to do was wait.

He shifted to wolf form. He would be able to hide more effectively in this body, and his animal senses would help alert him when the priest and his companions returned. He padded silently down the deserted dock, intending to find a hiding place in one of the alleys between the various warehouses, fish-sellers, and taverns located nearby, but as he passed one particular vessel—a small trading ship—he caught a whiff of blood mingled with the air's saltwater tang. Intrigued, he leapt aboard the vessel with lupine grace. Sniffing as he went, he traced the smell to the ship's hold. He shifted back to goblin form, opened the hatch, and climbed down the ladder.

Save for some crates and supplies, the hold was empty. Skarm shifted back to wolf form and sniffed the air. The smell of blood was stronger here, as was another smell: the faint sour-musty stink of decay. Skarm recognized it as the scent of a vampire, and not just any vampire—the one who'd accompanied the priest's friends on their rescue mission. He sniffed once more and caught a human's scent . . . a male. Skarm's lupine mouth stretched into a goblinish smile. Evidently the vampire woman had fed here and then disposed of the body before leaving. Too bad. Even drained of blood, the corpse would've made a nice snack for Skarm. He consoled himself by licking up the few drops of blood the vampire had spilled—they were almost dry, but still tasty enough—and then he returned to goblin form and climbed back up onto the deck. He was grateful the Dark Six had led him to this vessel: she would make a suitable vantage point to wait for the priest and his friends to make port again.

After a quick search to satisfy himself that there was no one else on board, he changed back into his wolf form and settled down on the deck, head on paws, eyes closed, alert for any sound or scent that would indicate his prey's return.

CHAPTER

THIRTEEN

Asenka had never been aboard an elemental sloop before. She wondered if she could get Baron Mahir to purchase one for the Sea Scorpions. The wind spirit that powered the craft was bound to a metal containment ring at the aft of the sloop and manifested as a glowing blue mass of swirling energy inside the ring. Wind issued forth from the ring to fill the *Zephyr*'s sails full to bursting. Yvka sat in a chair in front of the ring, one hand working the tiller while the other rested on the chair's arm, using a magical control built into the chair to command the elemental. In addition, the ship was constructed from soarwood—a substance so preternaturally smooth and light that it produced virtually no friction—and her runners slid over the surface of the sea as easily as if she were moving over solid ice. The craft was making phenomenal speed, so much so that Asenka, who'd spent the majority of her life at sea, needed to hold onto the ship's railing to steady herself.

"Where did you berth this craft?" Asenka called out over

the roaring of the elemental's wind. "I would've known if such a vessel had been kept at the main docks."

The elfwoman turned toward Asenka. "I find it best to keep the *Zephyr* away from prying eyes—not to mention greedy hands. I have access to a number of . . . alternate ports scattered around the Principalities. Let's just leave it at that." Yvka's voice was strained, her face grim. She looked away from Asenka and concentrated anew on piloting the vessel.

Asenka scowled. She understood that the elfwoman was concerned for her missing companions—especially Ghaji—but Asenka didn't appreciate being dismissed so casually. As commander of the Sea Scorpions, she wasn't used to being kept in the dark. She'd been reluctant to join the crew of the *Zephyr*, but she knew the elemental sloop was their only chance of catching up to the Coldhearts. The rest of the Scorpions had set sail at the same time the *Zephyr* had pulled away from the dock, and though their vessel was a fine one, there was no way she could keep up with the elemental sloop. That was the reason Asenka had joined the others aboard and ordered her second in command to captain the Scorpions' ship. Since she was a guest, she didn't feel it was best for her to push Yvka for too much information. She could learn more about these "secret ports" later, after they'd rescued Diran and Ghaji.

Still, wherever the elfwoman had kept her ship hidden, she couldn't have been too difficult to locate. After all, Makala had found her. The evidence lay right there on the deck before her: a large obsidian sarcophagus with strange runes carved into the sides. This was the object Makala had said she needed to move onto the *Zephyr* before she could accompany them on their rescue mission. Even knowing that Makala wasn't human, Asenka still had a difficult time imagining the slim, petite woman moving something so massive onto the ship by herself, but the sarcophagus had already been on the ship when Yvka sailed her from her hiding place and picked up the rest of them at the dock, which meant Makala had been able to move the object, presumably by herself, in a short amount of time.

Asenka gazed up the obsidian sarcophagus and shuddered. The lid was closed and Makala rested inside; asleep or awake, Asenka didn't know. Makala had shut herself in before the *Zephyr* left Perhata, saying that she could only tolerate sea travel while sealed within the stone coffin. She'd also made it clear that due to the enchantment on the box, she couldn't open it from within. One of them would have to open it for her. Given the sort of creature Makala was, Asenka didn't think it would be a bad thing if they never let her out, but since Makala was a friend of the others—or at least had once been a companion of theirs—Asenka decided to keep this opinion to herself. Still, she was glad the woman was shut away; it made her feel safer.

She recalled Makala's burning crimson eyes, once more heard her harsh, throaty voice. *I do not want to harm you, but remember what I said. I'll do anything to protect Diran.* Anything.

Asenka couldn't help shuddering anew.

Tresslar and Hinto stood at the bow of the ship, looking forward, their backs to the sloop's cabin, as well as to Makala's dark sarcophagus. On purpose? she wondered. Probably. As uncomfortable as she was looking at the thing, it had to be worse for Makala's friends, who evidently had known her when she was human.

Asenka decided to leave Yvka to her work, and still holding onto the railing for support, made her way to the bow. It was still night, but they'd sailed out of the fog and the stars shone brightly above, their light reflected like a scattering of diamonds on the surface of the Lhazaar. The sea air was cold, especially with the breeze kicked up by the *Zephyr*'s swift passage, and Asenka shivered as she joined Tresslar and Hinto at the bow. The halfling was swaddled in a fur cloak to protect him against the cold, as was the artificer, but as she drew near, she could've sworn that the air felt warmer.

As if reading her mind, Tresslar said, "It's a minor spell. It encompasses me—and anyone standing within a few feet of me—inside a pocket of warm air. It doesn't neutralize the cold by any means, but it should keep us from freezing. I've cast a somewhat similar spell on the entire vessel. That's what's keeping ice from forming on the deck right now. Standard stuff, really."

Asenka stood next to Tresslar and immediately felt even warmer. The artificer might be overly humble of his accomplishments, but there was no denying his skill.

"How far behind are your people?" Tresslar asked.

Asenka reached inside her cloak and beneath her tunic. She wrapped her fingers around the scorpion medallion that hung from her neck, closed her eyes, and concentrated. All the Sea Scorpions wore similar medallions. They didn't permit full telepathic contact, but they did allow their wearers to gain a sense of the others' approximate location.

Asenka opened her eyes and removed her hand from the medallion. "Not close enough. We'll arrive at Demothi Island two hours before the rest of the Scorpions join us."

The Sea Scorpions' vessel, the *Water Dragon*, was a well-made craft and swifter than the Coldhearts' *Maelstrom*, but she had only minor magical alterations to increase her speed and durability—nothing like what the *Zephyr* possessed. The best the crew of the *Maelstrom* could do was sail full out and catch up when they could. At least the winds were strong this night.

Asenka went on. "The big question is, will we intercept the Coldhearts before *they* reach the island?"

Hinto responded. "They left Perhata a half hour or so before we did. At our current rate of speed—and given that they're sailing an ordinary ship . . ." He paused and looked up at the stars, as if doing a quick mental calculation. "It'll be close. If we don't catch up to them before they reach the island, we'll get there soon after."

"You sound like someone who knows what he's talking about," Asenka said.

Hinto turned to the Sea Scorpion commander and smiled. "I was born aboard a ship. I've spent more time with my feet on a deck than I have on dry land."

Asenka nodded, accepting Hinto's assessment.

"What's so awful about Demothi Island?" Tresslar said. "It must be a particularly nasty place for Haaken to take Diran and Ghaji there instead of just killing them outright."

"That it is," Asenka said. "It's the most terrible place in the Gulf of Ingjald, perhaps in all the Principalities."

Tresslar snorted. "No offense, but during my youth I traveled the length and breadth of the Principalities. These waters contain more darkness than you could possibly imagine."

Asenka bristled at first, but from the artificer's tone it was clear that he wasn't trying to belittle her but simply state what he saw as fact. "Demothi Island is dark enough. According to legend, almost a thousand years ago an evil priest named Nerthach, a worshipper of the Keeper, traveled to the island and cast a massive spell to raise all those who'd died in the gulf. His motivation for doing so is unclear. Some say he wished to create an army so that he could conquer and rule, while others say he wished to let lose a plague of undead upon the region in honor of the dark god he worshipped. Still others say that he was simply mad. Whatever the reason, Nerthach cast his spell, and it succeeded, but not in the way he intended. Nerthach was transformed into a black-rock statue that stands in the center of the island. This statue possesses two large ebon gems for eyes, and it radiates an evil power that resurrects anyone who dies in the waters of the Gulf of Ingjald. The living dead gather in the waters offshore of Demothi, and when anyone is foolish enough—or unfortunate enough—to make landfall on the island, the undead rise forth from the sea to slay them."

Hinto's eyes widened after hearing Asenka's tale and he trembled. Tresslar appeared unmoved, though she thought perhaps his face was bit paler than it had been.

"That's quite a story," the artificer said.

"It's more than that. While no one in his right mind would approach Demothi Island, in the past I had cause to sail nearby once. I peered at the island through a gem of long-seeing and . . ." She trailed off. "Let's just say that I saw the legend was true."

"So you think Haaken plans to maroon Diran and Ghaji there?" Tresslar said. "On an island full of undead?"

Asenka nodded grimly. "I'm sure of it."

❀ ❀ ❀ ❀ ❀ ❀ ❀

Chagai found Cathmore and Galharath on the middle level of the psi-forge facility. This level contained the workshops where once psi-forged parts had been designed, built, and then assembled before imbuing the humanoid constructs with life. When House Cannith had abandoned the facility, they'd removed most of the materials in order to reuse them in other projects, so the workshops on this level were mostly empty, but Chagai's employer and his kalashtar assistant were here—along with a surprise. Inside one workshop, lying upon a table under Cathmore and Galharath's watchful eyes, was a construct whose body was covered with multicolored crystals.

As Chagai entered the workshop, he said, "Is that what I think it is?"

Cathmore nodded without taking his gaze off the creature on the table. "It is indeed. This is Solus, the only psi-forged this facility produced before it was shut down. As a matter of fact, he's the reason the facility was abandoned." Cathmore proceeded to tell Ghaji about how he and Galharath had discovered Solus, and what they'd learned about the psi-forged so far.

Chagai wasn't sure what to make of Cathmore's tale. As far as he was concerned, warforged were nothing more than ambulatory weapons, like a sword with legs and arms. They weren't alive, but if what Cathmore said was true, this creature had somehow absorbed the souls of the four living beings responsible for its creation. The idea was repugnant to Chagai. Orcs lived close to nature, and this monstrosity was about as far away from natural as it was possible to get.

"How was your trip to Perhata?" Galharath asked. "Did you find what you were looking for?" The smirk on the kalashtar's face said he already had a good idea how Chagai's journey had turned out. Chagai hated working with a telepath.

"I found who I was looking for. It was Ghaji." The orc turned to Cathmore. "You were right. Diran Bastiaan travels with him."

Cathmore's head swiveled toward Chagai with an almost audible snap. "You are certain of this?"

"I am."

A cold gleam came into Cathmore's eyes, and though he was a weak old man whom Chagai could slay with a single blow, the orc mercenary nevertheless felt a stab of fear upon seeing the master assassin's gaze.

"Excellent." Cathmore practically hissed the word. "You didn't harm them, did you?"

Galharath laughed. "Are you jesting? Chagai engaged the half-orc in battle, but he broke off and fled before he could get himself killed."

Rage flooded Chagai, and he reached for his sword. "The kalashtar lies! I simply wished to warn Ghaji that I was going to be coming for him." He glared at Galharath. "Had I wanted to slay Ghaji, I would have done so."

Chagai knew this last statement was a boast, a fact he was sure Galharath was well aware of, but if the kalashtar said anything more, Chagai intended to draw his blade and see which was swifter: his sword-arm or Galharath's mind.

The kalashtar's eyes narrowed, as if he were gauging the seriousness of Chagai's intent. He must've been convinced, because Galharath held his tongue—for a change.

If Cathmore noticed the exchange between his two associates, he didn't acknowledge it. "Good, good." He gazed once more upon Solus and placed one of his vulture-claw hands upon the creature's chest. "I think it would be prudent of us to put our new friend's abilities to the test. Galharath, can you manipulate Solus's mind so that he will do my bidding?"

The kalashtar thought for a moment. "Constructs don't have minds in the way you're thinking of. In some ways this makes them simpler to manipulate, but in other ways it's more difficult. As strong as he is, I won't be able to place him permanently under your control—at least not until I've had a chance to study him further—but I *might* be able to implant a suggestion within his mind that will allow you to command him for a short while. It will take some time for me to do, however."

Chagai's upper lip curled in disgust. He hated it when Galharath went on like that, mostly because he never had any idea what the kalashtar was talking about.

Cathmore seemed to understand, for he smiled. "That should do nicely, Galharath, thank you." The elderly assassin leaned down until his mouth was closed to the tiny opening in the side of Solus's head that served as one of the psi-forged's ears. "I'd like to introduce you to a former student of mine, Solus, and to an old friend of Chagai's as well."

Chagai saw what Cathmore had in mind, and he bared his sharp teeth in a mirthless smile.

* * * ◉ * * *

Haaken stood at the bow of the *Maelstrom*, hands gripping the railing. The ship's prow cut through the water, sending up showers of sea spray that quickly froze into a thin coating of ice that clung to Haaken's cloak and beard, but the commander of the Coldhearts didn't feel the cold. Instead he felt a mixture of elation and trepidation as the black shape of Demothi Island hove into view.

"Captain?"

Despite himself, Haaken jumped, and inwardly cursed himself for it.

"What is it, Barah?" Haaken barked.

The woman who served as Haaken's second in command took a half-step back, nearly slipping on the ice coating the deck, as Haaken turned to face her.

"The crew is starting to become . . . concerned, Commander. They're curious to know just how close we're going to come to the island."

Haaken understood his people's fear, for he shared it, but as their commander, he couldn't tolerate weakness—not even in himself. "As close as necessary to put our two prisoners ashore, Barah." He hoped that would settle the matter, and ordinarily it might have, but this wasn't some raid on a Perhatan merchant vessel. They were approaching the dreaded isle of the undead.

"And, uh, just precisely how close *is* that, Captain?"

Haaken should've backhanded Barah for questioning him, but considering the situation, he decided to allow her insolence to slide this time. "There's no need for us to make landfall. We can lash together some wooden planks to make a crude raft. We can then put the priest and the half-orc on it and give them a shove toward the shore. The tide should do the rest. Start some of the crew working on the raft."

Barah looked relieved that they wouldn't be going ashore. "Yes, Captain. Thank you, Captain." Holding fast to the railing, Barah headed off to get work started on the raft.

After staring at the dark mass of Demothi Island for a few more moments, Haaken could no longer bear the sight of the cursed place. When he'd first conceived of his plan to maroon the priest and the half-orc there, it had seemed wickedly appropriate. An entire island of undead creatures would be more than any priest could handle, but now that the *Maelstrom* approached the island, Haaken was having second thoughts. He'd never been this close to Demothi before, and while it might be his imagination, the closer the ship drew to the island, the more he thought he could sense an atmosphere of almost tangible evil emanating from it.

Haaken decided to go check on his prisoners and see if the amber sleep had worn off yet. He hoped so. He wanted both of them awake and fully aware when the raft carried them to Demothi's shore.

❂ ❂ ❂ ❂ ❂ ❂ ❂

"Ho, there! You two bilge worms awake? We've almost reached Demothi Island!"

Haaken was halfway down the ladder that led to the hold when he heard something *whsssk* toward him. Fiery pain erupted in his left earlobe, and he reached up instinctively to touch his wound. His fingers felt sticky blood, and that's when Haaken realized he no longer *had* a left earlobe.

"Nice shot," Ghaji said.

"Hardly," Diran replied. "I was aiming for his carotid. These glass fragments don't make for the most aerodynamic weapons."

Haaken hadn't brought a lantern with him, and he couldn't see anything in the hold, but framed as he was by the open hatch above him, not to mention the stars and moons beyond, he was a perfect target. He scrambled back up the ladder just as another glass fragment hit his shoulder. He felt the impact but no cutting pain, and he guessed his heavy cloak had turned away the glass shard. If that had been one of the priest's daggers, he'd be in serious trouble right now.

Haaken wasn't certain how his two prisoners had gotten free of the bonds nor where they'd come by the glass fragments the priest was hurling in lieu of knives. He intended to reach the deck and slam the hatch door shut and lock it before the priest and the half-orc could escape, but as he neared the top, he felt the ladder jerk, and he knew that someone, probably the half-orc, was coming up after him. Haaken tried to move faster, but his body was numb from the cold, and his limbs were sluggish. He was only partway out of the hatch when a strong hand gripped his boot and pulled.

Haaken nearly fell back into the hold, but he grabbed hold of the deck, raised his other foot and stomped down hard on the half-orc's hand. He heard Ghaji bellow more in frustration than pain, and then the half-orc released his grip on Haaken's boot, and the Coldheart commander was able to pull himself the rest of the way onto the deck.

Haaken spun, intending to slam the hatch, but as he reached for it, Ghaji's hand lunged out of the open hatchway, holding a broken wine bottle by the neck. Upon seeing the broken bottle, Haaken felt a surge of anger. That bottle had come from his personal stock, a rare vintage from Sarlona. The Coldhearts had slaughtered an entire shipload of Sarlonan merchants to get it! His rage was soon replaced by pain as Ghaji rammed the jagged edge into Haaken's sword hand. Haaken howled as broken glass sliced through his flesh and bit into the bone beneath. He yanked his hand away from the hatch and shoved it inside his cloak to staunch the blood.

"Coldhearts!" he shouted as he shoved himself backward, away from the hatch. "To me!"

The wind was blowing strong, and Haaken wasn't sure that his people had heard him. He was about to yell again when Ghaji leaped onto the deck and came at him, wielding the broken wine bottle like a knife.

"You have good taste in wine, Haaken. It nearly broke my heart to pour it out so we could use the bottles, though I admit we saved a few swallows for ourselves."

Ghaji leaned down and swung the broken bottle at Haaken's throat, but the Coldheart commander managed to deflect the blow with his forearm. Haaken followed by bringing a knee up and ramming it into the half-orc's gut. Breath whooshed out of Ghaji, and Haaken shoved him back.

Haaken knew Ghaji wouldn't be off-balance for long, and he shoved himself to his feet and started to run. Unfortunately, the deck remained coated with ice and his boots slid out from under him. He landed back-first onto the deck, and now it was his turn to have the wind knocked out of him. As he struggled to draw in air, he looked back toward the hatch and saw that Diran had emerged from the hold and was helping Ghaji to his feet.

Haaken felt a wave of frustration. He couldn't pull in enough air to shout for his people again, and he wouldn't be able to get up in time to defend himself against Diran and Ghaji. A few more seconds, and it would all be over . . .

"Don't move!"

Haaken looked up and saw Barah coming toward the hatch, three other Coldhearts in tow. They held their swords in one hand while holding onto the starboard railing with the other to keep from sliding on the ice-coated deck. Haaken had to admit they didn't make the most intimidating attack force approaching like that, but he was glad to see them just the same. The deck would prove just as slippery for the priest and half-orc, and they didn't have real weapons. They couldn't hope to stand against his people!

He turned to watch Diran and Ghaji's reaction and saw the priest reach into his sleeve and withdraw several shards of glass. His hands blurred as he hurled the makeshift weapons, and Barah's mouth opened wide to scream, but all that emerged was a wet gurgle followed by a spray of blood. A shard was embedded in her throat. Diran managed to strike the other two as well: one in the throat and the second in the eye. Barah fell to the deck, as did the two Coldhearts who'd had the misfortune to join her.

For the first time since meeting Diran Bastiaan that afternoon at the King Prawn, Haaken wondered if it wouldn't have been better if he'd swallowed his pride and just walked away.

Haaken was finally able to fill his lungs, and he put every ounce of air into shouting. "Coldhearts! To arms!"

He didn't wait to see if his cry for help had been heard. He slid himself starboard across the deck toward Barah. Her eyes were wide and staring, and though her body still twitched, Haaken knew she was dead, or close enough to it to make no difference, but right now he wasn't interested in mourning her loss. He was more interested in using her body as a shield against Diran's glass shards. He slid around behind her and propped her up using his wounded hand. It hurt likes blazes, but he needed his free hand to defend himself against Ghaji. He drew a dagger from his sheath, hunkered down behind the still-twitching form of his second in command, and waited for whatever would happen next.

* * * * * * *

Diran had been aiming for the throats of the three Coldhearts, and he would've considered himself lucky if he'd managed to take out even one of them, given how difficult the glass shards were to throw. He knew he had the Silver Flame to thank for all three of the Coldhearts going down—that or sheer dumb luck.

"Do you think the others heard him?" Ghaji asked.

Diran didn't have to answer, for more Coldhearts came at them from both directions, weapons in hand, gripping the rail to keep their footing.

"The cold works to our advantage," Diran said. "They can only come at us single file."

"What direction do you want? Fore or aft?"

Diran didn't have to think about it. "Fore. The wind's blowing in that direction."

"Then I'll take aft."

The two companions linked arms to steady themselves as they shuffled across the icy deck away from the open hatch and toward the starboard railing. They took up positions back to back—Diran facing fore, Ghaji aft—gripped the railing, and prepared to meet the oncoming Coldhearts.

It was an awkward, slippery battle, though it was made somewhat less so when Ghaji managed to liberate a sword from one of the attacking Coldhearts. When it was over, Ghaji had a shoulder wound from a sword thrust, and Diran's left hand was broken from when a Coldheart had gotten close enough to slam the pommel of his sword against it, but that Coldheart, like the others, was dead now. The only one who remained alive was Haaken. The Coldheart commander—or former commander, since all his people had been slain—still huddled behind the body of the woman Diran had killed with a glass shard to the throat.

"Is that all?" Ghaji asked, sounding disappointed. Blood flowed freely from his shoulder wound, but the half-orc warrior paid no attention to the injury.

"I believe so." Diran turned and placed his good hand on Ghaji's shoulder. He concentrated and felt warmth spreading outward from his palm to radiate through his friend's shoulder. Diran could sense the healing power of the Silver Flame reparing Ghaji's wound. When the task was complete, Diran concentrated on turning that power inward and healing his broken hand. Within a few moments, it was done. He flexed his fingers and found them nimble as ever.

"Thanks," Ghaji said. "What now?"

Diran noticed that his friend didn't take his gaze from Haaken. The Coldheart might not appear to be much of a threat at the moment, but after what the man had done to them this day, neither Ghaji nor Diran would underestimate him again.

"If Haaken truly is the last remaining Coldheart aboard, then there's no one sailing this vessel. One of us had better take the tiller."

"After we take care of Haaken."

Diran knew exactly what his companion meant by *take care*. "There's no need to kill him. We can tie him up and put him in the hold."

"We got out," Ghaji said. "He could too."

Before becoming one of the Purified, Diran would've slit Haaken's throat without thought or remorse, but he'd forsaken the shadowy path of the assassin when he'd taken his vows, and he no longer shared his body with the dark spirit that Emon Gorsedd had implanted in all the recruits of the Brotherhood of the Blade. The dark spirit muted its host's positive emotions while heightening the negative ones, making it easier for Emon's assassins to kill without conscience. Diran had broken free of the Brotherhood years ago and dedicated his life to the service of the Silver Flame. Diran thus avoided killing unless it was absolutely necessary. Haaken was no longer a threat so there was no need to slay him, but he knew Ghaji didn't see it that way.

"Perhaps we can locate his supply of amber sleep and use it to—"

The *Maelstrom* gave a sudden violent lurch and the sound of splintering wood filled the air. The impact knocked Diran and Ghaji off their feet and sent the two companions sliding across the icy deck. The vessel listed to port, and they continued sliding until they hit the railing on that side of the ship. They lay there for a moment, gripping the railing tight and waiting to see if the *Maelstom* was going to move any more. When it became clear that the vessel wasn't going anywhere, Diran and Ghaji stood as best they could on the tilted deck.

Diran looked in the direction of the bow and saw that the ship had run aground on a dark, forbidding, rocky shore.

"I believe we've arrived at Demothi Island," Diran said.

"Land ho," Ghaji muttered.

CHAPTER

FOURTEEN

They searched the Coldhearts'
ship and found Ghaji's axe and Diran's cloak and daggers in one
of the cabins—the one belonging to Haaken, Ghaji guessed, or
perhaps that should be *belonged*, for since the *Maelstrom* had run
aground, they'd seen no sign of the wounded man. If Haaken
had been tossed overboard by the impact, he wouldn't have
lasted long in these frigid waters, and even if he'd made it to
shore, without a fire to dry and warm him, he'd succumb to
the cold soon enough. Still, Ghaji would've preferred seeing
Haaken's dead body for himself. He'd been a warrior too long to
take anything for granted—*especially* the death of a foe.

Diran slipped his daggers into the various sheaths sewn into
the inner lining of his cloak. The priest carried blades fashioned
from all manner of materials: finely honed steel, polished silver,
sturdy iron, carved wood, smooth-hewn rock, delicate crystal . . .
each useful for battling creatures with varying weaknesses. Many
of the blades had been purchased—though as a wandering priest
Diran was hardly rich—while some had been gifts and a select

few had been crafted by Diran himself. The priest had a specific place for each dagger, though how he kept their locations straight, Ghaji didn't know. Give him a single weapon to keep track of, and maybe a second for back-up, and that was all he needed.

Ghaji also wore a pack containing supplies they'd scavenged from the *Maelstom*: rope, some rations, a few light-stones that while not as reliable as everbright lanterns, would serve well enough in a pinch. Diran didn't carry a pack, for it would interfere with drawing daggers from inside his cloak, but he did carry a waterskin looped to his belt, as did Ghaji. The half-orc had scouted their landing place from the ship's railing earlier, and from the look of the barren island, he doubted they'd find any fresh water there.

"Ready?" Diran asked when he was finished replacing his daggers.

"All ashore that's going ashore," Ghaji said.

They left the cabin and made their way back out onto the uneven deck. Dark clouds filled the night sky, blocking out the moons and stars. Waves crashed against the ship's hull, causing the slanted deck beneath their feet to shudder, making walking even more treacherous as they moved toward the ship's stern. Once there, Ghaji removed the rope from his pack and tied one end to the railing.

"You go first," he said to Diran. "I'll lower you down."

The half-orc was far stronger than Diran, who was a lean man at any rate. He knew he would have no trouble performing this maneuver.

Diran nodded, took hold of the other end of the rope, and looped it around his left hand. He then drew a steel dagger— just in case a very *un*welcoming welcome committee should appear—and climbed over the railing. The priest kept watch on the shore as Ghaji lowered him, but the precaution, wise as it was, turned out to be unnecessary. Diran's feet came down in the surf at the edge of the shoreline safely. The priest let go of the rope and Ghaji hauled it in. He gauged the distance from the railing to the ground once more, then untied the rope, rolled it up, and replaced it in his pack. He then stepped up onto the railing and jumped.

The half-orc landed with a splash next to Diran. The priest gave him a look and Ghaji shrugged. "I figured we might need the rope later."

Diran nodded, Ghaji drew his axe, and together they walked onto Demothi Island.

As soon as his boot touched the shore, Diran drew in a hissing breath.

"What's wrong?" Ghaji asked, almost activating his elemental axe out of reflex.

"I sensed an aura of evil emanating from this place while we were still on the ship, but now that we're here, it's even stronger—as strong as anything we've ever encountered."

A chill shivered down Ghaji's spine. Considering some of the evil, both supernatural and mundane, they'd faced together over the years, that was saying something.

As Ghaji took in his surroundings, he could easily believe that Diran's foreboding was well founded. The island was craggy and rough, the stony ground cracked and covered with jagged rocks. The only signs of life were tufts of dry grass that had managed to shove their way through the narrow fissures in the ground, along with twisted, gnarled trees that looked as if they'd never grown leaves or borne fruit, regardless of the season. Though Ghaji had no priestly training, he was half-orc and thus strongly attuned to the natural world, and all his senses were screaming that there was nothing natural about this place—nothing at all.

"We might be better off if we went back to the ship." Ghaji said.

Diran considered Ghaji's words. "You make a good point, but it's difficult to know how stable the Coldhearts' ship is after running aground. It might well collapse under us in the middle of a battle."

Ghaji glanced back at the *Maelstrom*. The ship listed to starboard, and there was a large hole near the bow, but otherwise the vessel looked as if she would hold together well enough. Diran had grown up in the Principalities and therefore knew far more about sea-going than Ghaji did, so the half-orc decided to defer to his friend's judgment.

Diran gazed inland and scowled. "Besides, if there's evil here, it is our duty to seek it out and destroy it."

Ghaji sighed. "I hate it when you say things like that."

The half-orc gripped the haft of his axe more tightly. He wasn't about to activate it now. Doing so would give away their location to whatever might be lurking on the island, and the light would also render his night vision almost useless. They'd proceed with stealth for now, and Ghaji would ignite the axe's flame when necessary.

Diran exchanged his steel dagger for a silver one, and the two companions began walking. Ghaji kept an eye out for threats while Diran, who only had the extremely limited nocturnal sight of a human, remained close to his friend and followed his lead. Ghaji knew that Diran wasn't without other resources to draw on, however. His training as assassin had taught him to pay close attention to all his senses, not just sight. Diran was doubtless listening for any noises beyond the pounding of the surf against the shore, scenting the wind for any smells in addition to the tang of sea salt, feeling for vibrations juddering through the rocky ground beneath his boots with every step . . . Diran might not have orc blood in him, but thanks to the training he'd gained at Emon Gorsedd's academy, the priest's senses were honed to as fine an edge as that possessed by any of his blades.

Diran had his priestly powers to draw upon as well. When Diran said he *sensed evil*, he wasn't speaking metaphorically, nor was he expressing the vague sensation that intuitive people sometimes had in dangerous situations. As one of the Purified, Diran sensed evil with the same clarity and certainty as someone else might see an object placed directly in front of their eyes.

They walked for some time across Demothi's barren landscape without encountering any signs of life beyond the dry grass and twisted trees dotting the island. No animals, no birds, no lizards—nothing—yet Ghaji couldn't shake the feeling that numerous eyes were monitoring their progress—malicious, hungry eyes.

Ghaji was so caught up in his thoughts that he nearly jumped when Diran spoke.

"This is it—the place where the evil that permeates this island is centered."

Diran pointed toward a dark object silhouetted against the night sky. The object was perhaps six, seven feet tall and wrought in the rough shape of a man. Ghaji was no priest, but now that they were this close, he could feel the waves of malevolent power emanating from the man-shaped obelisk.

"What is it?" Though he didn't intend to, Ghaji spoke in a hushed voice.

"I'm not sure. I'm not as familiar with the legends of this part of the Principalities as I am with others. Still, I vaguely recall reading something once about a dark priest who sailed to an island . . . a priest who was transformed into stone."

Diran stepped closer to the stone figure to examine it.

Ghaji made to accompany his friend, but Diran held up a hand to stop him.

"I appreciate your willingness to follow me, Ghaji, but it's best if only I approach."

Though he knew Diran was only taking a precaution, and a sensible one at that, Ghaji nevertheless felt a surge of anger at the suggestion he hang back. Remaining out of harm's way while a companion strode forth into danger was not the orc way, and it wasn't Ghaji's.

As if sensing his friend's feelings, Diran said, "Please. If this object is as powerful as I suspect, I'll need all my skill and power just to protect myself. I won't be able to safeguard us both."

Ghaji wanted to argue that he could look after himself just fine, thank you, but in the end he recognized the wisdom of Diran's words, gritted his teeth, and nodded.

Diran gave his friend a grateful smile before turning and walking toward the stone figure once more. Ghaji remained standing where he was, but he kept his axe at the ready, prepared to command it to burst into flame the instant anything even looked as if it was about to go wrong.

When he was within a foot of the statue Diran stopped, raised his free hand, and held it above the stone surface of the figure. Formed of the same dark rocky substance as the island, it didn't look as if it had been carved so much as arisen naturally from the surface of Demothi. While the statue possessed rudimentary human features—head, torso, arms, and legs—from the knees down it was nothing more than a mound of rock. The eyes were its most striking feature. Glittering black gems as large as an egg protruded from the statue's stony sockets.

"This is indeed the center of the evil on Demothi," Diran said. "The power radiates from this figure down through the ground and then spreads throughout the entire island, perhaps even extending for some distance beyond its shores, but for what purpose, I cannot say."

Ghaji heard a shuffling noise from behind him, and he whirled around to see what had caused it, elemental axe erupting in flame as he spun. The sudden light from his blazing weapon momentarily rendered his night vision useless, but his eyes quickly adjusted, and he saw a staggering humanoid shape lurching out of the night toward them. The creature was a bloated, wet thing, flesh puffy and discolored, body draped with dangling strands of seaweed. Its eyes and tongue were long gone, in their place clusters of tiny crabs that used the dead thing's skull as a home. The rancid stink of the creature assaulted Ghaji's nose—a sour reek of saltwater, dead fish, and rotting vegetation. It was fortunate that the half-orc hadn't eaten lately, because the gagging stench would've caused him to empty the contents of his stomach right then and there.

"Walking dead man," Ghaji said. He relaxed a bit upon seeing the undead creature shambling toward them. He'd encountered such creatures during his time as a soldier in the Last War, and he'd fought even more alongside Diran since then, though offhand he couldn't remember seeing any quite as disgusting as this one. Still, the living corpses, while unpleasant, were easy enough to dispatch. Diran could always repell the creature with his priestly powers, and if for some reason that didn't suffice, Ghaji's axe would make fast work of it.

"Don't you mean dead *men?*" Diran asked.

For a moment, Ghaji didn't understand what his friend was talking about. Then he noticed that the water-logged zombie wasn't alone. He'd brought some friends with him—several dozen, from the look of it. Ghaji squinted as he peered into the night beyond his axe's fiery illumination. Make that several *hundred.* The half-orc turned in a slow circle and saw that an entire army of walking dead was coming toward them from all directions, shuffling, stumbling, moving with spastic, jerky motions as if they were ill-fashioned marionettes controlled by a puppeteer with severe arthritis. While they varied in size and race—humans, elves, dwarves, shifters, gnomes, changelings— they were all in the same bloated, wet condition as the first zombie Ghaji had seen.

"It would appear that Demothi Island is a trap of sorts," Diran said, his tone emotionless and cool. "The undead wait underwater off shore, and once visitors reach the center of the island and are cut off from their vessel, the foul things rise forth to slay them. Clever."

"You'll forgive me if I don't share your admiration," Ghaji said. "Please tell me that you can repell a horde of zombies."

"We'll find out." Diran still held a silver dagger in one hand, and with the other he reached into a tunic pocket and brought forth the arrowhead-shaped object that was the symbol of his order. He held the silver arrowhead out toward the closest of the advancing sea-zombies and the metal glowed with an aura of blue-white light.

"In the name of the Silver Flame, I command you to turn aside!" Diran's voice boomed out, far louder than normal. Ghaji wouldn't have been surprised to learn the priest's words could be heard echoing across the entire island.

Several of the undead creatures stopped, hesitated, then resumed shambling forward.

Diran scowled. The aura shimmering around the silver arrowhead blazed more brightly, and this time when he spoke, his voice was loud as thunder.

"Be gone!"

The zombies didn't even pause.

The light surrounding the arrowhead winked out, and Diran lowered the holy symbol to his side. "The evil power emanating from the statue is too strong. We have no choice. Fight or die."

"I've been making that choice since the day I drew my first breath," Ghaji said. Elemental axe held high with its flames trailing bright against the night sky, the half-orc ran forward to meet the first wave of walking dead.

* * * ● * * *

Diran watched his friend hack zombies apart. Normally, undead flesh was dry, which made Ghaji's flaming axe a perfect weapon, but these zombies had come from the sea, and their skin, while just as lifeless as that of any other undead creature, was too wet to burn. Indeed, their entire bodies were suffused with saltwater, and only magical fire of a very high order could harm them. Too bad Tresslar wasn't here. He might well have a powerful flame spell stored in his dragonwand.

Diran drew another silver dagger from his cloak and turned to face the zombies approaching on his right. He'd had a great deal of experience fighting the undead, and not just as a priest. During the Last War, Karrnath had fielded armies of undead soldiers. The acolytes in the Brotherhood of the Blade employed zombies for quite a different purpose: as living mannequins on which to practice their deadly arts, so Diran was well aware that this was the sort of battle in which he was next to useless. If he couldn't repel the zombies by channeling the power of the Silver Flame, there was little else he could do. He could hurl one dagger after the other with deadly accuracy, but it would scarcely matter if his targets weren't alive in the first place. One zombie he could handle by deftly slicing through undead muscles and tendons until the creature, though still possessed of its mockery of a life, was unable to move, but more than one zombie came at them now, many, many more. Diran knew that if he and Ghaji were going to make it off Demothi Island alive, he would have to use his mind instead of his blades.

Ghaji grunted and Diran watched his friend slice through the torsos of three zombies with his axe. The top halves of the undead creatures flopped to the ground, but the bottom halves stood there for a moment as if stunned. The trunks and legs then began stumbling around erratically, lost without even the simple commands of a rotted zombie brain to give them direction. Ghaji ignored the meandering legs and attacked the next zombie that came at him.

Diran was grateful that none of the undead was recently reanimated, else their bodies would be too fresh and they'd move far more swiftly than these water-logged abominations, but even at their slow, shuffling pace, Diran estimated that he had only a few moments more before any of the zombies reached him. He'd have to think fast.

While Diran didn't know the specific details of the evil priest's identity or his motivations for raising an army of the dead, it was clear that something had gone wrong during the process. Maybe the priest was supposed to have been transformed into stone so that he would become the focal point for the necromantic energies that powered the army of sea-dead. If the statue was the source of the magic that animated the zombies, perhaps they could be stopped by destroying the statue.

Diran examined the stone figure of the evil priest once more, trying to determine if it had an obvious weak point. The dark gems that served in place of eyes? Doubtful. More than likely they were there in order to lure foolish treasure-seekers, greedy artificers, or power-hungry priests to the island. Diran wouldn't be surprised if there was a curse on the gems as well, but what else could there be? The statue had no other obvious features. No runes were carved into its surface, and there were no others gems or items of any sort embedded in the stone.

Diran glanced away from the statue and saw that a zombie— one with limp octopus tentacles dangling out of its open mouth—was nearly upon him. His thinking time was up.

After the priest's transformation, the statue had remained in human shape. Perhaps that was a hint as to its weakness. With no time left to consider, Diran gripped the silver dagger in his right hand tight and concentrated on summoning the power of the Silver Flame, willing the power to suffuse the dagger.

Argent light blazed forth from the blade. Diran stepped forward, and using all his strength, he rammed the knife into the statue's chest. The impact sent a jolt of pain shooting through his hand and up along his arm, and he released the dagger's hilt. He stepped back and saw that an inch or so of the blade had penetrated the statue, but that was all. The dagger still shone with the power of the Silver Flame, though, and Diran could sense the statue's evil aura reacting to the holy energy, massing its strength at the point of penetration and attempting to nullify the blade. Diran could also sense that if he didn't do something more and do it fast, the statue would succeed in resisting the Silver Flame.

Diran turned to call out to Ghaji, but his voice was choked off as a pair of slime-coated hands fastened around his throat. The priest found himself staring into the empty eye sockets of the tentacle-mouthed zombie. The undead creature possessed strength far greater than that of a normal zombie, undoubtedly due to its proximity to the ebon statue. Diran felt the creature's hands tightening around his throat, heard a roaring in his ears as the blood to his head was cut off, saw gray closing in on the edges of his vision, and he knew he was on the verge of death.

Diran still held a dagger in his left hand, and as his consciousness ebbed, he sliced at the zombie's right wrist with a single swift strike, then sliced its left. Instead of blood, brackish seawater spilled from the wounds, but Diran knew the injuries wouldn't pain the zombie. Despite the damage done to the zombie's wrists, the slimy fingers clasped around Diran's throat did not lose their strength. Consciousness began to ebb, and Diran prepared for his spirit to join with the Silver Flame.

Then a swatch of darkness detached itself from the night and swooped down to the zombie throttling Diran. His vision was too blurry for him to make out what the thing was, but it grabbed hold of the zombie's shoulders and yanked the undead creature away from the Diran. The zombie's skeletal fingers scratched Diran's neck as its grip was broken, and the priest drew in a gasping breath. He could feel himself on the verge of passing out, but he held onto consciousness through sheer force of will. He looked around to see who or what had saved him, but he only saw Ghaji some yards away, the half-orc swinging his elemental axe in great fiery arcs as he annihilated one zombie after another.

Diran didn't have time to worry about how he had been saved. The zombies had to be stopped. He tried to call out Ghaji's name, but the word came out as little more than a raspy whisper. He sucked in another breath and tried again. "Ghaji! Drive home the dagger!"

Ghaji turned toward Diran, frowning in confusion, but then he saw the glowing dagger protruding from the statue's chest, and his gaze lit up with understanding. Ghaji rammed aside an attacking zombie with his elbow and ran to the statue. Diran stepped aside as his friend approached and swung the flat of his axe at the dagger's pommel. A loud clang split the air, followed closely by the *chuk!* of metal being driven into stone.

The silver aura surrounding the dagger spread across the ebon statue until the stony remains of the evil priest glowed bright blue-white. The zombies stopped and stood frozen. Then, one by one, their slimy, sodden flesh began to liquefy and slide off their bones. Seconds later, the army of undead had been reduced to a collection of upright skeletons. Their bones quickly lost cohesion, fell apart, and tumbled to the ground, landing with wet plaps in the puddles.

The silver glow around the statue flared bright one last time before dimming and finally going out. Diran lowered his head and uttered a prayer to the Silver Flame. "Thank you for bringing us victory." When he lifted his head, he smiled at Ghaji. "Well struck, my friend."

"Looks like you're out another dagger. Unless you want me to try and pry it loose."

Diran shook his head. "Leave it where it is. The statue might become active again if the dagger's removed."

"Suits me," Ghaji said.

Diran reached into one of his cloak's hidden pockets, removed a bit of silver dust, and sprinkled it into the statue's eyes. "Divine light, ensure this being never rises again, and protect this island and the surrounding waters from the taint of its evil."

As Diran finished the rite of the Death of the Foe, Ghaji looked at him and frowned. "You're bleeding from scratches on your neck."

"I'm fortunate to still be alive. I was being strangled by one of the zombies when something pulled it away from me. I'm not sure what it . . ." Diran trailed off as coils of white mist drifted toward them on the night breeze. The coils joined to create a roughly human shape, and then the mist thickened and distinctly feminine features began to emerge. Within moments, a blonde-haired woman stood before them.

Diran felt his heart seize up in his chest, and he tried to say Makala's name, but he couldn't get the word past the sudden lump in his throat.

Makala smiled. "What's wrong? Zombie got your tongue?"

CHAPTER

FIFTEEN

I wondered if I would ever see you again," Diran said.

"I wondered if you'd ever *want* to see me again."

The two of them sat on a pair of rocks on the shore not far from where the *Maelstrom* had run aground. The *Zephyr* bobbed in the surf anchored nearby. The elemental sloop was both small and maneuverable enough that Yvka had been able to get her close to the island. The others—including Asenka, whom Diran was pleased had come along—were going through the wreckage of the Coldhearts' ship. They searched for survivors—or in Hinto's case, any plunder worth salvaging. Diran suspected at least part of the reason that everyone else aided in the search was to give Makala and him some time alone.

"You know, we all feel somewhat foolish for racing to your rescue." Makala gestured at a mound of bones sitting in a puddle of foul-smelling slime close by. Similar mounds of liquefied zombie remains covered most of the island. "From the looks of things, you were doing just fine on your own."

"This night would have had a very different outcome if you hadn't arrived in time to pull that zombie off me." He reached up to touch the scratches on the left side of his neck and found them tacky with partially dried blood. After the confusion following the zombies' destruction, Diran had forgotten about the wounds and hadn't gotten around to healing himself yet.

He saw how Makala's gaze fixed on his scratches, how her pupils widened and her nostrils flared. He lowered his hand, but her gaze remained on his neck.

"Am I going to have to reach for my arrowhead?" He meant it as a joke, at least partially, but it came out sounding more like a threat.

Makala tore her gaze away from Diran's neck with a start, and she shook her head as if to clear it. "I'm sorry. I can't help it."

"I understand. We both once played host to dark spirits of a different sort."

"That experience does help me resist the Hunger," Makala said, "but it's not the same. The dark spirits Emon Gorsedd forced upon us dwelled within our bodies. They whispered to us . . . manipulated us, but even so, they remained separate from us. The Hunger is different. It's *always* with me, and it never grows weaker, no matter how much I feed. The Hunger is me and I am it. We're inseparable."

Diran realized he didn't understand, not really. "I take it that you have killed to sustain your life."

She looked away from him and gazed out across the sea. Diran was struck by how pale she'd become. She'd always been fair-skinned, but now—here, in the moonlight—her flesh seemed white and smooth as marble. He wondered if he were to reach out and touched her if he'd find her skin cold as marble as well.

"I try to avoid taking life when I can," she said in a soft voice. "Let's leave it at that."

"As you wish."

They fell into an uncomfortable silence. They spent the next several moments watching the others crawl about the lopsided deck of the *Maelstrom*.

"The others are uneasy around me," Makala said. "I knew they would be, but it hurts." She gave him a quick smile. "At least you're not treating me like a monster."

"Try not to blame them," Diran said. "None of them has known you for as long as I have—and Tresslar and Hinto barely know you at all."

She gave him a sideways glance. "You forgot to mention Asenka." A hint of ice had crept into her voice.

"We only met today."

"She likes you, Diran. I can tell." A pause. "Do you like her?"

Diran felt uncomfortable with the direction this conversation was taking. "As I said, we just met. She seems to be a competent commander."

"Is that all you think of her?"

Diran looked at the eastern horizon and saw the first hint of dawn pinking the night sky.

"The sun will be rising soon."

"I know. I can feel it." Makala stood. She started to walk toward the water, but then she stopped and spoke without turning back around to face him. "I've learned a great deal about my . . . condition . . . over the last few months. It's hard to live with the Hunger but not impossible. If I can do it, Diran, I know you can. We could be together. Forever."

Without waiting for a response, Makala continued walking to the sea. Just as she was about to step into the water, her form blurred and she took to the air in bat form. She soared toward the *Zephyr*, once more assuming human shape as she landed upon the deck of the sloop. She then climbed into the obsidian sarcophagus and drew the lid closed over her. An instant later, a ray of sunlight broke over the horizon. It was soon followed by more, but despite their warmth, they did nothing to drive away the chill surrounding Diran's heart.

❋ ❋ ❋ ❋ ❋ ❋ ❋

Many miles to the west, across the Gulf of Ingjald and well into the foothills of the Hoarfrost Mountains, the first light of dawn also touched Mount Luster. Despite the mountain's name, however, the sun's rays did nothing to make its dull gray surface look any less dull or any less gray.

Inside the hollowed-out mountain, Aldarik Cathmore stood outside the workshop where Galharath continued to work on Solus. Chagai sat cross-legged on the floor, elbows propped on his knees, eyes closed, chin on his chest. The orc mercenary had learned long ago to rest when he could, and after his journey to Perhata and back—not to mention his "reunion" with Ghaji— his body needed it.

Chagai was unable to do more than doze fitfully, though, for Cathmore's constant fidgeting and fussing kept waking him. For an elderly human, the man seemed to have a vast supply of energy. He put Chagai in mind of a flame that flares most brightly just before going out.

Chagai spoke without opening his eyes. "Galharath will be finished when he's finished. Your pacing isn't going to make things go any faster."

Cathmore's footsteps stopped. "I appreciate your advice, but you'll forgive me if I ignore it. Your kind isn't exactly known for its wisdom, after all."

Chagai felt an urge to draw his lips back from his teeth, but he didn't want Cathmore to know that he'd gotten to him, so the orc resisted the impulse. "Wisdom is where you find it," he said.

Cathmore laughed. "It appears I have an orc philosopher on my hands!"

Employer or not, Chagai thought it high time that he taught the old man a lesson in respect. He leaped to his feet and rushed Cathmore, fist cocked and ready to strike. Chagai didn't see Cathmore move, but the elderly assassin now held a dagger, and what's more, it was pressed against the orc's throat. An acrid smell floated to Chagai's nostrils, and he knew that the blade as coated with poison. He didn't recognize the scent, but he had no doubt that whatever the substance was, it was deadly.

Cathmore's mouth stretched into a slow, wide smile, and his eyes glittered with an unsettling dark light that Chagai had never seen in the man's gaze before.

"Lower your hand, orc, or you'll be dead before your body hits the floor."

Chagai had been the one to attack, and to back down now would bring much dishonor to him. On the other hand, honor didn't mean a thing if you were dead.

Chagai lowered his hand.

Cathmore grinned at the orc a moment longer before slowly removing the daggerpoint away from his throat. "I assure you, Chagai, the next time you decide to test me will be your last. Do you understand?"

The orc answered through gritted teeth. "I do."

"Very good." With surprising deftness for one whose hands resembled vulture claws, Cathmore returned the dagger to its hiding place somewhere within the folds of his bearskin cloak. "At least your impetuosity has served to entertain me while we wait, and for that I thank you." The master assassin turned his back on Chagai and began pacing once more.

Chagai stood there for a moment longer before returning to the spot where he had been resting. He sat but this time he didn't lower his head or close his eyes. Instead he kept his smoldering gaze fixed on Cathmore and amused himself by imagining all the different ways he could make the old man suffer before he died.

* * * * * * *

Solus stood high atop a mountainous peak, white clouds drifting past at astonishing speed, though the air seemed still. Solus had only left the interior of Mount Luster a handful of times since the facility had been abandoned, but during those brief excursions into the outer world, he had learned that he did not experience existence the same way flesh beings did. He felt changes in temperature, but they meant little to him in regard to his own personal comfort, and while he also felt wind, he experienced it only as varying degrees of pressure against his solid body. He knew from the swirling, confused tangle of memories belonging to the four minds that he had absorbed that such physical sensations as the feel of sunlight on skin, of a breeze ruffling one's hair were far different and more intense that what he could experience on his own. He felt a pang of loss for something he had never known save through the memories of others.

Solus gazed down from his vantage point high upon the mountain and saw a city spread out below him, and beyond it, a slate-gray mass of water that stretched for mile after mile toward the eastern horizon. Though he had never seen such a sight before, the memories he had accidentally stolen from his makers whispered that he was looking at a vast body of water called the sea.

"Lovely, isn't it?"

Solus turned to see that he wasn't alone. Standing on the mountaintop next to him was a tall, lithe figure sporting a long brown ponytail braid woven with multicolored crystals. Solus felt no fear upon seeing the man, only mild curiosity blended with a sense of familiarity, as if he'd seen the man somewhere before, but that was impossible, of course. Aside from some representatives from House Cannith who'd come to investigate what had happened at the Mount Luster facility a few weeks after Solus's birth, the psi-forged had never seen another living being . . . or had he?

"Who are you?"

The tall man smiled, and Solus's stolen memories whispered that it was a warm, friendly smile. "My name is Galharath. I am your friend."

Solus did not possess facial features capable of expression, but if he had, he would've frowned. "How can this be so? I do not know you." Yet he couldn't escape the feeling that he *did* know this man, this Galharath, only he couldn't remember from where.

The man put a hand on Solus's shoulder, and the psi-forged saw that Galharath wore leather gauntlets containing more crystals embedded over the knuckles. The crystals pulsed with soft, gentle light—and they pulsed in time with the glow emanating from the larger crystal shard attached to the front of Galharath's vest. Solus thought this detail was important, but he wasn't sure why.

"You may not know me now, but you knew me once," Galharath said, "before your memories were taken from you."

"*My* memories . . . taken?"

"You still retain a few faint echoes of memory, the merest scraps of the knowledge you once possessed. I have some small skill with matters of the mind, and I've been working to restore your memories but without success. I have come to realize that your memories aren't simply damaged. They are gone, and this is the man who took them."

Galharath turned the palm of his free hand upward. Colors shimmered into existence above his hand and formed the image of a human male's face with long black hair and a lean, wolfish aspect. His gaze was hard and cold, the gaze of a man who felt no pity and gave no mercy.

"Is that him? The man you say took my memories?"

"It is. His name is Diran Bastiaan—a worshipper of evil gods whose only reason for existence is to spread misery across Khorvaire. He is the one who has your memories. Only by confronting him can we hope to get them back."

Solus didn't take his gaze off the face of Diran Bastiaan as he spoke. "How can we do that?"

"As I told you, I have some ability with matters of the mind. You also possess great strength of your own. Though Bastiaan is stronger than either of us alone, together we shall prove more than a match for his dark power."

Solus continued gazing at the image of Diran Bastiaan's face. He certainly looked like a man capable of the kind of evil that Galharath described, yet Solus couldn't help feeling that something wasn't right here, that he was missing something vital, though he had no idea what that might be.

"Your thoughts are in such turmoil, my friend." Galharath's tone was sympathetic and caring. "It pains me to think of the confusion that torments you so. Help me to heal you. Help me find Diran Bastiaan, and together we shall reclaim that which is rightfully yours."

Solus looked at the image hovering in the air above Galharath's palm for an instant longer before reaching out and closing his three-fingered hand around Diran Bastiaan's face, snuffing it out of existence.

"Where is this monster?" Solus asked.

Smiling, Galharath pointed to the city spread out below them.

● ● ● ◉ ● ● ●

Chagai got to his feet when he heard the sounds of movement coming from within the workshop. A moment later, the psi-forged strode forth with heavy footfalls, Galharath following close behind.

"Were you successful?" Cathmore asked, voice tight with barely restrained excitement.

"I was," the kalashtar said, "and we can speak freely. Our friend is now the sole inhabitant of his own private mindscape. He shall see and hear only what I permit—as long as I remain close to him, that is."

Solus didn't pause during this exchange. He continued walking toward the stairs at the far end of the workshop level.

"Perhaps you succeeded *too* well, artificer," Chagai said. "We'll have to get moving if we don't want the construct to leave us behind."

"Indeed," Cathmore said. "Let's go." The elderly assassin started hobbling after the psi-forged, Galharath and Chagai on either side of him.

● ● ● ◉ ● ● ●

Asenka stood toward the aft of the *Zephyr*, though not so close that she could overhear what Yvka and Ghaji were saying to each other. Though in truth, given the howling wind that poured forth from the elemental containment ring to fill the sloop's sails, she would've had to be standing right next to the two lovers to hear anything. Still, she wanted to give them their privacy, so she stayed where she was.

Hinto slept inside the *Zephyr*'s cabin, while Tresslar stood at the port railing holding his dragonwand out almost as if it were a fishing rod. Asenka had no idea what the artificer was doing, but he appeared to be in deep concentration, so she didn't wish to disturb him, and Makala . . . Asenka's eyes strayed to the obsidian sarcophagus resting on the deck between the containment ring and the cabin. She was close enough to the stone coffin that it would only take half a dozen steps for her to reach it. She wished they didn't have to keep the damned thing above deck, but the *Zephyr* was a small vessel built for speed, not hauling cargo, and there wasn't enough room below. She knew that the sarcophagus couldn't be opened from the inside, and that even if Makala did somehow get out, she wouldn't be able to withstand the light of the sun. Even so, she didn't feel comfortable with the thing—and the creature it contained—always present, and it seemed she wasn't the only one who felt that way, though perhaps for different reasons.

Diran stood at the bow of the *Zephyr*, gripping the railing to steady himself, his long black hair billowing behind him in the wind. His cloak barely stirred in the breeze, and Asenka knew that was because the daggers sheathed inside the inner lining weighted it down. The priest hadn't said much since coming aboard the *Zephyr*, and no one had made an issue of his silence. They'd also obviously made a point of leaving him alone. Asenka felt sorry for Diran. From what she gathered, this was the first time he'd seen Makala since her transformation into a vampire . . . a transformation that for some reason Diran felt responsible for. She wanted to go to him and be a sympathetic ear if nothing else, but she couldn't bring herself to disturb his self-imposed solitude, much as she might wish otherwise.

Asenka's thoughts turned to what had occurred so far during their journey back to Perhata. So swiftly did the elemental sloop travel that they'd already encountered the *Water Dragon*, still only two-thirds of the way to Demothi Island. Yvka had stopped the *Zephyr* long enough for Asenka to tell the Sea Scorpions what had happened and order them to return home. She felt somewhat foolish doing so, for it pointed up the fact that Diran hadn't needed her and her people at all. The priest's friends had proved quite capable of coming to his aid all on their own—if only to give Diran and Ghaji a ride back to Perhata.

Asenka still couldn't believe that Diran and Ghaji had broken the curse on Demothi Island by themselves. She didn't know why she had ever imagined she might be of any use to them . . . to *him*. She wasn't a war veteran or an adventurer. She was just the fleet commander for a third-rate barony in a region teeming with them. As the saying went in the Principalities, there are more fish in the Lhazaar than barons, but only just.

At least her baron wouldn't have to worry about Haaken and the Coldhearts anymore. Though not all of their bodies had been found, Asenka felt confident that they had perished either at the hands of Diran and Ghaji or when their ship had run aground. Either way, they were no longer a concern, and it would be some time before Baroness Calida could rebuild her fleet. Until that happened, Perhata would control the Gulf of Ingjald. Baron Mahir would certainly be pleased, even if the victory wasn't the Sea Scorpions' doing.

Though the sun was well above the eastern horizon now and the sky was clear, it was still quite cold aboard the *Zephyr*, and Asenka thought the wind stirred up by their swift passage was only partially to blame. She also noticed that thin patches of ice coated the deck and railing in numerous places—the first ice she had seen since the elemental sloop had set sail the night before. Since she didn't have anything else to do, she decided to go speak to Tresslar about it. Besides, it would give her a chance to find out just what the artificer was doing with his wand. She headed over to join Tresslar and, not wishing to break his concentration, she waited for him to acknowledge her presence. When he didn't, she spoke up.

"There are patches of ice on the ship."

Tresslar didn't turn to look at her. "Hmm?"

"I think something might be wrong with whatever warming spell you placed on the *Zephyr*."

That got the artificer's attention. He snapped his head around to face her, features twisted into a disapproving scowl. "What are you talking about? When *I* cast a spell, it . . ." He trailed off and rubbed his free hand over a tiny spot of ice on the railing in front of him. His expression softened, as did his tone. "Oh. I see what you mean. I'll tend to it at once."

Tresslar touched the golden dragonhead on the end of his wand to the ice on the railing. As near as Asenka could tell, the artificer didn't do anything, but a moment later tiny curls of steam issued forth from the dragonhead's nostrils—though there didn't appear to be any sort of opening in them. The steam touched the ice, melting it instantly. The wispy coils didn't evaporate, though. Instead they began to expand, spreading all along the port railing, then—Asenka looked over her shoulder—to the starboard railing. The steam, moving more like fog now, rolled down the railing and onto the deck, picking up speed as it spread. It coated the deck, the cabin, the mast and sails, and even the containment ring and Yvka's chair, though it never touched any of the people on the *Zephyr*. There was only one other thing that the steam didn't come in contact with: Makala's obsidian coffin. The warm white mist passed around the black sarcophagus, coming no closer than three inches to the unholy dark stone. Once it had covered the entire ship, the steam-coating lingered for several seconds before finally dissipating in the wind.

Asenka could feel the difference at once. The air around them was noticeably warmer, as was the deck beneath their feet.

"That was most impressive," Asenka said, and she meant it.

"Thank you, but it was nothing. A mere trifle." Despite Tresslar's words, it was clear her praise pleased him.

Since he seemed in a better mood now, Asenka decided to keep talking. "Earlier, I noticed you were holding your wand out before you almost as if it were a fishing rod."

Tresslar chuckled. "I suppose I *was* fishing, after a fashion. The golden dragonhead has the ability to absorb and store magical energy. I can then release this energy at a later time and use it for whatever task I wish. Though it's easier to simply cast the same sort of spell that was originally absorbed. Using heat energy to create heat, as opposed to trying to use it to try and create wind, like the elemental bound in the *Zephyr's* containment ring. That sort of thing."

Asenka wasn't exactly sure what Tresslar was talking about, but she nodded anyway. "So you were . . . what? Fishing for magic?"

Tresslar grinned. "Precisely. While the dragonhead needs to be in direct contact with an enchanted object to draw its full energy, it can absorb a certain amount of background magic. Many sea creatures possess mystic power to varying degrees, and the dragonwand is capable of taking in the magical residue they leave behind. It's not a great deal of energy, mind you, but I learned a long time ago that it doesn't pay to let the wand's energy level dip too low."

A faraway look crept into Tresslar's gaze, and Asenka wondered what the elderly artificer was recalling.

The dragonhead on the end of the wand was a beautiful piece of workmanship, with red gems for eyes and teeth made of crystal. "It's a most remarkable device," Asenka said. "I've never seen an artificer carry anything quite like it before."

Tresslar snapped back to the present. "And no wonder. I'm the only one in the Principalities—or Khorvaire, for that matter—who has anything like it." He looked down at the dragonwand, turning it this way and that, as if examining it for the first time. "It may well be the only object of its kind in all of Eberron." He spoke this last bit softly, as if talking to himself.

"I sense there's a story for the telling here."

Tresslar looked up at her, as if startled. "Well . . . yes, but it's not one I've ever told before." He glanced toward the bow where Diran still stood motionless, staring out at the slate-gray waters of the Lhazaar. "Not to anyone."

"A story might help pass the time until we return to Perhata."

Tresslar looked at her a long moment before finally saying, "Yes. I suppose it would."

CHAPTER

SIXTEEN

I was twenty-four, and I'd been sailing on the *Seastar* with Erdis Cai for almost two years."

Asenka blinked in surprise, unsure she'd heard correctly. "You mean Erdis Cai, the *explorer?*"

Tresslar gave her a small, sad smile, so unlike his previous boastful attitude. "The same."

"But the *Seastar* hasn't been seen in the Principalities since before I was born!"

Tresslar's smile grew a bit wider. "It was a long time ago."

"I meant no offense, but if you sailed with Erdis Cai, then you must know what happened to him and the rest of his crew. There are so many stories . . ."

Tresslar's smile fell away.

Asenka sensed there was another tale here, one that was difficult for Tresslar to speak of. Still, one story at a time. "So you were twenty-four," Asenka prompted.

"Yes, and the *Seastar* was headed for Trebaz Sinara."

Asenka almost interrupted again, but she stopped herself.

Trebaz Sinara . . . Every child in the Principalities had grown up listening to stories about the fabled island. According to legend, Trebaz Sinara was inhabited by the most terrible of monsters and surrounded by treacherous reefs that made landing there all but impossible, but legend also told that the island contained the hidden treasure of two thousand years of pirate raids—gold, precious gems, dragonshards, mystic relics . . . objects of unimaginable wealth and power. There were also said to be ancient tombs on the island, but who had built them, or what dark secrets they held within their sealed walls, remained a mystery.

Asenka knew that Trebaz Sinara was a real place, but she'd never spoken to anyone who had actually *been* there. Tresslar suddenly seemed less like a crotchety old man than a figure who had stepped right out of legend. As attentive as she'd been before, she was doubly so now.

Tresslar continued. "We'd sailed past the island numerous times on our way to Regalport or Orgalos, but we'd never attempted to make landfall before, though every time we passed Trebaz Sinara, Erdis made sure the *Seastar* always came in view of the island, even if it added days to our journey. He would stand at the railing and gaze out upon the deadly reefs that ringed the island, and though he wouldn't say anything, his eyes gleamed with desire, and we all knew that he was trying to imagine what riches and adventures might lie waiting for him there.

"Two weeks earlier we had put in to Skairn for supplies, and Erdis, who was something of a card sharp, had entered a high-stakes game of three-pronged crown between a number of prominent, not to mention notorious, sea captains. It was even rumored that several barons were in attendance. However, since Erdis was the only one of the *Seastar* present, I cannot confirm this. The game lasted for three days straight, and when it was over, Erdis had managed to double his money, but one of the players who owed Erdis had run out of funds, and he paid off his debt with a treasure map.

"I know what you're thinking: every lowlife gambler in the Principalities tries to pay off his or her debts with false treasure maps, but this debtor was a merchant lord of some repute and was also a longstanding acquaintance of Erdis's, so he accepted the map without even looking it over, though in truth Erdis was doubtful it would prove to be of any real value. Once back aboard the *Seastar*, and after getting some much-needed sleep, Erdis finally examined the map. He couldn't believe what he was looking at: the map depicted the northeastern tip of Trebaz Sinara, and what's more, it showed a route through the reefs. Erdis could no more resist the map's lure than a starving wolf can resist a plump, slow-footed sheep, so we set sail immediately. Two weeks later we dropped anchor off the coast of Trebaz Sinara.

"Erdis selected a landing crew of a half dozen men and women, myself among them. As ship's artificer, I often accompanied Erdis on dangerous trips, and I'm proud to say that my skills with magic saved his life on more than one occasion, but this time I was ambivalent to be going along. After all, this *was* Trebaz Sinara, and I feared there was no chance of our coming back alive. Still, it was my duty to go, and truth be told, I would rather have died than display cowardice before Erdis. He ordered a long boat lowered into the water. We climbed aboard and began rowing to the reef. Since Erdis preferred that I save my strength for working magic, I was able to sit and watch while others rowed. Erdis stood at the prow of the boat, map unfurled in his hands, and barked out orders to the rowers: 'Five full strokes, three port, seven starboard!' The rowers obeyed his commands instantly, and we began the long, twisting journey through the barrier maze of reef. How long it took us, I cannot say, but at last we won free of the reef and rowed the rest of the way to shore. The entire time we were in open water, I kept expecting some manner of monster to burst out of the sea and devour us, but none did, and I began to wonder if the stories of the terrible creatures that infested Trebaz Sinara were nothing but sea tales, perhaps originated by the ancient pirates who hid their treasure upon the island to discourage those who would attempt to search for it. Whichever the case, we made landfall without incident. We gathered our weapons and supplies, and set off for the island's interior, with Erdis leading the way, of course.

"From the start, it was clear that there was something strange about the island, or at least the northeastern portion of it. The landscape was a patchwork of different kinds of vegetation and soil. There were the usual trees that you expect to see in the Principalites: oak, elm, ash, fir, evergreen . . . but there were also trees that rightfully belonged to warmer climes: cypress, orange blossom, palm trees . . . Tropical fruit trees were abundant as well, and though it was summer, such fruit did not belong there, did not exist anywhere else in the Principalities, so far as any of us knew. The soil was just as varied. Sometimes it was a rich moist black, other times dry red clay, and sometimes it was cracked, barren, and lifeless as any desert. The air was still and stale, and as we trekked across the island following the path laid out in Erdis's map, we began to feel weighed down, as if some invisible force had settled on us and was slowly, inexorable pushing us toward the ground. Adding to the overall oppressive atmosphere was an eerie silence. Monsters or no, an island of that size, with all that vegetation, should've been teeming with birds, animals, and insects, yet we saw or heard no signs of such life as we walked.

"The crewmembers began to grow increasingly nervous, myself included, but when we told Erdis of our fears, he just laughed and asked if we wanted to live forever. We weren't surprised by his reaction, since his cavalier attitude toward danger was familiar to us all. Erdis was drawn to peril like a moth to flame, and in the end, I suppose, with much the same result."

The artificer paused, as if momentarily lost in thought, then he shook his head sadly and resumed his tale.

"We continued for some hours until we finally came to a rocky hillside and Erdis called a halt. He grinned, pointed to a cave opening in the hillside, and declared that we had reached our destination. By this time many in the landing party had begun to doubt the worth of Erdis's map, but upon seeing the cave, all their doubts were erased, and enthusiasm—which had been in short supply among us for some time—began to run high once again. Someone, I forget who, asked Erdis what lay inside the cave. Still grinning, Erdis said, 'That's what we've come to find out.' Erdis drew his sword, the rest of us took our own weapons in hand, and we followed our captain up the sloping hillside.

"The smell hit us before we were halfway to the cave entrance—the musky scent of lizard, combined with an acrid chemical stink that burned our throats and noses and made our eyes water. I'd never smelled anything like it before, but evidently Erdis had, for he whispered, 'Green dragon.'

"His words struck me like an arrow through the heart. I'd encountered more than my fair share of monsters since signing onto the *Seastar*, but I'd never faced a dragon before, and the thought of doing so terrified me. I was near to confessing my terror to Erdis and begging him to let me remain outside the cave when, as if sensing my fear, he turned to me and spoke first. 'This breed of dragon breathes poisonous fumes that result in agonizing death for any who are unfortunate enough to inhale them.' He put his hand on my shoulder then. 'But we have no reason to fear, do we, Tresslar? Not with our ship's artificer protecting us.'

"I wasn't at all confident that I could force myself to take a single step inside the cave, let alone protect Erdis and the others from the dragon's poison breath, but Erdis looked at me with a trust-filled gaze and squeezed my shoulder, and though my fear didn't vanish altogether, it did diminish to the point where it became manageable. All because of a single look and touch from the man. 'I'll do my best,' I told him, and he smiled. 'That will be more than sufficient. It always has been before.' Then he continued climbing toward the cave entrance and, after a moment's pause, I began following again, the others coming along behind me, their fears allayed as well.

"I still had concerns, though. I was a self-taught artificer with little formal schooling, and what I knew about dragons came almost entirely from drunken tales I'd heard from the *Seastar*'s crew. I knew most of their stories were lies, but the problem was I didn't know which few weren't, so as we finished our ascent to the beast's lair, I mentally went over all the dragon lore I knew—true or false—and prepared as best I could to justify Erdis's faith in me.

"There was a good-sized ledge jutting out from the cave entrance, and Erdis examined it closely before letting any of us climb onto it. 'This would be a perfect place for the beast to sun itself,' he whispered, more to himself than to any of us, 'but there are no claw marks in the stone, not even so much as a single scratch.' Erdis seemed troubled by this, and at the time I had no idea why. Now I know that he had been considering two possibilities: either the dragon had an alternate means of entering and exiting its lair, or the beast rarely left—if ever. Despite his misgivings, Erdis started toward the cave entrance, motioning for the rest of us to follow. Other captains might've let the low men on the pecking order go first, but not Erdis. He was always the first to face danger, and in those rare instances when he deemed retreat necessary, the last to flee it. I, as ship's artificer, was usually close behind, and that day in the dragon's lair was no exception.

"The sun had dipped close to the horizon by the time we reached the hillside, and little light came through the cave entrance. On my wrists I wore bracelets with a pair of light-stones set into the metal. I willed the light-stones to activate, but I made certain to keep their illumination at low strength: bright enough for us to see, but dim enough that we hopefully wouldn't draw undue attention to ourselves. The tunnel was more than large enough for us to move easily without having to crouch or squeeze through single file, and soon several of us—myself included—were walking alongside Erdis. The tunnel curved to the right and began to angle downward gradually, and though the slope was sometimes steep enough that we had to work to keep from sliding, we managed to maintain our footing as we continued ever downward.

"The air in the tunnel grew thicker and more acrid the deeper we went, and breathing became increasingly more difficult. I motioned for everyone to stop, and Erdis—undoubtedly knowing that I intended to do something about the gaseous air—did not dispute my right to call a halt. I slipped off my pack, rummaged through the contents until I found what I was looking for: a handful of pebbles. These weren't ordinary rocks. They'd been given to me by a locathah shaman when Erdis and the rest of us helped her tribe stave off an attack by a band of sahuagin. The fish-woman had enchanted the pebbles to allow surface dwellers to breathe underwater, and we were able to fight the sahuagin on their own terms. The pebbles had worked fine during the battle with the sea devils, but I had no idea if they could be adapted to function in our current situation. I pulled out my artificer's tools, worked on the pebbles for several moments, and when I was finished, I placed one under my tongue, counted to ten, then inhaled deeply through my nostrils.

"The air I took in was as clear and sweet as any I had ever breathed, and what's more, the gaseous fumes no longer stung my eyes. I had hoped as much, since the saltwater hadn't affected our vision when we fought alongside the locathah. Confident that the pebbles worked, I passed one out to every crewmember, including Erdis. Keeping a pebble stashed under one's tongue made speech difficult, but since we'd been proceeding in silence so far, I hoped this wouldn't prove much of a drawback. Thus we continued onward. Eventually the tunnel broadened and we saw a glowing green light ahead of us. I deactivated my light-stones, and we proceeded with cautious excitement toward the source of the verdant glow.

"We rounded a final bend and the tunnel opened into a vast cavern. Immediately we saw the source of the green light: both the cavern's stalactites and stalagmites were coated with some form of luminescent substance, a mold or perhaps some form of moss. Whatever it was, while its light wasn't bright as day, it was sufficient to illuminate the entire cavern—and most importantly, the cavern's sole occupant—a huge green dragon.

"Despite the pebble in my mouth, I found myself holding my breath at the sight of the awesome beast. The magnificent creature lay curled up on the cavern floor, head resting on its tail, eyes closed, greenish vapor curling forth from both its nostrils and the corners of its mouth. Even asleep, the beast exuded an almost palpable aura of power, and I was so awed by the dragon's sheer presence that I didn't notice what Erdis did. He leaned close to my ear, so close his lips almost touched my flesh, and whispered, 'No hoard.' Aside from the green dragon—and us, of course—the cavern was empty. While I'm sure that Erdis felt disappointed that there was no treasure, I later came to understand that he was more concerned because of how strange it was for the dragon not to have some kind of hoard. It was the one constant in all the tales about the beasts I'd ever heard.

For reasons known only to themselves, dragons have a need, a compulsion almost, to surround themselves with treasure, but this dragon had none.

"Then another mystery soon revealed itself. We didn't notice at first, for the air in the cave was hazy from the proliferation of fumes wafting forth from the dragon's snout, but the longer we stood there, the more we came to realize that the creature was wounded, terribly so. The wings folded against its back were shredded, their bones twisted and broken. Iridescent scales had been torn away in numerous places, exposing raw bloody flesh beneath. Fractured ribs jutted out from the creature's sides, and jagged fragments of bone protruded from its shattered limbs. We might've thought the dragon dead if not for its breathing, and even that we now realized was labored and irregular.

"Once more Erdis leaned close to my ear and whispered, 'This beast has come here to die. We should leave it in peace.' We might have done so, too, except the dragon chose that moment to shift its position. It didn't move much, merely lifted its head off its tail, stretched its neck, and then settled its head on its front feet, eyes closed the entire time, but the movement was enough to reveal that the dragon wasn't entirely bereft of treasure, for we now saw that around its neck hung a golden chain, and dangling on the end of it—"

"Was the dragonhead." Asenka nodded at Tresslar's wand.

"Yes. We were at least a hundred feet away from the dragon, but as soon as I saw the dragonhead, I could sense the mystic power emanating from it. The magic was strong, more so than anything I had come across in my young life. Erdis saw the dragonhead as well as I, and he turned to me and raised a questioning eyebrow. I understood exactly what he was asking me: Is the dragonhead valuable? Not in a monetary sense, for even if it were the most precious of rare artifacts, Erdis wouldn't risk his life and the lives of his crew to obtain a single object, but a *magic* object . . . that was a different story. I looked at him and nodded.

"A sly smile spread across Erdis's face as he turned back to examine the dragon. He pointed to me then two more of the crew. The message was clear: we three were to follow; the others were to remain behind. Erdis began moving toward the dragon, I came next, and the other two followed behind me. We went slowly and cautiously, for while the dragon appeared to be on the verge of death, still it *was* a dragon and not to be taken lightly. I don't know how long it took us to cross the cavern floor and reach the dragon. It seemed like hours, but I'm sure it took much less than that. Close to the dragon, the air was thick with greenish vapor, and if it hadn't been for the breathing pebbles under our tongues we would've died long before reaching the beast. When we had closed to within three yards of the creature, Erdis motioned for us to halt. Once again he leaned closed to my ear and whispered.

"'No blood,' he said. For a moment I didn't understand what Erdis meant, then I realized that the floor around the dragon was spotless. Though the creature was grievously wounded and its injuries were clearly wet with blood, the dragon wasn't actually *bleeding*. That is to say, blood did not seep from its wounds to spill onto the floor. At first I thought the beast might be some manner of undead thing, but its sides moved in and out as it breathed, vapor curled from its nostrils, and when it had moved earlier, it motion wasn't awkward and jerky like that of an undead creature, but rather smooth and natural, despite its wounds. Only magic of an extremely high order could be responsible for such a miraculous enchantment, and I looked at the golden dragonhead hanging from the beast's neck with newfound awe. A split-second later I realized that if we removed the dragonhead, there was a very good chance that the green dragon would no longer be protected against the progression of time, and its wounds would begin bleeding and death would soon come to claim it.

"I wanted to tell Erdis these things, but I was afraid to speak aloud and wake the dragon, so I hesitated, and in that moment, Erdis—sword gripped tight—crept up to the dragon's side and reached out for the golden dragonhead with his free hand. How he intended to get the object off the chain, I don't know. For at that instant, the dragon opened its eyes, or rather, I should say eye, for its left was nothing but a hollow, bloody socket.

"Erdis took several steps backward, but before he could do anything to defend himself, the dragon lifted its head, opened its mouth and released a blast of poison green gas that rolled over the four us like a cloud of thick, emerald fog. The vaporous cloud lingered for a moment before beginning to dissipate, and when the dragon saw that none of us had fallen, it spoke.

" 'I see that you have come prepared. Not that it matters, for all you've done is ensure yourselves a more grisly, though equally swift, demise.'

"Waves of fear pounded into me with each word, and if I hadn't been so completely consumed by terror, I would've turned and fled screaming for the cavern's exit. I understood then that I had experienced my first taste of dragonfear.

"When it finished speaking, the dragon rose onto all four feet, wincing in pain as it did so. Whatever the spell that kept its wounds from bleeding, it obviously didn't relieve the pain they caused. The creature drew its head back as if it were a serpent preparing to strike. Half of its teeth were either gone or reduced to broken nubs, but it still had more than enough left in its huge maw to slay with. As its one-eyed gaze was focused intently on Erdis, there was no doubt about whom it intended to kill first.

"The need for silence was long past, and I fought past my dragonfear to shout, 'Cut the dragonhead from the chain!'

"Erdis didn't respond, but as the dragon lunged, Erdis sidestepped, gripped his sword with both hands, and swung his blade at the golden object dangling from the chain around the dragon's neck. The strike was well aimed and severed the link holding the dragonhead to the chain. The object fell to the cavern floor. An instant later the dragon stiffened and let out a deafening roar of agony. As if some sort of internal dam had burst within the creature, blood gushed from its numerous wounds. Those of us closest to the dragon fled, as much from a sudden intense surge of dragonfear as to avoid the beast's death throes, but we needn't have bothered, for after releasing a single bellow of pain, the dragon slumped to the cavern floor and lay motionless. The dragonfear that had taken hold of us, Erdis included, subsided, and we stopped running and turned back to gaze upon the dying creature. I say dying, for though the beast did not move, its one good eye remained half open, and tiny curls of green vapor wafted from its nostrils.

"The dragon's right front claw twitched, its talons lightly scratching against the stone upon which it lay. At first I thought it was trying to get up, but then I saw the golden dragonhead lay less than ten feet from the claw, and I knew the beast wished to reclaim its magic talisman in order to save its life. Overwhelmed with sudden pity for the dragon, I stepped forward, intending to help it, but Erdis put a hand on my shoulder to stop me. I looked at him, and though he gazed at me with understanding, still he didn't release me, and I didn't try to break free. Instead, I turned back to look at the dragon. The streams of blood that had gushed from its wounds only seconds before had slowed to mere trickles, and I knew the dragon didn't have much time left.

"The beast spoke then. Its voice no longer echoed like thunder through the cavern, but came out instead as a soft rumble so quiet I had to strain to hear it.

" 'For more than twenty-six hundred years I have lain in this cavern, with only my pain for company,' the dragon said. 'The Amahau kept me alive all that time—much as I wish it hadn't—but now its work is finished. The Gatherer is yours now. Use it wisely.'

"I understood that the Amahau and the Gatherer were both names for the golden dragonhead, and though I knew this was hardly the time to quiz the dragon about the object, my artificer's curiosity was burning to learn more about the magical artifact, but before I could ask any questions, Erdis asked one of his own. " 'What is your name?'

" 'I am . . . Paganus.'

The dragon's eye closed then, and a last rattling breath escaped its scaly lips. After nearly three millennia—if the beast had been telling the truth—death had finally claimed it."

Tresslar fell silent after that and gazed out upon the sea. Asenka looked at the dragonhead—the Amahau—with new-found awe.

"What happened after that?" she asked.

Tresslar didn't respond right away, and she thought he hadn't heard her or that perhaps he had and merely intended to ignore her question, but then the artificer spoke once more.

"We left. I took the dragonhead, since as ship's artificer I was best equipped to handle it, and we made our way back to the *Seastar*. The return journey wasn't without its difficulties . . . after all, it *was* Trebaz Sinara, but all of us made it to the ship more or less intact, and we set sail. I began experimenting with the Amahau to learn its capabilities, and eventually I discovered how to use it to absorb and store magic. I affixed it to the end of this wand, and that's the end of the story."

Asenka very much doubted that last statement, but she sensed Tresslar didn't want to speak more about Erdis Cai or the crew of the *Seastar*, so she decided to ask something else. "Did you ever learn anything about the Amahau's origins or what the wounded dragon was doing hiding in the cavern for so long?"

Tresslar shook his head. "To be honest, I was never much of a scholar, but after Erdis and the rest of the crew . . . retired, I ended up working on Dreadhold. Because so many of the criminals incarcerated on Dreadhold possessed mystical abilities to one degree or another, the prison had a rather extensive research library for the artificers' use. From time to time I would visit the library to see what I could find about the Amahau or about a green dragon named Paganus, but I found only the most oblique references and very few of those. To this day, more than forty years later, I don't know where the Amahau came from or the full extent of its power."

Asenka gazed upon the golden dragonhead, its ruby eyes and crystalline teeth, and realized she was in the presence of a great mystery. After a time, she said, "Maybe it's better that you don't know more than you do."

"I've often thought the same," Tresslar replied.

They both fell silent after that and stood at the railing, side by side, watching the waves as the *Zephyr* sped across the water toward Perhata.

* * * ◉ * *

Inside the obsidian sarcophagus, Makala lay in darkness. The coffin's power insulated her from the effects of sea travel, so much so that she had no awareness that the ship was even moving. She wasn't asleep, at least not in the way that mortals understood the term. Just as vampires existed in a shadowy nether region between the worlds of the dead and the living, when resting, they hovered in a state between awareness and unconsciousness. The closest mortals could come to this experience was the delirium that accompanied a dangerously high fever. Makala's mind drifted in this ethereal twilight, images and sensations coming unbidden and leaving only distorted, fragmented memories of their visit upon departing.

Her reunion with Diran dominated her thoughts. The images that paraded through her mind were mostly of him, but at the extreme edge of her semi-awareness a voice whispered to her, as it had every day since she had been transformed into a vampire by Onkar, Erdis Cai's first mate. When she awakened, she would have no memory of this voice—she never did—but she would be changed a bit more by the dark words it spoke.

Makala . . . blood of my blood, flesh of my flesh . . . Soon you will be ready. Soon you will be worthy. Soon we shall be one. . . .

And then the voice—feminine, cruel, and so very, very cold—laughed.

CHAPTER

SEVENTEEN

Diran stood at the *Zephyr*'s bow as the elemental sloop approached Perhata. His lips were dry, the skin hard and cracked, and his cheeks were red-raw from windburn. He could've easily healed himself, but he didn't bother. He had long ago gotten used to ignoring pain.

"You should do something about those lips before they start bleeding. You don't want to be more of a temptation to our slumbering beauty than you already are."

Diran replied to Ghaji without turning to look at him. "I'm not in the mood for jokes."

"Since when has that ever stopped me?" The half-orc stepped up next to Diran and leaned forward onto the railing. "Sorry if my attempt at humor fell flat. It's the orcish way to try and cheer up a companion by provoking him."

Diran's cracked lips did their best to form a smile. "What's the companion supposed to do in response?"

"There are several acceptable responses, but the most common is to kill the idiot who's dumb enough to provoke an upset orc."

Diran couldn't stop himself from laughing.

Ghaji smiled. "From your reaction, can I assume you're not going to kill me?"

"Maybe later," Diran said.

It was late afternoon, and though the sky was clear and the sun shone bright, the air remained cold as ever. Ships of various types—two and three-masted merchant vessels, fishing boats, and small, sleek pleasure craft—plied the waters around Perhata as their owners went about their business. The wind rushing over Diran's face began to die down, and he realized the *Zephyr* was slowing. He glanced back and saw that the sails weren't as full as they had been a moment ago, and he knew that Yvka had commanded the wind elemental to decrease its output so that they could approach the dock at a safe speed.

"How are you?" Ghaji asked.

Diran faced forward once more. "Ever since that awful night in Grimwall, I've tried to imagine what it would be like to see Makala again . . . how I would feel . . ." He shook his head. "I didn't even come close."

"How *do* you feel?"

"As if I've betrayed her. I never should have let her go the night she was changed. I was too weak to do what had to be done."

"You loved her, Diran," Ghaji said. "Still do, unless I miss my guess. That's not a weakness."

"I am one of the Purified, and I swore an oath to fight evil in whatever from it might take." Diran paused. "Even if that form is my love for Makala."

"I don't understand."

Diran turned to look at Ghaji. "If I *truly* loved Makala, I never would've allowed the corruption of undeath to take hold in her. I would've slain her the moment I knew her transformation was inevitable. By allowing her to continue existing as a vampire, I've condemned her to something far worse than natural death. She might seem to be the same person now, but eventually her spirit will succumb to the darkness that dwells within her and she will be lost."

"Makala's as strong-willed a person as I've ever met," Ghaji said. "If anyone can resist becoming a monster, it's her."

"That's what I've tried to tell myself these last few months," Diran said, "but think of Erdis Cai. The man was a legendary adventurer who faced numerous perils and always managed to survive them one way or another. He had a strong spirit too, but that didn't prevent him from being consumed by evil after his transformation into a vampire."

"That's different. Erdis Cai wasn't simply bitten on the neck by another vampire. He was changed by Vol herself. No mortal can resist her power."

"But that's just it, don't you see? Onkar was Erdis Cai's first mate, and he was transformed by Vol at the same time Cai was. Onkar changed Makala, which means she's also infected with Vol's darkness, and as you said, no mortal can resist her power." He glanced over his shoulder, and though he couldn't see Makala's obsidian sarcophagus from where he stood, he nevertheless sensed its foul presence. "At least, not forever."

"If you truly believe that, then why don't you walk aft, open the coffin's lid, and expose Makala to the light of the sun? You wouldn't be killing her; you'd be setting her free."

Diran knew his friend was right. He also knew that he couldn't do it.

"I told you—because I'm weak."

"No, because you're *human*." Ghaji put his hand on Diran's shoulder. "No offense intended."

Diran couldn't help smiling. "So what's your excuse? You're only half human, after all."

Ghaji shrugged. "I guess I'm the half that can't bring himself to kill a friend . . .even when he should."

The two companions spoke no more on the matter, and the *Zephyr* continued toward Perhata's docks.

❋ ❋ ❋ ❋ ❋ ❋ ❋

Rather than finding a berth for the *Zephyr* at the docks, Yvka dropped off the others then sailed away. She planned to return the elemental sloop to the secluded location where she'd hidden her before—both to conceal her from those who might be tempted to steal the priceless craft as well as to protect Makala while she slumbered. Yvka promised to meet up with the others later at the King Prawn. Ghaji felt a bit nervous about the idea of Yvka being alone with Makala, even if the latter was sleeping, but he reassured himself that Yvka could deal with whatever threat came her way, including an attack by a vampire. Besides, Yvka would be safe enough as long as the sun was up . . . he hoped.

As Ghaji, Diran, Hinto, Tresslar, and Asenka walked down the dock to shore, Ghaji said, "So where were we before being so rudely interrupted by Haaken and his crew?"

"We'd decided to track down the barghest that attempted to steal Tresslar's dragonwand," Diran said.

"A worthy goal, if I do say so myself." Tresslar yawned, "but perhaps it might be best if we got some sleep first. We spent most of the night chasing after you two, and while we dozed aboard the *Zephyr*, I wouldn't exactly call a few catnaps a restful sleep."

"I'm not tired," Hinto said, "but then I'm not an old man like you, Tresslar."

"Old?" The artificer gave a derisive snort. "I prefer to think of myself as seasoned."

The others laughed, but Ghaji had to admit Tresslar had a point. Even though Diran's healing powers had countered the effects of the amber sleep, Ghaji still felt a weary ache in his bones. Diran's ability to heal could work miracles, but it didn't replace the need to attend to one's natural functions. Ghaji could use a soft bed right now, even if he was alone in it.

Ghaji expected Diran to protest, for the priest could drive himself quite hard at times, but instead Diran let out a weary sigh. "I suppose you're right, Tresslar. Much as I hate to postpone our hunt for the barghest, it *has* been an eventful couple of days. Besides, we'll be all the sharper after a bit of rest."

"I'll return to the Scorpions' barracks and have my people put the word out about the barghest," Asenka said. "Perhaps they can learn something of the creature's whereabouts."

Diran gave the woman a grateful smile. "That would be helpful. Thank you."

They held each other's gaze a few moments longer than necessary, and it was clear to Ghaji that Makala's return hadn't diminished Diran's attraction to the commander of the Sea Scorpions nor hers to him. Ghaji wondered if that was a good sign, or a sign of trouble to come. Both, he decided.

"I think we might have to postpone our rest," Hinto said. The halfling's voice held a note of fear, and everyone turned to see what had disturbed the diminutive pirate.

From the far end of the dock, a wolf came bounding toward them at terrific speed. It leaped at Tresslar and its jaws snapped closed around the dragonwand. The impact spun Tresslar sideways, and as the artificer hit the worn, wooden planks, the wolf yanked the wand free of his belt and dashed off.

Ghaji drew his axe, intending to hurl it at the fleeing barghest, but before he could draw back his arm to throw his weapon, a pair of silver daggers flashed through the air. Diran's knives struck the barghest between the shoulder blades, and the creature howled in agony. The barghest stumbled, its forelegs slid out from under it, and the dragonwand fell from its mouth as the beast collapsed.

Ghaji ran to the barghest without waiting to see if the others followed. He knew they would. The half-orc willed his elemental axe to burst into flame, and as he saw the wounded barghest scrabbling toward the dragonwand, clearly intending to retrieve it, Ghaji hurled his weapon. The axe tumbled end over end, flame trailing behind as it streaked toward its target. The axe blade struck the barghest in the side of its neck, and when the creature opened its mouth to scream, a gout of blood fountained forth instead.

"Ghaji!" Diran shouted. "Decapitate the beast!"

By the time Ghaji reached the barghest, its fur had caught fire. The flames rapidly spread across its body, which became slightly more humanoid as the barghest reverted to its natural form. Even wounded as it was, the beast continued to attempt to regain the dragonwand, now reaching for it with clawed fingers. Ghaji had no idea whether the barghest could command the wand's magic, but he wasn't about to let the creature get hold of it. He jammed his foot against the barghest's side to hold the beast in place, reached down, and yanked the axe free from the creature's neck. Blood gushed from the wound, and the barghest once more tried to cry out in pain but only managed to release a bubbling gurgle. Ghaji intended for it to be the last sound the beast ever made. He raised his flaming axe, ready to bring it down and end the barghest's infernal life.

Diran Bastiaan!

Ghaji grimaced as the voice thundered within his mind. He felt sudden pressure inside his skull, as if his brain were swelling rapidly, like a huge boil getting ready to burst. He forgot about the barghest, forgot he was holding his axe. All he could think about was the voice, and how much it hurt.

Return what you have stolen from me!

Ghaji's grip on his axe loosened, and he possessed just enough presence of mind to deactivate its fiery aura before the weapon fell to the dock. Ghaji followed his axe down, landing hard on his knees, though he barely felt the impact. He clapped his hands to his head, as if he were trying to hold his skull together, and clenched his jaw against the pain tearing through his mind.

Where are you? Thief! Monster! Face me!

Each word was like a hammer blow to the head, and Ghaji fell over onto his side, moaning, tears streaming from his eyes. He felt something warm and wet on his upper lip, and realized that blood trickled from his nostrils. He tried to rise but his body refused to listen. All he could do was lie there and wait for the voice of thunder to kill him and bring his agony to an end.

❧ ❧ ❧ ❧ ❧ ❧ ❧

Skarm was aware of the voice speaking in his mind, but he had more pressing concerns to deal with at that moment—like putting out the flames that were rapidly consuming his body. He had lost a great deal of blood and was very weak, but he was a supernatural creature, and though it remained an effort for him to do so, still he could move, if only barely. He pushed himself to the edge of the dock inch by tortuous inch—practically dragging his half-severed head—until he felt himself teeter and then slip over the side. The frigid water came as a welcome shock to his pain-ravaged body, and the flames snuffed out.

Skarm floated in the soothing embrace of the sea for several moments before his lungs began to scream for air. He swam toward where he judged the dock to be, and surprised himself when his clawed hands actually came in contact with wood. He grabbed hold of the support and climbed painfully to the surface. When his head broke water, he drew a gasping breath and then clung tight to the wet wood of the support as he continued to breathe. Hidden from sight by the dock above him, he was safe—for the moment, at least, but if the half-orc and his friends thought to search under it . . .

Then he heard the voice again, a voice speaking in his mind, he realized, calling for Diran Bastiaan. The barghest's mind was not like that of a natural creature, and though he heard the psionic shout, it caused him little discomfort—a blessing considering that every other part of his body was in utter agony. He had one other thing to be grateful for as well: whoever or whatever the psionic communication issued from, the voice was calling for the priest. That meant Bastiaan and the half-orc had bigger problems to worry about then tracking down a wounded barghest—and that suited Skarm just fine.

❀ ❀ ❀ ❀ ❀ ❀ ❀

Diran possessed no priestly powers that would allow him to block the shout in his mind, but he did know numerous meditation techniques—some learned at Emon Gorsedd's academy, some when he was studying for the priesthood—and he employed them now. He closed his eyes and pictured a pond, its surface smooth as glass. The voice spoke again and the pond rippled, but Diran imagined a soft breeze blowing across the water's surface, smoothing away the ripples until the pond was still once more. The pain the voice had caused receded, replaced by a feeling of peaceful calm. Then, and only then, did Diran reply to the voice.

I am at the docks. I shall await you here.

The voice didn't reply, but Diran felt the pressure begin to ease, as if his head had been held tight within a giant vise grip that was finally being removed.

He opened his eyes.

Ghaji was struggling to his feet near a scorched section of the dock. Of the barghest there was no sign. Tresslar hung limp in Asenka's arms as the woman worked to haul the artificer to a standing position. Hinto lay on his side, curled into a ball, trembling violently. All of them had bloody noses—Diran dabbed his fingers to his upper lip—as did he. His head ached as if he'd drank far too much of the bilgewater the King Prawn served in place of ale.

He hurried over to Tresslar. The artificer was unconscious, skin ashen, features slack on the left side of his face. Diran was no chirurgeon, but as a priest he'd been trained in both mystical and mundane aspects of the healing arts, and he knew the older man had suffered a stroke.

"Hold him as still as you can," Diran told Asenka. The woman nodded, and Diran gently touched his fingertips to the artificer's temples. He closed his eyes and allowed the healing power of the Silver Flame to surge through him and into Tresslar's body. When Diran opened his eyes, he saw that Tresslar remained unconscious, but the muscles on the left side of the man's face no longer hung slack.

"Let's lay him down gently," Diran said. "I've managed to heal the worst of the damage, but it will be some time before he awakens."

Together, Diran and Asenka lay down the unconscious Tresslar, then the priest turned his attention to the woman.

"Are you hurt?"

Asenka gave him a weak smile. "A headache, and I feel weak as a kitten, but I'll live."

Diran returned her smile. He could alleviate the aftereffects of the psionic assault with his healing powers, but he wanted to check on Ghaji and Hinto first, in case they were injured more severely.

Ghaji walked up, axe tucked beneath his belt, Tresslar's dragonwand held in his hand. "I'm really starting to get irritated with that barghest," he growled. The half-orc's complexion was a lighter shade of green than usual, and his upper lip was smeared with blood, but otherwise he appeared hale enough. Anticipating Diran's next words, Ghaji said, "I'm fine. See to the halfling."

Diran knew his friend would say he was fine even if he'd lost all four limbs and was about to lose his head in the bargain, but Diran agreed with Ghaji's assessment, so he walked over and knelt at the Hinto's side.

The halfling yelped when Diran placed a hand on his shoulder, but then he spoke in a stuttering, quavering voice, forcing out each word with an obvious effort. "I-I'm all right. J-j-just . . . afraid."

Diran was glad Hinto wasn't seriously injured, but he felt a wave of pity for his small friend. Maybe Ghaji had been right about the halfling not being able to endure Diran's chosen quest.

"Just lie still until the fear passes, Hinto. All will be well." Diran stood, wondering if he had just lied to his friend.

"Looks like we weren't the only ones who heard the voice," Ghaji said.

Diran saw what Ghaji meant. The docks were in an uproar, men and women shouting in confusion, crying out in pain, fleeing into the city streets or casting off lines in preparation of sailing away.

"Do you think everyone in the city heard it?" Asenka asked.

"I don't know," Diran admitted. "The voice called for me, so perhaps only those in my vicinity were affected." He didn't want to imagine the kind of power the owner of such a mental voice might wield if everyone in Perhata had heard the message.

"What do we do?" Ghaji asked. "Stand or run?"

"Stand," Diran said. "I told the voice that I was waiting at the docks. Besides, I'm not sure there's anywhere we could run even if we wanted to."

"Good," Ghaji said. "I'm too damned tired to run anyway."

Diran turned to Asenka, but before he could speak, she said, "Don't tell me this isn't my fight, Diran Bastiaan. I command the Sea Scorpions, and this is my city. That makes it my fight."

Diran smiled. "It seems as if our mysterious psion isn't the only one who can read minds."

"We should move away from Tresslar and Hinto," Ghaji said. "Neither is capable of fighting at the moment."

Diran hated to leave the two alone—Tresslar still unconscious and Hinto held tight in the grip of his fear—but they couldn't draw danger to them, either.

"Very well, let's—"

Return what you have stolen, thief!

The words lanced through Diran's brain like white-hot spearpoints, and he heard someone cry out in pain. He wasn't surprised when he realized it was him. Through eyes blurred with tears, he saw a large figure striding across the dock toward them. Man-shaped it was, made of stone and wood, the surface of its body encrusted with colorful crystal shards of varying sizes that pulsed with barely constrained energy. A warforged, Diran thought, but like none he had ever seen before.

Standing on shore, watching as the warforged advanced, were three other figures. Diran didn't recognize either the orc or the lean, graceful man clad in black leather, but the third figure was known to him, as familiar to Diran as his own face. Swaddled in a thick fur cloak against the cold, grinning like a shark about to sink its teeth into its next meal, stood Aldarik Cathmore.

Before Diran had time to fully register Cathmore's presence, a three-fingered hand made of stone closed around his throat, and he felt himself being lifted into the air. The warforged's pinpoint eyes smoldered with fury as he slowly tightened his grip on Diran's neck, and when next he spoke, its voice issued from its stone mouth.

"Return what you have taken, thief . . . or die!"

CHAPTER

EIGHTEEN

Can we have a third choice?"

Ghaji swung his flaming axe at the crook of the warforged's arm. During the Last War, he'd fought many of the living constructs, and he knew that they were most vulnerable at their darkwood joints, and though the darkwood was spelled to be fire-resistant on the surface, once that surface was broken, the wood underneath burned as easily as any other.

The axe blade bit into the joint of the warforged's arm with a loud *chuk!* and held fast. The warforged's head swiveled as he turned to look at Ghaji, but before the construct could react further, the half-orc hauled back on his weapon with all his strength, attempting to unbalance the warforged and break his grip on Diran. Given that the constructs were formed primarily of stone and metal, warforged were heavy and not easily moved, but Ghaji was determined to save his friend and gave it all he had. The half-orc's arm and shoulder muscles blazed with pain, but he refused to let up.

The warforged, which up to this point had been immovable

as a statue, began to lean toward Ghaji, and the half-orc gave one last mighty pull, shouting with the effort. It felt as if his arm muscles were going to rip free of their bones, but the warforged stumbled, and the hand clutching Diran around the neck sprung open.

The black-clad priest fell to the dock and gasped for air. Ghaji feared that his friend's throat had been crushed, but while he wanted to rush to Diran's side and tend to him, Ghaji knew he couldn't. The warforged would remain off-balance for only a second or two. Besides, Diran himself was best equipped to heal whatever injuries he might've sustained.

Ghaji's axe was still partially embedded in the warforged's arm, and he needed to pry the weapon loose to resume his attack, but before he could do so, the construct trained his pinpoint eyes of flickering energy on Ghaji, and the crystal shards affixed to his head—already pulsing with energy—shone more brightly. Ghaji felt himself rising into the air as if he was being lifted by powerful hands. He still had hold of his axe, and the blade slid free from the warforged's arm with unexpected ease. Ghaji looked down at himself, but he could see nothing visible that was holding him aloft.

The construct's eyes glowed like tiny twin suns, and Ghaji flew high up into the air and out over the sea.

* * * ⊙ * * *

Asenka watched as an unseen force lifted Ghaji into the air then hurled him far from the dock. The half-orc soared at least a hundred feet upward before starting to descend. From that height, hitting the water would be like slamming full force into a brick wall. If he hit the sea at the wrong angle . . .

Before she could see if Ghaji entered the water safely, a much closer splashing sound drew Asenka's attention back to the warforged. Thanks to Ghaji's axe-strike, flames engulfed the construct's arm, but now a stream of water rose forth from the sea to arc through the air and splash onto the flames, dousing them. Asenka knew that warforged wizards existed, though she had never encountered any, and she wondered if this construct was one. The warforged's actions didn't *seem* like magic though. He used no materials or tools, conducted no rituals, spoke no magic words . . . As near as she could tell this warforged simply willed something to happen, and it did. Disrupt a magic-user's concentration, interrupt his rite, make him mispronounce his mystical phrases, take away or damage his artifacts of power, and you could fight him, but Asenka had no idea how to even begin to counter such power as the warforged possessed. But she knew who might.

Asenka hurried over to Diran. The priest had risen to a sitting position, eyes closed, hand gently pressed to his bruised throat. As she watched, the blue-black color faded as the skin on his neck regained its normal hue, and his windburned cheeks and chapped lips—the result of his standing at the prow of the *Zephyr* for so long—healed as well. She offered her hand, Diran took it, and she helped him to his feet.

"Are you hurt?" she asked.

Diran rubbed his throat. "Not now. What of Ghaji?"

Asenka gazed seaward, but she saw no sign of the half-orc. "I don't know."

Diran's eyes narrowed in an expression that she was coming to recognize as one of controlled anger. "Stay with Tresslar and Hinto. I'm going to try and draw the warforged away from here."

The crystalline-studded construct had finished extinguishing the flames, but now he stood swaying from side to side, staring off into the distance as if stunned or confused.

Asenka grabbed his arm. "Wait!"

She pointed and Diran turned to see a squad of Sea Scorpions approaching at full speed from the shore end of the dock, a dozen men and women, all with weapons drawn and ready.

"Order them to back off!" Diran said. "There's no way they can hope to stand against a creature this powerful!"

Intellectually, Asenka knew he was right. Emotionally, she was proud of the people in her command. They were the best warriors Perhata had to offer, the best in the entire Gulf of Ingjald, and she was reluctant to admit there was any threat they couldn't handle.

As if Diran's words had brought him back to reality, the warforged turned to face the oncoming warriors. He seemed to study them for a moment before raising his right arm and stretching his three-fingered hand toward them. At first nothing happened, but then the wooden planks of the dock began to shudder beneath the Sea Scorpions' feet, and the wood exploded upward as a vast geyser of water erupted into the air. Men and women shouted as they were flung about like so many rag dolls. Most tumbled through the air to splash into the water on either side of the dock, but a few landed on unbroken wood in front of or behind the newly created gap. They hit hard, and the sound of snapping bones was accompanied by their screams of pain.

"Warforged!" Diran shouted.

The construct hesitated a moment before turning back around to face Diran and Asenka.

"I'm the one you want, not those warriors. Forget them. Whatever your problem is, it lies with me, so let us settle it—just the two of us."

The warforged stared at Diran, his expression—like that of all his kind—unreadable. The crystals covering his stone and metal body flickered on and off in a strangely tentative manner that to Asenka indicated indecision.

"Very well," the warforged replied in a hollow, emotionless voice, then it started walking toward them.

⊛ ⊛ ⊛ ◉ ⊛ ⊛ ⊛

Cathmore, Chagai, and Galharath stood on the shore, watching as their newfound friend went about his work.

"Our test seems to be going rather well, don't you think?" Cathmore said.

Chagai humphed. "Looks to me like he's just wasting time. If the creature is so powerful, he should've killed the priest by now."

"Be patient," Cathmore said. "After all, this is Solus's first battle. I'm sure he'll improve with experience."

Galharath didn't bother to respond to either of his companions' observations. He was too busy maintaining his mental link with Solus and monitoring the psi-forged. Solus was indeed powerful, but as Cathmore had said, the psi-forged lacked experience at applying his abilities to specific tasks. He had no concept of how much strength he possessed, and if it wasn't for Galharath helping to stabilize Solus's powers, the psi-forged could well destroy both the docks and the wharf, killing everyone in the vicinity—including Cathmore, Chagai, and himself. While Galharath didn't care all that much about preserving the lives of his companions, he preferred to retain his own corporeal existence.

Galharath had an additional concern about Solus. Now that the psi-forged had come in contact with Bastiaan, the deception that Galharath had created about him being an evil priest who had stolen Solus's memories was in danger of being revealed. Galharath had hoped that Solus would slay Bastiaan on sight, but that hadn't happened. The longer the priest remained alive, the greater the chance that Solus might probe his mind. If that occurred, Solus would learn the truth and slip free from Galharath's control, and if that happened, there was no telling how he would react.

Galharath had to do something and do it fast. The question was what.

A smile crossed the kalashtar's face. He'd thought of a solution as simple as it was elegant. Hopefully, it would also prove deadly for the priest.

With a small portion of his consciousness that wasn't involved in monitoring Solus, Galharath formed a tendril of psionic energy and reached out to Diran Bastiaan's mind.

* * * ◉ * * *

As Solus approached the man in black, he felt confused and uncertain. This was Diran Bastiaan, the monster who had stolen his memories, yet the human walked toward Solus with his arms held out to his sides, open palms displayed to show he carried no weapons. Solus might have little experience of the world beyond the walls of Mount Luster, but he knew enough to realize Bastiaan might be attempting to deceive him by pretending to be friendly. There was something else about the man that confused Solus. He sensed no ill intent on the man's part, felt no waves of negative emotion radiating from the man. He sensed only concern for others—the woman standing behind him, the small trembling one lying on the dock, the older human lying unconscious nearby, the half-orc that Solus had sent flying through the air, the men and women who'd been injured when Solus had caused the dock beneath their feet to explode. Bastiaan feared for their safety, all of them, without sparing a thought for himself. *This* was a monster? *This* was the villain he was supposed to destroy?

Solus halted, stopped by a new thought: Perhaps Diran Bastiaan wasn't the deceiver . . . perhaps *Galharath* was.

Before Solus went any further, he needed to speak with Galharath and clear this up, but as the psi-forged began to turn around, intending to walk back to shore and question the psionic artificer, Diran Bastiaan laughed. Surprised, Solus turned around to face the dark priest.

The laughter emerging from Bastiaan's throat was brittle and harsh, with a mocking edge to it. It was the laughter of a man who had nothing but the most profound contempt for the person he was facing . . . the laughter of a fiend delighted to behold the weakness of the victim standing before him.

Solus might not have his full memories to draw upon, but he recalled one thing very well: Rage.

He concentrated, reached into Bastiaan's mind, and commanded the monster's heart to stop.

Bastiaan's eyes flew wide and his laughter choked off. His features contorted into a grimace of pain, but his eyes held only surprise and disbelief. His body went limp, and he collapsed to the dock like a toy abandoned by a bored child.

The woman cried out in despair and ran to kneel at Bastiaan's side. She slapped his face lightly, and when he didn't respond, she struck him harder.

"Diran! Wake up! Damn you, wake up!"

Solus was more confused then ever now, for in the instant when he'd stopped Bastiaan's heart, his mind had touched that of the priest, and he'd sensed that Diran wasn't laughing of his own volition. Something—or some*one*—had been forcing him, but why?

Before Solus could consider this strange development further, the small man—who a moment ago had been lying on the deck shivering as if in the grip of intense cold—stepped between the psi-forged and the priest's body.

The little man drew a long knife from the sash around his waist and brandished it at Solus, the blade quivering in his hand.

"Guh-get away from hu-hu-him!"

Solus regarded the little man curiously. "You are smaller than I, and you have no special abilities that I can detect. You are not especially skilled with weaponry, you wield no magic, nor do you possess any powers of the mind. You cannot stand against me, and you are consumed by fear, yet there you stand, guarding Diran Bastiaan though it might well mean your own death. Why?"

The small man was so terrified, he had to struggle to force out an answer to Solus's question. "Buh-because Diran's my friend."

Solus probed the small man's surface thoughts and found no deception, only fierce affection and loyalty to the priest. If Diran Bastiaan truly was the monster Galharath had made him out to be, how could the priest have inspired such deep feelings of friendship in this small man, feelings so strong that he had fought to overcome his paralyzing fear to protect Diran, even at the cost of his own life?

Solus realized that he had made a terrible mistake. He reached into Diran's mind which, while in the process of dying wasn't quite dead yet, and reactivated the priest's heart. Diran's eyes flew open and his body spasmed as he drew in a deep, gasping breath.

Satisfied that the priest would live, Solus turned to regard the trio watching him from shore. He fixed his gaze upon Galharath and sent a simple thought to the kalashtar.

You lied.

Galharath smiled. *So I did.*

The psionic artificer furrowed his brow, and Solus felt a wave of energy surging toward him. He attempted to erect a mental barrier to defend himself, but he was inexperienced at psionic combat, and Galharath's attack broke apart into a dozen different streams of energy that snaked around Solus's barrier with ease. The streams coalesced as the psychic energy streaked toward the small green crystal that Galharath had embedded in the psi-forged's forehead. Solus felt the crystal grow hot as energy suffused it, then the shard exploded, taking a good chunk of the psi-forged's head with it, and Solus knew no more.

* * * * * * *

Diran came to with his head in Asenka's lap. She gazed down at him, smiling with relief as a single tear slid down her cheek.

"For a moment there . . ." She trailed off, leaving her thought incomplete.

Diran frowned. He knew something had happened, but he wasn't quite sure what. He'd been having a dream in which a silver flame burned bright and warm in the darkness, a flame that called to him in a soundless voice to come toward it . . . to come home. It had been such a pleasant dream that he was almost sorry he'd awakened.

He felt weak as a kitten, and when he tried to sit up, he needed Asenka's help. He looked around, trying to remember what had happened before he'd lost consciousness. He saw Hinto grinning at him, and behind the halfling stood a warforged whose body was covered by colorful crystalline shards. For some reason, Diran thought the shards should be glowing, but no light came from them now. The warforged's back was to him, and he stood with his arms held out in front of his face, as if trying to ward off some sort of attack. The construct stood motionless, and Diran had the impression that at the moment he contained no more life than a statue. He didn't think the warforged was dead, but why he should have that impression, he wasn't sure.

He turned to look seaward and saw Tresslar rise to a sitting position farther down the dock. The artificer grimaced and rubbed his temples. Diran had a vague memory of healing Tresslar, but he couldn't recall the specific injury that the man had suffered. Whatever it had been, it appeared the artificer would be all right, and for that Diran was grateful. Another memory came back to him then, an image of three men standing on the shore, watching as . . . as the warforged attacked.

Diran's full memory returned to him in a sudden rush, and he looked at the shore where Aldarik Cathmore had been standing, alongside an orc and a lean man Diran took to be a kalashtar, but no one stood there now. Cathmore was gone.

A splashing sound to his right drew Diran's attention, and he turned to see Ghaji haul himself out of the water and onto the dock.

"Sorry it took me so long to get back, but I dropped my axe, and the damn thing sank to the bottom." The half-orc looked around. "So . . . what did I miss?"

CHAPTER

NINETEEN

"Thank you for allowing us to bring the warforged to the Sea Scorpions' barracks," Diran said.

"Baron Mahir ordered me to conduct a full investigation into the warforged's attack,"Asenka said, then she smiled. "Besides, it's the least I can do for you after you healed my people who were harmed during the construct's rampage."

"Why are we doing *anything* with him?" Ghaji said. "Aside from disassembling him, that is. He nearly killed you, Diran."

"Actually, I believe he *did* kill me, but then he changed his mind and returned me to life."

Diran gazed down upon the warforged. The construct lay upon a table in the barracks' common room, eyes dark, body frozen in the same position it had held on the dock: arms held up as if to ward off an invisible assault. Diran's companions—with the exception of Makala, who still slumbered aboard the *Zephyr*—stood around the table looking at the creature that had come close to slaying them all.

"Solus," Hinto said.

Everyone turned to look at the halfling.

Hinto explained without taking his eyes off the warforged. "That's his name: Solus."

"How could you possibly know that?" Tresslar asked.

Hinto shrugged. "I don't know. I just do."

Tresslar snorted. "Nonsense."

"I'm inclined to believe you, Hinto." Diran examined the warforged's injuries more closely. His right arm was singed from the fire caused by Ghaji's axe, and the weapon had cut out a small wedge of wood as well, but by far the most serious damage had occurred to Solus's head. The explosion, whatever its cause, had blasted a fist-sized hole in the warforged's forehead, but where such an injury would've revealed ravaged brain tissue in a fully organic being, only solid rock was visible within Solus's head.

Hinto looked up at Diran, a worried expression on his face, but a hopeful look in his eyes. "You're a priest. Can't you do anything for him?"

"I'm sorry, my friend, but my abilities don't extend to healing damage done to constructs. Such work is the province of artificers."

Everyone turned to Tresslar.

"Don't look at me!" the artificer said.

"You told me once that you used to help repair the warforged that served on the *Seastar!*" Hinto protested.

"Yes, but I merely patched over a few holes, filled in some cracks, occasionally refit an eye or finger . . . but *this*—" Tresslar gestured toward the huge divot in Solus's forehead—"is another matter entirely. Such damage would require the attention of an artificer who specializes in warforged . . . assuming this construct can be revived at all."

"We don't have a specialist," Diran said. "We have you. You admit that you worked on warforged during the time you sailed with Erdis Cai. You must have had the opportunity to increase your knowledge during your years at Dreadhold. Surely there were some warforged among the prison populace."

"A few," Tresslar admitted. "Though warforged tend to commit fewer crimes than others." He leaned over Solus to examine more closely the warforged's head injury. He scratched his beard thoughtfully. "Warforged's internal workings are very different from ours. Their minds aren't physical things, and their personalities don't reside in organs like our brains. Their . . . selves, for lack of a better term, exist as an intricate matrix of mystical energies."

"It sounds like you're speaking of souls," Yvka said.

Tresslar shrugged. "If you like. The point is that while an injury like this—" he gestured to Solus's forehead—"would kill you or me, it isn't necessarily fatal to a warforged."

"So you *can* fix him!" Hinto said.

"I didn't say that!" Tresslar snapped. "I've never seen a warforged like this before." The artificer paused, and when he spoke next, his tone was apologetic. "I wouldn't know where to start."

"That's not the point!" Ghaji said. His voice was tight, and his complexion a darker green than usual, the equivalent of a human's face turning red with anger. "Why would we even *attempt* to repair him? We slay monsters; we don't nurse them back to health!"

Hinto turned to Ghaji, "He's not a monster!" The halfling's jaw jutted out in defiance. "He's just confused and afraid, but you wouldn't know what that's like, would you?" Hinto turned to regard the entire group. "None of you know!" He paused, and then softly added, "Not like I do." The little pirate gazed down at Solus with sympathy in his eyes then reached out and patted the construct's stone hand.

Diran looked at Hinto, concerned. It appeared their halfling friend had been more affected by his encounter with Solus than they'd realized. Diran wondered what long-term effects, if any, Hinto might suffer, and he decided to keep a close eye on the halfling for the time being.

"There's another matter to discuss," Yvka said. "Diran, you saw Cathmore watching from the shore as Solus attacked you."

Diran nodded. "Along with an orc mercenary known to Ghaji, and a kalashtar that I didn't recognize."

"Obviously, Cathmore learned of your presence in Perhata," Yvka said, "most likely from the orc, since he confronted Ghaji last night. I'd say it's safe to assume that Cathmore directed Solus to slay Diran, along with anyone else who happened to get in the way." The elf woman looked down at Solus's immobile form, greed shining in her gaze. "The question is how Cathmore came to control such a powerful creature as this—and if there are any more of them."

Diran didn't need to be psychic himself to know what Yvka was thinking. While she'd been of great help to them during their encounter with Erdis Cai, as an operative of the Shadow Network, her first loyalty lay with her employers. A construct like Solus, one possessed of vast psionic abilities, would be of great interest to the Shadow Network. The secret of his construction, and more importantly, how to make others like him, would be priceless to them.

"How Cathmore controlled the warforged is obvious," Tresslar said. "It was the kalashtar's doing, and unless I miss my guess, the green crystal embedded in Solus's forehead— the one that caused so much damage when it exploded—was the key to the kalashtar's control. When Solus threatened to break the hold the kalashtar had over him, the man willed the crystal to destroy itself, disrupting the energy matrix of the construct's personality."

"Such a deadly precaution is exactly Cathmore's style," Diran said bitterly.

"What I don't understand is why Cathmore would so openly observe his servant's attack," Asenka said. "Wouldn't he have wished to conceal his connection to Solus?"

"You're thinking of him like an ordinary criminal," Diran said. "Aldarik Cathmore is much more than that. He once was a member of the Brotherhood of the Blade, but he chafed at what he saw as the Brotherhood's restrictive code of conduct. The Brotherhood viewed assassination as a noble—and extremely profitable—profession, but Cathmore believed only in the exercise of power for its own sake. He clashed many times with Emon Gorsedd over their philosophical differences. Eventually he attempted to wrest control of the Brotherhood from Emon, but Emon defeated his half-brother and sent him into exile rather than killing him. At the time, I was impressed by Emon's mercy and restraint. Now, however un-priestly it might be, I wish Emon had chosen otherwise.

"Cathmore's ego is so strong that he doesn't fear exposure or capture, for he believes that he cannot be defeated by mere mortals. Unfortunately, he has the intelligence, skills, and experience to support his overdeveloped sense of self. As for why he was present during Solus's attack, he undoubtedly wanted to witness my demise—*and* to let me know that it was he who was responsible for my death." Diran paused. "You see, when Cathmore decided to overthrow his half-brother, he tried to garner the support of a number of students at the academy, myself among them. Because Cathmore trained the young students, he was our first teacher, and despite his coldness, we respected him a great deal. Many joined his cause. I . . . was tempted, but in the end, I remained loyal to Emon Gorsedd. However, I pretended to join Cathmore and spied on him for Emon. My efforts directly led to Cathmore's defeat." Diran smiled. "So you can see why he couldn't stay away during Solus's attack."

"Do you recall what I told you yesterday?" Yvka asked. "About how there have been reports of Cathmore buying supplies in Perhata? Some of those supplies could very well be used in artificer's work."

"Are you suggesting Cathmore has a facility for producing warforged like this?" Tresslar said. "That's impossible! The resources and expertise necessary to design and build such a facility are beyond any one individual, no matter how wealthy or powerful."

"Perhaps," Yvka allowed, "but during the Last War, the Principalities—while technically neutral—aided various factions by allowing them the use of both sea lanes and land. All for a handsome price, of course. It's possible that one of the Dragonmarked Houses established a secret creation forge near here, a forge that Aldarik Cathmore now controls."

Ghaji frowned. "It sounds as if you know more than you're telling."

Yvka grinned at him. "Always."

"This is most disturbing news," Asenka said. "If such a facility does exist nearby, then we must shut it down. We can't allow someone like Cathmore to create an army of warforged as powerful as Solus."

"My thoughts exactly," Diran said.

'So what are we saying?" Ghaji asked. "That for the time being we forget about our annoyingly persistent barghest friend and go after Cathmore, Chagai, and the kalashtar?"

Diran looked around to gauge the others' reactions, and when no one said anything in protest, he turned to Ghaji and said, "Yes."

Ghaji grinned, displaying his sharp teeth. "Good. After last night I've been itching for a rematch with Chagai."

"You shall have it," Diran said. "That is, *if* Tresslar can revive Solus so that we can question him and learn the location of Cathmore's stolen forge."

Tresslar scowled. "You're not going to let me say no, are you?"

Diran's only response was a smile.

"Very well," the artificer growled. "I'll need all of you to clear out and leave me alone to work." He turned to Asenka. "And I'll need some artificer's tools and supplies."

"Give me a list, and if what you want is to be found in Perhata, you'll have it—on the baron's expense, of course."

Tresslar nodded. "Good. Now everybody, if you wouldn't mind . . ."

Diran and the others filed out of the room, but Hinto remained behind.

"I'm staying," the halfling said, "and don't tell me I can't. I can be your assistant. Besides, Solus could use a friend at his side while you work on him."

Diran thought Tresslar would protest, but after a moment's hestitation, the artificer said, "Very well, but try not to get in my way."

⚬ ⚬ ⚬ ◉ ⚬ ⚬ ⚬

Skarm was tired of getting burned by that half-orc's flaming axe. He hurt so much that he was beginning to think it would be preferable to suffer Nathifa's wrath than to continue to try to steal the dragonwand for her, but then he realized how foolish the thought was. Better to suffer the pain of a thousand burns than to risk the unspeakable punishments his dark mistress was capable of doling out.

The barghest clung to the roof of the Sea Scorpions' barracks in his natural form. Three quarters of his fur had been burned away, and his flesh was a mass of suppurating blisters, but he'd heal soon enough, especially after he found a victim to devour. For the time being he'd have to content himself with the mild relief provided by the cool breeze wafting in from the sea. It was late afternoon, almost dusk, and the sun was riding low in the sky, something else to be grateful for. Even though the air was cold this time of year, Skarm didn't think he could stand the heat from direct sunlight yet.

His hearing wasn't as acute in his natural form as it was in wolf shape, but it was good enough to allow the barghest to overhear the discussion that had taken place beneath him. He hadn't witnessed the psi-forged's attack on the priest and his companions, but he'd heard it from where he'd clung to the piling beneath the dock. He understood that the construct and those who'd commanded it had come from Mount Luster—they were the "neighbors" that Skarm and his mistress had been aware of for some time. Skarm hadn't known they were in possession of a creation forge, however. Most interesting. Also interesting was the fact that Diran Bastiaan and his companions sounded determined to go after the current residents of Mount Luster, provided they could rouse the psi-forged and get him to tell them the location of his masters. Skarm was confident that they would succeed, especially since their artificer had the Amahau to rely on.

So far Skarm had had been unable to retrieve the Amahau on his own, and right now he was too wounded and weak to even think about making another attempt. Yet if the priest and his friends traveled to Mount Luster, they'd bring the Amahau with them—almost directly to Nathifa's doorstep—and by then Skarm would be fully healed and could make another try for the Amahau. Also, he thought his mistress would be interested to learn about the creation forge hidden within Mount Luster. Most interested, indeed.

Skarm made his way to the edge of the roof—every movement of his burned body an agony—and dropped to the ground. He clamped his mouth shut to keep from screaming in pain as he landed, then limped off to find a victim so that his healing might begin in earnest.

● ● ● ● ● ● ●

In a seldom used chamber within Mount Luster — one devoid entirely of furnishings — the air rippled and blurred. When space resumed its normal shape, the chamber was no longer empty. Cathmore, Chagai, and Galharath had returned home, thanks to teleportation capabilities of one of the kalashtar's crystals.

"I thought that went rather well," Cathmore said.

"You must be joking," Chagai said. "Not only did the construct fail to destroy Bastiaan, Galharath was forced to destroy it." For a supposed master assassin, you managed to miss your target most effectively, Chagai added mentally.

Cathmore was unfazed by Chagai's criticism. "True, the outcome was less than I'd hoped for, but our test was not entirely without success. The potential demonstrated by Solus was most impressive, and now that we have a better understanding of his flaws, we can make sure that the psi-forged we produce are more . . . tractable."

"We still have a long way to go," Galharath cautioned, "though I agree our experience with Solus will help us reach that day more quickly."

"You realize that Bastiaan, Ghaji, and the others will track us to Mount Luster?" Chagai asked.

Cathmore grinned. "Of course. We shall prepare an appropriate welcome for them."

Chagai scowled. "I thought the kalashtar said we can't produce our own psi-forged yet."

"Correct," Galharath confirmed, "but the facility's builders designed the forge to be adapted for use as a defense system." It might have been a trick of the light, but the psionic artificer's eyes seemed to glow momentarily. "With a few adjustments, the psi-forge itself can be turned into a weapon—and a most deadly one at that."

Now it was Chagai's turn to grin.

⊛ ⊛ ⊛ ◉ ⊛ ⊛ ⊛

The instant the sun vanished below the horizon, a knocking sound came from within the obsidian sarcophagus. Diran opened the lid partway, and Makala's hand emerged to grip the lid and push it the rest of the way open. Despite himself Diran took a step backward as Makala sat up and turned to look at him. The crimson fire of undeath danced in her eyes, mingled with an all-too-human sorrow upon seeing Diran's reaction.

"I'm sorry," Diran said.

Makala didn't acknowledge his apology. Instead she climbed out of the sarcophagus with a fluid grace that was as alluring as it was inhuman and stepped onto the deck of the *Zephyr*. Makala closed the lid of her resting place.

She looked around. "I see we're in a lagoon of some sort. Are we back in Perhata?"

"Close by," Diran said. "This is one of the Shadow Network's hidden ports. The lagoon is concealed by an illusion spell that makes it seem as if this area is nothing but desolate shoreline. Yvka brought me here so that I could . . . let you out."

"Thank you."

For several moments neither of them spoke. There was so much Diran wanted to say to her, but he had no idea how to begin. Finally, Makala broke the silence.

"I assume we had an uneventful trip back from Demothi Island."

"Yes, though our arrival was anything but." Diran filled her in on everything that had occurred while she'd slumbered. When he was finished, her eyes blazed with crimson fire, and her canine teeth had become more pronounced.

"Aldarik Cathmore . . . I never thought I'd see him again. At least, I hoped I wouldn't." Like Diran, Makala had remained loyal to Emon Gorsedd when Cathmore had attempted to take over the Brotherhood of the Blade, and she'd felt nothing but hatred for the man ever since. "You're going to kill him, of course."

Diran was shocked by how casually Makala spoke these words. "I intend to stop him from using the psi-forge for his own purposes."

Makala smiled, fully displaying her incisors, and she reached up to touch Diran's cheek with fingers cold as ice. "I understand that you follow a different path now, but surely even one of the Purified knows that you can't allow a beast like Cathmore to live. He may be human, Diran, but he's just as evil as any of the undead creatures that you've destroyed."

"And more so than some," he acknowledged, "but I'm not an assassin anymore, Makala. I kill only when I have no other choice."

Makala's smile widened a fraction more than seemed humanly possible. "That makes two of us."

A chill that had nothing to do with the cold late-autumn air skittered down Diran's spine.

"Where is Cathmore?" Makala asked.

"I believe he's taken possession of a hidden creation-forge facility somewhere in the Hoarfrost Mountains. Probably not too far from here, as he sends his orc servant into Perhata for supplies from time to time. Tresslar is working on restoring the warforged to consciousness so that we can question him and learn Cathmore's exact location."

"What if Tresslar doesn't succeed?"

Diran shrugged. "Asenka is confident Baron Mahir will give us the resources to track down Cathmore if we should need them."

Makala's smile vanished. "Asenka is quite a woman, isn't she? Strong, confident, beautiful . . ."

Makala's voice contained a hint of a growl, and Diran was suddenly uncomfortable. "She's an effective commander."

Makala leaned in close until all Diran could see was her crimson eyes.

"She wants you, Diran, and you her. Don't deny it."

Diran wanted to open his mouth to do that very thing, but he couldn't. His mind felt muzzy, as if it were wrapped in thick cotton, and his thoughts flowed sluggishly, like half-frozen tree sap.

"She's not good enough for you. You should just keep your relationship professional. In fact, it would be better if you didn't have anything to do with her at all."

Yes. Why hadn't he realized that before? It was so clear . . . Asenka was nothing compared to Makala. Nothing at all.

Diran reached for Makala, intending to take her in his arms, but then she smiled, revealing her fangs once more. Diran understood then what was happening, and he closed his eyes to shut out the crimson light shining in Makala's gaze. He took a step backward and turned away from her before allowing himself to open his eyes.

"Don't ever do that again," he said, still avoiding her gaze.

Makala said nothing for a moment, then she spoke as if nothing had happened between them just now. "If Tresslar fails to awaken Solus, you'll need another way to find Cathmore. If you don't mind, I think I'll conduct a search of my own."

An instant later, Diran felt a breeze and heard the sound of leathery wings beating the air. He looked up to see a large bat winging away from the lagoon, heading westward toward the Hoarfrost Mountains. He stood watching it for a long time.

CHAPTER

TWENTY

Darkness . . .

Soothing, silent.

No voices, no confusion.

For the first time since he had been brought into existence, Solus knew peace. Wherever or whatever this placeless place was, he had no intention of ever leaving.

Light stabbed into his eyes.

He tried to close them and shut the light out, but warforged eyes didn't function the same way that other creatures' did, and he had no choice but to allow the light in.

"Mfixzumedl . . . hear me?"

Solus swiveled his head in the direction of the voice and found himself looking at the blurry outline of a face. Male from the voice, and human, he guessed, though his vision was still too fuzzy to tell for certain.

"Yes, but I can't see you clearly."

"Your vision should be fine in a few moments," the man said, and then added, "I think."

Solus didn't find that particularly reassuring, but he saw no reason to make mention of it. Either his eyes would work efficiently or they wouldn't. "Where am I? Who are you?"

Another voice answered, this one also male but higher-pitched, as if it belonged to a child. "You're lying atop a table in the common room of the Sea Scorpions' barracks. We brought you here after your head exploded."

The voice came from his left, so Solus turned his head in that direction. This man was shorter than the other, and though the psi-forged's vision was no clearer than it had been a moment ago, he thought he recognized this man, not from his blurry features, but rather from his aura. A name came to the forefront of Solus's mind, and he spoke it aloud.

"Hinto."

The small blurry face broke into a grin. "That's right! How are you feeling?"

"I . . ." Solus didn't possess the facial muscles to frown, but if he had, he would've done so now. "The voices . . . I don't hear them."

The owner of the first voice spoke. "Voices?"

"When I was born, I absorbed the minds of my makers. Their voices have been with me ever since, sometimes as soft murmurs in the background of my thoughts, sometimes as deafening shouts. They are still present . . . I can *feel* their memories, but I no longer hear them speak."

"While I was repairing you, I detected an odd imbalance in your energy matrices. I suppose it was caused by these voices of yours. At any rate, I realigned your matrices, so they shouldn't give you any more problems."

"You mean just like his eyes?" Hinto said.

"I never claimed to be an expert on warforged! I was working primarily on instinct and intuition. To be honest, I'm surprised he's functional at all."

Hinto reached out and patted Solus's hand. "Don't mind Tresslar. He gets grouchy sometimes." The small man lowered his voice. "It's because he's old."

"Not so old that I didn't hear that!" Tresslar snapped.

Solus decided to try sitting up. His body moved sluggishly, as if reluctant to cooperate, but he managed the simple maneuver then turned to Tresslar.

"I appreciate your efforts. Thank you."

Solus couldn't see the expression on the man's face, but he could sense his irritation subsiding. "You're welcome. I can have another look at your eyes, if you like."

"That's not necessary." While his psionic abilities couldn't replace vision, in some ways they allowed him to "see" the world with more clarity and accuracy than mere eyes could ever provide. "You say my head exploded?" Solus reached up and touched his forehead. He found the area smooth and unbroken.

"It was the people you were with," Hinto said. "You turned to look at them right before the green crystal on your forehead blew up. I think they did something to make it happen."

"There were three men," Tresslar said, "a human, a kalashtar, and an orc. I believe the kalashtar controlled you through the green crystal and then detonated it when you broke free of his influence. Don't you remember?"

Solus concentrated. He could sense the memories of his four makers waiting for him to draw upon them if he chose, but his own memories—those that he had made since stepping forth from the creation forge—were hazy and jumbled.

"I recall bits and pieces . . . scraps of memory that make little sense."

"It's possible your memories became scattered, for lack of a better word, when I realigned your energy matrices," Tresslar said. "They may return in time, but then again, they may be lost forever. I don't know."

"Well, if your memories are gone, you'll just have to make new ones, won't you?" Hinto said.

Solus felt waves of cheer and good will emanating from the small man. His was a simple soul, but all the stronger for it. Solus didn't possess the physiognomy to smile, but he reflected the feeling of good will as he replied.

"I suppose so."

* * * ● * * *

Ghaji and Asenka were sparring in the barracks' central courtyard while Yvka cheered them on. Diran had yet to return from his trip to release Makala from the obsidian sarcophagus, and Ghaji was trying not to worry about his friend. The sun had set over an hour ago, and the stars glittered in the night sky like chips of ice. A series of glass globes set atop metal poles lit the courtyard, but while the minor fire elementals trapped inside the globes provided heat as well as light, Ghaji and Asenka's breath still misted the air as they fought. The illumination was more for Asenka's benefit than Ghaji's, and it was actually something of a detriment to him, given his night vision. Ghaji's preferred weapon was an axe, but he was proficient with any number of weapons. He wielded a longsword now to match Asenka. Ghaji was impressed by how well the woman handled herself, but then she had to be good to command a baron's warrior fleet, he supposed, even in a backwater city like Perhata.

Asenka closed and brought her sword around in a sweeping arc toward Ghaji's left. He blocked the blow easily and wondered if he'd been mistaken in his earlier assessment of her, but then Asenka, moving faster than Ghaji thought possible for a human, spun in the opposite direction and slammed her sword blade into his right side. His breastplate took the worst of the strike, but the impact still knocked the breath out of him.

Yvka laughed and clapped her hands. "That's another point for Asenka! It's now two to five. Be careful, lover—she's catching up!"

Ghaji had no breath to spare for a witty reply, which was fortunate since he also didn't have time to think of one. Asenka pressed her attack, coming at him with a series of rapid strikes that took all his concentration to deflect. He knew he could use his strength to overpower her if he wished, but at the outset they'd agreed that this would be a match of skill against skill. Five years ago, Ghaji would've won, but now . . . Half-orcs tended to have shorter life-spans than humans, though it varied from one individual to another. Ghaji was still in his thirties, but even so, he wondered if he was starting to get old.

Ghaji was spared from losing another point to Asenka when the barracks' door opened and Tresslar, Hinto, and the warforged stepped into the courtyard. The halfling held the construct's hand—or more accurately, one of his thick fingers—and it appeared the little pirate was leading him. Ghaji caught Tresslar's eye, and the artificer nodded to indicate all was well. Ghaji didn't allow himself to relax fully though—not after all the trouble the warforged had given them on the dock.

Cautiously, Ghaji, Asenka, and Yvka approached the construct. Yvka had been holding Ghaji's elemental axe for him, and now she gave him the axe in exchange for the longsword. Yvka appeared petite and delicate, but she was an elf and thus stronger than she looked—as Ghaji could attest from some of their more . . . *enthusiastic* encounters. She would be able to wield the sword without difficulty should the need arise.

The two groups met in the middle of the courtyard.

"It looks as if you've worked another miracle, Tresslar," Yvka said. "Congratulations." She openly admired Solus, and Ghaji knew she was calculating the construct's worth to her masters in the Shadow Network.

"Nothing that any other exceptionally brilliant master artificer couldn't do," Tresslar said.

Ghaji couldn't tell whether the old man was joking or not. "Whatever you did, I hope it purged our new friend of his homicidal tendencies."

"You have no need to fear me," Solus said in the eerie hollow voice that all warforged possessed.

"Of course not," Asenka said. "Why should we fear a being that's capable of hurling us all about like rag dolls simply by thinking about it?"

"Don't give him any ideas," Ghaji muttered.

"Solus is our friend now," Hinto said. "He's going to help us find Cathmore and the others."

"He's going to *try*," Tresslar amended. "The explosion that halted his attack also damaged his memories."

"I shall do my best to aid you," Solus said. "I have looked into Hinto's mind, and I have seen what Cathmore and his companions made me do. They are evil men and must be stopped." The construct looked down at the halfling who still had hold of one of his fingers. "Right?"

Hinto smiled as he gazed up at the warforged like a child looking at a beloved adult. "Exactly right, my friend."

Ghaji looked at Yvka and raised an eyebrow. It seemed Solus was following Hinto's lead in more ways than one.

"As soon as Diran returns, we can make plans for our departure," Ghaji said.

"He is already here," Solus said. "He's been watching us from the shadows all this time, waiting to see if I am still a threat."

The warforged pointed to the far end of the courtyard where the illumination of the light globes didn't quite reach, and everyone turned to look. At first nothing happened, but then a piece of the darkness broke free and came striding forward.

"I regret our last encounter, priest," Solus said as Diran joined them. "I hope you will forgive me."

Diran smiled. "I've had a great deal of practice at forgiving. I think I can manage to do it one more time."

"I hate it when you sneak around like that," Ghaji said. "At least now there's one of us you can't hide from."

Diran's smile fell away and his expression became grim. "Let us hope Cathmore has no more success hiding from our new friend than I did."

* * * * * * *

The night was more than halfway gone by the time Skarm entered his mistress's lair. His burns were almost entirely healed, thanks to a lone streetwalker in Perhata who'd reluctantly donated her life to fuel the barghest's healing. Unfortunately, dealing with his injuries had used up all the life energy he'd stolen, and Skarm was hungry once more. As he padded along the tunnel to Nathifa's chamber in wolf form, he kept alert for any vermin that might make a quick snack, but aside from himself, the tunnel was empty. Even rats and lizards were afraid to enter into the presence of his dread mistress, it seemed.

Skarm wasn't surprised to find Nathifa sitting at her table, gazing into the empty eye sockets of her obsidian skull. The lich didn't turn around or in any way acknowledge his return, but he knew she was aware of him nevertheless. He shifted to goblin form so that he could converse with her. But before he could say anything, Nathifa spoke.

"You have failed to obtain the Amahau."

Her tone was cold, utterly devoid of emotion, and that frightened Skarm far more than if she'd been angry. He knew it would do him no good to make excuses, but he couldn't help himself.

"I tried . . . several times, but I encountered . . . difficulties."
He hated hearing the wheedling sound of his own voice.

"I know all about your so-called difficulties. Espial has kept
me informed of your progress, or rather, your lack thereof."
Nathifa stroked the black skull's smooth round dome with slow,
gentle motions of her bone-white hand, as if the object were a
beloved child . . . or perhaps a lover.

Nathifa didn't take her gaze off Espial, and Skarm wasn't
sure whether or not to be grateful. When his mistress got like
this, she was difficult to read. He had no idea whether he was
going to be punished for his failures, or if she were so caught
up in communing with whatever spirit inhabited the obsidian
skull that she was going to ignore them. To be on the safe side,
he decided to keep talking.

"I know where the priest and his companions are going. They
travel to Mount Luster to confront those who have taken up resi-
dence there. The leader of the Mount Luster group is an old enemy
of the priest's named Aldarik Cathmore. The priest intends to
confront Cathmore, and his companions—including the artificer
who carries the Amahau—travel with him. I thought—"

"—that you could make another attempt to snatch the
Amahau while both groups are distracted by battle," Nathifa
finished. "I know. Espial has told me this as well."

Skarm scowled at the black skull. He'd never felt comfortable around the mystical object, and he certainly didn't like it
giving away his plans before he had a chance to propose them to
Nathifa himself, but Skarm's irritation was swept away by his
mistress's next words.

"It is a good plan, Skarm. Espial approves."

Skarm looked at the skull with newfound appreciation. Perhaps he would have to reconsider his feelings toward the thing.

"There's more going on here than we've realized, Skarm.
It's as if we were part a grand tapestry—all of us: you and I,

the priest and his companions, Cathmore and his allies . . ." Nathifa's voice held a dreamy lilt to it, as if she were under some sort of enchantment. "We are threads being brought together by a master weaver, one overlapping the other, about to be drawn tight to become the warp and woof of an ingenious design."

Nathifa rose from her chair and glided silently across the floor toward Skarm. It appeared even the endorsement of his mistress's vaunted magic skull wasn't enough to spare him from the lich's wrath. The barghest raised his arms to shield himself from the blow that was sure to come, but Nathifa moved past him and continued to the tunnel entrance.

"Don't just stand there. We have work to do."

Skarm lowered his arms and gazed at his mistress's retreating back in confusion. Since entering into Nathifa's service, Skarm had never known the lich to leave her lair, but unless he misunderstood, she intended to accompany him to Mount Luster. Nathifa disappeared into the tunnel, and a moment later she shouted Skarm's name.

The barghest shifted into wolf form and hurried to catch up to his dark mistress.

●　●　●　◉　●　●　●

Makala had been flying in bat form for hours. Had she been a natural creature, she would have become weary long ago, but weariness was for mortals. Of course, hunger was also a mortal sensation, and being undead did not spare her from it. It had been more than a day since last she had fed—she felt a pang of guilt for poor dead Eneas—and while her strength and endurance hadn't diminished appreciably in that time, the emptiness gnawing at the core of her being was becoming increasingly difficult to ignore. She could feel her tenuous control over the Hunger beginning to slip, and she knew that if she postponed feeding too long, the Hunger would take control of her. If that happened, she would become a wild creature, an animal concerned only with satisfying the basest of desires.

She pushed such concerns from her mind. Thinking of the Hunger would only make it stronger. Like Diran she had once been an assassin in the Brotherhood of the Blade, and like all in the Brotherhood, she had played host to a dark spirit implanted within her in order to blunt her natural human empathy and make her a cold and utterly dispassionate killer. She had been freed of her dark spirit some time ago, but she remembered what it was like to co-exist with evil. That experience helped her live with the Hunger without giving herself over to it, and she would have to rely on that experience once again this night.

Besides, she would feed once she found Cathmore . . . and then when she was finished, she would leave his desiccated corpse for the mountain scavengers to feed upon, and there would be a little less evil in the world.

Makala continued flying through the night air, allowing her senses to guide her rather than consciously choosing her direction. She could detect the scent of blood over great distances, whether it had been spilled or was still contained within a living body. She'd already sniffed out a band of elven hunters as well as a small enclave of kobolds who made their home in the mountains. Both times she'd been tempted to stop and feed a little to tide her over until she found Cathmore, but she'd resisted. She preferred to save her appetite for the main course.

She had other senses than smell to rely on, however. Her hearing was so sharp that she could pick up the soft whisper of blood as it pulsed through living veins, and she could feel the warmth radiating from a living body as if it were a miniature sun. If Cathmore was anywhere within these mountains, she'd find him.

She flew on, preternatural senses searching, searching . . .

As she flew, she tried to imagine the taste of Cathmore's blood as it filled her mouth and ran down her throat.

＊ ＊ ＊ ⊕ ＊ ＊ ＊

Like most orcs and half-orcs, Ghaji wasn't fond of horses—unless they were on a plate. That was all right, though, since by and large the beasts didn't care for him either. As much he disliked the smelly nags, he'd rather be sitting on the back of the most odiferous, foul-tempered horse than the so-called steed he currently rode: a nine-foot tall bird with long, powerfully muscled legs and tiny useless wings. The creature was called a stone-stepper because of its ability to gracefully navigate the rough terrain here in the foothills of the Hoarfrost Mountains, but Ghaji thought a better name would've been ass-breaker because of how uncomfortable it was to ride the monstrous avian. Asenka had supplied the mounts for them. The Sea Scorpions served as Baron Mahir's elite warriors on both sea *and* land, and when they needed to negotiate the mountainous terrain to the west of the city, they relied on the giant birds. According to Asenka, in the wild the creatures were fearsome predators and had phenomenal eyesight, during both the day and the night.

"Enjoying the ride, love?"

Yvka rode behind Ghaji, her arms wrapped around the half-orc's waist. Ghaji held tight to the stone-stepper's reins, though he knew he didn't have any real control over the creature. Luckily, the giant birds seemed content to move as a flock—or herd, or whatever—so he didn't have to do much more than hold on, which was hard enough given the stone-stepper's swiftly lurching gait.

"I've taken sword-thrusts to the gut that I've enjoyed more."

Yvka laughed and snuggled against his back. "At least it's cozy."

"That's the only good thing about it," Ghaji grumbled.

They traveled in a group of four stone-steppers. Diran and Asenka rode the lead bird, then came Hinto and Solus, then Tresslar who rode alone, and Ghaji and Yvka brought up the rear on their mount. All of them were dressed warmly against the cold night air—all save Solus, of course. Warforged needed no protection against temperature extremes. The stone-steppers' saddles were designed to carry two riders per bird, and the stone-steppers were both large enough and strong enough to carry a pair of riders with ease. Ghaji would've preferred to ride in a group formation rather than single file for better security, but Asenka had said that the birds wouldn't travel any other way. As the kidney-jarring journey wore on, Ghaji had to admit that single file worked best while navigating the uneven, craggy ground and squeezing through narrow mountain passes.

"I hope Solus knows where he's going," Ghaji said. "I'm not convinced Tresslar put the pieces of the warforged's head back together in the right order."

"Solus has done well enough so far," Yvka said.

The warforged had been calling out directions to Diran ever since they'd left Perhata, and though the construct occasionally seemed unsure which way to go, most of the time he spoke with confidence.

"Do you really think Solus can track the kalashtar's 'psychic trail,' whatever that means?"

"I'm no expert," Yvka said, "but I've seen psionic crystals before, and Solus is covered with them. They alone make him a very valuable piece of property." As if realizing she'd misspoken, the elf woman hurried to add, "I mean the crystals themselves are worth quite a bit. There would be no purpose to building a warforged with such crystals if he couldn't use them."

"I suppose," Ghaji said, "but possessing a tool is not the same as being skilled in its use."

Yvka didn't reply, and Ghaji didn't know if that meant she agreed or disagreed with him or simply didn't have anything to add. They continued to ride in silence, and Ghaji found himself remembering a conversation he and Diran had had while the Sea Scorpions' groom was getting the stone-steppers saddled.

"Do you trust this warforged?" Ghaji had asked. "He did almost kill you."

"Yes," Diran replied. "Solus managed to fight off the kalashtar's control and restrain himself. He showed mercy."

"Maybe, but what if Cathmore planned for Solus to fail? Maybe the old bastard knew Solus wouldn't kill you, and he only intended for the attack to lure you into coming after him." Ghaji thought of his encounter with Chagai, and how the orc mercenary had avoided engaging him in fight to the finish. "Lure the two of us. We could be riding into a trap."

Diran smiled. "What else is new?"

The seven companions rode on, the only sounds the scrabbling of clawed avian feet on rock, the creaking of leather saddles, and the strangely soothing trill the giant birds made as they traveled.

The stone-steppers' group song, along with the heat given off by their mount's feathered body, had almost lulled Ghaji to sleep when Solus called out, "There!"

Ghaji's eyes flew open, and he looked to see the psi-forged pointing toward a small mountain that rose like a black shadow against the night sky.

Asenka called out a command in a language Ghaji didn't recognize, and the stone-stepper she and Diran rode came to a halt. Though she gave no other command, the rest of the birds also stopped.

266

"It's called Mount Luster," Solus said, his normally emotionless voice tinged with excitement. "That's where I was created, and that's where we shall find Cathmore and the others." The psi-forged paused, and when he spoke again, his tone was almost apologetic. "At least . . . I think so."

Diran looked to the others. "Well? Do we give it a try?"

"Let's go," Ghaji said. "The sooner we get there, the sooner I can get off this damned bony-backed chicken."

CHAPTER

TWENTY-ONE

Galharath stood within the mouth of the psi-forge, his back to the table where Solus had been born, his hands grasping a pair of crystalline rings that hung in the air over his head. To the uninitiated, it would've appeared as if the kalashtar was simply holding the rings, but in truth they were bound to the invisible psionic energies surging through the forge, and if Galharath let go of them, the rings would continue to hold their position, as if held aloft by magic, but the power the rings allowed Galharath to tap into was far greater than any mere thaumaturgy; it was the full, unfettered strength of his own mind, made all the stronger by its connection to the psi-forge. The forge was powered by vast geothermal energies surging beneath Mount Luster, and now Galharath could draw upon that power too.

The sensations were beyond anything the kalashtar had ever experienced before. He felt intimately connected to all of creation while at the same time feeling as if he didn't exist. He knew pleasure beyond conception along with agony so intense there were no words for it. He was All, he was Nothing, he was *Everything*.

This must be what it feels like to be a god, he thought.

With the merest fraction of his awareness, he detected the presence of living beings approaching Mount Luster. The aura of one of these beings far outshone the others, like a blazing bonfire burning in the blackest of nights, and Galharath knew it was Solus.

"They're here," the kalashtar said, his voice a dreamy sing-song, as if he were halfway between sleep and wakefulness.

Cathmore stood outside the psi-forge's entrance, Chagai at his side. The old man rubbed his claw hands together with undisguised glee upon hearing Galharath's news.

"Excellent! Is everything in readiness?"

Galharath was barely aware at first of the old man's question.

Cathmore repeated Galharath's name more sharply, and the psionic artificer reluctantly allowed himself to recall the old man's existence.

"The psi-forge has been fully reconfigured into its defense mode. The inner walls of the facility have been shielded so that the psionic energies cannot be detected from outside. Solus will not be able to warn the others until it's too late. You may take up your positions now. I'll do the rest."

Chagai growled. "Who are *you* to be giving *us* orders, kalashtar?"

Galharath turned to look at Chagai. Through the orc's eyes, Galharath could see that his own eyes blazed with white light. He was pleased to see that the effect was quite intimidating.

Chagai stomped off to the corner of the chamber that had been assigned to him. Cathmore, however, lingered a moment.

"Be wary, Galharath," the elderly assassin said. "For most of my life, I have shared my body with my dark spirit. I know how difficult it can be to keep from becoming subsumed by power and losing one's individual identity. Make certain that it is you who controls the forge's energy, not the other way around."

With that, the old man hobbled off in the opposite direction from Chagai. Normally, Galharath would've been irritated by Cathmore's suggestion that he wasn't strong or skilled enough to maintain contol of the psi-forge, but the kalashtar was beyond such petty emotions now. Such things were a limitation of the flesh, and here, within the forge, he was pure intellect. All there was to do now was to enjoy this blissful state and wait for Diran Bastiaan and his companions to arrive, and once they had been dealt with, perhaps Galharath would take care of Cathmore and Chagai as well.

Galharath smiled, his teeth glowing from the psionic energy that surged like molten liquid through his body.

❧ ❧ ❧ ❧ ❧ ❧ ❧

The power roiling within the psi-forge cast flickering light throughout the cavernous chamber deep within the heart of Mount Luster. Despite the fitful illumination, none of the three present—not Cathmore, Chagai, or even Galharath—noticed a pool of thick shadow against one wall . . . shadow the light could not touch.

Skarm, in barghest form, huddled next to his mistress. He wished he could hide behind her, but he knew such a sign of cowardice would only incur her wrath, so he had to settle for crouching as close to her as she would allow. He understood that Nathifa's spell allowed them to see through the cloak of shadow she'd erected to conceal them, but Skarm still felt exposed. He wasn't afraid of the orc nor of the kalashtar who controlled the power of the strange creation forge. No, Skarm was afraid of the old man wrapped in the bearskin cloak who shivered as if he stood upon an open ice-field. The barghest, a creature of evil itself, could sense the foulness that dwelt within the old man, and it was a darkness to rival that of Nathifa herself.

Skarm started when Nathifa reached down with one of her skeletal hands and scratched the top of his half-goblin, half-lupine head.

"Patience, Skarm," the lich said in her sepulchral voice. "It won't be long now."

● ● ● ◉ ● ● ●

Makala swooped down to the mountain to confirm what she'd already sensed: Diran and the others had reached Cathmore's lair before her. They had left their mounts—some manner of giant flightless birds—tethered to stakes at the mountain's base and were making their way up single file along a winding trail.

Makala felt a very human wave of irritation. After leaving Diran at the lagoon and searching for half the night, she hadn't gotten here any faster than he had. She also felt a wave of shame at the thought of what she had attempted to do to him at the lagoon. She hadn't planned on using her mesmeric abilities to force Diran to forsake Asenka. It had just happened, and now there he was, and more to the point, there *she* was, walking right behind him. Shame instantly transformed into jealously, and the vampiress found herself dipping lower toward the party. It would be so easy to swoop down and snatch hold of Asenka's hair with her clawed feet, yanking the bitch off-balance and sending her tumbling down the mountainside. By the time Diran could reach her, she would be dead and broken, beyond healing.

As Makala drew closer, she saw that Diran and the rest had stopped walking and huddled together against the cold, watching Yvka. The elf woman knelt before the stone wall and ran her hands across its rocky surface. Everyone was distracted, including Asenka. Makala folded her wings and dove toward the woman, imagining the sound of her screams as she careened down the mountainside, but at the last instant, Makala swerved away and angled upward, wings beating furiously. She didn't look back, but she had the feeling that Diran was watching her, and worse, that he sensed what she'd been about to do.

As she rose toward the mountaintop, she debated winging eastward and returning to the lagoon where the *Zephyr* was anchored. She feared she couldn't maintain control over her more savage instincts—not where her feelings for Diran were concerned, at any rate—and she worried she might prove more of a hindrance than a help to him. While the night still had some hours left to it, she needed to be safely sealed in her resting place before the first rays of dawn touched the sky. She could always find temporary shelter here in the mountains. After all, there were numerous caves where she could spend the day in bat form if she wished, but she was reluctant to abandon the obsidian sarcophagus as it was her only way to safely travel across the sea.

In the end, her decision came down to one simple fact: she couldn't leave Diran to face Cathmore alone.

She'd been circling close to the peak of Mount Luster as she debated what to do, and she now saw what looked like seams carved into the mountain's stone surface. Curious, she flew down toward them, landed, and clung to the rock in bat form. Upon closer inspection, she realized that she'd found a set of shutters that had been disguised to appear as rock. This was a door or window of some kind, perhaps opening onto to a look-out station of some sort. She'd found her way inside.

Makala transformed into mist and curled through the seam and into Mount Luster.

● ● ● ◉ ● ● ●

"This is it . . . the place where we came out."

Solus pointed at a portion of the mountain that looked no different than any of the surrounding rock. Wind rushed across the face of Mount Luster, cold and biting. Diran's facial muscles were numb, but he didn't care. He did, however, keep his hands inside his fur cloak so they'd remain limber. He had a feeling he'd be throwing a few daggers before long.

"Are you sure?" Hinto asked. The halfling had ridden up the mountain trail atop the psi-forged's shoulders like a small child, and now Solus reached up, gently lifted the little pirate, and set him on the ground.

"I . . ." Solus's tone was uncertain at first, but then his voice became firmer. "Yes, I am."

Diran exchanged glances with Ghaji, and the priest knew his friend was thinking the same thing: if this was a trap, they were about to spring it.

"Let me take a look," Tresslar said. "The entrance—assuming one is here—is obviously hidden and likely warded as well." The artificer pulled the dragonwand from his belt and held it out before him. He waved it through the air in a slow figure eight once, then reversed direction and did it again. There was no outside sign of magic at work, but when Tresslar lowered his dragonwand, he said, "There's an entrance here all right, a good-sized one, too. This is probably where they brought supplies and materials in. It's well warded, as you might imagine. Whoever was responsible for the spellwork did a good job . . . worthy of the artificers on Dreadhold."

Diran's lips were too cold to form a smile. "High praise coming from you."

Tresslar scowled at the priest. "I said good, not great. I'll get us in."

The artificer stepped toward the craggy stone and touched the tip of his dragonwand to its surface. The red gems that formed the dragonhead's eyes burned with crimson light, and the stone surrounding the snout began to glow with pulsing green energy.

"What's happening?" Asenka whispered in Diran's ear.

Diran tried to ignore how good the warmth of her breath felt against his flesh. "Tresslar is using his dragonwand to absorb the magic of the wards on the entrance, nullifying them."

"And he's done," Tresslar pronounced. The artificer stepped back, and the crimson glow in the dragonhead's eyes quickly faded. "All we have to do now is figure out the mechanism to open the door. It's not magical, that much I know."

"Let me have a look," Yvka said. "After all, you're not the only one who knows a thing or two about hidden entrances."

As an operative of the Shadow Network, she'd had to find her way into any number of places where intruders weren't wanted, Diran imagined. He'd undergone similar training in the Brotherhood of the Blade. If Yvka wasn't successful, he'd take a look.

Diran sensed movement off to his right, and he looked up in time to see a shadowy shape swoop upward, gaining altitude as it soared away. His hands emerged from the folds of his cloak holding daggers made of silver, but he didn't hurl the blades at the retreating dark shape.

"Looks like your friend has decided to join us," Asenka said. She too gazed up into the night sky, watching the bat as it flew toward the summit of Mount Luster.

"I'm sure she was just letting us know she's here," Diran said.

"Right," Asenka said, "which is why she nearly hit me . . . and why you have a pair of daggers in your hands."

Diran didn't respond. He couldn't.

"Found it!" Yvka said.

Diran was grateful for the interruption. He turned with the others to look at Yvka. The elf woman pressed her palm against a part of the wall that looked no different than any other, but there was a soft click and a stone lever slid out of the rock next to Yvka's hand. She took hold of the lever and pulled downward. There was a second click, the wall shuddered, a grinding sound filled the air, and a large section of stone began to rise before them. They were in!

"Wait!" Solus cried out. "Something is wrong! I sense great power . . . the stone masked it from me, but now that the door is opening, I can feel it! Psionic energy, far stronger than anything I've ever known. We have to—"

Galharath reached out, took hold of their minds, and they were lost.

● ● ● ◉ ● ● ●

Diran found himself standing in a chamber that he hadn't seen for decades, though it felt as if he'd been here only yesterday. Long room, high ceiling, wooden floors, empty save for a large mahogany chest with double doors . . . He was back at Emon Gorsedd's academy, inside the Proving Room.

"Welcome home, Diran."

Though he'd been alone an instant before, Aldarik Cathmore now stood before Diran. The man appeared just as Diran remembered him: lean, handsome, looking like he was in his late thirties. Cathmore wore the same outfit he always did for sessions in the Proving Room—long-sleeved light brown shirt, tan pants and boots.

Diran didn't know what magic was at work here, and he didn't care. He reached for a pair of daggers sheathed at his belt, but his hands brushed only soft cloth. He looked down and saw that he wore the gray tunic of a new student at the academy. He felt around for his cloak and found he wasn't wearing it. No belt sheaths and no cloak meant no daggers. He was unarmed.

Cathmore smiled. "Missing something?"

Diran realized then that he wasn't just dressed as a student; his body was that of a much younger man . . . a boy. Though he retained his adult memories, his physical form had regressed to the age he'd been when he'd first entered the academy, or at least, it *seemed* that way. Diran remembered Solus's warning as the entrance to Mount Luster started to open. *I can feel it! Psionic energy, far stronger than anything I've ever known!* Somehow the kalashtar working with Cathmore had to be responsible for this.

"This isn't real," Diran said.

"That depends entirely on one's definition of reality," Cathmore countered. "You are real, I am real, and the power that gives shape to all this—" the master assassin gestured at the room surrounding them—"is real. If you die here, I'm afraid that will be real, too."

"That's a two-edged sword, isn't it? If I can die here, then so can you."

Cathmore laughed. "Your mind is as sharp as I remember, Diran. I'm tempted to offer you a chance to join me. Together, the two of us could destroy my half-brother and his vaunted Brotherhood. Then by using the power of this facility, we could create an army of psi-forged even stronger than Solus—mindslayers who would obey our every command. We could establish our own Brotherhood, one far more powerful than anything Emon could ever dream of!" Cathmore paused then sighed. "But I won't bother. I know the spineless followers of the Silver Flame have warped your mind with their foolish beliefs. Everything we taught you, Emon and I . . . wasted." He shook his head. "It's enough to make me weep."

"Where are my friends?" Diran demanded.

"Oh, they're around, but you shouldn't worry about them. You have problems enough of your own to deal with. Do you remember our first session here?"

"How could I forget? I only wish I'd been smart enough to slit your throat instead of hitting you in the shoulder with that dagger."

Cathmore's eyes glittered with cold anger. "Indeed, and if you'll recall, there was a third party present."

Cathmore did nothing that Diran could see, but now there was a body lying on the floor nearby. Male, naked, bronze-skinned, concentric tattoo on the top of his bald head, a droopy black mustache on his lip. The man's eyes were swollen and black-tinged, as were his lips. Diran recognized Bruk: one of the raiders responsible for killing his parents, and the man he'd poisoned in the Proving Room so many years ago.

Diran whispered the raider's name, and as if the word were a signal of some sort, the dead raider's eyes snapped open. The eyes were white and filmy, with no sign of iris or pupil. Bruk's swollen lips parted in a grotesque parody of a smile, revealing discolored teeth that were sharper than they should've been. Moving with slow, spastic motions, Bruk maneuvered himself into a sitting position and then rose to his feet.

Diran reached for his silver arrowhead charm, but it was gone, along with his daggers. No matter. The arrowhead was merely a symbol. The true power came from the Silver Flame itself. Diran raised his hand and opened his mind and soul. Silver flame ignited in the palm of his hand to form a blazing arrowhead shape. Argent light washed over the undead creature that had been Bruk, but instead of being repelled, the raider simply stood and grinned at Diran.

Diran allowed the silver light he held to dim and wink out.

"*I* make the rules here," Cathmore said. "Your parlor tricks will have no effect unless I say they do." He turned to the undead raider. "Now I believe Bruk has a score he'd like to settle with you."

Still grinning, the zombie reached out with hands that looked more like animal claws and started toward Diran.

❋ ❋ ❋ ❋ ❋ ❋ ❋

It was still night, but it was no longer cold, and the rocky terrain of Mount Luster had been replaced by grass and trees. Ghaji looked around, confused.

"Where am I?" he said.

"You mean, where are *we*."

He turned to see Yvka standing by his side, which was odd because he could've sworn she hadn't been there an instant ago. Nevertheless, he was relieved to see her.

"Weren't we about to enter the mountain?" he asked. "What happened to everyone else?"

"I think we *are* inside Mount Luster," Yvka said. "We just can't see it. We're trapped inside some kind of illusion. The others are probably here too, but we can't see them because whatever is causing this illusion won't let us." She reached up and stroked his left cheek. "You look younger, too. There's no gray in your hair."

Ghaji ignored her comment about his hair. An illusion? Everything seemed so real—the cool breeze, the birds' nightsongs, the rustling of leaves . . . And if he were truly his younger self, why did he still carry his elemental axe? "Do you think Solus went crazy again?"

Yvka shook her head. "I doubt it. It's more likely this is Cathmore's doing . . . or rather the kalashtar he's working with."

Ghaji frowned. "Something just occurred to me. If everything around us is an illusion, how do I know that you're real? How do you know I am?"

Yvka smiled, stepped forward, and kissed him long and

slow. When she stepped back, Ghaji grinned. "All right, you're real. So . . . how do we get break free of the illusion?"

Yvka shrugged. "I don't know. I've had occasion to use certain devices during my career that can create illusions, but never anything like on this scale. I wouldn't know where to begin. Too bad Tresslar isn't here."

Ghaji felt that there was a reason the artificer—or any of their other companions—wasn't present, though he couldn't quite put his finger on it. There was something familiar about this place . . . and then it hit him.

"I've been here before! During my early days in the Last War, I served with a mercenary group led by Chagai. This valley was the site of the last raid I went on with them before I left the group."

"Before you betrayed us with your weakness, you mean."

Ghaji and Yvka spun around to see Chagai standing several yards away—not Chagai as he was now, but rather as he had been when Ghaji had served under him: younger, stronger, in his prime. Ghaji was certain the orc warrior hadn't been present before, and neither had the cottage that the mercenary leader stood in front of. It was a cottage that Ghaji had visited only once but had seen many times since in his dreams.

"I see you brought a friend with you," Chagai said, "and she's an elf." The orc wrinkled his noise in disgust. "Is she your woman, Ghaji? I can smell her stink on you."

Ghaji snarled and drew his elemental axe. He willed the weapon's flame to activate, but nothing happened.

Chagai grinned, displaying a mouthful of sharp orc teeth. "You're not in control here, Ghaji. I am. You participated in the raid on the shifter's cottage, but your heart wasn't in it. You're a coward and a weakling, Ghaji, a halfbreed ruined by the taint of human blood running through your veins. You never should have been born, and that's a mistake I intend to rectify now."

The cottage door burst open and a male shifter stepped outside, features transformed into his full bestial aspect. The man's eyes were completely white, his forehead split open. Blood from the ghastly wound trickled down the sides of his face, and Ghaji remembered that it had been he who dealt that killing wound so long ago. This was Ruelo, the wood-wright the orcs had been sent to kill, and whose entire family they had slaughtered.

As Ruelo's animated corpse came charging toward Ghaji and Yvka, three other figures emerged from the cottage, and Ghaji knew the wood-wright wasn't the only shifter looking for revenge.

❋ ❋ ❋ ❋ ❋ ❋ ❋

As soon as the sensation of vertigo hit him, Tresslar understood what was happening. Of course, Solus's warning helped, too. They were being subjected to a psionic assault of some sort, and while Tresslar was hardly a psionicist, he knew enough to attempt to mount a defense against such an attack—*and* he still had hold of the dragonwand. It all came down to speed now. If he could cast a spell before the psionic attack fully took hold of his mind . . .

The momentary dizziness passed, and Tresslar found himself standing within a cavern before the dead body of a large green dragon.

"Damn," the artificer muttered.

He'd been too slow. He looked down at his hand and saw that it was empty, and more startlingly, that it had become the hand of a far younger man, one in his early twenties. It seemed that not only did he find himself inhabiting a memory, he was—outwardly at least—the same age he'd been then. He knew he was still a man in his seventies, and he still held the dragonwand, but as long as this illusion had a grip on him, he would be unable to draw upon the wand's magic. If only he'd been faster . . .

A coughing-gagging sound came from his right, and he turned to see Asenka standing next to him. The woman's eyes were wide with alarm, and she had her hand to her throat as she struggled to breathe.

Tresslar felt the pebble under his tongue, and he realized what was happening. The air in the cavern had been tainted by the dragon's toxic breath, and Asenka didn't have an enchanted pebble to help her breathe. It didn't matter that they weren't *really* here, and that the air wasn't *really* filled with deadly gas. Their minds had been made to believe it, and their bodies would react accordingly. If Tresslar didn't do something to help her, she would die.

Tresslar quickly reached into his backpack and withdrew a pebble. He took hold of Asenka's face with one hand and slipped the pebble beneath her tongue with the other.

"You'll be all right now," he told her. "Just try to breathe normally."

It took several moments for Asenka's panic to subside, but eventually she got hold of herself enough to ask, "What's happening?" She frowned at him. "Who are you?"

That's right, Tresslar thought. Though her appearance hasn't changed, I look like a young lad to her. "Do you remember the story I told you aboard the *Zephyr*, about how I came to find the dragonhead on my wand?"

Asenka frowned. "Tresslar?"

The artificer nodded. "We've become trapped within that memory. Though why you should be here too, I'm not certain. Perhaps it's simply because I told the story to you recently. At any rate, here we are."

Asenka looked around the cavern, grimacing as she saw the bloody remains of the dead dragon. "We're actually *inside* one of your memories?"

"Technically, this memory has been used to create a psionic illusion to ensnare our minds. I assume the same thing has happened to our companions."

"Why?"

"We came to Mount Luster to prevent Cathmore from using the psi-forge. I imagine he's trying to stop us."

"You think you're smart." The voice boomed through the cavern, echoing off the walls, and seeming to vibrate through their very bones.

They turned to see that the dragon—Paganus, Tresslar recalled—had raised his head and was glaring at them with a single milky-white eye.

"If you're so damned clever, how come you never learned what the Amahau was or why I had it? How come you've never taken the time to fully investigate the Amahau and discover its true power? Is it because you're not as intelligent as you like to others to think—or is that you've been afraid all these years? Afraid of finding out what it was that you stole from me?"

Despite the knowledge that this wasn't truly Paganus they faced, the dragon's words still cut Tresslar deep—for while the beast might not be real, his accusation was all too accurate.

Before Tresslar could stammer a reply, Paganus roared, spraying blood from his wounded throat, and attacked.

❖ ❖ ❖ ❖ ❖ ❖ ❖

Hinto was very confused. One second they had been standing outside the mountain, and now it seemed that he and Solus were *inside*, though he didn't remember actually entering. The two of them stood within a large cavern, facing a strange object made entirely of crystal. The thing glowed with a pulsing inner light that spilled into the chamber, the eerie illumination only serving to make the cavern's darkness more ominous.

The shadows reminded Hinto of the terrible nights he had endured aboard the *Proud Pelican*, shipwrecked in the Mire. He felt the first stirrings of panic—a cold, jittery sensation just below his sternum, but he gritted his teeth and fought his fear. Whatever was happening, his friends . . . especially Solus . . . were counting on him, and he was determined not to let them down again.

Speaking of friends, Hinto couldn't see any of them, just Solus.

"That's because they aren't present," the psi-forged said, "or rather, they are, but we currently exist on separate psionic frequencies. We share the same physical space, but not the same mental space."

Hinto had no idea what his new friend was saying, but the specifics didn't matter. He understood enough: Diran and the others were here, but he couldn't see them, which meant they couldn't see him, either. It was like being lost in a thick fog at sea. Two ships could pass right by each other and never know the other was there.

"An apt comparison, my friend," Solus said.

"So this place . . . is where you were born?"

The psi-forged nodded. "That is the creation forge where I was imbued with life, or at least an image of it. I believe Galharath is standing within the true forge, using its power to boost his psionic abilities to create this illusion, as well as those that our friends are currently experiencing."

"Galharath?"

"The kalashtar who repaired the psi-forge for Aldarik Cathmore. My full memories—such as they are—have returned. I believe exposure to the forge's energies has restored my mind to its previous state, completing the repairs Tresslar began."

"That's wonderful!" Hinto said. "Is your vision restored as well?"

"No. I will need to continue to rely on you as my eyes."

"But you remember everything about how to use your powers, right?" the halfling asked. "That means you can fight Galharath!"

"It's not that simple, my friend. Galharath attacked before my mind was restored, and I was unable to shield us from his assault. I am trapped within his illusions as surely as the rest of you."

"But you can fight your way free . . . can't you?"

"Perhaps with time, but Galharath isn't going to give me the chance."

"Too true."

Hinto turned to see that they were no longer alone in the cavern. Four people stood shoulder to shoulder, glaring at Hinto and Solus with dead-white eyes: a human and three kalashtar. Though the halfling pirate had never seen any of them before, he knew who they were. Perhaps Solus had psionically shared the knowledge with him, or perhaps it was Galharath's doing. Either way, Hinto recognized Banain, Evalina, Turi, and Karnil—the telekineticist, artificer, psionicist, and House Cannith overseer who had been responsible for the creation of the psi-forge and Solus's birth. It was they whose minds Solus had accidentally absorbed in the first confusing moments after he emerged from the psi-forge.

It was Karnil who had responded to Solus's statement, and the short human—not much taller than Hinto, really—took a half step forward, as if to differentiate himself from the others and make clear he was their leader. "None of you will succeed. Why not surrender now, Solus? Cathmore can still make use of you. You need not share the fate of your new companions."

"I will die before allowing myself to be used by anyone again," Solus said.

Hinto felt proud of his friend, and he knew he had to do

whatever he could to give Solus the time he needed to counter Galharath's illusions.

The halfling drew his long knife and stepped forward. "I'll see to these four, Solus. You deal with Galharath."

"Do not do this, Hinto," Solus warned. "Those four may be illusory, but they have power enough to kill."

All four of the memory-ghosts grinned.

"That we do," Karnil said.

"Don't worry about me," Hinto said. "I've sailed the Lhazaar all my life. I've weathered rough seas before."

Karnil trained his dead gaze on the halfling pirate, and Hinto felt as if the man were peering into his mind. "You have, haven't you? None were as rough as those you weathered in the Mire."

Hinto watched in ever-increasing horror as the ghostly quartet changed. Their forms blurred, shifted, and merged until they had become a multi-headed, multi-limbed conglomeration of human and kalashtar, but the transformation didn't end there, Their arms lengthened, became sinuous, fingers withdrawing as hands formed lamprey-like mouths. Hinto understood what was happening: they were becoming like the creatures that inhabited the Mire, that in a very real sense *were* the Mire. The same creatures that had snatched up and devoured the crew of the *Proud Pelican* one by one, leaving Hinto the only survivor.

Fear—overwhelming, crushing, paralyzing—whelmed into him, and he felt his knees go watery and start to buckle. Blackness nibbled at the edges of his vision, and he knew that he was on the verge of losing consciousness. He wanted to give in to the darkness, let it bear him far, far away from the nightmare that stood before him, but if he did that, he would be abandoning his friends—not just Solus, but Diran and the others, all trapped within illusions that were undoubtedly just as horrible as this one. It had been Diran, Ghaji, and Yvka who had rescued him from the Mire, and though they hadn't encountered Tresslar until after that, the grouchy old artificer had saved Hinto's life numerous times in the months since then. No matter what happened, no matter the cost to himself, Hinto would not let his friends down. Not this time.

He raised his long knife, shouted a battle-cry, and dashed toward the tentacled monstrosity.

● ● ● ◉ ● ● ●

Secluded within the cloak of darkness she'd erected, Nathifa watched as the priest and his companions struggled with the illusions created by the kalashtar. She knew that Skarm, who huddled close to her like a frightened child, saw only mortals stumbling about in an empty chamber while their tormenters watched in mocking amusement, but she had been a powerful sorceress in life and she'd only grown stronger in death. She could see the mindscapes that the kalashtar had devised, and she couldn't help admiring his diabolical creativity. Perhaps when this was over, she should attempt an alliance with him? No . . . all that mattered was getting her hands on the Amahau. That's what Espial had told her, so that's what she would do.

From the look of things, it wouldn't be much longer before she at last got her bloodless hands on the dragonhead. In the meantime, she'd remain hidden in darkness and enjoy the show.

CHAPTER

TWENTY-TWO

Makala moved silent as a shadow through the interior of Mount Luster. To human eyes, she would've appeared lithe and graceful, but she felt clumsy and heavy-footed. The moment she had entered the mountain facility, waves of mental energy slammed into her, forcing her to retake human form and walk when it would've been so much more efficient to fly. As a vampire, she possessed mesmeric abilities of her own, but it took all her concentration to resist the vast psionic power radiating through Mount Luster. Still, it gave her a destination, for whatever the source of the mental energy, she was certain Diran and the others would be at the center of it—and undoubtedly in quite a bit of trouble.

She made her way through corridors and down stairwells, the waves of psionic energy growing ever stronger and more difficult to resist, until she reached a large cavern. At the heart of the chamber lay a glowing crystalline structure that she sensed was the source of the psionic storm that raged through Mount Luster, but what drew the focus of her attention was what the glowing light revealed: Diran, Ghaji, Yvka, Tresslar Hinto, Solus, and *that woman*—all of them stumbling about the cavern, pantomiming actions as if in the throes of a waking dream. There were three others—a kalashtar at the center of the crystalline structure, an orc laughing as he watched Ghaji fight imaginary foes, and the only one Makala recognized: an old man wrapped in a bearskin cloak, eyes gleaming with cold malice as he watched Diran move about like a puppet on a string.

Cathmore.

The kalashar might've been the one operating the device that held her companions in thrall, but Makala knew that Cathmore was the one ultimately in control. She recalled something he had taught her when she was but a child. *Cut off the serpent's head and the body dies.* She intended to put that lesson to good use this night. She would kill Cathmore and sate her hunger at the same time. It would be an appropriately ironic end for the master assassin, for he was far more of a monster than she could ever be.

Makala moved across the cavern floor silent as a passing cloud, approaching Cathmore from behind. Makala thought she could've made all the noise she wanted, though, for the man's attention was completely focused on Diran. This was going to be too easy.

Just when she had closed to within striking distance and was about to leap upon her prey, she felt someone's eyes upon her. She looked to the kalashtar standing inside the crystalline device, unimaginable energies surging around him. He looked back at her, his eyes blazing with light. He grinned and Makala's world changed.

● ● ● ◉ ● ● ●

As Bruk came at him, Diran side-stepped, spun around, and ran toward the mahogany chest. In the real Proving Room, the chest contained numerous weapons, and Diran hoped this illusion matched the reality. He threw open the doors and was relieved to see that the chest was as full of weapons as he remembered. He heard Bruk coming up fast behind him, and he knew he didn't have time to be choosey. He reached into the chest and grabbed hold of the first weapon his fingers came in contact with—a warhammer. He whirled about just as Bruk lunged for him. Diran swept the hammer in a vicious arc at the undead sea raider.

The hammer smashed into the left side of Bruk's face, just below the temple, crushing the eye socket and reducing the eye itself to jelly. Bruk cried out—not in pain, but in frustration—and staggered backward, momentarily knocked off balance. Diran didn't expect the blow to stop him, but if the illusions adhered to their own cause and effect pattern—and so far they seemed to—then perhaps he could neutralize the undead raider.

Diran dropped the warhammer and turned back to the chest. He snatched up a dagger, spun around, and hurled it at Bruk's remaining eye. Though he presently wore the form of his younger self, a self who had yet to undergo his assassin's training, he still possessed his natural ability and his adult memories. The blade flew straight and true and buried itself in Bruk's right eye. The raider howled in rage. He reached up and yanked the dagger free in a spray of blood, vitreous fluid, and chunks of brain.

Cathmore smiled grimly. "Very good, Diran. You couldn't repell the zombie with your priestly powers, so you chose to blind him, giving you the advantage. Now you can whittle away at him bit by bit until you've rendered him incapable of harming you. As one of your former teachers, I must confess to feeling a certain measure of pride at this moment. But if you'll recall, I told you that *I* am in control here, not you."

Cathmore waved his hand and Bruk's eyes were restored. The zombie turned to look at Diran and grinned.

"You're going to die here, Diran," Cathmore said. "The only question is how long you'll manage to postpone the inevitable."

Before Bruk could resume his attack, the air shimmered and a young blond girl wearing a gray tunic and sandals appeared behind Cathmore. Diran's breath caught in his throat as he recognized Makala—not as she was, but as she'd been when they'd first met, so many years ago at Emon Gorsedd's academy.

Cathmore turned and smiled at Makala. "It's about time you arrived, my dear. I was beginning to think you were going to miss all the fun."

Makala returned Cathmore's smile, revealing her elongated canine teeth. "The fun's just beginning, and by the way, you don't have as much control here as you think."

Before the master assassin could react, Makala hissed and launched herself at him.

❋ ❋ ❋ ❋ ❋ ❋ ❋

Flames or no flames, Ghaji's axe was still honed to a fine edge and his arm was as strong as ever. He hacked away at the undead shifters as they came at him, severing limbs and lopping off heads, until the family that he'd once helped slaughter years ago—father, mother, and their two children—lay in a grisly scattering of mutilated body parts.

"Don't take this the wrong way, love," Yvka said in a queasy voice, "but I think I'm going to be sick."

Chagai applauded. "Now *that's* more like a full-blooded orc. Why couldn't you have fought like that when you were under my command?"

Ghaji's chest heaved as he struggled to catch his breath, and with his free hand he wiped a smear of gore from his cheek. "They weren't real, but *you* are. I wanted to finish them off so I could finally put you out of my misery."

Ghaji lifted his axe and rushed forward, but something grabbed hold of his ankle, and he tripped and fell onto the grass.

"Ghaji, look out!" Yvka shouted.

Ghaji thought she was warning him that Chagai intended to attack while he was down, and he rolled over so that he would be able to defend himself, but then he looked down and saw what had tripped him: one of the shifter's arms—the father's, it appeared—had wrapped its hand around his ankle. Other body parts came crawling, sliding, tumbling, and oozing across the ground toward him, moving with nightmarish speed. Clawed fingers dug into his skin, fanged teeth sank into his flesh, loops of intestine coiled around his throat and limbs like grisly serpents, binding him, choking him . . .

Yvka rushed to his side and began slicing at the animated remains of the shifters with a jade-bladed knife. The weapon was no doubt magical, provided to Yvka by her masters in the Shadow Network, but whatever its properties, it caused no special damage to the attacking body parts, and they continued their work unfazed.

Ghaji tensed his neck muscles, struggling to keep his airway open, but as strong as he was, the intestine wrapped around his neck was stronger, and he knew he was fighting a losing battle. Chagai's mocking laughter rang in his ears, accompanied by a roaring sound that he knew heralded the approach of his death.

"No . . . honor . . ." he gasped out.

Chagai stopped laughing. "What did you say, half-blood?"

"No . . . *honor,*" Ghaji repeated, more loudly this time, using up the last of his air.

Yvka, tears running down her face, desperately slashed at the shifters' remains with her jade knife. Ghaji wanted to take her hand and tell that it wasn't her fault, that as a warrior he knew this day would come, but he couldn't move, couldn't speak. All he could do was watch his lover cry as his vision began to dim.

Then the pressure on his throat eased, and he was able to draw in a breath. Yvka kept hacking away at the body parts as Ghaji breathed in and out, relishing such a simple, life-affirming act. Now when Yvka's knife struck, the wounds began to rot, the decay spreading until the affected body part collapsed to dust. Within seconds, the shifter remains were no more.

Ghaji sat up and rubbed his throat as he turned to face Chagai. The orc glared at him with fury in his eyes and perhaps a hint of shame as well.

"Stand up," Chagai growled, "and let's finish this like orcs."

Ghaji rose to his feet, axe gripped tight.

❂ ❂ ❂ ◉ ❂ ❂ ❂

Tresslar might not have his dragonwand in this illusion, but that didn't mean he was helpless. He grabbed Asenka by the elbow and yanked her out of the way as Paganus's head lunged at them. Despite the beast's ravaged condition, he moved swiftly, his wounds no impediment to motion, and his jaws snapped closed on the empty air where the Sea Scorpion commander had been standing only a second before.

"Stay behind me!" Tresslar warned Asenka.

Then, hoping his illusory backpack contained the same objects it had when he was a young man, the artificer reached inside and pulled out a small diamond wrapped in spider-silk. Relieved, he tossed the gem into the air over their heads. The diamond hovered above them, its position fixed, and a shroud of webbing descended from it like a curtain of gauze to envelop them. As the bottom edge of the protective web stretched to the ground, Tresslar reached into his backpack and removed a small stone wrapped in a mesh of thin bronze wire. Tresslar thumbed a tiny switch he'd attached to the wire-mesh, then crouched down and tossed the stone onto the ground just as the web sealed itself around Asenka and him.

Paganus had pulled back his head for a second strike, but he hesitated when he saw what the artificer had done. The dragon cocked his head to one side.

"You can't possibly believe that such feeble magic can protect you from *me*," Paganus rumbled. "I can claw through that webbing as if it were naught but air."

"It's not meant to defend against physical attack," Tresslar said. "It protects against heat. You see, I've had a lot of years to think about what I did the first time we met and to consider what I might have done differently. I'm sure you're aware that the gas you breathe—the gas that fills this cave—while deadly poisonous, does not burn, but the breath of a green dragon *will* ignite when combined with certain other elements. That small catalyst stone was given to me by an alchemist I did a good turn for once in Cliffscrape. Of course, I modified it to make it a wee bit stronger."

Tresslar snapped his fingers, the wire-mesh encasing the catalyst stone began to glow, and Paganus roared as his lair exploded.

* * * ☉ ☉ * *

Solus didn't know what to do. Though the conglomerate creature Hinto attacked possessed no physical substance, any damage it appeared to do to the halfling would be inflicted on his mind, with results as devastating as any bodily wound. More so, in fact, but if Solus went to his friend's aid, that would leave the psi-forged open to attack by Galharath. Hadn't Hinto told him to deal with Galharath while he engaged the conglomeration in battle? By helping Hinto, Solus would be going against his friend's wishes, and more, he would be dishonoring the halfling's sacrifice, and he sensed that this was important to Hinto, that the small man was fighting a battle much greater and more personal than simply cutting away at an illusory monster. It was a battle that Hinto needed to fight, and Solus should give his friend that chance.

The others—Diran, Ghaji, Yvka, Tresslar, Asenka, and someone else whom Solus had never met but who was well known to the rest, a woman named Makala—all of them struggled with their own separate battles. They faced the same danger that Hinto did: that their minds would be destroyed by Galharath and the power of the psi-forge.

Solus knew then what he had to do. No matter what else happened, Galharath had to be stopped.

As if sensing Solus's decision, the kalashtar gazed out from within the cradle of the psi-forge and directed a thought his way.

There's nothing you can do, Solus. You are merely a construct, imbued with a semblance of life. While I . . . I have become a god!

Solus had little direct experience in using his psionic abilities in battle, but he had more than his own memories to draw on. He had the memories of his four creators, those who had designed and constructed the psi-forge and who knew the device far better than Galharath ever could. That knowledge would become his weapon.

He looked upon the crystalline structure—the main chamber, the struts rising toward the cavern's ceiling, the ones that reached down through the cavern floor to draw upon the thermal energies beneath the mountain. He saw the physical components of the device, but he also saw the intricate lattice of psionic power that made up the true heart of the psi-forge. He saw Galharath not as a being of meat and bone, but rather a luminous creature of pure thought . . . and what's more, he saw precisely how the kalashtar was integrated into the psi-forge's energy lattice, and he saw what he needed to do.

Solus focused the power of his mind into a single tight beam of telekinetic energy and sent it hurtling toward the crystalline ring clasped in Galharath's right hand. The beam sheared off a portion of the outer ring near the top, so small that it would've been impossible to detect with the naked eye, but it was enough to do the job.

The ring shuddered in Galharath's hand, and the kalashtar looked up at it in alarm. A memory came from one of Solus's creators—which, he couldn't say. The memory was of the way a glass goblet would vibrate when subjected to certain frequencies of sound . . . vibrate enough to shatter.

The ring in Galharath's right hand burst apart in a shower of crystal shards.

The kalashtar screamed.

❋ ❋ ❋ ❋ ❋ ❋ ❋

Diran held out his hand and silver light flared to life in his palm. Makala hissed as the argent illumination poured over her, and she threw herself away from Cathmore, turned her back to Diran, and covered her eyes.

"Are you *mad?*" she screeched. "You're protecting a monster!"

Diran hated to see Makala in pain, but he couldn't let her slay Cathmore. "It's you I'm protecting—from yourself."

Cathmore laughed. "How deliciously self-righteous!"

Diran ignored the master assassin and spoke calmly to Makala, though he did not allow the silver fire burning in his hand to go out. "It's one thing to feed, quite another to kill. Cathmore may deserve to die, but I won't let you become a soulless murderer."

"Why not?" Cathmore spoke in a jovial tone, as if he were enjoying himself enormously. "That's what the Brotherhood trained her to be."

Makala continued to huddle on the floor, her back to Diran. "Put out that damned light!" she shouted. "Let me do what has to be done!"

Cathmore continued to grin at Diran, but his voice took on a cold edge. "You can't save her. She's a killer at heart . . . just as you are. No matter how much you try to deny your true nature, it will always come to the fore, one way or another. The Diran Bastiaan I trained as a boy was too intelligent not to recognize such a basic fact about himself. Forget your friends and your pathetic excuse for a religion. Become once more who you truly are."

Cathmore took a step toward him, and his grin fell away. His voice was completely devoid of emotion as he continued, almost as if Cathmore wasn't speaking, but someone—or *something*—else was.

"I'm old, Diran. Not many years remain ahead of me. When I die, the spirit inside me will need a new home. You gave up your dark spirit some time ago, Diran, but it's not too late to return to the way things were."

Cathmore took another step forward.

"You can become the new host for my spirit, and you don't have to wait for me to die . . . we can make the transfer now."

Confusion, fear, and anger warred in Cathmore's gaze as he spoke, and Diran understood what was happening.

"It's not you talking now, is it, Cathmore? It's your dark spirit, desperate to find a new host before you die and it's forced to return to whatever foul netherworld spawned it. How does it feel to know that at the end of your life, the spirit you've relied on for so many years cares no more for you than a sea rat cares for a sinking ship?"

A wave of vertigo hit Diran. The Proving Room shimmered and grew blurry before disappearing altogether. When the dizziness passed, Diran found himself in a large cavern, his adult self once again. Makala had also been restored to her true age, though she still crouched with her back to Diran to hide from the light of the silver flame blazing in his hand. Diran took a quick look around and saw his companions were present as well—Ghaji fought with Chagai, axe against sword, while Yvka looked on; Tresslar and Asenka huddled close together, as if to protect one another from some unseen threat; and Hinto and Solus stood before a glowing crystalline structure that Diran knew had to be the creation forge which had birthed Solus. Inside stood Cathmore's kalashtar ally, screaming as blood poured from numerous wounds to his face and neck. Crystal shards of varying sizes were embedded in the man's ravaged flesh.

Diran wasn't certain how they'd all ended up in the cavern. Perhaps the kalashtar had used his mind powers to direct them to come here, and they had no memory of doing so. It didn't matter. All that was important was that Solus had triumphed over the kalashtar and broken the man's hold over all of them.

All at once the kalashtar stopped screaming, his eyes went wide, and the light emanating from the crystalline structure began to fade. The kalashtar held onto a single crystal ring that hovered in the air above him, but he released his grip on the ring and fell to his knees. Diran thought the man was going to die, but he remained on his knees, staring blankly, a thin line of drool running from a corner of his mouth.

Diran turned to Cathmore.

"It's over. You've lost."

Cathmore's gaze was clear, and Diran knew his dark spirit had returned control to the master assassin. The old man looked uncertain, as if he couldn't bring himself to believe what had happened, as if he were hoping that this was another of the kalashtar's illusions that any moment would be dispelled to reveal that he, Cathmore, was the ultimate victor.

Diran closed his hand, extinguishing the silver fire he'd brought into existence. He then drew a pair of steel daggers and flipped them into throwing position.

"Surrender or die, Cathmore. Your choice."

Cathmore's uncertainty faded and was replaced with cold hatred. "I'll never surrender to you."

Makala grabbed Cathmore from behind.

"That's just what I wanted to hear," she said.

Before Diran could stop her, she bared her fangs and sank them into Cathmore's neck.

Diran had no choice. He hurled his daggers.

* * * ◉ * * *

Ghaji ducked just in time to avoid Chagai's swing, though from the way Yvka gasped as the broadsword passed over his head, Ghaji had come within a few hairs of losing his scalp. Though he was in an awkward position, Ghaji swung his axe at Chagai's unprotected side. He knew his weapon probably wouldn't penetrate Chagai's enchanted mail shirt, but he hoped the impact would at least break a couple of the bastard's ribs.

Before his axe could hit Chagai, the night-shrouded valley vanished, and Ghaji saw they stood inside a large cavern. The sudden change of scenery distracted Ghaji, causing him to angle his axe head upward so that the flat of the weapon struck Chagai in the side instead of the edge. There was still plenty of strength behind the blow however, and the breath gusted out of Chagai's lungs as the impact sent him stumbling to his right.

Ghaji wondered what had happened to break the illusion of the night valley, and whether it meant good or ill for him and his companions, but he knew he didn't have time to be concerned with such matters now. Twenty years ago he'd allowed Chagai to live, and that was a mistake he intended to rectify.

He stood, willing his axe to ignite, and he was gratified to see flames flare to life around the elemental weapon.

Chagai regained his balance and turned back to face Ghaji, bringing his broadsword around for another strike. Ghaji ran forward, gripped the flaming axe in both hands, and raised it high over his head.

"This is for Ruelo and his family!" Ghaji shouted.

Chagai's eyes widened as Ghaji brought his fire-flecked axe blade down and split the orc's skull in two.

❋ ❋ ❋ ❋ ❋ ❋ ❋

"Soon . . . Soon . . . *Now!*" Nathifa commanded.

Skarm didn't hesitate. He leaped from the cloak of darkness, donned wolf form, and dashed across the cavern floor toward the white-bearded artificer.

❋ ❋ ❋ ❋ ❋ ❋ ❋

As much as Tresslar wanted to believe that he was responsible for ending the psionic illusion they'd been trapped in, he knew he had nothing to do with it. Still, he was pleased that his notion for defeating Paganus had worked, even if only in an illusion. Tresslar had answered a question that had nagged at him for forty years, and how many people were fortunate enough to receive an opportunity like that? There was no time for such idle thoughts: just because the illusion had ended didn't mean the danger had.

Gripping his dragonwand—and wasn't he glad to have it back?—he turned to Asenka.

"Are you hurt?" he asked.

The Sea Scorpion commander looked dazed, but she shook her head, appearing none the worse for wear.

Tresslar glanced around the cavern, hoping to determine what was happening and where he might be needed.

A gray shape came streaking at him from the cavern's shadows. Tresslar was still somewhat disoriented from having been in the grip of illusion, and so he hesitated, unsure whether the wolf running at him was real or not.

The beast leaped, closed its mouth around the dragonwand, and tore the magic weapon out of Tresslar's hand. The wolf raced away toward a stairwell at the far end of the cavern, and though Tresslar thought it might be his imagination, he swore he saw a dark form trailing the creature, as if one of the cavern's shadows had decided to break loose and accompany the beast. Then the wolf entered the stairwell, and the dark shape—assuming it truly existed—vanished as well.

Tresslar stared in stunned amazement. For four decades he'd possessed the dragonwand, using it during his voyages with Erdis Cai, then concealing it during his lengthy tenure on Dreadhold, and now, after all those years, it was gone.

● ● ● ◉ ● ● ●

The blades Diran threw were made of steel, not wood or silver, and thus would not cause Makala any serious injury, but he wasn't aiming for Makala.

The first dagger struck Cathmore just above the throat apple, while the second slid into the master assassin's left eye socket, penetrating deep into the brain. Cathmore stiffened as blood gushed from his wounds, then he fixed his remaining eye on Diran and slowly smiled with trembling lips. The smile fell away, the eye glazed over, and Cathmore died. The master assassin went limp, but he did not fall, for Makala had hold of him from behind, her head at the juncture of his neck and shoulder, her mouth pressed to the side of his throat as she drank the dead man's blood.

Diran prayed that he'd been fast enough. For the moment Makala's fangs had pierced Cathmore's neck, she'd opened herself to the dark spirit that dwelt within the old man, but if Cathmore had died *before* the dark spirit could enter Makala though the blood of its former host, then there was a chance the evil entity would be cast out before it could infect her. *If* he'd been swift enough.

"Makala?"

As Diran spoke her name, he reached back into his cloak and withdrew a dagger made of pure silver from one of the sheaths sewn into the inner lining.

For a moment, she continued enjoying her grisly repast, but then she lifted her blood-smeared mouth from Cathmore's ravaged neck and smiled at Diran, revealing crimson-flecked teeth.

"I'd forgotten how *good* it feels to have the darkness inside." Her voice was soft, almost a purr.

Diran felt as if he'd taken a blow to the chest. He'd failed her—again.

"Please, Makala . . . let me help you."

Makala spoke with mocking amusement. "Help me how, *lover?* You can't cure me. So what will you do? Kill me?"

Diran hesitated for only a half second. Forgive me, he thought, then threw the silver dagger at Makala, but before the blade could strike, she lifted Cathmore's body and used it as a shield. The dagger *thunked* harmlessly into the dead man's chest.

Diran reached for a second silver dagger, but Makala's reflexes were far faster than his. She hurled Cathmore's body at him then her form faded to mist.

Diran leaped to the side to avoid the old man's body, throwing his dagger at Makala as he did. The blade flew straight and true, but it was too late. The dagger passed through the space where Makala's heart had been. The blade fell to the ground with a metallic *tink*, and Makala's dark laughter echoed through the cavern air. Though it quickly faded, Diran continued to hear it in his mind long after.

CHAPTER

TWENTY-THREE

Any luck?"

Diran turned to see Ghaji striding across the rocky ground toward him. The half-orc was clad in a thick fur cloak, his axe tucked beneath his belt. The clouds in the gray sky had a dark-ish undercast, and though it was not yet winter, Diran thought there was a good chance it might snow soon.

The priest was annoyed to see his friend approaching, but he tried to keep his tone neutral as he replied. "What do you mean?"

Ghaji stopped when he reached Diran and took a quick look at their surroundings to check the area for threats—an action Diran knew from their long association was second nature to the half-orc. Evidently Ghaji saw nothing to concern him in the desolate, rocky hills, for he turned his attention back to Diran.

"This is the third day you've come out here alone—without telling anyone, I might add. You're searching for Makala, aren't you?"

There was no point in denying it: Ghaji knew him too well. There were a couple of rocks nearby large enough to sit on. Diran took one, Ghaji the other.

Now that they'd sat, Diran found himself still reluctant to talk about Makala. "Have you heard anything from Yvka?"

Ghaji's eyes narrowed, as if he were well aware that his friend was stalling. "She stopped by the King Prawn this morning to, uh, get some rest."

Diran grinned.

"Anyway, she told me her 'friends' have taken possession of Mount Luster—and they've taken custody of Galharath. No doubt they're going over the psi-forge facility inch by inch to glean all the information they can. I get the impression that Yvka's risen in status in the Shadow Network thanks to her association with us. First she was able to deliver Grimwall to them and now Mount Luster."

"I don't like the idea of the Shadow Network possessing the capability to create psi-forged," Diran said. "Imagine the destruction an army of constructs like Solus could cause."

"Warforged aren't mindless machines, you know," Ghaji pointed out. "Creating them is one thing. Controlling them is another. Besides, according to Solus, the psi-forge's energy matrix—whatever that is—was damaged when he attacked Galharath. There's no guarantee that the Shadow Network's artificers can repair it."

"True, but if the Shadow Network can restore Galharath's mind, they might be able to get the kalashtar to cooperate with them."

Solus's attack had done more than damage the internal workings of the psi-forge. It had reduced Galharath to a drooling idiot. Diran had attempted to heal him several times but without success. Whatever injury had been done to the kalashtar's mind was beyond Diran's power to repair. Galharath had been taken to Perhata and locked up in the baron's prison, where he'd remained for the last few days . . . until the Shadow Network had taken him. Diran wondered how the Network had managed to get Baron Mahir's cooperation, and he wondered what Asenka thought about having to give up the prisoner. He suspected she was less than thrilled.

"If you couldn't heal him, I doubt very much the Shadow Network can," Ghaji said.

"How's Solus doing?" Diran asked.

He'd spent so little time in Perhata these last few days—mostly just to sleep and restore his supplies—and he hadn't seen much of the psi-forged.

"His vision is still blurry, despite Tresslar's attempts to fix it, but Solus doesn't seem to mind. He's happy enough with Hinto to guide him. You ask me, they make an odd pair."

Diran smiled. "People have said the same about the two of us, you know."

Ghaji snorted but otherwise didn't reply.

Diran was pleased that Hinto had formed a bond with the psi-forged. They complemented each other well: Hinto helped Solus maintain mental stability, while the psi-forged helped the halfling emotionally. Diran had a feeling theirs was a partnership that would last, but only time would tell.

"How fares Tresslar?" Diran asked.

Ghaji shrugged. "He's still mad as a nest of hornets over the loss of his dragonwand, though he tries to downplay it. You know he'd rather die than admit how much he's come to rely on the thing. He says he's working on a way to locate the dragonwand, but it might be mere bluster. Still, he *has* been spending a lot of time in the artificer's workshop Baron Mahir has granted him use of, so who knows?"

"How are *you* feeling, my friend?" Diran asked. "By defeating Chagai, you've had the opportunity to lay an unpleasant part of your past to rest."

"You'd think so, wouldn't you, but the truth is that I don't feel much of anything. Killing Chagai didn't bring back any of the people we killed during the time we served together, and I'd put our association behind me the day I left him lying wounded on a field in the Eldeen Reaches. The world's a better place with him gone, though, that's for certain."

"As one of the Purified, I must remind you that all life is sacred," Diran said, then he smiled. "However, in this case, I can't help but agree with you."

"What of you?" Ghaji said. "Cathmore was a large part of *your* past."

Diran considered his reply for a time before speaking. "Of all the teachers I've had over the years—my father, Emon, Tusya—Cathmore is the only one I wish I'd never had, but I can't deny that I learned from him, that the man I am today was shaped at least in part by his teachings. However, I do not feel any joy that he's dead, nor do I feel any relief. No matter what we do, or who we outlive, the past remains with us—always."

"Which brings us back to Makala," Ghaji said softly.

"I suppose it does." Diran let out a long, slow sigh. "I should've killed her the moment I realized she'd been tainted by the vampire's curse."

"How could you? You love her."

"If I truly loved her, I would've done what needed to be done. Instead, I told myself that I should allow her to choose, that she was strong enough to bear the curse if she so wished." He shook his head. "I was a fool."

Before Ghaji could respond, a woman's voice cut in. "You wouldn't be the first fool for love, and I doubt very much that you'll be the last."

Diran and Ghaji looked up at the same time to see Asenka approaching. She wore a thick fur cloak with the hood down, and the sunlight—what little there was of it, at any rate—accented the highlights in her strawberry-blond hair.

The half-orc scowled. "Did you follow me all the way from Perhata?"

The commander of the Sea Scorpions smiled as she reached them. "That I did."

Ghaji's scowl deepened. "My senses must still be suffering from the after effects of Galharath tampering with our minds." He stood up and turned to Diran. "See you back at the King Prawn for dinner?"

Diran had intended to continue searching for Makala until he was too weary to continue, but he nodded and said, "I'll be there."

Ghaji put his hand on Diran's shoulder for a moment, and then, after a nod to Asenka, the half-orc warrior turned and began the trek back to Perhata. When Ghaji had gone a dozen yards or so, Asenka sat on the rock he'd vacated.

"You know he let me follow him," she said.

Diran smiled. "Yes."

"He's a good friend."

"The best I've ever had," Diran said as he gazed at the half-orc's retreating form.

They sat in silence for a time, listening to the moaning of the wind as it blew through the hills.

After a while, Asenka said, "You're not really searching for Makala out here, are you? At least, that's not all you're doing. She's more likely to be holed up in Perhata, since that's where . . ." Asenka trailed off, as if realizing she was about to say something she shouldn't.

"Where the greatest supply of food is located," Diran finished for her. "You're right, of course. I've been coming out here to 'reacquaint myself with solitude,' as Tusya, the priest who was my mentor in the Church, would put it. When one wishes to hear the voice of the Silver Flame most clearly, one must first calm the unquiet mind."

"Is it working?"

Diran smiled. "Not in the slightest."

Asenka laughed then immediately apologized. "Sorry, I know it's not funny."

"You have nothing to be sorry for. Laughter is a sound of life, and while it might not have mystical healing powers, it's a powerful medicine in its own right." Diran broke off and stared into the distance, seeking Ghaji, but the half-orc was no longer in sight. "It's a medicine I could use more of. For a man who's dedicated himself to combating evil and preserving life, I spend far too much of my time surrounded by death."

"Aren't life and death two sides of the same coin?" Asenka said. "One can't exist without the other."

"I suppose," Diran allowed, "but that doesn't mean I have to like it."

"No, it doesn't." She paused as if trying to decide how best to proceed. "You've been doing more out here than just getting to know solitude again, though. You've been hoping to lure Makala out into the open. That's why you haven't gone too far into the hills. You want to remain close to the city."

Diran turned to regard the Sea Scorpion commander, impressed anew by how perceptive she was. "Yes. Whether she's hiding here in the hills or in Perhata, I'd hoped that she'd seek me out."

The dark spirit Makala had inherited from Cathmore would bring forth the cruelest aspects of her nature, which alone would cause her to want him dead, but she'd also realize that now Diran wouldn't rest until he had freed her from her dual curse—the vampire's taint and her symbiosis with the dark spirit—and so in order to preserve her own life, she would have to end his.

"I take it that you haven't seen her," Asenka said.

Diran nodded. "And I don't understand why."

"I do. Somewhere inside her, maybe so deep that even she's not aware of it, she still loves you."

"And you know this because . . . ?"

Asenka looked at him for a long moment before answering. "Because if I were in her position, I'd feel the same way." She stood before Diran could respond. "Well, I'll leave you and solitude alone with each other. Did you mean what you said to Ghaji, about returning to Perhata for dinner?"

"Yes."

"I'll see you then." Asenka started to go.

Before she'd taken more than a few steps, Diran said, "There's something else Tusya used to tell me."

Asenka stopped and turned back to look at him. "What's that?"

" 'Solitude's all well and good at times, but it's a damn poor conversationalist.' "

Asenka grinned then returned to sit on the rock next to Diran once more, and after sitting quietly for a time, they began to talk.

CHAPTER

TWENTY-FOUR

Skarm lay on the floor in his true form, half dozing. Since returning to her mountain lair several days ago, Nathifa had done nothing but sit at her table and stare into Espial's obsidian eye sockets. For the most part, Nathifa remained silent as she gazed into the skull's eyes, but occasionally she muttered barely audible words: *Yes, no, I understand . . .* The Amahau, still attached to the head of the artificer's wand, rested on the table next to Espial, but Nathifa hadn't so much as looked at the artifact since placing it there. Skarm knew better than to expect any gratitude from his mistress, but after all the trouble—not to mention the physical agony—he'd endured in order to retrieve the damned thing for her, the least she could've done was show a little excitement over finally having the Amahau in her possession, but no . . . she only had eyes for Espial.

Skarm shivered. In the last day, it seemed Nathifa's lair had gotten much colder than could be accounted for by the outside temperature, and the shadows that clung to the chamber's walls seemed to have grown darker, thicker . . . and at times they had appeared to ripple slowly, as if they had begun to take on a life of their own. The barghest hoped it was his imagination, but he knew it wasn't, and not for the first time since entering into Nathifa's service, he wondered just what Espial was and what fell secrets it spoke to his mistress.

Nathifa sat up straight, the sudden motion startling Skarm.

"It seems we have a visitor," the lich said. She turned to face a pocket of shadow near the head of her bed, and Skarm peered in the same direction. The barghest saw nothing out of the ordinary at first, but then a form emerged from the shadows, and a blond, pale-skinned woman stood smiling at him. He recognized the woman as the vampire that had been present at Mount Luster. Skarm wasn't especially afraid of vampires—not when he had a lich for a mistress—but there was something about this one that caused the fur on the back of his neck to stand up. The barghest sensed that while she was a vampire, she wasn't *only* a vampire.

Nathifa didn't rise from the table, but the atmosphere in the chamber became charged with dangerous potential, like the air just before a violent storm was about to erupt.

"I'm impressed," Nathifa said. "I didn't sense your presence until you entered the room. Normally, I would've been aware of you long before that."

The vampire shrugged. "I know a few tricks. What I don't know is who you are or why I'm here. I . . . felt drawn to this place, almost as if I were summoned here."

Now it was Nathifa's turn to smile. "You were. I've been waiting for your arrival."

The vampire scowled. "You brought me here?"

The lich shook her head. "Not me—the one I serve."

She lifted Espial off the table, turned it around to face the vampire, then she glided across the floor toward the blond woman. The vampire looked at the obsidian skull with suspicion, but she didn't shy away when Nathifa raised the object so that its hollow eye sockets were even with the vampire's eyes.

The vampire gazed into Espial's eyes for some moments, remaining perfectly still the entire time. Then she blinked several times and turned to Nathifa.

"I see," she said.

Nathifa grinned, showing rotted teeth and dead-gray gums. "I thought you might." The lich looked down at Skarm, who'd observed the entire scene from his position of the floor. "Get up, you lazy thing! It's time for us to go." She smiled at the vampire once more. "*All* of us."

Skarm transformed into his goblin form as he rose to his feet. "Go where?"

Nathifa didn't answer right away. Instead, she tucked Espial under her arm, returned to the table, and snatched up the dragonwand with her free hand.

"Trebaz Sinara," the lich said. "Where else?"

Skarm tried to keep the sarcasm out of his voice as he replied. "Where else, indeed? But we lack one very important component for sea travel, my mistress: a ship."

"I know where we can get one," the vampire said.

"Is it swift? We shall have need of a fast vessel," Nathifa cautioned.

"Don't worry. This ship *is* fast." Makala grinned. "Fast as the wind."

❂ ❂ ❂ ❂ ❂ ❂ ❂

In an icy throne room far to the north, a bleached-white claw with long black nails stroked the smooth dome of an obsidian skull—one that was an exact match for Espial—and laughter brittle as ancient bones defiled the air.

During the Last War, Gaven was an
adventurer, searching the darkest reaches
of the underworld. But an encounter with
a powerful artifact forever changed him,
breaking his mind and landing him in the
deepest cell of the darkest prison in
all the world.

THE DRACONIC PROPHECIES

BOOK I

When war looms on the horizon, some see it as more
than renewed hostilities between nations. Some see the
fulfillment of an ancient prophecy—one that promises
both the doom and salvation of the world. And Gaven may
be the key to it all.

THE STORM DRAGON

The first EBERRON hardcover by veteran game designer and
the author of *In the Claws of the Tiger*:

James Wyatt

SEPTEMBER 2007

FORGOTTEN REALMS®

A world of Adventure Awaits

The FORGOTTEN REALMS world is the biggest, most detailed, most vibrant, and most beloved of the DUNGEONS & DRAGONS® campaign settings. Created by best-selling fantasy author Ed Greenwood the FORGOTTEN REALMS setting has grown in almost unimaginable ways since the first line was drawn on the now infamous "Ed's Original Maps."

Still the home of many a group of DUNGEONS & DRAGONS players, the FORGOTTEN REALMS world is brought to life in dozens of novels, including hugely popular best sellers by some of the fantasy genre's most exciting authors. FORGOTTEN REALMS novels are fast, furious, action-packed adventure stories in the grand tradition of sword and sorcery fantasy, but that doesn't mean they're all flash and no substance. There's always something to learn and explore in this richly textured world.

To find out more about the Realms go to www.wizards.com and follow the links from Books to FORGOTTEN REALMS. There you'll find a detailed reader's guide that will tell you where to start if you've never read a FORGOTTEN REALMS novel before, or where to go next if you're a long-time fan!